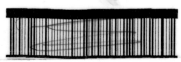

Quartet  Qrime

AT NIGHT ALL WOLVES ARE GREY

GUNNAR STAALESEN

At Night All Wolves Are Grey

Translated from the Norwegian by David McDuff

QUARTET QRIME

First published in Great Britain by Quartet Books Limited 1986
A member of the Namara Group
27/29 Goodge Street, London W1P 1FD
First published in Norway by Gyldendal Norsk Forlag, Oslo, 1983

British Library Cataloguing in Publication Data

Staalesen, Gunnar
  At night all wolves are grey.
  I. Title   II. I market er alle ulver gra. *English*
  823[F]   PT8950.S7/

ISBN 0 7043 2558 6

Typeset by MC Typeset, Chatham, Kent
Printed and bound in Great Britain
by Chanctonbury Press Ltd
Bradford, West Yorkshire

Note: *Varg* in Norwegian means 'wolf'. The expression *varg i veum* means 'persona non grata', 'outlaw' or 'pariah'.

1

I met Hjalmar Nymark in the café I had begun to frequent that winter Solveig left me.

I had noticed him before. He had a strong face, with a prominent, crooked nose, dark, eager eyes set far back in their sockets, and an aggressive chin. I would have estimated his age at around seventy. His hair was almost white and was combed straight back, receding in a deep V over each temple. He was in the habit of sitting with a rolled-up newspaper in one hand. I hardly ever saw him read the newspaper; instead, he used it in order to emphasize the points in the conversation, bringing it down abruptly on the table.

He was powerfully built and this gave him a stocky appearance, in spite of the fact that he was nearly six feet tall. He had a paunch of the type common in old, burly men: not loose flab but simply muscles that were in the process of drying up. He usually sat a table or two away from me. Most often he was alone but from time to time he had company. Sometimes we would bump into each other in the doorway and, after a while, I could tell that he had come to recognize me. His eyes had a humorous gleam in them and once, when I was on the way in and he was on the way out, he said as he passed me: 'Going into the watering-hole?' Then, before I was able to reply, he was gone.

The café was only three doors along from the building where I had my office and I started to look in there three or four afternoons a week. Even at the entrance you couldn't help noticing some of the café's distinguishing characteristics for, at no matter what time of the day or night you were about to go in, someone would always be on their way out, and those who emerged from the place were seldom very steady on their feet. The doorman was helpfulness personified: he would point out the direction you should take, or stand there holding you upright until your taxi arrived. Most people required a taxi.

Just inside the door there was something that gave the establishment an almost international feel. A glass hatchway connected through to the tobacconist's next door, making it look as if that was where the local bookie had his premises. But, here, the most you could expect was to hand in your football pool coupons shortly before five on a Wednesday afternoon.

The reek of beer and cigarette smoke gave the place a strongly

1

masculine atmosphere. Most of the customers drank beer, often in impressive amounts. The faces around you were heavy, often with age, but even more frequently with alcohol. Here old salts got together in order to reminisce about the days when most of the work in the port was done by hand. Here, after closing-up time, came the market stallholders with their large red hands, the furrowed skin of which still retained streaks of fish blood. Here, too, came retired factory workers in plain workshirts that were buttoned right up to the neck, coughing painfully and unpleasantly into the foam in their beer-glasses, drinking up, striking the table with their fists and demanding more. A little office worker, balding on top, in a white shirt and anaemic tie, carefully unfolded his copy of an evening paper, ducked down behind his half-litre and put off his arrival home to his wife by another half-hour. Young, talk-hungry lads from the country, who by early afternoon had advanced so far towards evening that they couldn't get in anywhere else, were guided to a hospitable table where they scattered the last of their banknotes around them and clinked their glasses in front of one another's red-cheeked faces, before crawling out of the door on all fours some two hours later, helped on their way by the doorman, and possibly a waiter or two if they got too rowdy. A few women – most of them well over fifty – found empty seats and familiar faces at most of the tables. They drank their beer from smaller glasses and sat with their coats on until time wore on and they undid them, letting their heavy breasts protrude inside the blue mohair sweaters that had been fashionable twenty years earlier.

From the north-facing windows the afternoon light filtered in through curtains that were yellow with nicotine. Between the windows brownish ceramic reliefs hung against a green background. At the very back of the café, where the serving counter was, a large mural depicted the bustle of the docks in faded blue against a background of yellow plaster, to make the majority of the clientele feel at home. Powerful hands raised heavy barrels towards the dark sides of ships.

The cloths on the table were coloured ones and, when you came in from outside, it sometimes looked as though they had been arranged in some form of pattern; but, after you had been sitting down for a while, you observed that they were changed solely according to the whim of chance – as soon, in other words, as too much beer or cigarette ash had been spilt on them. The waiters glided between the tables in burgundy-coloured jackets, dispensing capacious glasses to the elect and changing tablecloths with an efficiency that would have impressed an undertaker.

The food they served here was plain and simple, with no refinements beyond the odd sprig of parsley or a crumpled lettuce leaf or two, but it was good, wholesome stuff that filled you up without burning a hole in your pocket. I ate lunch there occasionally but most often I made do with a glass or two of beer. I would buy a couple of evening papers at the tobacconist's next door and take them in with me to read, find a small table against one of the walls at the back and sit there on my own.

So, three or four days a week, the afternoons went by, like the strokes of oars in quiet waters. The minutes trickled down on to the surface of the water and now and then you would rest on the oars, just to watch the time go by – like the columns of print in the newspaper in front of you: yesterday's news that was already on its way to becoming ancient history.

After a few months, several of the other regulars had begun to say hello to me and one day at the end of April, I got into conversation with Hjalmar Nymark.

2

The afternoon we started to talk was one of cold, penetrating rain mixed with small, grey splotches of sleet. That year, spring had come at the end of March. Now, we were on our way backwards through the seasons again and the weather was more reminiscent of November than April.

I had spent the day writing postcards to friends and acquaintances. The last one was to a fellow called Veum who lived somewhere up between Stølen and Skansen. He would surely be glad to hear from me. Afterwards I had called the ciné bureau's automatic answering service in order to hear a thirty-second synopsis of one of the films that was currently playing in town. In spite of repeated dialling, all I got was the engaged tone. I didn't make any more calls. It wasn't wise to put too much strain on the phone bill.

The day before there had been an ad in one of the papers:

WE'RE GETTING ESTABLISHED! Harry Monsen Ltd, Detective Agency, have now opened a Bergen branch. International contact network, lastest electronic equipment. Twenty-four-hour surveillance, personal investigations, all types of detective work undertaken. First-class personnel, one hundred per cent confidentiality.

I had studied the ad closely. I speculated about what they meant by 'first-class' and 'one hundred per cent'. Perhaps I ought to call them up and ask them – or at least wish them luck. The ad gave their telephone number. They even had car phones. All I had was a telephone that had gone to sleep and a Mini which I couldn't afford to trade in for something better but which had long ago been ready for the eternal scrapyards. There were no two ways about it: I was headed for harder times.

It was the sort of day when you needed to brace your nerves with a drink or two and once I was out in the rain I turned up the collar of my coat, pulled my hat well down over my eyes and quickly traversed the short distance along to the café.

The café had one other distinctive feature. No matter when you entered it, it seemed full and yet there always seemed to be a vacant seat somewhere, once you'd taken a look around. This afternoon, however, it appeared that the rain had driven everything that moved off the streets in search of shelter and I was only just able to squeeze myself in behind a tiny table stacked with white porcelain ashtrays with adverts for Italian vermouth on them.

A waiter came to remove the ashtrays before asking me what I would like. I ordered a half-litre of pilsner and a whale steak and looked round the room. A fog was rising from wet clothes, hand-rolled cigarettes and smoky old pipes. Broad shoulders leaned forward over white plates, large hands grasped glasses that were half full and drained them in a single gulp before their owners turned their mighty torsos around and looked in the direction of the waiter in the way a nervous man looks back over his shoulder.

Hjalmar Nymark came in out of the rain, pushed back his wet hair and shook the water from his coat. He looked around him. There were no free tables but, right next to mine, there was an empty chair. Calmly, he approached. As he came to a halt in front of me, he nodded to me amiably and said: 'I can't see anyone I know. Is there room for me here?'

'As long as you don't require too much elbow room.' I moved my chair closer to the pillar against which the table had been placed. Then I got up and we shook hands. 'Veum. Varg Veum.'

He offered me a hand that was neither as large nor as powerful as I had expected. 'Hjalmar Nymark.'

He moved the empty chair over to the table and hung his wet overcoat over its back; then he sat down. When the waiter arrived, he ordered half a litre of pilsner and a plate of Norwegian stew. He fished the rolled-up newspaper out of one of the pockets of his coat and sat holding it.

'Terrible weather,' he said.

I nodded my agreement.

'But they do say that the summers are going to turn out colder during the eighties.'

'Sounds promising,' I said.

He gave me a searching look; he was quite open about it, didn't try to cover it up. 'And what's your line of business, Veum? No, wait – let me try to guess first. I used to be quite good at that, once.'

'Good at what?'

'Placing people.'

'Look at the back of the bottom shelf. That's where I belong.'

'Among the fringe professions?' he chuckled.

'I'm not so sure I'd describe it as a profession,' I replied, giving him a wry smile and running a hand through my hair. The grey in it wasn't much more than a hint as yet but, by the time the cold summers of the eighties were over, the snow would never leave it.

He studied me, taking in my blonde hair, my spring-pale Janus face,

5

my blue Levi shirt worn open at the neck, my slightly threadbare jacket, the blue V-necked sweater underneath it, and continuing down to my brown corduroy trousers. He cast a glance at my overcoat which was draped over the back of my chair.

'From the way you're dressed I'd put you somewhere at the lower end of the university's employment scale – a post-doctoral fellow or something of that sort. Or maybe something to do with a library.'

'The general impression's a bit down-at-heel, in other words?'

'Not exactly down-at-heel. But not particularly well-off, either. And not fashion-conscious, either, but that's probably because you can't afford to be. All the same . . . There's something that doesn't fit. You've got the look of a freelance about you. An unsuccessful freelance, of course.'

'Of course.'

'But that green hat of yours – I find it a bit confusing. It gives you an outdoors look, as if you were an engineer, or something of that kind.'

Our food arrived and I was glad of the interruption. Something was needed to take the edge off all these impressions.

Hjalmar Nymark broke the crispbread between his fingers as though it were a communion wafer but he dipped the broken pieces in his stew and didn't share them with anyone but himself.

'I can just see you in some little office somewhere, one belonging to a wholesale hardware business, let's say. You certainly can't afford a secretary and I don't really think you're kept all that busy but . . .'

I decided I had had enough and said curtly: 'I'm a detective. Private eye.'

For a moment he just sat there, gaping over his plate. Then he swallowed down what he had in his mouth, took hold of the rolled-up newspaper that lay beside him, batted the edge of the table with it lightly, and said: 'The very devil!'

'You can say that again. Actually, he has the office next to mine but not even he ever feels like popping his head round the door.'

He threw up his hands. 'Well, then – *you* ought to be the expert around here. What am I, do you think?'

I cast a rapid look at him: white shirt with broad tie, slightly spotted brown suit of an early-sixties cut; fingers that had nicotine stains on them, with bitten-down nails. 'Old age pensioner,' I said.

'Right. But what was I before that?'

I pointed my fork at him. 'Judging by your powers of observation, I'd say you were – a policeman.'

'Correct.'

'So we're probably both experts of a kind, really.'

'Yes. In a sense we're colleagues.'

'Except that I'm a bit down on my uppers and you've been an OAP for years.'

For a while, we ate on in silence. Then I said: 'How long have you been an OAP?'

'Ten years. I retired in '71.'

'And how do you make the time pass?'

A gleam came into his eyes and he looked at me with a faint, mischievous smile. 'Oh, I go sniffing around a bit. Do a bit of looking into old cases. Ones that haven't been cleared up.'

'Were you in the Crime Department?'

'Mm.' He nodded and we continued to eat.

He told me no more that day but later on it often used to happen that we had lunch or a glass of beer together.

3

At that time I was living a regular sort of life. Five days a week I was in the office. I was doing a couple of jobs for an insurance company. The work brought in enough money to enable me to keep my head above water – low water, anyway. Three or four days a week I looked in at the café and, more often than not, it was Hjalmar Nymark I sat there talking to. I spent the other evenings going for long, steady jogs over gravel and asphalt in sun, rain and sleet. The beers I had at the café used to result in my taking some chasers from the bottle of schnapps (in Norway we call it *akvavit*) I kept at home but the arduous bouts of running helped to keep the score even: if I was going to pieces, at least I was doing it slowly.

Every other weekend I had a visit from Thomas, who was ten now, looked at me with well-mannered, serious eyes and told me about football matches I hadn't seen and books I hadn't read. My marriage to Beate was on the way to becoming a memory as remote as that of the places where I'd spent the summers of my childhood. The biggest event that year – before I met Hjalmar Nymark – had been when the dentist, who had the office next to mine, had hired a new female assistant. After a few weeks she began to smile at me whenever we passed each other in the corridor.

At the beginning of May, summer began. The sudden heat laid the town flat and people went around with faces that looked liked boiled beetroot, longing for the cold weather to come back. They had their wish fulfilled. By about the seventeenth of the month the summer was over and the grey skies returned. After a few days it was as though the sunshine had never been and would never return.

On one of those days – when the sky lay on top of the town like a grey, woollen blanket – I received a telephone call from a man who didn't want to give me his name.

'Do you take on any kind of detective work, Veum?' he asked.

'It depends,' I replied.

'What kinds of work don't you take?'

I was feeling tired, so I said: 'Why don't you just tell me what it is you want me to do?'

'I think – I've got this feeling . . . that my wife's being unfaithful to me.'

I made no reply. On the other side of Vågen the old sailing ship *Statsråd Lemkuhl* was swarming with tourists. She reminded me of a stuffed swan full of lice.

'I need . . . I want to be sure,' continued the voice on the other end of the line.

'What of?' I asked, absent-mindedly.

'That she's being unfaithful to me! My wife.'

'That's the kind of work I don't take.'

There was a moment's silence. Then it came, violently: 'Why the hell didn't you say so in the first place?' He recollected himself and asked, a little more calmly: 'Is that on principle or is it a personal preference?'

I couldn't help laughing. 'Let's say it's both, then we're on the safe side.'

'I'll go to the other agency!' he yelped.

'Go ahead. I'm sure they're not bothered by things like that.'

'Things like what?'

'Principles.'

'Huh!' he said, bringing the conversation to an end and slamming down his receiver. I sat there looking at mine. It was only when I'd put it down that it struck me that that was a threat I hadn't heard before.

I closed the office early that day and went straight to the café. Hjalmar Nymark was already there and, when I appeared in the doorway, he waved me over to his table. He was sitting on his own.

The three or four weeks in which we had known each other had passed quickly but it felt as though we had been friends for years. We had a lot to talk about. Without exactly confiding in each other, we none the less found it easy to talk.

Our conversations had frequently centred on old criminal cases, both solved and unsolved ones, yet in the course of them we seemed to have covered most of the things two men whose ages lie thirty years apart can talk about.

Sometimes he would get genuinely serious. On one occasion he asked: 'When were you born, Veum?'

'1942,' I replied.

'So you don't remember anything of the war?'

'Not much.'

After that he sat looking gloomily into space for a long time and said nothing further.

On another occasion he said: 'Listen, Veum. The name Peacock. Does it mean anything to you?'

I shook my head slowly.

He went on: 'Peacock Paints Limited. They had a factory on Fjøsangerveien. There was a nasty explosion there in 1953. The whole place was burned down and a lot of people were killed.'

'An accident?'

He nodded heavily. 'So they said. I was in on the investigation. It

9

was a difficult case.'

A bit later that same evening he suddenly said: 'There are some cases you get really obsessed with. They get a hold of you and you can't stop thinking about them. They never let go.' He batted the edge of the table with his newspaper. 'Never!'

Somehow I got the idea that there was a connection between these two statements. It was as though he were trying to show me a jigsaw puzzle but didn't have all the pieces.

As was nearly always the case when we talked together, his eyes had a gleam in them and he spoke in a humorous tone of voice which said that yes, these were tragic things we were discussing but, for God's sake, Veum, it's history – history! On the occasions when the gleam in his eyes disappeared, and he became completely serious, I realized that something else was involved. Something that hadn't yet become history, something that was still alive – at least for him, at any rate. It was as if he were trying to tell me something but couldn't quite bring himself to take the plunge.

'Rat Poison. Does that mean anything to you, Veum?'

I shook my head. 'Rat Poison?'

'That was what they called him. During the war.'

'Wait . . . Does this have something to do with Peacock?'

He looked at me with eyes that were dark and inscrutable but made no reply. After a while he began to talk about something else.

On this May afternoon he seemed restless. He was drinking faster than usual and I couldn't afford to keep up with him. He kept talking anxiously about fire-blight and, even though there was every reason for anxiety on that score this year, there was still something odd about it.

'Ach, I feel old, Veum!' he broke out, suddenly.

'Well, we all have days when we . . .'

'I'm never going to get it all done. Haven't enough days left.'

'You've plenty of days left. You're strong and healthy and you . . .'

'But the years are going by, Veum – and the wolf's catching up with me.'

'The wolf?'

'*Time*, Veum. Time, slinking through the streets, baring its fangs at you. One day it'll snap at you and one day – one day it'll leap up and have you by the throat. And then you'll be out of it. Struck off the register.'

Cautiously, I said: 'But perhaps there are other registers – to get one's name on to?'

He put the newspaper down and slammed the flats of both his hands down heavily on the table, making his beer-glass jump between them. 'I don't think so,' he said, darkly.

I looked around me. The downpour outside had made the café dark and autumnal. Daylight had never been all that flattering to the place and the faces around us gaped like open wounds. Eyes that were turbid with wounded solitude and frustrated pride, mouths that slobbered over their glasses, churning out meaningless words, while time passed, mercilessly and inexorably.

It occurred to me that the image he had presented to me was an appropriately poetic one. I could see it in my mind's eye: a shaggy wolf with sharp fangs, a lonely hunter, deadly and irrefutable. The wolf of Fenris, eternally on the hunt. They were its home, those streets that were waiting for us out there. The wolf had been driven out of the forests and the wide open spaces. But in the town it still hunted through the asphalt-covered streets, over the glistening cobbles and along the gaping drains – time, the wolf. Perhaps it was as well to stay indoors.

I looked at Hjalmar Nymark. His strong face was impassive, locked. His dark eyes were far, far away. He was sitting erect behind the table with his head tilted back slightly and his gaze directed straight over my head, at some infinitely distant point. One of his hands was crooked round the rolled-up newspaper, while the other lay at the foot of his beer-glass like a dead rabbit.

'Forget it,' I said. 'Tell me about Peacock instead . . .'

Suddenly he was all there again. 'Why do you want to know?' he asked, suspiciously.

I shrugged my shoulders and made a gesture with my hands. 'It sounded – interesting.'

He gave me a dogged look. Then his face relaxed, not into a smile but rather as if it had suddenly opened. He said: 'I'm sorry. I'm not quite my usual self today.'

He looked round. 'This place is getting on my nerves. Let's go back to my flat. I've got a bottle of something there, and I'll tell you . . .'

We drank up, rose to our feet and left. Outside the rain was drifting in from the sea like cobwebs: long, sticky threads that clung to your hair, skin and clothes and made you feel sad and heavy. Up on the mountainside the trees were swelling, green and expectant, and in the gardens up towards Fjellveien the first pale lilacs had clung fast like slumbering, blue-white bats. But the flowers' heavy, cloying scent did not reach us where we stood in the rain, on a windswept stretch of pavement that ran alongside an abandoned wharf. I couldn't help looking round to see if the wolf was anywhere about. I couldn't see it but, if I stroked my hand over my face, I could feel where it had clawed at me.

This was the first occasion on which Hjalmar Nymark and I had both left the café at the same time.

4

Hjalmar Nymark lived on the third floor of an unpainted apartment house at the lower end of Skottegaten. His flat consisted of two small rooms, a kitchen and a cramped WC you entered from the outside hallway. A narrow door led from the kitchen out to a fire escape and, through the grey-white curtains, you had a view over the houses down in Nøstegaten and out along Puddefjorden, where the Askøy ferry pitched faithfully and reliably out through the rain.

We each went into the kitchen and got ourselves a glass before going into the living-room, where Hjalmar Nymark produced an unopened bottle of brandy from a squat, brown-lacquered sideboard. Here the windows faced away from the sun, up towards Klosteret.

Hjalmar Nymark filled our glasses to the brim, without adding water. '*Skål*,' he said.

'*Skål*,' I replied. The grape liquor tore at my throat, sinking slowly through my body, and then opening out like a red-brown rose of warmth somewhere down in my stomach.

Hjalmar Nymark sat in a deep, brown armchair with light-coloured arm-rests made of lacquered wood. I occupied a grey-green chair that was upholstered all over. Against one wall, by the sideboard, stood a spindleback chair and between us was a small table with a well-used cloth running across its centre. A few old, yellowed family portraits stood on the sideboard and near them lay a small pile of well-thumbed, dog-eared paperbacks. Beside the black stove there was a stack of newspapers and a box for firewood, which was empty. A pale green door led into the other room. Beside the door there was a television set and a black portable radio stood on the floor.

'Taking a look round?' said Hjalmar Nymark.

'It's an old habit,' I said, smiling wryly.

He nodded. 'I know what you mean. The places people live in often tell you more about them than bears thinking about. A good investigator will always carry out a proper on-the-spot inspection, not just to find clues but also to get some sort of picture of the person concerned.'

He took a gulp from his glass, and said: 'As you can see, I'm a bachelor. There aren't any flowers in here – no baskets containing balls of wool, no bowls of fruit, no pictures of grandchildren on the wall.

Those people over there are my parents and they both died a long time ago. This isn't a home, just a place I spend the night in. A place where I can get in out of the rain. And have a drink. *Skål* again, Veum.'

I raised my glass and took a sizeable swallow.

He hesitated for a moment. 'Have you ever been married?'

Silently, I nodded.

'Any children?'

'One. A boy.'

'That's probably what a man misses most.' He hadn't switched on any lights yet and in the semi-darkness his face looked swarthy, almost Mediterranean, against his grey-white hair. When you looked straight into his face it appeared rectangular because of his firm, prominent jaw and broad temples. The skin was stretched taut over his massive facial structure and he leaned towards me with eyes that were black.

Then he straightened up again in his chair and said, in a sober voice: 'Now and again, when I'm out taking a walk in Nordnes Park and sit down on a bench to rest for a bit, some little toddler – one who's out with his mother – will come up to me. Up he'll come, toddling on his little legs that are barely able to carry him, and he'll smile and stretch out his arms to the old man sitting on the bench. I'll lift him up and sit him on my knee and he'll laugh and pull my nose. Either that or he'll want to get down again and go back to his mother because the old man suddenly seems too close. And his mother will smile in that self-confident way all mothers of young children do when their charges aren't crying. And on they'll go. It's at times like that that I realize what I've – how old is your son?' he asked, breaking off.

'Ten.'

'Are you divorced?'

Again, I nodded.

'Now and then I sometimes wonder which is worse: to have once been happily married, only to get divorced. Or to have lived alone all one's life without really ever having shared anything with anyone.'

'Surely it varies,' I said. 'Suddenly being alone again can be both a shock and a liberation. But when the initial terror or sense of freedom has died away, all that's left is loneliness, really. But I think I've found a kind of rationale for that now.'

'But it's a bitter life, Veum. When you're seventy years old, and haven't all that many years left to look forward to, you feel bitter about having lived the whole of your life on your own. It's . . . nineteen years now since I slept with a woman.' His gaze grew distant. 'In a cold hotel room; a woman in her late forties, wearing a stiff dress with the kind of rustling petticoat that can stand up by itself on the floor. I was in Haugesund working on a case and I met her in the restaurant over a glass of beer. Later on she came up with me to my room to have a drink and we . . .' He made a gesture with both arms. Laconically, he added: 'I could have had others, too. I could have paid for a woman, the way other men do. But . . .' His mouth tautened into a hard smile. 'I didn't want it to be like that. I wanted it to be something you did because you had warm feelings for another person, something to share with someone. Otherwise it wasn't worth it, and now – now, it's too late. 1962 – that's a long time ago, Veum. Little boys have grown up and had their first women in that time.'

I thought back. To 1962, when I was twenty years old and had long ago had my first sexual encounters. One career had just come to an end and another had only just begun. So it is that life passes its threads through us and invisibly but inexorably sews its pattern.

'How long is it since you . . .' He didn't finish the question.

I sipped my drink and smiled wryly over the reddish-brown liquid. 'About six months ago, in Stavanger.'

He peered down into his own glass before suddenly glancing up at me and there was something of the old, humorous gleam in his eyes again. 'So we both had our last love affair in Rogaland.' After a little while it came, like an afterthought: 'Yes, Bergen's a cold town.'

'No colder than most,' I said. 'But you often feel more alone in the town you were born in, because it shouldn't *be* that way. In other towns it's – from a certain point of view – natural that you should be alone. At the same time your loneliness gives you fresh hunting-grounds, a sudden freedom you don't have in the town you come from.'

Hjalmar Nymark rose to his feet, went over to the wall and switched on a small table lamp. It filled the room with a gentle, yellowish light. Outside the dusk was flooding in stiff torrents against the window-panes. Inside two men – one of them seventy and the other nearly forty – sat with two glasses and a bottle on the table between them, talking about loneliness.

We drank in silence for a while.

I said: 'You were going to tell me about Peacock, weren't you?'

He looked at me with another kind of distance in his eyes. 'Don't you even remember their adverts? A peacock with its tail spread out. On placards, in all the colours of the rainbow. There used to be a big one painted on the wall facing north that you couldn't miss when you were driving along Fjøsangerveien.'

I shook my head. 'I must have been too young. All I can remember is Bjercke's "The Painter" – and that healthy, wholesome-looking fellow in the striped sweater with the toothpaste smile who looked as though he were trying to get us to clean our teeth with Fenom.'

He got up and went through to the room that lay beyond the pale green door. When he came back, he was carrying a brown, oblong cardboard box tied up with string. He put the box down on the floor. It smacked heavily against the carpet.

'This is all the stuff I've collected about Peacock,' he said, sitting back down at the table, pouring himself another glass of brandy and filling mine up, too.

'It looks pretty heavy,' I said. 'What's in it?'

He opened the blade of a penknife and cut the string around the box. He felt inside and pulled out a handful of papers. One of them he held out to me. 'A lot of it's newspaper cuttings. I've also got transcripts and copies of all the hearings and technical investigations that took place after the fire.'

A yellowed newspaper cutting lay on the top of the pile. The typesetting showed it was a set of headlines from the early 1950s. The street sales ghosts hadn't yet taken over the newpaper layout departments in those days and, even though this was undoubtedly a front-page story, the headlines contained plenty of information. The banner read: '15 KILLED IN FIRE-EXPLOSION.' Underneath, in smaller type, were the words: 'PEACOCK PAINTWORKS ON FJØSANGERVEIEN BURNS TO GROUND.' From the text it emerged that people in the neighbourhood had heard a loud explosion at about 2.25 p.m. Immediately after it had been discovered that the building was on fire and, when the fire brigade had arrived at 2.35, the entire structure was in flames. The production room had been worst affected and all fifteen people who had been killed in the blast had been working there. The administrative wing had sustained the least damage. Extensive rescue work had been carried out in order to extricate possible survivors and a dramatic photograph showed firemen helping the injured out of the burning building amid garlands of cascading water.

A reference to a column on page eight led me on to the next cutting. Two women were photographed standing in front of the blackened site of the fire, one of them young with dark hair in a bun, the other older with horn-rimmed spectacles, a mouth like an owl's beak and a hairstyle that looked like a daisy. The caption read: 'Office clerk Elise Blom and secretary Alvhilde Pedersen, who both escaped from the fire without injury, in front of the burned-down factory building on Fjøsangerveien.' The photograph was accompanied by interviews with, among others, the two women in the photograph; all those interviewed confirmed unanimously that the explosion had been completely unexpected and 'a shock', according to Miss Pedersen. The factory's owner and director, a man named Hagbart Hellebust, had been in Oslo when the explosion had occurred; on the telephone he had been unable to say anything except that he was deeply shaken by the disaster and that he had the very greatest of sympathy for the dead and their families. It also emerged from the piece that several of the employees had performed acts of sheer heroism during the period before the fire brigade arrived and that the death toll would have been even higher had it not been for the contribution they had made. The fire chief said it was impossible at this stage to hazard a guess as to the cause of the explosion.

I thumbed my way further through the pile. Several cuttings from other newspapers told the story of the fire without differing to any significant degree. The reports on the technical investigations were so exhaustive and peppered with specialist terminology that it was impossible, merely from a brief look through, to obtain any proper idea of what they had revealed.

I looked up at Hjalmar Nymark who was watching me with the expression of someone who was showing off a unique collection of old photographs. I said: 'Did they ever find out what caused the fire?'

He nodded. 'It was a leak in one of the production tanks. The gas that seeped out was highly inflammable and it wouldn't have needed more than a spark from the generating plant to set off the explosion. That was the theory they put forward as to what happened.'

'I see. But?'

He was looking at me as though wondering how far he could trust me.

I went on: 'Yes, I'm assuming there's a *but* – otherwise you wouldn't have collected this material.'

He nodded. 'It's a funny thing, Veum. I started working in the Crime Department in 1945 and I've lost count of all the crimes I've helped to investigate since then. Everything from the most run-of-the-mill break-ins to murder, rape, child abuse.' His face was grim now. 'I've seen some sorry fates, I can tell you. A policeman's life is that of an outcast. When you spend at least twelve hours of every day – overtime included – poking about in other people's wretchedness you tend to get a bit thick-skinned after a while. Women who've been subjected to battering every single day for the last thirty years, infants of only three or four months old who've been hurled from wall to wall, repulsive females who've been unfaithful to their meek-and-mild husbands for years until one day the meekness suddenly runs out and they find themselves on the floor with a knife in the vicinity of their heart. Or drunken bums who've stolen a bottle of beer off a brewery lorry, and whores who weigh thirteen stone and have fleeced some trusting grass-widower of a week's pay. The whole gamut, Veum. Girls of sixteen who've been raped and have stayed up all night crying and will maybe never be able to look at a man again, a fourteen-year-old car thief who's smashed an automobile into a telegraph pole out in Fana somewhere and is sitting with the lower part of his body firmly jammed in the wreckage and will never be able to move it again. The whole bag of tricks. But – of all the cases I've worked on – there haven't been many that made such an impression on me as the Peacock fire did.'

'Why do you think that is?'

'Because – because I *know* we're never going to get to the bottom of that case. And there's nothing that irritates a policeman more than to feel that a case has gone unsolved.'

'But . . .'

'And because,' he went on, ignoring me, 'because it was so easy to see the *pattern* in it all. The poor drunk with the bottle of beer got six months on Jæren. Hagbart Hellebust went scot-free.'

'The factory owner?'

'That's right.'

'But he was in Oslo when the explosion took place.'

'Correct. But if anyone was responsible, he was.'

'How do you know?'

He gave me a weary look. 'If I'd *known*, I wouldn't have kept this cardboard box in the house all this time and Hagbart Hellebust wouldn't be where he is now. That was the really damnable thing about it all. There was no evidence.'

'And where's Hagbart Hellebust now?'

'Doesn't the name mean anything to you?'

I had to think for a moment or two. 'It does ring a bell somewhere – a distant one – but I can't place it.'

'How about Hagbart Helle, does that sound more familiar?'

I nodded. 'Of course.'

Hjalmar Nymark poured us another round and then sat back with the bottle in his hand. 'What do you know about him?'

I hesitated for a moment. 'Not very much. I know he left the country some time in the early 1950s and settled down in the Caribbean or thereabouts and I know that he owns a steadily growing fleet of ships that sail under flags of convenience. One of those shipowners who after the war didn't bother to preserve even a semblance of national feeling but were pretty sure what they thought of taxes and the welfare state. But I've no clear picture of him. As a person, I mean. He seems a bit – shadowy.'

'Shadowy is right!' In his excitement, Hjalmar Nymark waved the bottle about, making the brandy slosh around inside. I was afraid he might hit the edge of the table with it, the way he usually did with his newspaper. 'Not a single photograph's been taken of him since 1954 and, when he does visit Norway, he shuns publicity like the plague.'

'Evidently a man who values his peace and quiet. Is he married?'

'Oh, yes. He's seventy-three and married to a woman who isn't yet forty. She's British, so far as I know. He met her in Barbados. That's where he lives.'

I raised my glass. 'That's where we should be.'

'Not on your life!' He leaned forward over the edge of the table. 'I can't abide the sun. As far as I've been able to manage it, I've tried not to spend one moment more than necessary away from West Norway.' He gazed out of the window. 'A long, rainy West Norwegian summer – that's my idea of happiness.'

'You must be a happy man, Nymark. Not everybody gets their wishes fulfilled as easily as that.' I could feel a tingling sensation in the

17

top of my head. I was starting to get slightly drunk.

'Yes, Hagbart Helle made his fortune out of the Peacock fire and that's a fact, Veum,' he continued quickly.

I leaned back in my chair with my glass in my hand. 'Hear ye, hear ye – the Story of Hagbart from Norway!'

'You might very well call it that, it's a real old-fashioned success story.' His 's's were slightly slurred. The brandy was having its effect on him, too.

'Hagbart Hellebust was born in Bergen in 1908. His father came from somewhere up the coast, Bulandet I think it was, and worked as a dyer. His son began in the same trade but went further up the colour chart, so to speak. He went into paint. Like a lot of successful businesses, Peacock began as something of a one-man firm. There's one thing you can definitely say about Hagbart Helle: he knew how to start from modest beginnings. He did it twice. Peacock soon became a household name and the business grew. What had begun as a wooden shed out on Sjøgaten became a large factory on Fjøsangerveien and Hagbart was able to trade in his attic on Ladegårdsgaten for a villa in Hop. But that was typical of the family. For a few years he had his younger brother, Yngvar, working with him but Yngvar started up in hosiery and soon had a flourishing business of his own. By the way, he still lives in Bergen.'

'Does he allow himself to be photographed?'

'Oh, I think so. When Hagbart Helle comes to Bergen – he only comes once a year and he stays for one day only. That's the first of September, his brother's birthday. There's a family get-together.'

'But, otherwise, he stays in the sunshine?'

'Yes. The Fjøsangerveien fire could have been a disaster for him, of course, but he turned it to his advantage and managed to get paid the whole of the insurance money. The total amount was never made public but I can guarantee that it was a pretty substantial one for 1953.'

'In other words it wouldn't even cover the electric light bill nowadays?'

'Probably not. Hagbart bought himself a share in a ship, quite a large share.'

'Here in Norway?'

'Oh, yes. Here in Norway and in complete accordance with all the regulations. He just changed horses, that's all. Turned himself from a factory owner into a shipowner in the space of a couple of days. And then suddenly, about a year later, he popped up, like a jack-in-the-box, in the Caribbean. By then he'd sold his share in the shipping company here in Norway – it went bankrupt some years later, actually – and settled down in Barbados with a little white ship in his pocket. Bulk cargo. That was where the easy money was in those days, then as now. And on the funnel of that ship the oceans of the world saw for the first time the emblem that was later to become so well known: two

18

white 'H's against a blue background. That double H has followed him around ever since. He timed his appearance well – a year and a half before the Suez crisis. That was what he used to build himself up. Like that of a lot of other shipowners, his income can be charted against the fluctuations of the crisis in the Middle East. The high points are the years 1956, 1968 and 1973.'

He grew quiet. We sat in silence for a while, sipping our drinks and listening to the rain beating against the windowpanes. Somewhere in the building someone turned down the volume on a TV set.

Down on the street cars went by at regular intervals but it was a quiet street and the intervals were long.

When Hjalmar Nymark eventually broke the silence, his eyes were dark and embittered once more. 'I said just now that no other case made such an impression on me as the Peacock fire did. I'll tell you why. I've seen a lot of corpses in my time. Bodies that have lain in cars at the bottom of the sea for days, charred corpses dragged from houses that burned down, old folk who've lain rotting in their beds until the smell finally alerted the neighbours. But that night at Peacock . . . fifteen charred corpses, Veum. I still sometimes have nightmares about what I saw that time. And I was no youngster then, either. I was forty-two years old and I'd been exposed to a bit of everything, during the war, for instance. But that . . .'

He looked round the room as though he were gazing out across another, considerably larger and gloomier. 'The big production hall was charred completely black. The bodies of those who had been standing nearest the spot where the actual explosion occurred had been spattered all over the floors and walls and what was left of the roofing. Of the bodies that remained intact, several were those of men who had been moving away from the site of the explosion – towards the exit. One of these men had even got out of the production room and out on to the stairway. But the stairway had burned down, too, and he hadn't succeeded in getting out. Of the eighteen men who were working in there, only three got out alive. One of them was blind for the rest of his life and the others had severe burns.'

'But they survived?'

'They did but I wouldn't have liked to have been one of them. Two of them are dead now and you'll find the wretched remains of the one who's still alive down in the docks somewhere. He's one of the regulars down there and he looks plain bloody terrible, Veum.'

'What's his name?'

'Olai Osvold. But they just call him "Bombsite".'

I smiled, wryly. They certainly knew how to give a man a name.

'Did you succeed in discovering anything on the site of the fire?'

'As I told you before, the cause of the fire was an explosion in one of the production tanks. They found something that *could* have been a construction defect and the gas that would have leaked out as a result

19

was highly inflammable. The results of the whole inquiry were sent to the company's insurers and they didn't protest. And, as I'm sure you know, those people don't pay out money if they can see any way of avoiding it. It wasn't just a question of the insurance on the factory. There were a lot of life insurance policies involved as well.'

I nodded. I knew. They occasionally paid me fees and it was never money easily earned.

He went on: 'The prosecuting authorities also studied the report. To see if there might be a possibility of bringing an action on grounds of negligence, infringement of the safety regulations, that kind of thing. But they found it impossible to take that step on the basis of the material we had managed to collect. The man who was responsible for seeing that the regulations were observed, that all the machinery was checked and all suspected leaks immediately reported, was the works foreman. He was a fellow called Holger Karlsen and he was one of the men who lost their lives in the fire.'

'So . . .'

'So, nothing. The case was dropped and all subsequent attempts to get it taken up again met with refusal.'

'So, somebody did try to get it taken up again. Who?'

'Me. Listen . . . Holger Karlsen's widow came to see us. She was still off-balance from the blow she'd sustained – she'd been left to cope single-handed with a four-year-old daughter to look after. She was confused and talked incoherently but she maintained that when he'd been setting off for work that morning, her husband had said he was quite certain there was a leak in the plant and that he was going to take the matter up with the management again.'

'*Again?*'

'That's right. She'd taken him to mean that he'd mentioned it the previous day as well but they hadn't talked about it any more and she couldn't tell us anything precise. Hagbart Hellebust categorically denied that Karlsen had ever been to see him and his testimony received the backing of the other administrative personnel. No one had heard anything about it.'

'But a leak of that kind – it wouldn't be easy to prove its existence, would it?'

He shook his head, heavily. 'Not immediately, no. The construction defect could have been so small that no one might even have suspected a leak at first. But the defect would get bigger and, if you were lucky, you'd notice a smell of gas. There are also instruments you can use to measure that sort of thing but the equipment they used in those days was far less sensitive than that in use today and a higher concentration of gas in the atmosphere was necessary before it registered anything – such a high concentration that the danger of an explosion would already be present. Holger Karlsen had worked in the paint business for fifteen years and he ought to have had enough experience to know what he was talking about. But . . .' he threw up his hands. 'What Holger Karlsen thought or did, we shall never know – they didn't even need to cremate him.'

'But if his widow told them that . . .'

'His widow! Who the hell was going to pay any attention to what some confused female suffering from shock kept babbling on about? She was merely out to clear her husband's posthumous name – if it were to get out that the fire had been due to negligence on his part, his life insurance policy might go up in smoke, too. That's what they said, anyway?'

'Surely it wouldn't?'

'*That's what they said*, I'm telling you. I talked to her many times later on, after she recovered from it all, and I tried – as I told you – to get the case taken up again, but it came to nothing. Because there was one other thing . . .

'As a matter of protocol, all fifteen bodies had to be identified. First, they had to be sorted out one from the other, as far as was possible – the ones that had been blown to pieces, I'm talking about. We went by the teeth, initially. Then, if that wasn't enough, we followed other distinguishing marks: remains of rings, watches, belt buckles, that kind of thing. I told you we found one of them right on the stairway. That was Holger Karlsen.'

'I see.'

'And when we did a post-mortem on him, we discovered that his lungs were practically free from smoke particles and that the back of his head bore the marks of a nasty blow.'

'*I see*,' I repeated, with more gravity this time. 'And how did you explain that?'

'We explained it,' he said, acidly, 'by supposing that some of the roofwork had collapsed as he'd been trying to get out, that it had struck him on the head and killed him outright. You have to remember that it was a fire-explosion and that the fire spread within the space of a couple of minutes, possibly even less – and something like that *could* quite easily have happened. The only thing I found odd was that it was Karlsen it happened to.'

'Agreed. But nobody else thought likewise?'

He shook his head.

'Were you in charge of the investigation?'

'No. It was an older colleague of mine. He's dead, too, now. One of the most difficult things about a case like this one is that so many of the people who were involved in it are either dead now or so old that they've forgotten most of what happened. And we only did the spadework. A commission of public inquiry was set up to study the incident, too.'

'Why?'

'Because fifteen men had lost their lives and there was a general

21

election that autumn.'

I put my glass down. It was empty. Outside it had grown completely dark. 'Have you got any more?'

He surveyed me gloomily. 'The only sure things I've got are Holger Karlsen's widow's statement and the body of Karlsen himself. The rest of it is so uncertain that . . . it builds mainly on a hypothesis that has never been confirmed. And when you build on hypotheses, what you end up with are hypotheses, too, aren't they?'

'Is there anything – anything I can try to do for you?'

He shook his head firmly. 'No, no. You must forgive an old man for poking about in cases everybody's long since forgotten. All I'm telling you is a story, Veum – a little bedtime story.'

'Then tell me about your hypothesis, too.'

He looked at his watch. He had to hold the dial right up to his face in order to see the hands. I noticed that he looked terribly tired. I didn't feel exactly on top of the world, either. The pleasant stage of tipsiness had passed: now the brandy lay like a sour clot somewhere in the region of my midriff. He said: 'If I'm to do that, I'll have to tell you about Rat Poison and about things that happened in the war. And that's a long story, too. I don't think I can manage it. Not tonight.' He slowly transferred his gaze from the cardboard box to the door of his bedroom. The bottle before him was empty and there was only a drop left in his glass. 'Why don't we meet again tomorrow in the café and I'll tell you about it then.'

I got up. It was a heavy burden to lift and the floor felt like a quagmire underneath me. 'Same time?'

'Maybe a bit later,' he mumbled. 'Is that all right for you?'

I nodded.

He came out from behind the table, offered me his hand and shook mine firmly.

'Thanks for listening to me, anyway. Think no more about it. It's just . . . a muddle. I'm just an old . . . man.' His words were coming with more and more difficulty, slower and slower, and his footsteps were heavy as he escorted me to the door.

I clambered my way down a dark shaft in the centre of the building, emerged through the squeaking doors and felt rain on my face: wet, black rain. A dark shop window stared at me from the other side of the street, like an empty eye-socket in a face grown old. I turned up the collar of my coat, bowed my head into the rain and began to walk.

5

My cups of coffee the next morning had the acrid flavour of old sou'westers. Outside the windows of my office there were occasional brief glimpses of sunlight in between the heavy downpours. There was no let-up in the overcast conditions inside my head.

Hjalmar Nymark came to the café around six o'clock, as he had promised. He entered quickly and he was looking back over his shoulder as though someone were on the point of following him in. He remained standing just inside the door, looking inquiringly from face to face until his gaze came to rest upon me. He gave me a rough nod and there was suddenly something huddled and uneasy about him, something that hadn't been there before. He kept glancing about him and he studied each person who came in through the doorway with sharp eyes. The rolled-up newspaper was rotating nervously in one of his hands and it took him barely five minutes to drain his first half-litre.

When he ordered another, I asked, cautiously: 'Is anything the matter?'

He scowled at me and bit his lower lip. 'Did we get through a whole bottle of brandy yesterday?'

I nodded. 'We certainly did.'

'I can feel it. It doesn't take me the way it does other people – I don't get a hangover, it's more . . . nerves. Fear. I get the feeling there's someone following me.'

'Following you?'

'Yes,' he said, heavily. He looked down into his beer-glass. When he lifted his face again he was gazing reflectively over my left shoulder. 'Perhaps it would be better . . . Perhaps it would have been better just to let sleeping wolves lie.'

'What do you mean?'

He gave me a dark look. 'I'm not sure now that it's really a very good idea to go digging up corpses that are twenty-eight years old. Or even older. A man gets tired more quickly at my age. I've seen too much. Too much misery and far too little happiness. I think there have got to be limits to the amount of experience an individual can absorb, don't you?'

I let one of my fingers slide down the moist exterior of my glass. It left a smooth trail from rim to bottom. I said: 'You said yesterday you'd tell me about – Rat Poison.'

Once again he looked around him. Then the turned his gaze towards me again. 'Are you sure you really want to know?'

'Absolutely,' I replied.

'Very well, then.' He seemed to straighten up in his chair, as though he were taking his seat on a rostrum. But the audience he was addressing couldn't have been a large one for he talked in a subdued voice, so softly that hardly a word escaped further than the table at which we sat. 'How old were you when the war ended, Veum?'

'Only two or three. I remember practically nothing of it.'

'What did your father do during the war?'

'Oh, he was one of the silent majority. One of the people who didn't do anything much at all. He sold tickets on the trams, just as he'd done before and as he went on doing afterwards. In his spare time he read about Nordic mythology but I doubt if he had much time for the Nazis. I think it's a safe bet that he was a Social Democrat. But he died when I was only fourteen, so . . .'

'All right. This won't take long – I don't want to paint too rosy a picture of the part I played in the war either. But I was – well, one of the activists. As you know, there's still a lot of debate about who really started the resistance movement; but I can tell you that here in West Norway, at any rate, it was folk from the Labour Party and the Communists, led by Peder Furubotn. I knew Furubotn slightly from earlier days – my father was a furniture maker – and I got involved in the movement early on. But, by the time Furubotn was setting up his headquarters in Valdres, I was back in Bergen, and I more or less lost touch with *that* cell. In the meantime, the Home Front had been organized and several other cells, too, and I witnessed quite a few dramatic incidents. There was one time, in the Evanger area . . .' He broke off. 'Am I boring you?'

'No, no – for God's sake, no. Please go on.'

'All right. The leader of the group I belonged to from 1942 until 1945 was a man called Konrad Fanebust who later became mayor of Bergen. He's probably one of the most important war heroes in this part of Norway and the work he did was invaluable. But that time, in Evanger, we ran into a German ski patrol. Fanebust was there, there was myself, a man called Jakob Olsen and a couple of lads from Voss. Olsen was killed instantly and Fanebust got a bullet in his shoulder. He went off the ski-track and fell and broke a leg. We returned the Germans' fire while one of the lads from Voss made a temporary splint for Fanebust and got him on to a ski-sledge. Then we set off. The weather was terrible, there was a blizzard, it was late spring and the river level was rising. All the same, we managed to get across to the opposite bank and up into the mountains. There was a hut up at Hamlagrø we used to use, and there we were able to attend to Fanebust's leg and bullet wound properly. He was lucky to pull through but he was worth his

24

weight in gold.

'For the next four months, after we'd got him back to the Bergen area again, he directed operations from his bed, even though the fracture was a compound one and he's never really ever recovered from it, not even now. My role in the cell was as a kind of security chief. I did intelligence work. Of course, I'd had experience of police work from before the war but during the war I worked – on the outside. It was while I was doing that intelligence work that I got on to the trail of Rat Poison.'

'Who – or what – was Rat Poison?'

He was far, far away. The newspaper hung limply in his hand. He hadn't touched his beer. 'Try to imagine Bergen during the war. A blacked-out town. Now and then you'd hear an explosion, or the sound of a German car tearing through the streets. Or the noise of marching feet as one of their boot-clad patrols went by. All of a sudden the air-raid sirens would start to howl and then you'd have to hurry away to the nearest air-raid shelter in whatever clothes you could manage to struggle into. Women and children, the old and the sick. The bombs would start falling. First, you'd hear the distinctive whining noise. Then it would go completely quiet. Deadly quiet. And then there would be the explosion. The earth would shake beneath you – or it might be so far away that you could hardly hear it at all. Either was equally terrifying. When the raid was over, and the all-clear sounded, you'd go home again. Down on the wharves there would be a great glow of light: a ship in flames, houses on Nordnes burning to the ground, desperate folk trying to save what few possessions they had, weeping and cursing, the sound of oaths in German and Norwegian, the screams of the dying and wounded . . .'

His face was bitter now; his nervousness had given way to the embitterment these memories of forty years ago still aroused in him. 'But most of the time the streets were dark, the houses shut up behind lowered blinds. It was in them that we met, laid fresh plans, printed illegal newspapers and leaflets, sat in front of home-made radio sets and listened to London. And through those dark streets a car would come quietly purring and pull up at the edge of the kerb, filled with men in dark overcoats with pale, narrow faces. Then someone would give a sign and the car would empty. The men in the long overcoats would run up to one of the houses, clutching pistols, thunder up the stairs, position themselves in front of a door, a swift order would be given and the door would be kicked open, there would be a shout, someone would be trying to gather things together at the last minute, someone else would reach for a gun, shots would be fired but it would all be soon over. One of the Norwegians would lie dead or wounded on the floor, the others would be put up against the wall and soon be on their way to detention. The Gestapo.'

He almost spat the word out. '*Gestapo*. Can you think of an uglier word? It hisses like – like the brood of snakes they were, hellish black creatures of the slime . . . they didn't even look like ordinary Germans, they were little and shrunken, like devils. Even today I get seized by terror just thinking about them. We never had one hour's peaceful sleep, Veum. The mornings were the worst time. That was when they used to come, in the grey light of dawn. At the wolf hour, do you know when that is?'

I nodded.

'It's the last hour before daybreak. The time when most people die. That was when they used to arrive, as if they were death's own messengers. The Gestapo.'

He stopped talking for a moment, took a gulp from his glass and put it down firmly. 'And the worst of it was that the enemy was right there in our midst. The Gestapo had their collaborators and what was most abominable about what happened in those dark years was that it was Norwegians who informed on Norwegians, it was Norwegians who pointed their fingers at other Norwegians and said *him* and *her* and *here* and *there*! Without their informers the Gestapo would never have been as efficient as they were.'

His gaze was bitter. 'There was a special breed of sewer vermin that lived in the dark streets of Bergen and they were worse than the mangiest rats. They were the men who shunned the light of day, the ones who saw a chance to profit from the war, make money out if it – or who exploited the situation for their own ends. Murderers and grave-robbers and profiteers. And one of the worst of all those bastards was the man who ordinary people knew only by the name Rat Poison.'

'Who was he?'

'Rat Poison was a shadow, a ghost. No one could ever get near him and it's one of the tragedies of the post-war era that it's never been definitely established who Rat Poison actually was.'

'Does that mean that . . .'

'Whatever I think of Rat Poison, I see a character out of pulp fiction, a bit like those drawing of villains you used to see on the cover of *Detective Magazine* before the war: hat down over the eyes, overcoat collar turned up and a shifty look from a face that had almost demonic features.'

He took a swallow and continued: 'Nobody knows for certain when he began to operate but the first sign I picked up of anything that might have been his trail was in connection with a couple of cases of large-scale informing I was working on during the autumn of 1942. But the real peak of his career was in the years from 1943 to 1945.'

'And did you get on to his trail?'

'It was like doing ordinary intelligence work, the only difference was that it was illegal and was, for that reason, both less effective and more difficult. Most of my leads came through interviews with witnesses or

26

people who'd happened to be around at the time. But Rat Poison wasn't content merely with informing. He also killed people and he was an extremely dangerous murderer. He had a natural talent for killing and he never left any evidence. But some of the witnesses' statements . . . Catching Rat Poison became one of our highest priorities but we never succeeded, neither then nor later on. And we did absolutely all that we could to succeed. Tracking down informers was important – that way they could eventually be eliminated.'

'Eliminated?'

'That's right. There was a war on, remember, Veum. We weren't playing games. But I did my utmost to see that we had firm evidence before we took that step.'

'But what was this trail you were talking about?'

'It became clear quite early on that the man who was Rat Poison had one remarkable distinguishing characteristic: he had a limp, probably in his left leg. There was that and the fact that he often hid out in the area to the south-east of Bergen, let's call it the Os-Ulven area. But there wasn't much else. The bit about the limp was important. People noticed it as early as 1942 and, in nearly all the subsequent murder cases, there was someone who had seen a lame person, even if that was the only thing they had noticed. It was often as though he were invisible when he carried out his operations.

'Really?'

'Yes. His favourite method was the "accident". Nine out of ten of all the people we suspected Rat Poison of having murdered died from what might be called natural causes – if you can call being run over, falling down a flight of stairs and breaking your neck, drowning and so on, natural. But there were so many of these deaths that they began to attract attention. In the course of 1943 eight people, all of whom occupied central positions in the resistance movement, died in this way. Only one of them was shot, in the usual fashion. In 1944 there were twelve such deaths, plus one shooting. And a woman in her fifties, who acted as a courier, was strangled. Before the liberation in 1945 he killed another three people – two straightfoward murders and one "accident". We reckoned that altogether he was directly responsible for the deaths of twenty-six resistance workers; and, indirectly – by means of information – for the deaths of something like fifty others.'

'But what happened after the war was over?'

'We worked flat out attempting to trace him. We mopped up several nests of informers after the liberation, you know, and we interrogated all those whom we arrested very thoroughly. But it turned out that no one on the other side knew who Rat Poison was either. A German officer confirmed that Rat Poison had occasionally functioned as a link-man between one of the informers and the Gestapo. The man had had a limp but he had worn a stocking over his face. The officer said he was a man of about five foot six and quite powerfully built. The man had received a large sum of money and they had met each other on the road along Svartediket. The man with the limp had been on his way out of town, the German had been heading into town. On another occasion their meeting had taken place at Sydneshaugen, in a narrow close up near Dragefjellet. They had also met on Nordnes and on Sandbrekkeveien over in Fana. All their meetings had taken place under cover of night and the man had always worn a stocking mask. In the end we came to the conclusion that not even the Gestapo had known his true identity. They'd just made use of his help. The German officer had brought the payment with him and delivered it each time, after the information had been given and checked. In a way he must have operated as a kind of freelance, a lone wolf.'

'But . . .'

'You see, what made the whole investigation quite impossible was the fact that no one, except perhaps the murder victims themselves, had even seen him. And, secondly, there was no firm evidence that they really *were* murders, those accidents. They *could* have been accidents, if they'd just been isolated occurrences and hadn't formed any kind of a pattern.'

'But . . .'

'*But*,' he said grimly, 'I had a hunch. A very strong hunch.'

'Aha. Tell me about it.'

Once again his gaze went searching round the room. He said: 'There was a man called Harald Wulff. He came from somewhere up in the Ulven area. He was born in 1914, on a little farm up there, and between the wars he worked as some kind of an electrician. He joined the Nazi Party early on, back in 1934. I remember he was one of the people we brought down to the police station after the theatre riot in 1936. That was the time the Nazis held a demonstration against Nordahl Grieg's *But Tomorrow!* Officially, he was never regarded as anything more than a small-time Nazi. In 1946 he was sentenced for treason and went to jail but he got out again, on probation, only three years later. There were a few people who thought they *might* have seen Harald Wulff near the scenes of a couple of the accidents I was investigating. People who knew him from the confrontations of the inter-war years. But none of them was ever a hundred per cent certain. Wulff was in a pretty exposed position, after all. He had a limp, you see.'

'Really?'

'When he was fourteen he'd been involved in an accident and ever afterwards he'd had a limp – it was his left leg that was affected. In 1945 we interrogated him as thoroughly as it was possible for us to do. I was personally in charge of the interrogation, together with Konrad Fanebust, who was a trained lawyer – but it was like trying to draw blood from a stone. He wouldn't say a word, didn't make a single confession. There was only one other line of inquiry left open to us.

That was to concentrate on the murders that had been carried out with a pistol – we found the bullets that had been used in three of those cases. They were all the same calibre and had been fired from the same pistol – a Luger 505. A German pistol, in other words. When we arrested Wulff in 1945 he was living in a wretched little boarding house out on Nordnes. We found nothing in his room. His parents were both dead and he didn't have any other family. The farm in Ulven had been taken over by new tenants: even so, we took the place apart, searched it from top to bottom. No pistol. It still hasn't been found. It's probably lying at the bottom of Vågen, or some lake or other. And we never found Rat Poison.'

'And was that the end of the matter?'

'I swore I'd never give up my hunt. Whenever anyone mentioned Rat Poison, I used to note down what they said. Even though the case had been dropped a long time ago, I continued the investigation on my own. Right up until 1971.'

'1971? What happened then?'

'In January 1971 a man's body was discovered out at the far end of Nordnes. His face had been badly mutilated but he was identified all the same. It was Harald Wulff.'

'Did you see him yourself?'

'I was entirely certain it was him. The man was of similar build but he was a bit older; he had the same leg defect but it was his face that presented the real problem – it was just a mess.'

'Who identified him?'

'A woman he'd been living with.'

'But did that mean the case was solved, then?'

'You mean, did we know who had done the murder? No. And, to tell you the truth, I don't think much was done to get to the bottom of it, either. I resigned from the force two months later, in March, and by that time the case was already on ice – "active abeyance", it's called – that means that if no fresh evidence turns up, nothing more will happen. Most people assumed that it had been the work of former resistance workers who'd taken the law into their own hands and I don't think there was anyone who thought that unreasonable. There are a lot of folk who still carry the scars of the things that happened back then.'

'So Rat Poison finally got his just deserts. If it really was him.'

Hjalmar Nymark nodded. His energetic face flamed red and his eyes continued to search restlessly round the café, as if he were still unable to give up the hunt for the man they called Rat Poison, or his ghost.

'But wait a minute,' I said. 'What's all this got to do with the fire at Peacock?'

He looked at me for a moment before replying. Finally, he leaned towards me and said: 'In 1953 Harald Wulff got a job as an office messenger at Peacock.'

'An office messenger?'

'Men like him didn't find it easy to get jobs in the years immediately after they left prison. He got that job through the State employment agency.'

'You mean he . . . could have had something to do with the fire?'

'It was a bit odd, at least, don't you think? The fire was officially written off as an accident. If it really was the work of Harald Wulff, and if Harald Wulff really was Rat Poison, then it was his *pièce de résistance*, if you can call it that. Fifteen charred corpses.'

'But what would he have stood to gain by it?'

Hjalmar Nymark shrugged his shoulders. 'The satisfaction of revenge, perhaps – revenge on society, on the other people, people who'd been on the right side. Or pehaps he just did it for profit.'

'You mean somebody might have paid him to do it?'

'Something like that.' He gave me his dogged stare. 'Harald Wulff was one of the heroes of the Peacock fire. One of the ones who went back into the sea of flames to rescue others. He escaped with a few minor burns but he was singled out for special merit in the report. He didn't have much in common with the slippery customer Fanebust and I had interrogated back in 1945.'

'Was that what you meant yesterday when you said you had a hunch, or was it a hypothesis?'

'The hypothesis was this: that Harald Wulff really *was* Rat Poison, something we never managed to confirm. If *that* were true, there was a possibility that he might have had something to do with the fire. But those were two completely unverifiable assumptions and no prosecuting authority in the world, let alone Norway, would have been prepared to make out a case on grounds like those. We interrogated Wulff again but the climate wasn't the same in 1953 as it had been in 1945. We had to go more carefully and Wulff himself was more aggressive. He alleged he was being subjected to persecution, admitted he had made a mistake and had taken his punishment, but claimed that justice now demanded that he cease to be hounded for the rest of his life.'

'What about Hagbart Helle? Where did he stand during the war?'

Hjalmar Nymark gave me a sly look. 'He went scot-free after it was all over, like a lot of other people in his social circle. The authorities were very careful in their dealings with the business community. In spite of everything, a certain number of jobs had to be maintained, even during the war. People had to live, after all. Then again, it was important to build up a stable and secure commercial life during the difficult years of the immediate post-war period. The authorities turned a blind eye to a lot of different forms of – collaboration. Let's just put it this way: Hagbart Helle certainly didn't *lose* anything by the war and the business he owned was, if anything, more secure in 1945 than it had been in 1939.'

'So there weren't any verifiable links between him and Harald Wulff?'

He shook his head emphatically. 'No *verifiable* ones,' he said. 'If there'd been any we'd have stepped in at once. The commission of public inquiry was headed by Konrad Fanebust who, that year, was deputy mayor. No one had more interest in running Rat Poison to earth that he and I did, and I remember we stayed up late into the night going over everything we had in the way of evidence, both from the interrogations we'd carried out in 1945–6 and from the investigations into the causes of the fire. There *was* just one thing . . . and it . . .'

'Yes?'

'It, more than anything else, made us certain that we had a case.'

I nodded. I knew what he meant. 'Because what distinguished Rat Poison's activities was . . .'

'You've got it. What distinguished Rat Poison's activities was that there *was* no evidence. He had struck again, eight years after the war had ended. But that, at least, made me feel sure of one thing . . .'

'And that was . . .'

'That Harald Wulff really *was* Rat Poison. Can you understand now why I've never been able to stop thinking about the Peacock fire case?'

I nodded. 'What happened to Wulff later on?'

'He got another job, in a printing works. After that he had various other odd jobs. In 1959 he moved in with a woman he'd met while he'd been working at Peacock. They never married but they lived together until he died. I showed you a picture of her yesterday, in one of those newspaper cuttings. The youngest female clerk, Elise Blom. She was the only woman mentioned in his obituary. After the Peacock fire she got a job on the town council and she works there still. She was the person who identified Wulff in 1971.'

'Are there any photographs of him?'

'Of Wulff?'

I nodded and he fished his wallet out of his inside pocket. It was a brown leather wallet of the kind that people carry around with them all their lives, as if that is where they keep their souls. He searched through its numerous compartments and eventually extracted a yellowed newspaper cutting. He handed it to me cautiously, as though he were afraid it might disintegrate into dust in the air between us.

I looked at the cutting. It was a none-too-clear photograph taken during the post-war treason trials. Five men were pictured on their way into a courthouse and the caption stated that the three in the middle were the defendants, while the other two were plain-clothes policemen. The last of the three defendants was Harald Wulff. As he walked, his face was partially concealed behind the man in front of him and not all his features were visible. His face was long and narrow, almost horse-like. His nose and the area above his eyes were strongly marked, protruding slightly. He had large ears. His dark hair was parted on the left and combed back so that a long, dark lock fell forwards to the right. I didn't recognize any of the other four men in the picture.

I studied Harald Wulff closely before handing the cutting back. 'Well . . .' I threw up my hands.

'Precisely, Veum. Well . . .' He mimicked my gesture. 'That's the way all stories that mean anything end. With a *well* . . .' Again he caricatured my gesture. 'There's no such thing as a happy ending. Perhaps there isn't any justice, either; perhaps there are only old fogeys like myself who can't shake off the idea that we were right in those days, we must have been right!'

He stared angrily at his beer-glass. It was empty. As if to make sure there wasn't still a drop of beer left in it, he raised it to his mouth and turned it upside down. A few flakes of foam dribbled out but that was all. Then he put the glass down firmly on the table and rose to his feet. 'Well, Veum. Now you know everything I know. The main points, anyway. I'm off home now. I'm still off-form. Be seeing you!'

I made as if to get up but he nodded in the direction of my glass which was still half full. 'No, don't get up. Enjoy yourself while you can.' He gave me a grim smile, put his coat on and walked out of the café holding his rolled-up newspaper in one hand. The door swung to behind him.

A few seconds later, through the half-open windows that were screened from the side street by greyish yellow curtains, I heard it. The noise of an engine revving, the screech of brakes, tyres skidding over ice-smooth cobbles, something hard and metallic striking something else – and then: the horrible sound of a human body hitting the ground after having been thrown through the air. The engine hammered into life again and I heard the vehicle swerve off round the corner.

I got to my feet so quickly that I overturned the table. Everybody in the café was staring at the windows, the expressions on their faces registering varying degrees of astonishment, depending on how drunk they were. I passed the doorman and rushed outside. At the far end of Strandkaien I saw a large, dark blue van swing round Murhjørnet and disappear from view. I ran on, round the corner.

The little side street was empty. At the intersection with Strandgaten two people came into view: their faces looked scared. The newspaper kiosk just round the corner lay overturned on the pavement but that didn't necessarily mean anything.

What did mean something was that in the middle of the street, his face to the cobbles, lay Hjalmar Nymark. His rolled-up newspaper had partially unrolled in the gutter, where the squally wind was making a couple of its pages flutter like the wings of a dying bird. They were the only things that moved.

6

I got down on my hands and knees beside Hjalmar Nymark. I didn't dare to move him, in case he had broken his neck, but I knelt down and made sure he didn't have anything in his mouth that could prevent him from breathing. My fingers fumbled along his throat. The pulse was there but it was unsteady. There was a thin trickle of blood from one of his ears and his nose looked as though it must have broken in his collision with the ground. There was something pathetic about the old man's powerful, motionless body which a few minutes ago had been so alive: so alive, and so afraid.

The drizzle deposited a weightless layer of tiny drops on us. And the gutter ran with a soft purling as the newspaper slowly absorbed the water and lay still.

The doorman from the café came over to me. 'I've called an ambulance,' he said. 'Is he . . .'

'Not yet.' I kept my hand in position on the side of his throat. His pulse was fainter now.

I looked around in desperation. The little street was strangely deserted. The two people along at the intersection had stayed where they were, as if to emphasize the fact that they had nothing to do with what had happened.

Then the ambulance arrived. The two ambulance men got out in a swift, experienced fashion. One brief glance was enough to tell them all they needed to know about the situation. Supporting Hjalmar Nymark's neck, they lifted him on to the stretcher and into the ambulance. I followed them inside.

'Are you coming too?' one of them asked.

'He's a friend of mine.'

He waved me towards a seat at the back. Then he reached for an oxygen apparatus that hung from the ceiling above our heads.

I leaned forward to the driver's seat. 'Do you have a radio phone?'

The driver nodded as he set the vehicle in motion.

'Tell the police they should be on the lookout for a big blue van that drove off in the direction of Nordnes. At any event, it went round Murhjørnet,' I added.

'Anything else?'

I hesitated. 'Tell them that Veum sends his greetings and that I'll stay at the hospital until . . .' I had no idea of what might lie in store for me. 'Until the situation becomes clear.'

He delivered the message over the radio phone without any further questions, started the siren and increased our speed with a light pressure on the accelerator. We passed the first intersection as the yellow light was changing back to red and the street buildings raced past us as if we were at the cinema and something had gone haywire in the projection room. Even so, I saw everything that we drove past with astonishing clarity: people turning to stare at us, cars swerving aside and the faces of drivers glancing round at the moment we passed them.

The other ambulance man, a lad with closely cropped fair hair and a boyish down on his red cheeks, held the oxygen mask at the ready right in front of Hjalmar Nymark's face. The broad vertebrae barely moved up and down, and now and then a gurgling sound came from somewhere inside his body. None of us spoke.

We drove straight to Haukeland. When we reached the top of Kalfaret, Hjalmar Nymark suddenly raised his head and looked about him with a bewildered stare which eventually came to rest on me. His voice was broken and faltering: 'Ve . . . Veum?'

I nodded and smiled: a thin, metallic smile.

He was trying to say something else, searching for the words. I bent over him. The young ambulance man was listening intently. The driver was watching in the mirror.

Hjalmar Nymark said: 'Veum . . . If I die . . .'

I nodded to show that I understood and then shook my head to indicate that he wasn't going to die.

'Find out . . . what really happened to Docker Johan . . . in 1971 . . .'

Then he closed his eyes and passed out. As we swung in through the hospital gates he suddenly opened his eyes and said: '1971. Docker Johan.' Then he passed out again.

The two ambulance men quickly ferried Haljmar Nymark into the building on the stretcher. Trained medical staff were there to attend to him and I followed them into the lift and upstairs without anyone protesting.

Hjalmar Nymark was wheeled straight into the operating theatre. A kind-looking woman with black hair, olive-coloured skin and dark brown eyes showed me into a small waiting room which contained furniture bought at a mission jumble sale and pot plants that looked as though they were relics from the First World War.

Under one of the tables there was a meagre selection of yesterday's newspapers. Somehow, it felt right. I even felt as though I was an item of yesterday's news myself.

7

Nobody disturbed me. The small waiting room was separated from the corridor outside by a thin wall, the upper half of which contained windows. Through those glass windows I could see busy, white-clad people hurrying past. None of them cast so much as a glance in my direction. As long as I didn't get in anyone's way I could sit here for as long as I wished. Perhaps that was what it was like if you were a patient, too. If you said nothing to anyone, but just lay quietly wherever it was they had wheeled you away to, nobody would disturb you, until one day they noticed you were covered in flies.

Detective Inspector Jakob E. Hamre peeped through the glass pane in the door before knocking and coming in. 'Just as I thought,' he said. 'Got yourself a new office, Veum?'

'I couldn't wish for a quieter one,' I replied. 'Sit down. Is there anything I can get you? A glass of naphtha, perhaps? Or some valium? Or something for your heart?'

He gave me a searching look and sat down on one of the chairs with a faint smile. 'The same old Veum, eh? Never learn your lesson, do you?'

'Oh, but I do – I just keep it to myself, that's all.'

Jakob E. Hamre was immaculately dressed in a light-coloured doubled-breasted overcoat worn over a grey suit, black shoes, light blue shirt and dark blue tie. He was only a couple of years younger than I was but from the way he looked it might have been ten and he was a lot more handsome than I was. Jakob E. Hamre was one of those policemen who remind you of boy scouts but who can be as crafty as old pimps when they want to be. His handsomeness was of a slightly impersonal variety – the kind of man every mother-in-law dreams of but who leaves most daughters cold.

'I got your message,' he said. 'So I've come to see for myself. Do you know anything about all this?' He surveyed the toe-caps of his shoes almost modestly; then, however, his eyes came up and battened on my face, steady and vigilant.

'Have you found the van?' I asked.

He nodded. 'It was parked away out on C. Sundtsgate and had apparently been stolen.'

'Hm. Well, Hjalmar Nymark and I are friends, I suppose, that's all.

Or acquaintances. I haven't known him all that long but we've talked a fair bit together and we have quite a few things in common.'

'Such as?'

'He and I are both detectives, after a manner of speaking. He used to talk a lot about cases from the old days.'

He leaned forward, interested. 'You mean Nymark spent his time poking his nose into old criminal cases?'

I nodded, slowly. 'I'm not sure how much time he spent *poking his nose* into them but he certainly thought about them a lot. How is he, anyway? Have you heard anything?'

He shook his head. 'I was told to wait. They've got him in there on the operating table right at this moment. What cases did he used to talk about, Veum?'

'Rat Poison, some person they called Rat Poison, does that ring a bell with you?'

He shook his head, to indicate that it didn't.

'What about the Peacock fire, then?'

There was a faint gleam in his clear eyes now. 'Not really.'

'No, it didn't ring much of a bell with me, either. Rat Poison was a notorious informer and probably also a hit-man during the war. His true identity was never discovered. Peacock was a paint factory on Fjøsangerveien that burned down in 1953. Fifteen people were killed and the man Hjalmar Nymark suspected of being Rat Poison was employed as an office messenger up there when the whole thing took place.'

'What was is name?'

'Harald Wulff.' He had taken out his notebook and was now writing the name down in it. I added: 'But he's dead.'

'I see.' He stopped writing. Then he gazed into space. 'Tell me, what were you talking about with him earlier today?'

'We were talking about this man – Rat Poison. He . . . he seemed nervous, as though someone might have been following him. But he put it down to the after-effects of the brandy. We drank a whole bottle of the stuff together yesterday, he and I.'

'I see.'

'So, then he left . . . I was sitting right next to the windows that give on to the street at the side when it happened. I heard the revving of an engine, brakes screeching and then the sound of his body hitting the ground.'

Once again he leaned forward. 'So it wasn't an accident, you mean?'

'Like hell it was. Somebody ran him over, Hamre, and whoever it was meant to do it.'

'Why?'

I shrugged my shoulders and threw up my hands.

He said: 'A police detective makes quite a few enemies in the course of his life. Maybe it was one of them waiting for Hjalmar Nymark out

36

there in the side street.'

'He said something in the amublance on the way here.' I hesitated slightly. "*If I die*, he said –" . . .'

'Yes?'

'He said if he died I was to find out what happened to Docker Johan in 1971.'

'Docker Johan, in 1971?' He had his pen out again. 'Wasn't there any more than that?'

'No. Just that.'

'We'd better . . .'

He was interrupted by an elderly nurse who came in from the corridor and turned to him. 'The doctor would like you to go in, Inspector,' she said in a formal tone of voice. She didn't look at me at all. There weren't any flies crawling over me yet.

Hamre nodded briefly and left me. I stayed where I was, keeping an eye on the corridor outside. The forms out there slid silently by, like figures in a puppet show for the deaf. Everything was peaceful. The only sound I could hear was the pattering of the rain on the windowpanes – a velvety creature that wanted to come inside.

A quarter of an hour later, Hamre returned. He looked relieved. 'It's OK, Veum. He's badly injured but he'll live.'

'How badly?'

He thumbed through his notebook and read out: 'Fracture of the cranium. Severe concussion, one ear-drum perforated. Fracture of the right arm, just above the wrist. One rib broken, four fractured. Damage to the right kidney. Fracture of the left femur and right ankle. Internal and external lesions, including a fracture of the nose.' He looked up. 'He's had his profile softened for him.'

'Is he conscious?'

He shook his head. 'No. They've given him something to make him sleep. The doctor said he needs a lot of sleep but has a strong constitution for his age and will almost certainly pull through.'

Hamre fastened up his coat. 'Is there anything else you can think of, Veum? Didn't he say nothing about where he was planning to go after he left the café?'

'He just said he was going home.'

'Did you often meet there?'

'Two or three times a week, maybe.'

'Did you ever visit his home?'

'Only once – last night. He showed me some old newspaper cuttings relating to the Peacock fire.'

He nodded. 'I'm going to do some checking up on all that, too. Can you come and see me tomorrow morning – at about eleven, let's say?'

I nodded. Then I said: 'Did you know Hjalmar Nymark, Hamre?'

'No. At least, not personally. He retired from the force in 1971 and I was stationed somewhere else in those days.'

'Where?'

He raised his eyebrows, ironically. 'Stavanger.'

'Then perhaps you know a police officer called Bertelsen?'

He gave me an ironic look. 'Yep. I know him. But I wouldn't have thought he was exactly your type, Veum.'

'He wasn't.'

We ushered each other out into the corridor and found our way downstairs.

When we got outside the building, we stood still for a moment. Hamre pointed to a black Volkswagen. 'Can I give you a lift home, Veum?'

'Thanks, but I think I need some fresh air.'

'Just as you like.' He shrugged his shoulders. 'See you tomorrow, then.'

'Yes, see you then.'

He walked towards the car. Suddenly, a thought struck me, and I shouted after him: 'Hamre . . .'

He turned round. 'Yes?'

'1971,' I said. 'That was the year Harald Wulff died. The year something happened to a man named Docker Johan. And the year Hjalmar Nymark retired.'

'Really?' said Jakob Hamre, looking thoughtful. Then he gave me an absent-minded nod, got into his car and drove away.

'An eventful year,' I said to myself.

8

Next day the fog came drifting through the streets like ghosts. Grey tentacles clutched at me from the corners of houses and a cold rush of air from the sea flooded up through my alley, a wind that belonged to autumn.

Jakob E. Hamre was at his desk talking on the phone when I entered his office. He waved me towards the uncomfortable chair and carried on with his telephone conversation. As he talked, he made notes on a piece of paper in front of him. 'Two litres of milk, a yogurt, a kilo of wholeground rye bread – and eggs. I'll see what I can do. Yes. As usual, I hope. Fine. Have a good day.'

I looked around me. How long was it since the last time I had sat here? It must have been two or three years and the office hadn't changed. It was just as I remembered it: a room you forgot even before you left it. Featureless walls of an indeterminate colour, bookshelves containing files and statute books, the same old view of the same old bank building. I'd been in quite a few such offices in my time; they were usually rooms you couldn't get out of fast enough.

The knot of his tie was a bit loose but, otherwise, Jakob E. Hamre was as immaculate as ever. His handsome face stared at me calmly and inscrutably; his well-groomed hair fell over the right-hand side of his forehead in neatly planned fashion. There was an elegance about Jakob E. Hamre which implied that he really belonged on the other side of the street: the helpful bank manager, turning down your application for a loan with a melancholic look on his face.

'How is he?' I asked.

'Oh, he'll pull through. It's possible that we may be able to talk to him later today.'

'And what about the person – or persons in the van?'

He shook his head, regretfully. 'We've nothing so far. We're getting the usual eye-witness testimonies, of course, but there's not much that's definite to go on. A elderly lady says she saw the blue van parked with a man sitting at the wheel but she didn't get a close look at him and she's unable to give us anything approaching a description. The analysis of the fingerprints has led us nowhere so far. We'll go over the van again, of course, but . . .'

'Who did it belong to?'

'It was owned by a sports goods shop. They never used it in the afternoon.'

'And those cases I mentioned?'

Hamre leaned back in his chair, placed his hands on the edge of the desk and stared down at them for a moment, as though he were wondering whether his fingernails were short enough. Then he gazed musingly into space and said: 'I've been making a few inquiries – in the building. People who knew Hjalmar Nymark. It seems that . . . Hjalmar Nymark was an excellent policeman in many ways. But he had one basic fault. He had a tendency to get a bit too personally involved in some of the cases he worked on. That wasn't always a very wise thing to do. And, particularly towards the end of his time here, he had a couple of hobby-horses he just wouldn't leave alone. One of them was the Peacock fire.' He threw up his hands and gave me a look of resignation. 'But who on earth has time to bother about fires that are twenty years old when we've barely the resources to deal with today's problems?'

'But what about the other case? Who was Docker Johan?'

He sighed. 'That was the last case Hjalmar Nymark worked on before he retired. It, too, came to be an *idée fixe* with him.'

'In what way?'

Hamre gazed out of the window. 'How many cases like that do we get every year? One or another sample of the town's flotsam and jetsam disappears. Some of them have simply taken the train to Oslo. Others we find floating in the sea a few weeks, or years, later. Some drink themselves to death and lie forgotten in some wretched rented room or other until someone finally begins to wonder where they are. And, of course, some of them are murdered: it's a tough world to survive in. There are a lot of cases like that and they don't usually come very high on our list of priorities. Not, at least, until it's been established that some crime has been committed. The case of Docker Johan was one like that.'

'Tell me about it.'

He produced a file from the heap of documents on the left-hand side of his desk and began to thumb through it. 'Johan Olsen, born Bergen, 1916. Former seaman and holdworker. Illegal activity during the war. Alcoholic. Conviction for vagrancy in 1960, otherwise nothing in police records. He vanished in January 1971 but wasn't reported missing until February.'

'Who reported his disappearance?'

'A woman. Her name was Olga Sørensen and she was his – occasional – cohabitant, to use a modern expression.'

'And why didn't she report the matter until February?'

He shrugged. 'She probably assumed he'd simply taken off somewhere, wandering around.'

'And what was the result of the investigation?'

Thumbing over a couple of sheets, he murmured: 'He was never found. Officially he's still missing. But for all we know he may be alive and well – in the Canaries or somewhere like that, where sun and brandy are more easily available than they are in our latitudes.'

'Are there any photographs of him? Any descriptions?'

He rummaged deeper through the file, produced a photograph and handed it to me. It was one of those photos they take of you down at the police station and use to surprise you later on: a mugshot and profile, done in garish lighting. You look the way most people look in the photographs in their passports. The only difference is that you're actually *in* the crime album.

Johan Olsen, also known as Docker Johan, had an oblong, horse-like face, not at all dissimilar to that of Harald Wulff. His ears were smaller, however, and his eyes were further apart. He was unshaven and his tight-lipped mouth had a bitter, slightly contemptuous look.

'Here's the description.' Hamre handed me a sheet of paper.

I read it quickly through. Johan Olsen had been five feet seven inches tall, his eyes had been blue and his hair dark blonde. Apart from an old injury to his left knee, which made him limp, he had had no particular distinguishing features.

I read the last sentence over again twice, in order to make quite sure that it said what I thought it said. Then I looked Hamre steadily in the eye and a crawling, uneasy sensation took hold in my stomach. 'I can see why Hjalmar Nymark was interested in this,' I said.

'What do you mean?'

'Haven't you read it? Docker Johan had a limp in his left leg. So did Harald Wulff. And Harald Wulff disappeared – if that's the right word for it – at exactly the same time as Docker Johan. In January 1971.'

9

'I've got the material on Harald Wulff here,' said Hamre, taking out another file. It was somewhat fuller than the one on Docker Johan. With the index finger of his right hand he tapped a third file, which contained more than twice as much material as the two others put together. 'And this is the stuff on the Peacock fire. I've even managed to dig up that.' There were traces of cobwebs on one corner of the Peacock file. As he tapped it, a cloud of dust rose into the air. 'So you see, we're carrying out a thorough investigation.'

'I don't doubt it.'

'Good. Well . . .' He opened the file that contained the material on Harald Wulff. He thumbed quickly past the yellow forms from the legal proceedings during the treason trials. They were bound together with transcripts of the hearings. 'This is old stuff,' he murmured. 'But here . . .' The last chapter of Harald Wulff's life was held together with large paper-fasteners. He opened a brown envelope and withdrew from it a large handful of photographs. With a neutral gaze he surveyed them and then handed them to me.

The photographs of Harald Wulff were not a pretty sight. In one of them he lay naked on his back and one could see that his body was covered in blue marks and extravasations. He had received a thorough beating up. But one didn't have to look at his body in order to realize that. His head had taken the worst of it. His face had been kicked to pulp. With a brutality the like of which I couldn't remember having witnessed before, someone had turned his features into an unrecognizable mass of bone, cartilage, torn flesh and blood. His bristly hair was caked in blood and one of his arms was clearly broken. Splinters of bone protruded from his forearm and the fingers were spread out.

The other photographs were close-up shots and some of them were so close they made your stomach heave. One of them focused on the ring he was wearing on the fourth finger of his left hand. The design on the ring was quite clearly visible. It was a wheel cross.

Three or four of the pictures showed from various angles what the body had looked like when it had been found. It lay on the gravel, surrounded by patches of dirty snow; in one of the photographs some boathouses could be glimpsed; in another, black, leafless trees.

I put the photographs down on the desk. 'Not exactly Sunday school stuff,' I said. 'How were they ever able to identify him?'

Hamre leafed through the papers. 'There was a woman who lived with him. Er . . . Elise Blom.'

I nodded in recognition at the name. 'She worked at Peacock.'

He looked up from the papers. 'Really? Yes, that's right and so did Harald Wulff. As an office messenger, if I'm not mistaken?'

'Yes.'

He went on: 'Well, it was Elise Blom who identified him.'

'In that condition?'

He gave me a patronizing look. 'A woman who had lived with him for . . .' – another glance down at the papers – 'twelve years. There are other distinguishing marks besides the ones we carry around on our faces, Veum.'

'Yes, yes. I was really thinking of . . . It must have been something of a strain for her.'

'And the ring. That was definitely his.'

'It could have been put on somebody else.'

'Yes, but there was absolutely no reason for us to doubt Elise Blom's testimony. What's more, she was questioned thoroughly during the investigation . . .'

'Did she report him missing?'

'There wasn't time for that. Harald Wulff went to the cinema – so he said – on 13 January 1971. He didn't go home that night but, according to Mrs – or *Miss* – Blom, that wasn't all that unusual. He was a bit unpredictable that way. Nerves from the war, she said. There were periods when he could hardly sleep at all and then he would roam about the streets all night. But not on the night in question.'

'No?'

'He was discovered as people were on their way to work out there at around seven o'clock on the morning of 14 January. There's a slip road that leads down to the warehouses along the north side of Nordnes and he was found lying right at the end of it, just before you come to the warehouses. There were the traces of a struggle in the snow nearby but no one in the neighbourhood had heard anything unusual. It's not one of the quietest parts of town, you know.'

'I know. I grew up out there.'

'He had a post office ID card in his inside pocket and a wallet containing 180 kroner. We called at his address and that's where we found Elise Blom.'

'Hjalmar Nymark took part in the investigation, you said?'

'That's right.'

'Was he able to identify Wulff?'

'*He* hadn't slept with him, Veum. In fact, it was nearly twenty years since he'd set eyes on him. Attempts were made to find someone who could confirm Elise Blom's statement but it turned out to be impossible. The two of them lived a very withdrawn kind of life – no

43

friends, no family. As if they were living in a kind of exile.'

'Listen – when Docker Johan vanished, did anyone think of letting *his* woman view Harald Wulff's corpse?'

He shook his head. 'There was no reason to. For one thing, Harald Wulff was discovered in mid-January, and Docker Johan wasn't actually reported missing until a month later – *that* investigation didn't get a very high priority, as I've told you. For another, by mid-February the investigation of Harald Wulff's murder was practically over.'

'So soon?'

'Yes.' He thumbed through the pile of documents relating to the investigation. 'We tried to map out his circle of acquaintances – including those he'd had during the war – but it wasn't easy. There was, of course, quite a lot of forensic evidence at the scene of the crime, including some footprints in the snow, the footprints of two people in addition to Wulff himself, and the tyre-marks of a car that had been standing parked outside the old depot barracks. But the investigation didn't yield any positive results. Besides . . .'

'Yes?'

'Whether one likes it or not, one's got to accept it. As I've told you, I had nothing to do with this investigation. I wasn't even in the same town.'

'What is it one's got to accept?'

'This is a rather special type of murder, don't you think?'

'Is it? What do you have in mind – the degree of brutality?'

He nodded. 'It all points to a sudden outburst of rage – or an act of revenge. Harald Wulff was a notorious collaborator and it's evident from the case documents that he was strongly suspected of being the man known as Rat Poison whom you mentioned yesterday.'

'Precisely.'

'Well, the obvious thing to suppose was that it had been the work of an old adversary, or two, from the "right" side, so to speak, who had finally decided it was time to settle old scores. And there were certainly quite a few people – even among the police – who considered that Harald Wulff had only got what had been coming to him.'

'So the case was dropped?'

'It was given every chance but after more than a month of concentrated but fruitless investigation, as well as sporadic follow-up inquiries whenever anything that seemed significant turned up – those lasted a further five or six months – it was decided to put the case on ice for a while. Cases of that nature are never dropped, Veum. At least, not until the period of limitation comes into effect.'

'So it just becomes one more unsolved case of murder?'

'Yes, but you won't often hear it referred to in those terms – either in the dailies or in the weeklies. Harald Wulff wasn't – to put it bluntly – a murder victim anyone felt particularly sorry for.'

'What about the woman he left behind – Elise Blom?'

He shrugged his shoulders. 'Well, I suppose everyone has someone who feels sorry for them. But it came out at the hearing that she knew all about his wartime background, so – but I suppose not all choices of lifetime companion are without their problems.'

'Where was she on the night Wulff was murdered?'

'Out playing bingo.' He added, quickly: 'And I can assure you that thorough forensic investigations were carried out in their home, too. There was nothing that suggested she had had anything to do with the murder.'

'Well, well,' I said, raising my hands in the air.

'And to tell you the truth, Veum, I can't see that any of the things I've managed to find out up till now – either about Harald Wulff, the Peacock fire or Docker Johan – have anything whatever to do with Hjalmar Nymark's being run over by a van yesterday afternoon. In other words, we're working on the hypothesis that this is just one of those ordinary hit-and-run cases that occur from time to time. The most serious crime was when whoever it was failed to stop and just drove on. It might have been someone with too much alcohol in his blood, or perhaps it was just someone in a hurry.'

'But the van *was* stolen?'

'Probably. But, of course, we'll check carefully with the staff of the sports shop.' He sighed. 'All those traffic lights – they're not exactly ideally situated and that side street there, between those two intersections, that's a dangerous stretch of road. The drivers cross the first intersection and see the green light coming on at the second. So they step on the gas, close their eyes and hope for the best. Usually there's no problem. But now and again someone gets in the way.'

'And this time it was Hjalmar Nymark.'

'Yes.'

'Well.' I shrugged my shoulders. '*You're* the ones who're dealing with the case. Just tell me though . . .'

'What?'

'Is there anyone in this building who ever worked on the Peacock case?'

'Dankert Muus. He's the only one. And he was only a young whippersnapper in those days.'

'Dankert Muus,' I said, reflectively.

'Yes. Do you know somebody else of that name?'

I got up. Hamre began to tidy away the papers that lay before him. 'All right, Veum. If any more corpses should turn up . . .'

'Corpses?' I said.

He gave me a disarming smile. 'Just a figure of speech. I'm sorry if it upset you.'

I thought about it. 'No. Not today. You'll find me in the phone book for a while yet.'

I left him sitting at his desk with the light at his back.

45

10

The door to the office next door was slightly open. Inside I could see Dankert Muus sitting behind his desk. He was poring over a heap of documents that might easily have been the score of the march for the entrance of the bureaucrats, if thickness were anything to go by.

Dankert Muus was sitting in his shirt-sleeves. His brown jacket was draped over the back of his chair and the knot of his necktie was loose. The general impression would have been quite a casual one had it not been for the grey pork-pie hat which someone had once jammed on top of his head and which, it was a safe bet, he never took off, not even in the bath. It had become part of him. At any rate, I'd never seen him without it.

He must have sensed that someone was watching him, for I suddenly met his eyes below the brim of his hat. It felt like a flame-cutter hitting me on the forehead. Abruptly, he snapped: 'What the hell are you staring at?'

I opened the door all the way and pretended I had been about to come in. 'I was just thinking it must be a while since we last . . .'

He pointed at the floor in front of me. 'Not one inch over that threshold, Veum! I'm warning you! I've told you once and for all: I don't want to see you, I don't want to hear you, I don't want to talk to you. Not one single word.' His voice suddenly acquired a velvety softness. 'Not until you're sitting where you belong, on the other side of my desk, and I can award you a first-class indictment with bells and knobs on. Got it?'

'Message received,' I said, leaning lightly against the door-frame. Dankert Muus glowered at me and I said: 'Do you remember anything about the fire at the Peacock paintworks?'

I watched the question sink slowly into his skull; I could see it bouncing to and fro in the great echo chamber that was in there. 'Peacock?' he repeated, softly. Then he remembered where he was. 'I'll give you peacocks, you dolled-up parrot! I don't answer questions from third-rate amateurs. Didn't you hear what I said?'

He stood up threateningly behind his desk and I withdrew hastily into the corridor. That pale grey face with its washed-out eyes, the wide jaw and mouse-coloured hair under the pork-pie hat – they didn't make a pretty sight and it was one that didn't get any prettier as he came out from behind his desk and started moving towards me. But, in the end, he contented himself with an irritated grunt before kicking the door shut in my face with a bang.

I remained standing there, staring at the name-plate on his door. *Detective Inspector D. Muus*. White letters on a blue-grey background. It looked about as inviting as he did.

The next door I came to was also half open. It must be open day down at the police station. The next thing you knew they'd be offering guided tours of the place.

Vegard Vadheim was standing in front of his bookshelf, turning the pages of a large, red statute book. He was thin, dark-haired and stooping, and there were one or two grey curls behind his ears. He had once been a long-distance runner for the Norwegian national athletics team and the 10,000 metre finals at Melbourne, 1956, had been the international high-point of his career. Some years later he had published a couple of books of poetry. We had never really been on a collision course with each other and, in fact, I even found it possible to have a reasonable civilized conversation with him now and again – civilized, that is, by comparison with the standards observed by the rest of the building's inhabitants. 'Hi,' I said, and he looked up.

His dark eyes surveyed me thoughtfully. Vegard Vadheim always looked thoughtful. In spite of the fact that it was twenty years since he had last published anything, I always had the feeling he was mulling over some stanza or other, as if he were forever on the trail of the *mot juste*, the correct formula. By inclination he was a poet but experience told me that he was also first and foremost a realist. I said: 'When did you first come to Bergen, Vadheim?'

He looked at me in wonder. 'When did I first come to Bergen? Have you taken up journalism, Veum?'

'Not yet. It's about Hjalmar Nymark.'

He at once grew serious. 'Yes, I heard about the accident. That was nasty. But he'll pull through, won't he?'

'Yes. Listen . . .'

He looked at me with interest. 'I smell a rat, Veum. Are you trying to tell me someone deliberately ran him over?'

I shrugged my shoulders. 'I don't know. But he had a lot of stories to tell, Nymark did. A lot of ballast on board.'

He passed a hand through his hair. 'You'd better come in, Veum.' He put down his book and seated himself on the edge of his desk. He motioned me to sit down on one of the chairs but I remained standing, leaning against the wall.

'Did you know Hjalmar Nymark?' I asked.

'Oh yes. We worked together, befored he retired. Later on I used to see him now and again. We don't often get retired policemen calling on us here, Veum. We're far too busy as it is. And they know it.'

'You mean there don't ever seem to be enough of you?'

'Yes,' he said, shortly. 'I first came to Bergen at the beginning of the 1960s. For several years Hjalmar Nymark was one of my closest colleagues. He taught me a great deal.'

'In other words you mean that – that you . . . tell me, was Hjalmar Nymark a good policeman?'

Vegard Vadheim gave me an acid look. 'A good policeman? It depends on how you define it. We probably have completely different ideas about it. In fact, there's a lot of disagreement about it in this building . . . But I'll answer your question. *Yes.* In my opinion Hjalmar Nymark was a very good policeman. I learned to trust his judgement. He knew a lot about people and he was always on their side, if you know what I mean. Far too many of us just make do with going by the book but people must always come first, Veum. No one's infallible. Not even policemen. And not every law represents an eternal truth.'

'Did you know Hjalmar Nymark well?'

'As well as one ever knows one's colleagues, short of becoming personal friends with them. He was a reserved sort of chap in many ways. He lived for himself, had few real friends, no family. I think he must have led a damn lonely life but that was the way he wanted it. We used to have lunch together sometimes, or my wife and I would invite him over to our place but . . . We had a lot of respect for each other, during working hours. The rest of the time we didn't see much of each other.'

'When you knew him did you ever notice that he seemed to be preoccupied by one or two cases from the old days?'

'What do you mean?'

'Things that happened during the war. An informer – and murderer – known as Rat Poison. A fire at a paint factory with the name of Peacock, in 1953. Fifteen people were killed. A disappearance – well, that was later on, in 1971. And a murder that also took place in 1971.'

'I think you're getting things mixed up, Veum. Take number one on your list. Nymark used to tell us a lot about what went on during the war. He did occupy a central position in the local resistance movement, after all. What he told us was certainly interesting but you know how it is. Everyone's got some story or other from the war days. It gradually gets to the point where you stop paying attention to details after a while. But I do remember that name – Rat Poison. And I even remember the murder you mentioned just now, the one that took place in 1971. There were a number of people, and Hjalmar Nymark was one of them, who thought the murder victim was Rat Poison, isn't that right?'

I nodded. 'Yes. The case was never solved.'

'No. It wasn't. That was a brutal episode but, in many ways, a typical one. It was an execution of a kind that often takes place in the criminal underworld. Stool-pigeons are executed that way. Or narcotics dealers who can't pay for the consignments they've received. Perhaps it also happens to former Nazis. It's not at all improbable.'

'But what about the man who went missing?'

'Who was that?'

'Someone called Docker Johan who disappeared at roughly the same time as the murder took place. Someone who had the same physical defect Harald Wulff and Rat Poison had. Someone who's never turned up again since.'

'I don't remember that case . . .'

'No. That's probably because of the low priority it was given. Dockers come and dockers go. Shipowners are a bit different.'

He looked at me, sadly. 'I'm sorry. I don't know anything about it.'

'That fire in 1953. Hjalmar Nymark thought Harald Wulff might have had something to do with it. Wulff worked as an office messenger there. Nymark had an idea that the fire might not have been a tragic accident after all but something much more serious: a crime, in other words. And these cases occupied his mind night and day. Right up until the day he was run over, that same day, even, he used to talk about them. He hadn't forgotten them. It was nearly thirty years since the Peacock fire and exactly ten years since Docker Johan's disappearance and the unsolved murder of Harald Wulff but he . . . I don't know for certain but I have a feeling that he was still pursuing some kind of an investigation into those matters. And then he was run over. It's a miracle he's survived, actually. Can't you see – the possible connection?'

Vegard Vadheim gave me a long look. 'It doesn't sound very likely to me but – yes, I can see the *possible* connection. But . . .' He threw up his hands. 'Why are you coming to me with all this? It's Hamre who's in charge of the case and I can assure you, Veum – Hamre's a first-rate policeman. If there's anything at the bottom of this, he'll find his way to it. I . . .' He stretched an arm towards the telephone.

'I've just been in there talking to him. He wasn't very interested. Of course, you can always try talking to him about it. And . . .'

The door opened and a woman came in bearing a pile of documents. 'Here it is. I think I've got it now.' As she caught sight of me, she halted in the doorway. 'Oh, I'm sorry – I . . .'

She was in her early thirties with long, blonde hair, a large, slightly crooked nose and a cautious smile which in a surprisingly short time became genuinely cheerful. Her eyes had a sparkle in them and she extended a slim hand. 'Hello. Your name's Veum, isn't it?'

I cleared my throat. 'That's right. At any rate, it isn't Dr Livingstone. But . . .'

She laughed gently. 'No, we haven't met. But I once tailed you. In a green Mazda. My name's Eva Jensen.'

'Ah, that time. Well, in that case . . .'

'Did I interrupt something?'

'No, I was just on my way out.'

Vegard Vadheim had abandoned his perch on the edge of the desk and stood smiling faintly. 'Do you still do any training, Veum?' To Eva Jensen he said: 'Veum and I used to keep each other up to scratch when he worked in the Child Welfare Office and was in the Town Hall running team.'

'I do a bit of running,' I said. 'If the summer's a good one and I'm feeling in a good mood . . . Will I see you at the Bergen Marathon this autumn, then?'

'Possibly, Veum, possibly.'

'Well, so long.' I nodded to them both. Eva Jensen was dressed in blue: blue shirt-blouse and blue corduroy skirt. Her smile stayed with me until I was out on the street. A few years earlier I might have fallen in love, perhaps. But not now. I was a ruin, an abandoned fortress, a field that had been ploughed over long ago. That was the way I felt, at any rate, and that was the way I had felt since last November.

Occasionally, when I met policemen like Hamre, Muus and Vadheim in the course of my professional work, I used to wonder what their private lives must be like.

Jakob E. Hamre's private life was probably, I thought, an orderly one. I saw him with a pleasant wife who baked healthy, wholemeal bread for him, and two small red-cheeked children, the younger of whom he took to the playground in the afternoons; I imagined that he went to parent-teacher meetings at the older child's school in the evenings. I saw him discussing football and politics with the neighbours over a cup of coffee, going for walks in the hills above the town on Sundays, taking his wife to the cinema or the theatre once or twice a month, maybe even going out to dinner with her once in a while. He only made love to her occasionally but when he did it was quite a passionate business, though I wouldn't have been surprised to learn that he got up and gave his hair a comb after it was over.

Dankert Muus, on the other hand, was the type who expected everyone to spring to attention as soon as he came home and welcome him with dinner on the table and the daily newspaper neatly folded beside father's place on the settee, for leisurely reading during afternoon coffee. I saw him spending his evenings in front of the television screen with his legs on the table and bottle of beer within arm's reach as he grunted his comments on the news, the weather forecast or the evening's television play. His hat still on, a grey growth of stubble covering his chin and jowls, the nearest he ever got to passion was when there was a football match to watch.

To judge by the glint of pain in his eyes, I assumed that Vegard Vadheim was a man with a lot of problems in his love life. For some reason I always imagined him in a dimly lit kitchen at a table set for two, with red wine in glasses. On the other side of the table sat a woman with sensitive features and long, blonde hair. They were leaning towards one another over the table and they were talking about serious matters. Now and then the picture would alter: she would get up, stare out of the window, out into the autumn darkness, while he put his arms round her waist; in the next picture she was on her way out of the door and he was sitting at the table again, staring sadly after her. In my mind's eye I saw him standing over his bed, packing his suitcase and folding the clothes neatly away inside it, taking down the last copies of the two collections of poetry he had written, throwing in a couple of sports medals, going into the children's room and standing there for a while, stroking the hair of the sleeping children, and then leaving. And I could see him walking down a narrow staircase inside a dark house but the blonde was out of the picture now. A man in three stages.

Perhaps none of this was real. Perhaps it was mere fantasy. Sometimes, when you're on your way out of a house, your head is filled with images.

And Eva Jensen?

She was a smile, slowly fading.

11

How do you pass the time when it's June and the days are dark, the rain is slapping like dirty wash-rags against your windowpane, your best friend is in hospital, the local First Division team is rapidly on its way back down into the Second Division again, your bottle of schnapps is empty and you can't afford to buy a new one?

I sat in my office trying to write down what I could remember of the things Hjalmar Nymark had told me and the things I had discovered at the police station later on.

I attempted to draw up a form of chronological chart, starting back in the 1930s. I jotted down the things I had been told about Harald Wulff's activities during the period from 1943 to 1945 – that was always assuming, of course, that he *was* Rat Poison. I drew a circle around the year 1953 and wrote down the names I'd heard associated with the Peacock fire: Harald Wulff (again), Elise Blom – heavily underscored twice (because she later moved in with Harald Wulff), Hagbart Helle (or Hellebust), Holger Karlsen (d. 1953) and Olai Osvold (Bombsite). Out in the margin, at a slight angle so that it also covered the war years, I wrote one more name: that of Konrad Fanebust. Then I skipped a few years, until I arrived at 1971. There I wrote: 'Harald Wulff – dead? Docker Johan – disappeared?' And, finally, I drew a large, thick arrow pointing towards the foot of the sheet. There I wrote: '1981 – Hjalmar Nymark run over.'

I sat staring at the sheet of paper. It told me nothing. Nothing more that I already knew. If there was a pattern there, it was well concealed and the clues were ten years old, at the very least. If, indeed, there were any clues.

If someone had suggested I go and look for the famous needle in the haystack, I would have willingly used up my emergency funds on that instead.

I pulled open my desk drawer, took out my office bottle and checked that my memory was correct. The bottle was, indeed, empty.

There was nothing I could do. Not until I had managed to have a word with Hjalmar Nymark, that was. And that looked as though it was going to take some time.

A week passed before they would allow me in to see him. In the interim I talked to Hamre on the telephone a couple of times, only to have confirmed what the newspapers – by their silence – had already told me: that nothing had happened.

On the day I went to visit Hjalmar Nymark in hospital I bought a bunch of lily of the valley, a bag of grapes and a book about unsolved criminal cases I found in the second-hand bookshop on Markeveien (so as to have a pretext for getting into more serious conversation).

Going to a hospital at visiting times is rather like going to a funeral. As you stand in the line of people on their way into the hospital grounds, all with the same holy relics under their arms – boxes of chocolates or bunches of flowers – you feel like a member of some large, mysterious brotherhood . . . the well. Even so, there is no one who, on arriving at a hospital at visiting time, doesn't feel ever so slightly unwell, doesn't experience some slight sensation of pain – be it in the stomach, the heart, or merely the back of the neck. There's something there that's not quite right. You can't be completely certain. Perhaps a doctor will come along and make you roll up your eyes because he thinks he has spotted a familiar symptom. Perhaps they'll put you on a trolley and wheel you into the operating theatre before you've even had a chance to deliver your box of chocolates or your bunch of flowers.

Hjalmar Nymark was in a ward on the third floor. Out in the corridor the patients were lying lined up in rows. Those of them who had been lucky, and had been put near the windows, could lie looking out at the large city centre apartment block into which no one could afford to move: a fitting monument to the ingenious dispositions of the oil age in this country which, according to all the predictions, ought now to be one of the richest in the world.

At the far end of the corridor I came to a long, narrow recreation room which terminated in a small, parlour-like recess right out in the furthest corner of the building. The cigarette smoke drifted like sea-mist over the patients who lay with their backs and necks propped up on lop-sided turrets of pillows as they watched the end of children's hour on TV. Most of them looked well over eighty.

Hjalmar Nymark lay about halfway down the left-hand row of beds. In one hand he was holding a cannula, and a phial of clear liquid was suspended above his head. He looked as though he had lost about twenty pounds. The skin of his face was moist and yellowish, and his eyes had a strange dullness that had not been there before. One half of his face bore the purple marks of the major injuries he had sustained and every conceivable part of his anatomy was covered in plasters and bandages. He lay on his back, staring vacantly out into space. Both his legs were in traction, the wrist of his right arm was in plaster and the fingers of his left hand were splayed out like a dead crab.

I entered his field of vision slowly, so as not to startle him. He

53

looked at me without reacting to my presence. This was not the big, energetic man I had come to know – the one who had thumped the table with his newspaper to lend emphasis to his words and who had risen to his feet like a tornado when he had finished talking. This was some strange, out-of-town cousin, a pale relative, a shadow on an overcast day.

'Hello, Hjalmar,' I said, as gently as I could.

Hjalmar Nymark looked at me, opened his mouth and closed it again. The man in the next bed gave an idiotic laugh. I looked at him. He wore spectacles the lenses of which were about two feet thick, his mouth had no teeth and he was in plaster from his neck down to his stomach. But it wasn't me he was laughing at. He was probably still enjoying life, in spite of it all. There are people like that, reassuringly enough. In heaven, they'll be the ones who'll get seats in the front circle, while the rest of us will have to make do with standing in the back balcony.

'Don't you know who I am?' I asked, a bit long-windedly.

He nodded, slowly. 'V–V–V. . .' he said.

'I've brought you . . .' It seemed absurd for me to be standing there holding those small, fragrant lily of the valley, so full of fresh, exuberant life, with their dark green leaves and tiny, yellowish-green stamens which were going to shed their pollen in vain on floors that were scrubbed with cleaning fluid every morning. It would have been tantamount to an insult to place the little bag of grapes under that sagging mouth. I just put the book down on the night table without any comment.

I sat down on the chair that stood next to the bed and he followed me with his eyes. Far away inside them there was something watchful, alive, but it was a long way off and you would need a powerful torch to find it.

He didn't manage to say anything that evening but the following day he greeted me with a hint of a smile and the day after that he succeeded in pronouncing the whole of my name.

By the end of a week we were able to carry on a cautious sort of conversation but, as soon as I attempted to steer it round towards what we had been talking about before he had been run over, his face closed up and his gaze shut me out. I tried again, and suddenly – for one abrupt and unexpected moment – it was as if a part of the old Hjalmar Nymark had come to life in him again. He clenched his left hand into a balled fist, so tightly that his knuckles showed white and his dark eyes flashed.

'Forget it, Veum!' he barked. 'There's nothing more to talk about! Do you understand? Let dead wolves lie, do you understand?' His eyes seemed almost young, as dark and vulnerable as those of a rejected lover. 'Do you understand?'

We didn't take up the matter again and it was as if a kind of

54

stagnation had set in inside Hjalmar Nymark. He did get better but it wasn't a genuine recovery. The people at the hospital said he'd made wonderful progress but I couldn't observe any great change.

And so June went by, like wet footprints on fresh asphalt. The days quickly evaporated and July came in the way it usually did.

July that year was grey and rainy. I spent five weeks on the island of Sotra, in a log cabin I'd managed to borrow from a distant relative who liked the idea of someone looking after his summer home while he himself took his vacation in sunnier climes. I had mentioned my plan to Hjalmar Nymark before taking up the offer, just in case he thought he might miss my visits too much but, in fact, he seemed almost relieved when I told him about it. Perhaps it was that my presence merely reminded him of things he would rather forget. Perhaps if I stayed away for a while he would really get better. In any event, I packed a suitcase with schnapps, fishing tackle and running gear and went off to settle down for a while on the outermost rim of Norway, where the Atlantic comes snarling in over bare, sloping rocks that are heavy with herring and there is a pungent aroma of seaweed in the air.

The cabin was situated on top of a steep knoll. At the foot of a sheer drop there was an old boathouse and a pier and, beyond the little strait, a few windswept islets formed the last defence against the ocean.

Far, far out on the horizon the sea became sky but you couldn't always see that this was so. On these grey summer days, with insipid rain in the air and a sun that was never anything more than a hint somewhere beyond the clouds, it was as if you had been wrapped up in a large, grey and waterlogged length of canvas which someone had thrust underneath the patch of land on which you were sitting.

The days floated by with a tranquillizing symmetry. I got up when I felt like it in the mornings, spent a couple of hours over breakfast and coffee, drove to the nearest grocery store and did my shopping, rowed the distant relative's boat out to the nearest of the islets, found a suitable spot for catching coalfish, threw out my bait and more often than not pulled in my dinner.

Every evening without exception I went running and the distances I covered grew greater and greater. At the same time my need for alcohol grew less. When the bottle of schnapps was empty, I didn't buy another and the crate of beer I had bought lasted the whole five weeks of my stay. That was the way it was out here: you had to buy your beer by the crate – maybe they figured people drank less that way, or something. During my last week I drank nothing but milk, coffee, tea and water. Slowly I felt the strength returning to my body. It had been a long, bewildering year, with regular trips to the bottom of those bottles of schnapps I kept in the office.

I spent my holiday alone. Thomas had gone to America with Beate and her new husband who had been awarded a scholarship to cover a two months' study trip over there. I still thought of him as 'Beate's new husband' even though he had now been married to her longer that I had been. I received two postcards from Thomas during my holiday. One of them was from Disneyland and said he had never had such fun in his life before. The other was an authentic photograph of the corpses of Tim Evans, Bob Dalton, Grat Dalton and Texas Jack after the legendary gunfight at Coffeyville, Texas, on 5 October 1892, and, on the obverse side of the card, I read that my son would never forget this trip as long as he lived.

The distant relative sent me a postcard from his sunny climes to tell me that the brandy was cheap, the woman were willing and the sun shone all day. I didn't hear from anyone else.

In the evenings I would sit at the large window of the living-room nursing a glass of beer or a small glass of schnapps (for as long as it lasted) and read books that were so fat you needed the whole of a summer holiday to get through them. Or else I would just sit staring out across the islets at the endless sea, the way people always stare at the horizon, as if there were a secret opening out there that led to a new and better world. Now and then a large ship would cross the expanse of open sea out there and, down towards the south, a lighthouse would send its regular messages to the surrounding world: 'blink – blink blink – blink . . .'

In the neighbouring cabin lived a family with two small children. The father was a big, lanky man with spectacles. The mother was one of those agile, transparent blondes who become almost invisible when they get into a bikini. In the evening I caught glimpses of them by the light of the paraffin lamps they used. After their children had gone to bed they would sit close to each other, staring out at the same sea as they made small talk about nothing in particular. They looked wonderfully content. During the daytime they would emerge dressed in brilliantly coloured rainwear and whenever we passed one another on the track that led down to the main road they would smile pleasantly, nod and say 'hello' to me, and on days when they were really feeling bored the two children would come over and exchange a few words with the lone wolf who lived on the knoll.

On three of the days it was sunny. Then they sat out on the verandah in front of their cabin until the sun went down and the children were allowed to stay up late. They had long drinks in their glasses and when it began to get chilly they would put on capacious sweaters and sit ever closer together. I could hear their gentle voices from where I sat – on some flat stones down in front of my cabin, with a warm cup of coffee between my fingers and an old crab trap at my feet. From our respective vantage points we would watch the sun sink slowly towards the horizon, round as a large balloon, so round you half expected it to bounce back up again. But down it would sink, into the depths, and the darkness would come slowly drifting in like a black pestilence from the sea.

There weren't many evenings with sun, however. The newspapers said it was the wettest summer since the early 1920s and a lot of people were of the opinion that we were entering a new Ice Age. The more optimistic consoled the rest of us by saying it was nonsense to call it an Ice Age, it was simply a period of wet summers and low annual mean temperatures, and would last no longer that twenty or thirty years. Those of us who lived that long could look the future intrepidly in the face, in other words.

On some evenings, as the rain dripped like tallow towards the quiet surface of the water, I rowed around and hauled crabs out of dark traps. Afterwards, I would sit eating until daybreak: the kind of endless, peaceful crab-feasts you can only have when you are alone.

Finally, the days began to shrink. The evenings grew darker and there was a cold nip in the air when you went outdoors in the morning. I stayed on for some extra time and it was eight or nine days into August when I finally tidied the place up, fastened the shutters and locked everything securely.

As I crossed the Sotra Bridge a south-westerly wind was blowing in from the side. Up north, Askøy lay neatly packed in cotton wool so it wouldn't get damaged in transit. As I approached the town, fronds of mist lay like fangs along the mountain-sides, as if they were trying to devour the last remnants of the summer that had hardly been.

I parked my car on Tårnplass and looked in at my office on Strandkaien. The mail had been accumulating and a lot of people seemed to have been keeping the postman busy distributing advertising material during the time I had been away on holiday. My mailbox contained nothing more personal that a demand for a payment to a life insurance scheme I had long ago considered it pointless to continue. I went up to my office and let myself in. The dust had been gathering like the low-pressure systems along the Norwegian coastline. Otherwise, everything was in order. The bottle in the office drawer was as empty as an election promise and the only change in the townscape outside my windows was that the new hotel they were building out on the wharf had lent the other side of Vågen a new and more handsome appearance, as though a mouth's knocked-out teeth had finally been replaced by crowns.

When I telephoned the hospital to find out how Hjalmar Nymark was, I was told he had been discharged.

12

'Discharged?' I said, possibly a little louder than was necessary. 'I suppose you mean transferred. To a nursing home, or some such place.'

'Just a moment, sir, I'll put you through . . .' said the voice, breaking off in mid-sentence.

A new voice took over. It sounded much more authoritarian and I saw before me one of those big, hefty matrons who give you a motherly dressing-down if you so much as turn over in your sleep without ringing to ask for permission first. 'Sister Pedersen here, what is it you want?'

'Ah, Mrs Pedersen, my name's Veum and I'd like to visit my good friend Hjalmar Nymark who's . . .'

'He's been discharged. He was discharged today.'

'But he - do you really mean *discharged*? Sent home?'

'Yes, he's gone home, that's correct.'

'But was he able to walk? The last time I saw . . .'

'He had to use crutches but he was completely mobile.'

'Completely mobile? But he lives on the third floor of a house in which there's no lift. How do you suppose . . .'

'I'm sorry, Mr – who was it?'

'Veum.'

'It's naturally to be regretted – but the overcrowding here during the holiday period is really quite a problem. We're having to send patients straight home from the operating theatre in taxis, if it's at all defensible.' I could hear her sifting through some papers. 'But if it will help to put your mind at rest I can tell you that we've been in touch with the Welfare Office and a home help has been arranged for Mr Nymark, on a daily basis, so . . . There are other people in a worse position than he's in. If you're a relative of his, I dare say you could go . . .'

'Yes, I'm going to see him. Immediately.'

'Very well. Was there anything else, Mr Veum?'

'No, there . . .'

'Goodbye, then.'

'Goodbye.'

I hung up cautiously, thinking she might call back and give me a telling-off. Then I got moving.

The cramped, grey apartment house Hjalmar Nymark lived in didn't look particularly inviting. I clumped up the dark staircase. It would certainly be no easy matter for a man of seventy on crutches to get up here. And, if a fire were to break out here, he wouldn't be worth any more than a thirty-year-old dossier in the police archives.

The bulb in the lamp on the second-floor landing had gone. As I groped my way towards the third floor, I became aware of someone standing up there. I paused with one foot on the step above. The eyes that met mine were at once hostile and concerned.

'Are you a relative of his?' she barked. 'If you think I find this amusing . . . They told me the door would be unlocked and I'd be able to go straight in. The client's supposed to be bedridden, or at least a bit wobbly on his legs.'

I was up beside her now. She was rather less awe-inspiring close to, since she was some four or five inches shorter than me. Her lips were thin and pursed, her eyes were sharp and she smelt faintly of eucalyptus drops. She was wearing a grey-brown, knee-length double-breasted coat which had wide flaps over the pockets. Her legs were in the position of a moderately accomplished goalkeeper who was waiting while the other side's star scorer prepared to take a penalty kick. Her ruby-red handbag had long straps, a feature that gave it excellent potential as a hand weapon. I kept a wary eye on it.

Cautiously, I asked: 'Are you the home help?'

'Yes and I haven't got all day. I've two other clients still to see to and one of them's an old lady of ninety who's blind and partially disabled and *has* to have help with her evening meal every day without fail. And they said at the Welfare Office . . .'

'What sort of arrangement did you make with them?'

'This Hjalmar Nymark – he's just been discharged from hospital and they told me at the Welfare Office . . .' – she inspected me, suspiciously – '. . . that he didn't have *any* relatives and so he'd have to have a visit every day – except weekends, of course. We don't work then.'

'And so what happens at weekends?'

'Nothing. If they haven't any family and there's no one else to look after them.'

'And what about the old blind lady?'

'Oh, that's when her daughter comes.'

'So *that's* when her daughter comes.'

'Yes. She lives on Stord, you see.'

'And isn't there any room for her in a nursing home anywhere?'

She shook her head, silently. Then her gaze slid to one side, in the direction of the door. The door was brown and through the narrow slats of glass we could see the light from Hjalmar Nymark's hallway. In the centre of the door was one of those old-fashioned bell-knobs that are still to be found in some districts of Bergen. You turn a handle and a bell rings inside: a hoarse, rasping sound.

The home help said: 'The man in there can hardly walk. That's why the people from the hospital were going to arrange for the door to be left unlocked. I was supposed to go straight in. But it's locked. And I haven't got that much time.' She motioned towards her wrist watch.

I looked at the door. If one were determined enough, it would only take ten seconds to open it. 'Have you tried the bell?'

'Of course. And I've knocked, too. I've been down to the floor below but there's nobody in.' She gave me a perplexed look. 'If you were a relative of his . . .'

I shrugged my shoulders. 'So what are we going to do? There's only one thing for it. We'll have to break in.'

She opened her eyes wide. 'But – but what if one of the wardens . . .'

I pushed her gently to one side and took a step towards the door. I took a quick glance at the lock, then raised my right leg and gave the door a flat kick, right next to the keyhole. The door-frame creaked and plaster came showering down from the ceiling. The home help looked up with a worried expression on her face and took hold of the stair-rail. The door didn't open.

I gave it another kick. Quite a lot more plaster came showering down from the ceiling this time. It settled over us both in a grey-white powder and now it was my turn to look up. If I continued this way we would soon both be standing in the open air. The door's lock still held.

'Okay,' I said and decided to settle the matter for once and for all. A fresh kick smashed the pane of glass nearest the lock. With the toe-cap of my shoe I kicked the sharpest fragments of glass clear, put my hand inside, took hold of the door-knob and opened the door from inside. The lock gave a little click as it gave way.

I stood to one side and suggested to the home help that she should perhaps go in first, as she had the authorities on her side. Anxiously, she stared at the doorway and motioned to me to go on ahead.

I went inside and heard her rapid footsteps following right behind me. She might not be first on the scene but she wasn't going to miss anything either.

The flat was completely quiet, the hallway soundless and pitch dark. I opened the door into the living-room. It was empty. 'Hjalmar?' I said.

No one replied.

The home help was breathing heavily behind me. 'Is he . . .'

I crossed the living-room floor, went over to the pale green door, knocked quickly and opened it before anyone had time to answer.

It's a funny thing. When you open doors like that one, you nearly always know what you're going to find inside. You know it at the very instant of opening. It's as if death had a powerful aura all of its own.

Hjalmar Nymark was lying in bed. His eiderdown was thrown partly to one side. His pillow lay on the floor. One of his arms hung limply down from the bed, not quite touching the floor. His new crutches stood propped up near the bedside table. On the table itself there was a glass of water. It was part empty.

His face betrayed nothing. It was alien and altered, like a wax mask that had partly melted. There was a sweetish, cloying smell in the room and it was impossible not to notice the film of dust on the furniture. Hjalmar Nymark had died in surroundings that were in keeping with the kind of life he had led – surrounded by nothing, with nobody present but himself.

I turned away. I met the eyes of the home help behind me. She wasn't looking anxious any more. Quite suddenly she had acquired a sober, matter-of-fact air, one that was almost comforting. I walked away from the doorway, into the living-room. Into the dark I said: 'Well, I suppose we'd better telephone somebody.'

13

I remained standing where I was, with my back to the pale green door. There on the sideboard right in front of me were the portraits of Hjalmar Nymark's parents. They were sepia-tinted photographs that had been taken around the end of the last century; it occurred to me that Hjalmar Nymark had been a man with three generations inside him and that his parents had belonged to a fourth. They had probably been born some time during the 1870s about the time of the Franco-Prussian War, the Paris Commune and the birth of parliamentarianism. When the First World War broke out they had been older than I was now. Bergen had been a town without cars, young trees had grown on Fløyen and, if you wanted to take a trip to the country, you went to the other side of Store Lungegårdsvannet by boat.

I studied Hjalmar Nymark's father. That was where Hjalmar had inherited his facial structure: square and massive, with a powerful jaw. The father's hair was curly and rose straight up from his broad forehead. His face wore a solemn expression, the kind people put on when they went to the photographer's back in those days.

The mother looked more delicate. Her face tapered away towards her chin, like an ice-cream cone, and her forehead was covered by a light, creamy topping of blonde curls. Her eyes looked shy and there was a pensive line around her mouth.

And now their child was lying in that room through there. He had joined the ever-growing ranks of the forefathers and all that remained of him was an empty skull and a dead, meaningless mask of a face.

I looked around me. The place looked dusty and unlived in. He had lived here for a whole lifetime. Now other people would move in, cover the floor with a new carpet, splotch loud paint on the walls, put gaudy, flowery curtains in the windows, decorate the place with flowers and pictures, and move in furniture you would have to be a specialist in yoga to feel at home with.

The home help emerged from the bedroom. She glanced quickly at the clock. 'I don't think there's anything we can do,' she said.

'No,' I said, lamely. 'Apart from calling the police.'

Her broad face seemed to flatten out. The skin on her cheek-bones grew taut and I had a feeling she was seeing her time-table going up in smoke. 'The police? But why? You don't really think . . .' She looked

62

up at me, inquiringly.

I said: 'He was a policeman himself. A couple of months ago he had an accident. He was run over. I think it would be stupid not to call the police.'

She nodded.

I said quickly: 'I wonder if you would do it? I'll stay here.'

She nodded. 'All right. Do you suppose we'll have to make statements?'

'That won't take long,' I said. 'You didn't meet anyone on the stairs when you arrived, did you?'

She looked at me in astonishment.

'On the stairs? No.'

'No one at all?'

She shook her head and moved towards the door. Then she came to abrupt halt and grew reflective. 'Except . . .'

'Yes?'

'I didn't meet anyone on the stairs. But someone came out of the building when I was approaching it from the street.'

'Someone came out of the building?'

'Yes. He made off in the opposite direction, so I didn't get a close look at him.'

'A man.'

'Yes. He . . .' She bit her lip, thinking back. 'There *was* something odd about him.'

'Yes?'

Then her face suddenly cleared and she said: 'Yes, I know what it was! He was trailing one of his legs along, as though he – yes, as though he had a limp.'

Something cold and sinister wrapped itself round my chest. 'Are you sure he . . . that he definitely had a – limp?'

'As sure as I'm standing here. Is it important?'

'I don't know. But for God's sake, whatever you do, don't forget to tell the police about it. Promise me you won't forget.'

'I certainly won't. Of course, I'll tell them,' she said. Then she cast a vague look in the direction of the bedroom, made a motion with her free hand, clutched her handbag tightly in the other and left the flat.

I stayed where I was and took another look round. The flat had acquired a new significance. I studied it. Was there anything that wasn't as it ought to be? What about the doors of the sideboard, wasn't one of them slightly open, as if someone had recently opened it and then not re-closed it properly? Wasn't the pile of newspapers beside the stove even more disorderly than when I'd been here last? And what about the bedroom?

An idea struck me.

I went into the bedroom, trying to avoid looking directly at Hjalmar Nymark. Getting down on my hands and knees, I looked under the bed. I got up again and opened the wardrobe, stood on tiptoe and peeped into the top compartment, shifting a couple of cardboard boxes. I moved the two suits and four shirts to one side and rearranged the shoes on the bottom. Then I dragged a stool over to the wardrobe, got up on it and looked around the top. Right at the back, against the wall, there was an old sweater. Otherwise there was nothing but dust up there.

I got back down on to the floor and just stood there for a while, letting my gaze take in the whole room. The final possibility was the bedside table. I opened its drawer. Inside were an old Bible and a magazine containing so-called 'true-life' crime reporting. I opened the cupboard underneath. It contained a used pocket handkerchief, a scrap of old newspaper and an empty tube of adhesive. That was all.

I drew myself up and stared straight at Hjalmar Nymark. His eyes were rigid and glassy. They betrayed nothing.

I went back into the living-room again and examined all the places in there where something might be hidden. There was nothing.

I went into the hallway, searched the cupboard, the bookshelves and a little chest of drawers. Nothing.

Now only the kitchen was left. I opened the refrigerator first. It contained fresh milk, a carton of six eggs, some tubes of processed cheese and a polythene pack of tomatoes. That was all. The kitchen cupboards, the drawers and the small pantry all yielded the same meagre results.

I stood at the kitchen window, staring down at Puddefjorden. Over on Laksevåg an oil rig the colour of red lead stood out in sharp relief against the built-up area along Damsgårdsfjellet, where the autumn tints had not yet set their seal of death on the vegetation. The sky above the peak was a leaden, crushing grey. It was one of those August days that boded winter and death.

Slowly, I went back into the living-room. I was pretty certain. The cardboard box in which Hjalmar Nymark had kept the newspaper cuttings and all the other material related to the Peacock fire was no longer in the flat.

14

The home help returned. The police were on their way, she said. We each took a chair and sat poised on the edge of it without saying a word, like two distant relatives who have met each other for the first time in many years and can't find anything to talk about.

We heard them out in the hallway and we rose to our feet before they entered the living-room. It was Hamre, Isachsen and Andersen. They greeted us in low voices, as if they were already at the funeral, and went quietly into the bedroom. When they re-emerged, their faces looked melancholy. Hamre was stroking his chin with a troubled expression and gazing at me, neutrally. 'It's always sad,' he said.

No one contradicted him.

The home help immediately began to say that she didn't have much time to spare, that she had two other clients waiting, and asked if she might be allowed to make her statement before I made mine.

'Statement?' said Hamre, giving me an inquiring look.

I opened my mouth to speak but she got in ahead of me. 'Yes, that's what it's called, isn't it?'

Isachsen and Andersen moved around the room, taking care not to touch anything. Isachsen's pale freckles were almost invisible in the poor light. Andersen was breathing heavily after climbing all those stairs. His large abdomen bulged tight against the jacket of his suit which was almost at bursting point. Isachsen's face wore its customary sour expression and he completely ignored me.

Hamre was still looking at me. 'Is there any reason for supposing there may be anything suspicious about this man's death?'

I stared back at him. 'You know the previous history. And what about this? The home help was told quite emphatically by the Welfare Office that the door would be unlocked when she arrived. Well, it wasn't. We had to break in.'

'Just a moment, Veum. Why did you come here today, in particular?'

'I arrived back from holiday on Sotra this morning. When I called the hospital I was told Nymark had been discharged. I came straight here and found – er . . .'

'Lie. Tora Lie,' said the home help, looking as though she were about to offer me her hand for me to shake it.

'I see . . .' said Hamre. All three of them were listening to me now. Isachsen, it was true, was gazing out of the window, as though he weren't really interested but I could see from his tense posture that he was all ears.

'Mrs Lie says she saw a man leave the building as she was arriving. A man with a limp,' I added, meaningfully.

'Yes, yes,' said Hamre, impatiently. 'But . . .'

The man in there – Hjalmar Nymark. His pillow's lying on the floor, as though someone had used it to . . . I would want to find out what the cause of death was. If it turned out to be suffocation I'd find that very suspicious.'

Hamre closed his eyes patiently, as if telling me to stop trying to teach him regulation police procedure, and then opened them again.

Quickly, I said: 'And the last time I was here, Hjalmar Nymark showed me a cardboard box containing old material from the investigation into the fire at Peacock. Newspaper cuttings, case documents, technical reports and so on. I can't find that box anywhere now.'

'Taken a good look round, have you?' he said, acidly. 'Gone nosing everywhere, putting your fingerprints all over the place, so no others can be found?'

'That's a lot of rot, you know it as well as I do. If there *are* anyone else's fingerprints here you'll soon find them. Anyway, it isn't certain that whoever was in here needed to do much looking. When Hjalmar Nymark fetched the box that time, he went in here – into the bedroom. The box was either under the bed, on top of the wardrobe or under the bedside table. My bet would be under the bed. Whoever took the box . . .'

'*If* anyone took it,' Hamre said, interrupting me. He was looking pale. There couldn't have been much sun where he'd spent his summer holiday, either. The stubble was clearly visible on his chin and there was something grey and drawn about him that didn't exactly promise fair weather. He turned to the other two men: 'You'll be responsible for calling in the necessary personnel and for conducting routine investigations in the flat. I'll take Veum down to the station and take a statement from him.' To Tora Lie he said, in a friendly tone of voice: 'You're free to go and attend to your other clients now but please contact me at the police station later on today.'

The home help smiled gratefully. Hamre nodded sharply in the direction of the door and gave me a frozen look. 'Come on, Veum.'

I followed close on the heels of Tora Lie as she walked out through the door. In the doorway I turned round and looked back. Jon Andersen was studying the portraits of Hjalmar Nymark's parents with interest, while Peder Isachsen stared sullenly up at the frame of the window, as though he expected to find incriminating evidence there. Through in the bedroom Hjalmar Nymark lay on his *lit de parade*, looking like something somebody had left behind.

I went out of the room and along past the front door with its broken panes of glass. Somewhere on the stairs below I could hear Tora Lie saying something and Hamre replying in a low voice which nonetheless managed to be friendly – that was his way of doing things. I followed them down with an uncomfortable sense of always seeming to arrive on the scene too late – that was my way of doing things.

15

When we arrived at the Crime Department, Hamre told me to wait. I sat down on one of the chairs facing the duty desk where an ageing, bespectacled police sergeant sat bent forward, reading the sports pages of one of the morning papers. His face wore an absent-minded expression and I wasn't surprised. The local First Division soccer team had suffered a bad defeat the day before and now the Second Division team was on its way out, too.

The reception area of a police station is not unlike a waiting room. Those who are waiting there may not be fatally ill but most of them look as though they are. Some sit nervously twiddling their thumbs. Others quietly murmur long, memorized statements to themselves, like the 'explication' of the Ten Commandments you had to learn for your confirmation exam in the old days. Vagrants come and go, some of them pretty shabby-looking, others not at all without finesse. It's like watching life's shadow side on parade. And in the front row of the front stalls sits Versatile Veum, the hope that never fades.

In a way it was like waiting to see the dentist when you don't have an appointment. The people sitting beside me were called in one after the other and ushered out again. For long periods I was completely alone. On a couple of occasions Hamre came out into the reception area but made no signal for me to follow him. He moved with swift steps: an efficient and energetic young man at the peak of his career. I sat there wondering what it felt like. I'd never been up there. Perhaps I wouldn't be able to take it. I'd probably suffer from giddiness.

Other policemen went by like a procession of more or less unsuccessful caricatures. Dankert Muus went lumbering by like a love-sick elephant. Ellingsen and Bøe had joined forces again but Ellingsen was still limping on the leg he had broken a couple of years ago. He'd got out of bed too early that morning, they said – perhaps his wife had kicked him out. Her name was Vibeke and I'd known her slightly at school. According to my calculations, it was ten years since I'd seen her but it amused me – in my more cheerful moments – to let Ellingsen think it happened more often. That was the reason he didn't acknowledge my presence as he went past, either. Bøe, on the other hand, did at least offer me a sidelong glance and a discreet sign of recognition which he made with his eyebrows. He was slimmer than

Ellingsen, leaner in the face and had a sparser covering of vegetation on top. Jon Andersen went one better: he came over and actually exchanged a few words with me. 'We're busy checking,' he mumbled.

'What?' I asked.

'You know,' he said, cast a nervous glance in the direction of the man at the duty desk, and pottered off again.

Eva Jensen walked by without noticing me. I watched her as she went. She had a springy kind of walk. Perhaps she played handball or ran for the police athletics team. I saw no sign of Vadheim.

At length, Hamre emerged again. He turned to me with a meaning look and indicated with one crooked finger that I was to follow him.

I followed him up to the third floor, along the corridor and into his office. Closing the door behind him, he pointed to the chair. I looked up at the clock. Two hours had gone by. I was beginning to feel hungry. Hopefully, this wasn't going to take too long.

He sat down at his desk and came straight to the point. 'We've been having a word with the two porters who accompanied him home from the hospital.'

I leaned forward. 'And?'

'They couldn't be sure. They went with him right to the top. He was supposed to be able to manage by himself, but – he had problems getting up there on his own.'

I tensed up inside. 'I can imagine. But they just went up with him and then left him there. More or less the way they put out the dustbins in the morning.'

He threw up his hands. 'I don't like it any more than you do, Veum. But *those* fellows couldn't do anything to change the situation for better or for worse. They had their instructions. And the hospital administration isn't any better placed to help, it has its hands tied behind its back by wage agreements and labour environment laws, by tight budgets and understaffing. And then there's the fact that this is the holiday period. They *had* to have him go home.'

I said bitterly: 'I bet they did. Well-fed administrators who sit grumbling about budgets well-fed politicians have made for them. Have you ever heard of a politician starving to death, having a home help visit twice a week, lying rotting in a little flat because nobody's discovered that he's dead? Have you ever heard of that happening to a politician?'

'No.'

'Just pity the poor devils who've made the mistake of growing old in this so-called Welfare State. Pity the poor devils who start counting up all the income tax they've paid on their earnings over the years and then wonder what they're going to get back in return now that they really need it.'

'You know how it is, Veum. Everybody wants what they haven't got. There aren't even enough of us in this building, you know. You ought to see the overtime rosters.'

Wearily, I said: 'I know, I know. But there are people far worse off than you. People who've retired on a pension, say. Or young folk queuing up for work at the time of their lives when they're most vulnerable. We take care to see to it that the old die as soon as possible. The young, far too many of them, take either to drugs or to alcohol. *We*'ve no reason to feel bitter, Hamre, people like you and me. Our only problems have to do with personal relationships or troublesome overtime rosters. But those kind of problems are a luxury, Hamre. Don't you know what I mean?'

He looked at me heavily, and said: 'You're eating into my overtime right now, Veum. To take up from where we were before you interrupted me . . .'

'I'm sorry, I . . .'

'It's okay.'

'You see, Hjalmar Nymark and I, we . . .'

'I said it's okay, Veum. Will you allow me to go on now?'

I shrugged my shoulders. 'Nobody has any time to spend hearing about friendships. They've hardly got time to make any themselves. It might upset their schedules.'

He went on: 'So they helped him up to his flat and followed him inside. They took their time about it and asked him if he'd like them to make him something to eat. But he said it was all right, he'd just like to lie down for a while and wait for the home help to arrive. They helped him into his bed. And then . . . then they left.'

'Leaving the door unlocked, as they'd been told to?'

'Well, that's just the point. They weren't too sure. You know how it is when two people are supposed to do something. One thinks the other's doing it and the other thinks the first's already done it. So they couldn't swear to anything but one of them thought he'd left the door off the latch and then merely pulled it to behind him.'

'I see.' I sighed, adding: 'But at least we can *suppose* that it was open and yet when the home help and I arrived – it was locked.'

'I understand she got there first?'

'That's right. She was standing up there when I arrived and she . . . Hey, you're not going to tell me you suspect *her* of . . .'

'We don't suspect anyone, Veum.'

'As I've told you, she said she saw a man leaving the building just as she arrived outside it. A man with a limp in his left leg.'

He winced. 'Really, Veum. Don't let's start getting melodramatic. I can understand that you're badly upset by the death of a close friend but I can assure you *we* don't exactly appreciate having our retired colleagues dying in circumstances like these, either.'

'No. You must admit it's odd, though. First he gets run over and then – on his very first day out of hospital he's found lying dead in bed.'

'The cause of death is the first thing we'll have to find out.'

'I'll bet you ten to one he was suffocated.'

He shrugged his shoulders.

I went on: 'The pillow. It was on the floor. Surely the most normal place for it to be would be under his head? An old, disabled man lying in bed – and a pillow. Anyone could have killed him – a child, a woman . . .'

He scratched his forehead. 'The post-mortem will tell us that. In the meantime we shall, of course, do everything we can to get to the bottom of this. We'll go over the flat with a fine-tooth comb. We'll interview the home help thoroughly – get a description of the man with the limp, issue a wanted notice. I can assure you, we'll do all in our power. You can rest easy.'

'And then there's the cardboard box containing the newspaper cuttings. I'm positive he hadn't hidden them anywhere outside the flat. He was run over so suddenly and – I think he would have told me about it. If the box isn't in the flat, you've got the motive for the murder.'

'That all very well, Veum – but you must see that, so far as we know, you're the only person he ever showed the box to.'

'There are others, there must be, I'm sure of it. Why don't you make inquiries?'

'As I told you, we'll . . . But you know how it is: a theory isn't worth the paper it's written on – unless it can be substantiated by evidence or by testimonies that are identical . . .'

I nodded, bleakly. What I was telling him wasn't exactly very inspiring. I ought to have thought of that earlier. When Hjalmar Nymark had been run over, I ought to have borrowed the key to his flat, removed the box and put it in a safe place. The material in the little cardboard box had been unique. If it had disappeared, I was afraid the lid would now slam shut on the Peacock case for good, that Rat Poison's identity would remain a mystery for ever, and that Hjalmar Nymark had taken the last shreds of curiosity about those matters with him to the great beyond – where the only dossier anyone delves into is the ultimate, absolute one and where all mysteries are solved for once and for all.

'Is that all?' I asked Jakob E. Hamre.

'That's all.'

'Will you let me know when the report on the post-mortem becomes available?'

'I will. For old – friendship's sake.'

I knew why he paused before uttering that word. It was more a polite way of putting things than anything else.

16

Days on which sudden deaths occur are days that grind to a halt. Some hours later, I was sitting in my office. For most people, the working day was over and the town was in the process of draining empty. By a miracle, someone had managed to sweep the sky clear of clouds. A few woolly, miniature sheep still floated over Askøy, their underbellies tinted by the sinking afternoon sun. A golden light filled the town, insinuating itself between the steep façades of the houses, creating abrupt reliefs in the road surface and making shiny windowpanes glitter.

After leaving the police station I hadn't been able to do anything that demanded much effort. I had eaten my evening meal at the cafeteria on the first floor and had read through the day's papers up in my office on the third. Now I sat with the window slightly open, listening to the sound of the dying weekday slowly filtering into the room. Not everyone had finished work yet. For some people a new working day was just beginning. Down on the market square the preacher was getting ready for action.

As long as I could remember he had been there, with the same thin face, the same windswept hair, and the same enthusiastic ring in his voice as he talked about Jesus. He was like a figure carved from the innocent landscape of one's childhood, when everything was simple – black and white. God was a man with a white beard surrounded by pink clouds, and death was something remote and incomprehensible that really didn't have anything to do with oneself. It was something that happened to cowboys and Indians in a fairytale America. Something that happened to grandparents when they were very old.

The preacher was probably in his fifties and, when I thought about it, I realized he could hardly have been there when I'd been a boy. Even so, it *felt* as though he'd always been there. Preachers had come and gone – Salvation Army officers and hypocritical Swedes with Elvis haircuts had confessed the sins of their youth; young blonde girls in knee-length pleated skirts had sung duets about joy and salvation. But now they were gone. Only this preacher was left. In an age without faith, he was the last of the Mohicans. He smiled – but wasn't there a bitterness about his lips, as he did so? His enthusiasm – didn't it really conceal a sense of disappointment at the constant interruptions he had to suffer from intoxicated youths and old drunks?

He had set up his loudspeakers now and had plugged in his electric accordion. He played a few tentative notes before breaking into:

He has opened up the Pearly Gates
So I may step inside!

I went over to the window and looked down. Now he was speaking. Nobody was stopping to listen. Someone walked quickly past him without looking either to right or to left. A couple of young girls wandered past, bent double with suppressed laughter. Down on Strandkaien, right below me, a couple of Japanese tourists came to a halt and it wasn't long before they had their cameras out. Folklore recorded on film. The last of the Mohicans, encountered alive and well on Bergen's market square.

It was at moments like this that I felt a kinship with him. He down there, alone, talking enthusiastically about Jesus. Me up here, his only true listener. And he was unaware of my existence.

When he had finished, he packed up his gear, indulged in a little small talk with one of the vagrants who was passing, filled his car at the gas station and drove off home. I stayed sitting at my desk while the darkness slowly filled the town, the office and myself – until we fused into a single darkness, a single substance, a single thought . . .

I must have dozed off. When I opened my eyes again, red and green neon lights were blinking off and on at me, like Christmas-tree lights in the dark.

Slowly, I put on my overcoat, locked up the office and went home. There wasn't anything else to do.

17

Finally, when most people had returned to their jobs and the schools were just about to re-open, summer arrived without warning, pulling out all the stops and blushing crimson like an infatuation in old age. The heatwaves came flooding in over the town and they really were waves for, every so often, they would recede as though to re-gather their strength, and then the air would contain cold glimpses of the summer we had put behind us and the autumn that was still to come.

Jakob E. Hamre telephoned the very next day. 'Just to save you the trouble,' he said.

'You don't say,' I said.

'We've had the report on the post-mortem,' he said.

'And what does it say?'

For a moment he was silent. Then he said: 'Heart failure.'

'What?'

'The cause of death was heart failure. Quite simple and not at all unusual – for a man of his age. Particularly after the strain he'd been under during those last few months. The doctor said it could even have been a delayed reaction to the accident itself. His body had already been weakened. In a way . . .'

'Yes?'

'In a way it was almost a blessing in disguise. A man like Hjalmar Nymark wouldn't have been able to tolerate the kind of life he'd have had to have lived with all those injuries. It's probably just as well that it was all over so quickly.'

'I suppose that's one way of looking at it.'

'Yes.'

'And what about the rest of the investigation?'

He said quickly: 'It's still underway.' Then, a little more slowly: 'But we haven't made any real progress. So far, there's nothing to suggest that a crime's been committed.'

'But what about the man with the limp?'

'The home help was the only person who saw him and when we interviewed her again she wasn't sure any more whether he really did have a limp or whether it might have just looked that way.'

Irritably, I said: '*Looked* that way? And what about the cardboard box, have you found it?'

His voice sounded weary: 'No, Veum. We haven't found it.'

'So you're carrying on with the investigation?'

'Yes. I just thought you'd be interested to . . .'

'I am, Hamre. Thanks for calling. I'm sure they'll have made a note of it on the other side of the Pearly Gates, in the remote filing cabinet that contains the card with your name on it. Have a good day, Hamre.'

'You too, Veum.'

And with that I put down the receiver.

A week later, the death notice appeared in one of the daily newspapers. It was as simple as it probably could have been:

Our old friend
Hjalmar Nymark,
died suddenly, aged 70.
Friends and colleagues.

The funeral was to be held the following day. I tore the notice out of the newspaper and placed it in the centre of my desk on top of the gigantic pile of papers and documents relating to all the many cases I was working on. It lay there alone, in other words.

On the day of Hjalmar Nymark's funeral the summer came to an end once more. The sky had put on a grey shirt and there was a melancholic feel of early autumn in the air. It suited the occasion.

The gravel of the paths that led between the graves of Møhlendal Cemetery crunched beneath my feet. Old gravestones leaned backwards like old folk with lumbago. The letters that were carved on them sent their brief messages up into the universe – a name and two dates: a whole lifetime swallowed up by facts. Everything and nothing: a handful of letters and eight numerals. All the joys and all the defeats. All the laughter and all the sorrows. Loves and disappointments. Tenderness and loneliness. The inscriptions said nothing about all that. It was simply *there*, somewhere behind all the names and dates, in the ground underneath the leaning stones, the windswept flowers and the overgrown paving.

Over by the chapel a small group of people was waiting. The chief of the Crime Department was there. We had never been introduced to each other. He was a bureaucratic-looking man with thick spectacles. Vadheim was there, looking even more melancholic than usual. We were joined by several older policemen, most of them retired. Jakob E. Hamre came hurrying along at the last moment, his overcoat flapping behind him and his hair ruffled by the sudden gusts of wind. Inside the chapel Hjalmar Nymark was waiting in a white coffin. When it was time, we went inside. I counted eleven people – they were all men and none of them, apart from Hamre and myself, was under fifty.

Hjalmar Nymark's death notice had borne testimony to a life lived in solitude. No family, no names of friends or relatives, just the anonymous 'Friends and colleagues'. The coffin bore a wreath from the Police Federation and there were two bouquets of flowers. One of them was from me.

The priest was a man in his late fifties and the sermon he delivered was about as personal as a Xerox copy. If any of us had a lump in our throats, it wasn't because of him.

At the end, he threw some earth on the coffin. 'Earth to earth, ashes to ashes, dust to dust . . .' The scene-shifters pulled the right rope and the coffin containing Hjalmar Nymark disappeared down into the crypt. Later it would be cremated, his remains transferred to an urn and stored in a suitable place. There he would rest, until things got too crowded, his grave was dug over and he himself became merely a name in the church records. The steep, rocky face of Ulriken would watch over him for a quarter of a century or so, rain and snow would fall, more people would die and gather round him, as though they were lining up to sing in a heavenly choir; perhaps I myself would have joined their ranks by the time his grave was dug over. We know nothing about death: about when it may arrive, about what it may conceal. A van turning a corner, a pillow on the floor . . . And then suddenly it's there, mysterious and powerful, as inevitable as the storms of autumn, as unstoppable as the eternal cycle of the years.

As always happens, a few people remained standing around outside the chapel after the proceedings were over. I said hello to a couple of Hjalmar Nymark's former colleagues. None of them had seen him for a long time but, even so, they were sad he was gone.

I went over to Hamre who was showing signs of wanting to be on his way again. He gave me a pained look, as though I were his guilty conscience.

I said: 'Well, anything new?'

His mouth was taut and pale as he replied. 'No. There are no good reasons for wasting valuable manpower on this case, Veum. Nothing suggests that any crime has been committed. It's maybe true that he died in unfortunate circumstances but only barely. The cause of death *was* heart failure. There weren't any signs of suffocation – as there would have been if the pillow had been used as a murder weapon. The two hospital porters can't swear that they left the door unlocked – on the contrary, they're very uncertain about it. As for that cardboard box – well . . .' He shrugged his shoulders meaningfully. 'Nymark could have disposed of it himself, before his accident. You said yourself that he seemed depressed that day you met in the café. People do things like that when they're depressed: they tidy up the past, throw it into the dustbin or toss it into the stove and set light to it.'

'And what about his being run over?'

'Well, *that*'s an entirely different matter, of course. That was a crime. Even if it was an accident, it should have been reported.'

'So that case hasn't been dropped yet?' I said, conscious of the sarcasm in my voice.

'No.'

'You're working flat out on it?'

He gave me a resigned look. 'Really, Veum. You know what we have to contend with. We . . .'

'Spare me the lecture, Hamre. I just want to know what's going on, that's all.'

There was a glitter in his eyes and he pushed a hand through his tousled hair. 'For God's sake, Veum! If anything fresh comes to light we'll follow it up. But we can't produce fresh clues from nowhere, not now, so long after the event. We did all that we could early on, when the evidence was fresh and the witnesses were reliable. We appealed in the press and on radio and TV for the person to report to us. There was no positive response. And the van was stolen. There were no fingerprints on it – at least none that told us anything. There wasn't a shred of evidence anywhere. Anyone could have done it. He or she is quite literally invisible.'

'Invisible?' I echoed.

Vadheim was approaching, in the company of the chief of the Crime Department. Reflectively I said, in such a soft voice that only Hamre could hear: 'As if he'd returned to the past he came from . . .'

Hamre gave me a sceptical look. Vadheim and the crime chief had come to a halt. I met the crime chief's eyes through the thick lenses of his glasses. His dark hair was sleeked back and his forehead was lofty and pensive. He extended a hand and introduced himself. I did likewise. Then he added: 'I've heard about you, Veum.' Somehow, though, he didn't look as though what he had heard had made him particularly happy and we didn't take the subject any further.

I said: 'I was a close friend of Hjalmar Nymark.'

'Is that so?' said the crime chief in a friendly tone of voice.

'I hear you've stopped the investigation.'

'Well, we have and we haven't. You know, Veum, cases of sudden death never really get dropped. If something new turns up, then . . .'

'Something new? Like what? More corpses?'

'Well . . .' There was a humorous glint behind the thick lenses 'That's putting it a bit strong.'

Hjalmar Nymark's 'friends and colleagues' were now about to depart from the little square in front of the chapel. The three police investigators were making me feel nervous, as though I were a boy scout who had got into a theological dispute with three old bishops. We began to walk towards the gates that led out to the street. Above us, bristling up the side of Ulriken, were the steel supports of the new funicular railway which had at last been set working again in the aftermath of the 1974 disaster. The only trouble now was that nobody wanted to ride on it, the fare cost as much as a ticket for the circus, and the company was on the point of going bankrupt.

Outside the gates Vadheim asked me if I wanted a lift back into town. I thanked him but told him I felt like a walk. I needed the fresh air. Vadheim and the crime chief both nodded and said goodbye in friendly fashion, while Hamre merely grunted an indistinct farewell. Then they all got into the car. Hamre taking the wheel.

I walked across Årstadvollen and down Kalfaret. A wind had risen and there was a damp trace of drizzle in the air. In the part of town through which I was walking people lived in big, desolate villas, some of them so spacious and impractical that living in them must have felt like spending one's life in an outsize suit of armour. This wasn't the district in which Hjalmar Nymark had lived. He had passed his life in a cramped little flat with faded wallpaper on the walls at the top of an apartment house and there he had died.

But had his death had natural causes?

As I followed the pavement along Kalvedelsveien, looking down over the Hansa Brewery and out across Store Lungegårdsvannet and the mountains on the other side of town – Løvstakken, Damsgårdsfjellet and, furthest along, Lyderhorn with its long, narrow, mounting profile – I promised myself I wasn't going to let the matter rest where it was.

I was going to get to the bottom of what had happened.

If Hjalmar Nymark hadn't died from natural causes, I would find out what had really happened, even if I had to travel twenty, thirty years back in time to run the culprit to ground.

When I arrived down at the town gate the rain came down, like grey slops from the pail of an ill-tempered washerwoman somewhere up behind the clouds.

18

At the station cafeteria I had a cup of coffee and a roll. Around me sat people with suitcases and rucksacks on the floor beside them. It was August – early autumn in the mountains. The last of the summer tourists were still on the go. Perhaps they were dreaming of sunny places up above the clouds. Or perhaps they were simply seeking out the high ground, the way animals do during major floods. The rain pencilled long, transparent stripes on the windows that looked on to the street, making the view blurred, as though you were seeing through gelatine.

I crossed the street and approached the identical building that lay next along: Bergen Public Library. These two buildings – the railway station and the library – had been constructed from the same material: large blocks of dark granite. Perhaps this had been done so that these redoubtable monuments to two of humanity's virtues – restlessness and the thirst for knowledge – might survive the apocalypses which those who had lived at the beginning of the century had had the imagination to envisage. Here they stood, waiting for the neutron bomb. When all the human beings had been destroyed, perhaps they would continue to stand here: the railway station, with its eternal draughts, chilly and uncomfortable, even in midsummer; and the library with its shelves bulging with a knowledge that had turned out to be of little use after all. Invisible trains would pull out of the station, following eternal time-tables, along tracks that had long ago fallen into disrepair; and, through the empty library, the ghosts of timeless borrowers would flit silently from shelf to shelf, never removing a book, never reading a word.

There weren't any draughts in the library. An eternal twilight reigned there, as though all the years the books contained had leaked out, filling the place with the mist of time, the half-light of history.

I asked if it would be possible for me to see copies of the *Bergen Times* for the period April-May 1953 and an obliging little dark-haired woman in large spectacles and green corduroy slacks went down into the archive for me and came back lugging a bound series of all the issues for the second quarter of the year in question. If I had gone to the university library I could have obtained it all on microfiche but that always confused me. You missed the contact with the paper, you missed the smell, still clinging to the yellowed pages, of printers' ink that once, long ago, was fresh, the type set by compositors who were dead and gone, the pictures taken by photographers who were old age pensioners now and the stories written by journalists who had long ago sharpened their last pencils.

I quickly found my way to the front-page stories about the Peacock fire. Several of them I recognized from Hjalmar Nymark's collection of press cuttings. I noted down the names I came across and thumbed through the remainder of the week's issues, the ones that had followed the first dramatic days. Two days after the explosion the paper gave a complete list of those who had been killed. I jotted down their names.

Then I found my way to the death notices. I noted the names of relatives. For a long time I sat looking at one of the notices; it was Holger Karlsen's. He was the person who had been landed with the moral responsibility for the explosion – the works foreman who hadn't noticed anything was wrong.

My beloved husband,
my good, devoted father,
our dear son
Holger Karlsen,
suddenly taken from us,
aged 39.
Sigrid.
Anita.
Johan – Else.
The Family.

Sigrid – in 1953 her last name had been Karlsen – would it be possible to track her down now? Was she still alive, and, if she was, would she be willing to talk to me?

To end with, I surveyed the lists I had made. I had underlined the names I considered most interesting. They were more or less the same as those I had included on a similar list I had made back in June. Elise Blom – she had worked at Peacock, and later on had lived with Harald Wulff. Olai Osvold (the man they called 'Bombsite') – he had survived the explosion. Then there was Sigrid Karlsen who might possibly be able to tell me something I still didn't know. Finally, there was Konrad Fanebust – he had led the commission of public inquiry into the explosion and might be able to supplement the information Hjalmar Nymark had given me.

I ended by adding one more name to my list – that of Hagbart Helle(bust). Beside his name I entered a date: 1 September. That was the one day in the year he spent in Norway and I had already earmarked it in my diary.

Now I had an outline, the beginnings of a plan. But I needed some more satisfactory background material and I thought I had a pretty good idea where I could get it.

Using the telephone in the cloakroom I called the *Times* and asked if Ove Haugland was in his office. He was and I arranged to look in and have a word with him.

19

A newspaper's offices are like a beehive. Each tiny office is like a cell in which the worker bee produces his black-and-white honey for the delectation of the afternoon readers who hurry greedily from page to page in search of a scandal – or, just possibly, an item of news.

I found Ove Haugland in his fourth-floor office, one floor above the main editorial department. These narrow little cubicles must have been designed according to some special principle for they seem to lead you in one direction only: towards the typewriter. The room compels you to concentrate and, when someone comes into it to be interviewed, it at once seems too small. When a women's liberation group arrives with an armful of manifestos protesting about the latest male-chauvinist gaffe made by a reporter, it gets positively overpopulated and then anything can happen.

The last time I'd seen Ove Haugland he'd reminded me of Montgomery Clift, after the car crash. He still did but he'd grown noticeably thinner in the face, there was a faint streak of silver in his dark hair and he was sitting at his typewriter wearing a pair of thick-lensed reading glasses: like Montgomery Clift in the screen version of *Miss Lonelyhearts*.

He sat hunched over the machine, staring at the last sentence he had written and leafing absent-mindedly through a thick reference book that looked as though it were probably an income tax guide.

I knocked on the frame around the open door and he looked up abruptly, over the top of his glasses. There was dark stubble on his chin and he was dressed in a pair of dark Terylene trousers and a grey-and-white striped shirt that was open at the neck. Over one of the chairs hung a moss-green sweater and a brown tie. A blue overcoat hung on a peg behind him. The window of his office looked out on to the back yard. In one of the windows on the opposite side of the building a heavily built man stood staring out into space as he spoke into a dictaphone. He looked as though he were talking into a telephone that was out of order.

Ove Haugland got up with a clumsy movement, and said: 'Hi.'

I stepped inside and the office shrank. The chair on which I sat down didn't have anything on it but, on the floor beside it, there was a pile of old newspapers, so perhaps he had cleared those off it before I'd arrived. On a small table in one corner there was something that looked like a personal file in a dirty grey plastic case. Red and green filing cards peeped out of it and I could see the torn edges of old newspaper cuttings, computer print-outs, photocopies and the like.

A row of fat books stood on the bookshelf above his desk – trade directories, shipping registers, tax guides and the sort of literature that might be supposed to interest someone who had the reputation of being the newspaper's expert on financial matters. Two years previously I had given him some information about an item that would have turned out to be a real scoop for him, if only the editor hadn't dithered so long about getting it into print that it had ended up appearing in both the other Bergen papers and half the Oslo media as well. Perhaps that had taught him a thing or two. Perhaps that was why his hair had started to go grey.

I remembered his wife, too. I had seen her around town. She had the kind of dreamy, lilac-coloured eyes you never really get to the bottom of and I was never quite sure whether she was looking at me or just wondering where she had seen my face before.

About him there was something melancholy, possible even bitter. I made a mental note not to ask after his wife. It was best to stay on the safe side.

I took a look round and said: 'Nice place you've got here. A few more square feet and I'd almost feel at home.'

He gave me a crooked smile. 'I thought you had a view, Veum.'

'Mm. That's about all I have.' I looked out at his view. The man with the dictaphone had disappeared from view. 'It's a bit more distracting than yours, perhaps.'

He peered blindly at the window. 'To tell you the truth, it's a while since I paid any attention to it.'

I said: 'All right, I'll come straight to the point. It's possibly a little before your time, but . . .'

He looked at me with curiosity. 'Yes?'

'Tell me . . . What do you know about Hagbart Helle?'

He gave a long whistle. 'Hagbart Helle . . . What do you want with him?' He glanced at the clock.

'Am I cutting into your time?'

'No, no. I was just looking to see what date it is today. But today it's only the – yes.'

He nodded, with a slightly disappointed look. 'Oh, you know about that, do you? It's the one day in the year he comes home. It's the day when his brother, who owns a knitwear factory, celebrates his birthday. For several years I've been trying to get an interview with Hagbart Helle on that day but it's always been impossible. He refuses to make any kind of public statement and he tries in general to avoid all forms of publicity. Photographs, for example . . .'

He swivelled his chair round and began to thumb through his file. He produced a press photograph and handed it to me. It was grainy and blurred, and bore signs of having been taken with a telescopic lens that hadn't been properly focused. Sitting in the back of a large, black car was a man with a thin, hook-nosed face and hair that was nearly white; he was leaning forward slightly, as though he were staring ahead of him or having a word with the driver. I looked up inquiringly.

Ove Haugland nodded. 'Hagbart Helle. The only recent photograph of him I have.'

He handed me another photograph. A serious, dark-haired young man was staring stiffly into the camera; the jacket of his suit placed him at the end of the 1930s and he had an expression on his face like that of a crestfallen snail. 'Helle as a young man.'

I looked from the one photograph to the other. The resemblance between them wasn't very great but, then, they had been taken with an interval of almost half a century between them.

Ove Haugland went on: 'Some years ago I wrote a series of articles about these overseas shipowners of ours. One or two of them are among the richest men in the world – they depend on there being wars and the state of the stock market, it's true but even so . . . And Hagbart Helle's quite a big fish even by their standards.'

'What would you say he's worth?'

He threw up his hands. 'What was the origin of the universe? It's anyone's guess. A hundred million kroner, a billion? Impossible to say. It would require an investigation taking several years to find out. You'd have to go through all his shareholdings in businesses, credit institutions and shipping firms all over the world, count up the properties he owns in more countries than you've ever been in . . .'

'Oh, yeah?'

'I would have thought so.'

'I've worked at sea.'

'Ships on more seas than you've ever sailed and so on and so forth.'

'So he's – what you might call – a powerful man?'

'If money is equal to power, then Hagbart Helle's a powerful man – yes, Veum.'

'And money *is* equal to power. More's the pity.'

He threw his hands up again.

'And what enabled him to acquire all that wealth?'

'What was the origin of the universe? What . . .'

'I'm not interested in the universe. I'm interested in . . .'

'Hagbart Helle.'

'That's correct.'

'But why, Veum?' He suddenly leaned forward and stared me intently in the face. 'Why are you interested in him?'

I looked away over his shoulder, out of the window, in the direction of the window on the opposite side of the building. A woman went by with a folder under her arm. Perhaps she'd just finished typing out the message on the dictaphone. Only his signature was now required. The world was waiting.

'You've got your job to do, Veum – if you can call it that. And I've got mine. The first of September's not that far off. How about letting me have a little story to mark it with?'

I nodded. 'I'm always prepared to do a deal. You give me something and I'll give you something.'

'Very well, Veum. Why are you so interested in Hagbart Helle?'

'It's names that interest me. His used to be Hagbart Hellebust, you know.'

For a second or two his jaw dropped. Then he regained his composure.

'Perhaps you'd better tell me what it's all about.'

'All right. It's an old case with a lot of loose ends and it's one I only got involved in by accident. It concerns a factory fire that took place back in the spring of 1953. The factory's name was Peacock, the building was over on Fjøsangerveien. Fifteen people lost their lives in the blaze and the factory's owner received a tidy sum in insurance. He invested the money sensibly, and . . .'

'I know that story. I've made a thorough study of Hagbart Helle's background.'

'I see. Or Hellebust, as he used to be called back then.'

'And?'

'There's not much else. A friend of mine, a policeman . . .'

'Funny kind of friends you have.'

'He's retired now. He took part in the investigation into the fire, together with Konrad Fanebust, among others.'

'Hellebust and Fanebust. I suppose he calls himself Konrad Fane nowadays?'

I said: 'No. Don't tell me you don't know who Konrad Fanebust is. Mayor of Bergen for . . .'

He raised one hand in a mock defensive gesture. 'Konrad Fanebust, distinguished Bergen politician and businessman, mayor of Bergen from 1955 to 1959, director of shipping firm Fanebust & Wiger together with his partner William Wiger – but Wiger died when his house burned down some time around 1972–3, and Fanebust has been sole director of the company ever since.'

'You left out the war-hero bit.'

He gave me a melancholic look. 'That's right, I did. Konrad Fanebust, distinguished Bergen war hero of the fearless struggles with the Nazis along Sørfjorden during April 1940 . . .'

'Thanks, that'll do.'

'All right, back to Helle. Is there anything else you want to know? Have you got anything on him?'

'On him?'

'I'm assuming that when you got mixed up in this it was because you'd caught wind of something. If it concerns the fire, that case will soon be statute-barred on grounds of age and, if you have any evidence, you should submit it to the prosecuting authorities well before the first of September, so they can have a decent reception committee waiting for him out at Flesland when he arrives. I'd give a lot to be there with a photographer, Veum. If you can promise me that bit of news, I'm yours forever, anytime, anywhere.'

'You're still talking business, aren't you?'

Something resembling a thoughtful expression came over his face. Then he smiled with embarrassment, and said: 'Yes.'

'Very well. What I'm really after . . . I'll be quite frank with you. I've got absolutely nothing on Hagbart Helle. Nothing at all. What I'm really after is some idea of – what kind of a man he is. Is he just a tax exile, or a smart businessman, or an idealist, or – what?'

Ove Haugland's smile became slightly sarcastic. 'You and I, Veum – we're the idealists. Look at our threadbare jackets, our down-at-heel shoes, the shiny knees in our trousers. Top-flight international businessmen aren't idealists. Patrons, maybe – if it'll pay them. And goodwill does pay. But they never do it out of idealism. They take an interest in science and culture – as objects of investment, never out of a love for beauty or a thirst for knowledge. Men like Hagbart Helle are brutal, unscrupulous rogues – otherwise they'd never have got where they are. You can't get to the top in the international financial world today without quite literally stepping over a few dead bodies.'

Reflectively, I said: 'Fifteen dead bodies, on Fjøsangerveien.'

'For example. But if *that*'s what you're after, you'll have to have proof.'

'I know. So that's all you've got?'

'I'm afraid so, Veum. If I had any more, I'd gladly let you have it. But the man's a sphinx – the Greta Garbo of the financial world. You've seen his photograph there. That man doesn't spend his time opening museums he's provided the money for, or naming super-tankers or making speeches at conferences. That man spends his time sitting at his desk counting money, money, money.'

I sighed. 'Okay. But there was something else. It's not really your department . . . but do you think you could look in your photo library and see if you have a picture of a man who was known as Harald Wulff?'

He rolled the name on his tongue. 'Harald Wulff, eh? Is he some relative of yours?'

'Only in *riksmål*. He was a Nazi collaborator during the war and he had a job as office messenger at this factory Hagbart Helle owned at the time it went up in flames.'

He gave me an inquisitorial look. 'Got hold of something there, Veum?'

I added: 'And he died in 1971.'

He looked at me resignedly. 'All right, all right. I'll go and see.' He got up. 'It'll take me a minute or two.'

'Wulff with two f's,' I said.

'And Harald spelt with a Q?'

I remained there alone, staring out of the window. There was no one visible at any of the other windows. Perhaps it was lunchtime, or perhaps they'd all just gone home.

Ove Haugland returned with two photographs. One of them was the photograph Hjalmar Nymark had shown me, in an enlarged format. The other was a picture of Wulff on his own on the witness stand during the court proceedings. The angle was approximately the same but the facial features were more clearly visible: the long, horse-like face, the powerful nose, the large ears and the dark lock of hair that fell forward over his brow, almost like a mane. His name ought to have been Horse, not Wulff.

'May I borrow these?'

'Sure. Nobody has any use for them here. But bring them back when you come to tell me the news, all right Veum?'

I promised I would do just that, thanked him, and left.

20

I took the lift to my office. As I was stepping out of the lift, I bumped into the dentist's new assistant. Her dark hair was swept tightly to the rear of her head and gathered at the back in a pony-tail. She had a talent for two things: smiling and blushing. That was how I figured it, anyway, since there was no other reason she should do both every time she saw me.

I held the lift door open for her and said: 'You must come and visit my office one of these days. Inspect the view.'

She looked along to my office door. 'In there, you mean?'

'Yes.'

'Surely the view's no different from the one we've got?'

'Ah, there's always a new perspective to be gained from someone else's office,' I said, making it sound like some old Norwegian proverb.

She smiled, blushed and walked past me into the lift. The arrow that indicated which floor the lift was at spun round in a circle. I watched it, as though I were expecting it might stop suddenly and start moving back round again. But things like that just don't happen.

I passed through my waiting room as though I were my own ghost. No one leapt up from a chair in alarm, no blondes came towards me clutching tear-soaked lace handkerchiefs. Silence brooded over the place like a hen on a porcelain egg.

I let myself into my office, blew the dust off the telephone book and thumbed through it until I came to the Karlsens. They filled slightly over a page. To my surprise, I even found one called Sigrid – and only one. She lived in Yttre Markevei. That wasn't quite my part of Nordnes but I knew it well enough.

There was no reason to delay matters. I dialled her number and listened to the telephone company's favourite tune. But no one answered.

While I still had the phone book in front of me, I looked up another name. Konrad Fanebust was easy to find. He had both a business address and a private home number. His firm's offices were in Olav Kyrresgate; he himself lived in Starefossveien.

Then there was Elise Blom. There weren't as many Bloms as there were Karlsens and there was no Elise. Not on your life. If it had been as easy as that I would soon have been out of a job. People could rent a phone book instead of a private detective and it wasn't at all certain that they'd get less for their money.

My girlfriend at the Census Office, the one I usually got no more than a sour comment or two from, was able to help me, however. She must have been feeling rested after her holiday for she didn't even ask if she could have time to think about it. Within the space of a minute she had given me the address at which Elise Blom had lived since 1955. It was that of a house – her own – in Wesenbergssmauet.

'So she owns it?'

'That's what it says here. She bought it in April 1955.'

'But she's not on the phone?'

'It doesn't look like it.'

'Hm.'

'Will that suffice?'

'What would I do without you?' I said and I meant it. I was going to have to revise my theory a little. A phone book wasn't enough. You needed a good friend at the Census Office, too.

I said: 'I wish you a long and happy life at the Census Office. Convey my greetings.'

'Who to? To . . .'

'The Census Office.'

'Oh. I thought . . .'

'How is she, anyway? Your sister, I mean.'

I could hear her radiating enthusiasm.

'Oh, she's fine, Veum. She's just had a baby.'

'Tell her I wish the little one a long and happy life at the Census Office, too. If you should ever think of quitting. But don't do it. And stay well.'

'You, too.'

Yes, she must have had a really good holiday. Either that, or she must have enjoyed being an aunt.

I tried Sigrid Karlsen's number again. This time there was somebody there. A woman's voice, of indeterminate age, said: 'Yes, hello?'

I cleared my throat and said: 'Hello. Er, my name's Veum, and I'm ringing because . . . It may sound a little stupid but were you ever married and was your husband's name Holger Karlsen?' I spoke his name clearly, so there wouldn't be any room for misunderstanding.

Her reply came hesitantly. 'Ye – es. What is it about?'

'Listen. I'm ringing in connection with – it's so long ago now – with that fire at Peacock. There are certain things connected with it that I want to talk to you about.'

Her tone was still uncertain. 'I don't quite understand. What did you say your name was?'

'Veum. I'm – well, an investigator, and certain things have come to light. I realize that it must be very unpleasant for you to talk about this matter but I think we may have – how shall I put it? – certain interests in common.'

'Are you from the police?'

'No. I run my own private firm.' I hoped that way of describing my occupation lent it just that little bit of respectability. I cast a shamefaced glance around my private firm. I could hardly invite her to come up for a tour of inspection. 'But I was wondering if you remember a policeman called Hjalmar Nymark.'

'Ye – es?'

'He's dead. And just before he died he told me a number of things.'

Her voice hardened. 'Which the police have known all along?'

I replied quickly: 'No, no. It was more to do with certain theories he had, theories constructed on hypotheses.'

'But what did you mean when you said we might have – certain interests in common?'

'I meant that there are grounds for believing that it may at last be possible for your husband's name to be cleared.'

'If it's money you're after, Mr – er – Veum, I can assure you that . . .'

'It's absolutely nothing like that, Mrs Karlsen – I swear to you. All that interests me is your view of the case, your thoughts about it, things you might be able to tell me. I need your testimony, one might say. That's all. And that is, of course, if you don't find it too painful to go raking up the past again.'

'Believe me, Mr Veum – *that's* not so important. I shall never be finished with that business. I've been raking it up for the past twenty-eight years, so . . .'

'I wonder if I might drive over to see you?'

There was a slight pause. 'It would be a little difficult today. But if you cared to drop by tomorrow, quite early?'

'What do you consider early?'

'Nine, half-past? I'll make some coffee for you.'

'That sounds wonderful. So we have a date, then?'

'That'll be fine.'

We said goodbye and hung up. As so often before, I sat there staring out of the window. Now it was afternoon. Vågen lay flat and grey and there was the mountainside with its dull August tint, already diluted by a few browny-green areas where the very earliest leaves had begun to wither prematurely from the months of rain we had had. The sky overhead was greyish-white, opaque.

Such was the day on which Hjalmar Nymark was cremated and on which I arranged my first interview in connection with the case.

21

I woke up to another grey day. August hung with a crestfallen look above the town, like a seabird with oil in its feathers. The clouds floated above Askøy like black seaweed and there was already the first hint of rain in the air.

Sigrid Karlsen lived in a narrow, three-storeyed wooded house that seemed to keel over slightly at the top. It was white but the paintwork was old.

The front door was open. A dark hallway led along to a ground-floor flat, the door to which bore the name of someone else. A flight of stairs led up to the first floor. Up there was where Sigrid Karlsen lived, behind a green door the upper part of which was inset with narrow panes of glass that were fluted with rectangular patterns. I rang the door-bell. Soon I heard movement inside and the door was opened by a small woman with a cautious smile.

'Mrs Karlsen? I'm Veum.'

She opened the door wide. 'Come in.'

We entered a narrow little vestibule in which there was no room for anything much except a bureau and a mirror. The bureau had a conspicuous scratch on one of its corners and there was a crack running across the mirror.

She extended her hand in greeting. 'Sigrid Karlsen.'

'Varg Veum. I'm pleased to meet you.'

'Here, I'll take your coat.'

'Thanks.'

'Let's go through into the kitchen. This way.'

Obediently I followed her. We entered a small, white-painted kitchen. There were blue checked curtains at the window, the table was covered with a light-coloured cloth and a heavenly smell of coffee was coming from the stove. The kitchen cupboards had blue doors and on the wall above the refrigerator hung a calendar with a picture of a boy and a dog running across the kind of flowery meadow that only exists on calendars of that type. A radio stood on the kitchen table filling the room with schmaltzy music that was interspersed with soothing small talk.

The kitchen faced north and above the roofs of the nearby houses we could see the spire of Nykirken. Sigrid Karlsen pulled out a chair and set cups, saucers and a plate for each of us. There were biscuits in a dish and she asked me if I would like cream with my coffee. I politely refused and she poured coffee into the cups. As she sat down on the other side of the table, she said: 'I was a little surprised. When you phoned.'

'I can understand that. It's so long ago, after all.'

'Yes . . .' She gazed out of the window, thoughtfully. Her eyes, behind her large, silver-rimmed spectacles, were blue; her hair was blonde, with a suspicion of grey in it. Her features were regular and girlish, and only the fine wrinkles around her eyes and mouth betrayed her age which I put somewhere midway between fifty and sixty. She was small and neat, wearing a blue cotton dress with a light beige cardigan. If she used make-up, she was very good at it.

She withdrew her gaze from the window and looked at me again, a little shyly.

'I know this part of town well,' I said. 'I grew up on Nordnes, only a bit further out.'

'Really? Yes, I've lived here since just after the war. We were living here when . . . Holger had received the promise of this flat just after the war was over. We could just about manage the rent. He had a good job and we'd been saving as much as we could. We had a good life here.'

I looked out of the window. 'You probably saw me once upon a time when I was a lad, running around out there, as you were sitting in here at your kitchen table. I remember we used to do our shopping round here from time to time. There used to be a fish shop down this way, isn't that right?'

'Yes.' She smiled faintly. 'There were several shops here, in the old days. There aren't many of them left now.'

'No.'

'But you must tell me . . .'

'Yes. But I think I'll let you begin, if you don't mind.'

'Very well. What is it you want to know?'

'I want you to tell me everything you can remember about the events that took place before and after the tragic fire.'

She nodded, slowly. 'I think I . . . ' She got up and poured some more coffee. Then she said: 'I'll go and get . . .' She went into the living-room, leaving the door ajar, and I caught a quick glimpse of a dark room with old-fashioned, patterned wallpaper and a TV set that didn't really look as though it belonged there.

She came back holding a framed photograph. She handed it to me and I sat there looking at it.

'That's us on our wedding day. That was in 1947.'

It was a posed, ceremonial photograph. The two young people stared stiffly at the camera with smiles that looked as though they had been retouched afterwards. I glanced up at her. She hadn't changed all that much but it *was* over thirty years ago. In the photograph there was something fresh and girlish about her, something that was bright and sunny. The man at her side was taller and darker that she was. He had a lean, sharp face, with a strong chin. It was a handsome face but he looked awfully uncomfortable in his black suit with its large lapels, and the white carnation in his buttonhole looked out of place there. I could easily imagine him in a boiler suit. His dark hair was combed back from his forehead and cut short over his ears.

She said: 'He was twenty-nine. I was four years younger than him.'

Her wedding dress had been white and voluminous, her bride's bouquet overlavish. 'Nykirken hadn't yet been rebuilt then, just after the war, so we got married in St Mark's. But we held the reception up at the Galley Cooks' and Stewards' School. It was November and the weather was clear.'

I nodded. 'And he was the works foreman at Peacock?'

'Yes. He'd just got the job and his wages had gone up such a lot that we thought we could afford to get married. We'd known each other since 1942. The Easter of that year.'

She nursed her cup in both hands. 'It seems like another century now, that time after the war. They were lean years but we were glad the war was over and we felt optimistic about the future. Holger and I were young and happy, and we thought the future was ours. We had Anita in 1949. It was a difficult birth, I was a little too slender in the hips but it turned out well all the same. Oh, when I think back . . . I can see him as he used to be, early in the morning, before he went to his job. He used to sit there – exactly where you're sitting now. He was – I thought he was a wonderfully handsome man. I was so terribly in love with him.' Quietly she said: 'And still am.'

'He . . .'

'He'd be wearing a checked work-shirt, brown shoes, a belt that was slightly too long for him – he was so thin, the poor man. He would have bread and coffee, and when Anita woke up he'd sit with her on his knee, laughing and playing the clown. He was a good father and he devoted time to his daughter. That wasn't quite usual in those days and the other men in the neighbourhood used to stare at him when he went for afternoon walks with Anita in the pushchair . . .'

She put her cup down. 'So, then he used to walk to work – or take the bus. The number six from Haugeveien. And he wouldn't get back until dinner at five. But, even though he'd be tired and – you know, in a place like a paintworks there weren't the same sort of controls on the materials they used as there are nowadays – he often used to have a headache – he would always go out for a walk with Anita, every single afternoon, practically. He was a good man. He grew up in Viken, the youngest of eight children – and then for him to go and die so young and have his name dragged in the mud as it was. There were people who would still ring me up years after it happened, Veum. The widows

93

of other man who'd lost their lives up there. They used to ring me up and threaten me and tell me that Holger – that they hoped – he was being tormented in hell because he had murdered their husbands. One of them – one of them used to send me flowers – every year, on the day of the fire – for nine or ten years afterwards! The first time it happened I had no idea who they could be from and I opened the envelope that was with them. "Happy Anniversary" it said on the card inside. "Greetings . . ." Later on I just used to throw the flowers in the dustbin. I'd phone the florist's and ask them not to send any more but she'd just use another. I rang the police but they couldn't do anything about it, they said. In the end it stopped of its own accord. The poor woman, she was ill, of course. But those were bad years I lived through, after it happened. I was on my own with Anita and it was a long time before the insurance company was willing to pay out any money. They claimed that – but there, at least, the police were helpful. They said that nothing could be proven, either about Holger's guilt – or about his innocence. And, if nothing could be proven, the insurance company were obliged to pay up. I had a word with a lawyer and he helped me. But it took a lot out of me. It really did. I hope I never have to go through anything like that ever again. And the worst of it was that I – I *knew* he was innocent. I knew what he'd said and I did *know* the man, after all – better than anyone else did.'

'Tell me what he said.'

She looked beyond me, almost thirty years back in time. 'He never often used to complain. He was a union shop steward for some time but he was never one of the revolutionaries. He was a Social Democrat by nature.'

'Like most Norwegians.'

'Yes, that may be so. Anyway, he was always one for co-operation. For as long as he could see a way of negotiating his way towards a solution, he'd try to avoid conflict. But, of course, there were certain situations that sometimes arose – during wage negotiations, for example. And then he could be stubborn, he would stick to his guns. But he never complained, especially at times like those. Something would come over him – a kind of sadness. His forehead would break into long, worried creases, his eyes would go dark and his mouth would take on a grim, almost angry expression. You have no idea how handsome he looked. There were times when he looked like a young poet, like Rudolf Nilsen, perhaps. But he wasn't a poet, of course. He was a man who sat at negotiating tables and there it was all figures – hours of work and weekly wages.'

She broke off, poured fresh coffee into our half-full cups, and then sat back, apparently listening to the music on the radio, where an accordion ensemble was playing 'The Dream of Elin' with plenty of high-speed suction.

Then she said: 'That's exactly the way he looked during those last days before the fire.'

'Worried, you mean?'

'Yes. And he wasn't well. I could see. He was pale and he was off his food. One night – or perhaps it was early one morning – when he thought I was still asleep, I heard him going to the toilet and being sick – without bringing anything up. I suggested he ought to go and see the doctor but he just shook his head. Then I asked him if there was anything that was troubling him. He looked at me with that sad gaze of his. I could see the muscles working in his jaw. But he didn't say anything. Not until he came home from work that afternoon. Suddenly, while he was having his afternoon coffee, he burst out: "I'm going to have a word with the management tomorrow!" I can remember those words as if it were yesterday – "I'm going to have a word with the management tomorrow! I'm sure there's a leak. I'm not the only one who's been feeling ill." He told me that several of the other men who worked in the production hall had been suffering from headaches, dizziness and nausea lately, and he was convinced there must be a leak somewhere. Gas leaking out.' Her voice broke slightly as she said: 'There would have been the danger of an explosion, too.'

I nodded. 'And the following day . . .'

With a sudden anger she burst out: 'The next day he went to the management and told them about it!' She grew calmer. 'It was a funny sort of day. I remember it as if . . . It was April and we were having some real April weather. One moment the sun would be shining, the next it would be raining cats and dogs. I'd been out at the shops and, on the way home, there was a break in between the showers, so I walked around Nordnes for a while. I don't know if you remember what it looked like out here in those days?'

'Oh, yes.'

'The bombsites that were left after the air raids. The reddish brown remains of foundations, with new vegetation growing on top. I remember the plump, yellow pussy-willows that day. The bushes were full of them. And the sun had warmth in it, the wind came in sudden gusts and ruffled your hair. Anita was sitting in her pushchair and I thought: it's spring at last. What a glorious summer it's going to be – with my child and my dear, good husband. I felt like the happiest woman in the world. And it was just on that day that he didn't come home for dinner.'

'No?'

'No – and that had never happened before. He'd never come home so late, he'd always . . . I'd made stew and sago pudding with redcurrant sauce for dessert. I rang the paintworks but all they could tell me was that he'd left work at the usual time. He didn't get home until about eight, before I'd got Anita off to sleep. She used to be so fidgety. I heard him down at the foot of the stairs, his steps sounded heavy. He was fumbling with the lock. I was sitting in there, in the living-room, in the dark. He came in here first and I could see him quite distinctly in the light before he came along to the door and caught sight of me. He . . . His lower lip was sticking out like a sulky child's. His hair was tousled and he was walking in a peculiar, swaying sort of way. When he reached the door, he stood still and leaned against the lintel, and guilty conscience was written all over his face. I had never seen him like that before. I realized he was drunk and he stank of beer. All he could say was: "They wouldn't listen to me." "Who?" I asked, irritable with anxiety. "The management," he said, almost snarling. Later, when we'd got Anita to sleep and I'd made him some strong coffee and we were able to sit down in the living-room and get some peace and quiet . . . he told me he'd gone to see the management and had told them of what he suspected. But the management had told him to go away and had said they'd look into the matter themselves but that any halt in production was out of the question.'

'Did he say who it was he'd talked to?'

'When he put it like that – when he merely said "the management" like that – there could only have been one person he was referring to.'

'And that was?'

'Hellebust. The company's director.'

'Who subsequently denied your husband had said anything at all?'

Her eyes flashed. 'Yes. Precisely!' Her small fists clenched and unclenched and, all of a sudden, the veins at her temples became clearly visible. 'And the day after that . . .' Tears came to her eyes and her voice became indistinct. 'The day after that it was all over – for me too, Veum.'

Silently, I nodded.

'And it was such a beautiful spring day, too! There weren't any showers that day. The sun was blazing but I still felt anxious when he set off for work, because of what had happened the previous day. There was something bitter and determined about him when he set off and I felt pretty sure that – I got so scared because I . . .'

'Because you . . .'

'I always get scared in situations where there's any conflict involved. And that day I was convinced Holger had decided to go on strike, call the men out on strike – if the management wouldn't give in.'

'But do you know . . .'

'No, I don't know what happened. Hellebust was in Oslo that day, so it couldn't have been him he talked to – and so . . . When they phoned to tell . . .' She swallowed several times. 'I just stood there holding the receiver, completely paralysed. I couldn't move, I couldn't utter a word. I just let the receiver go – it hung there, dangling. I couldn't even scream. It was as if I had been struck dumb. I opened my mouth and my body screamed but around me everything was silent. I could hear Anita prattling away to one of her dolls in her bedroom and the radio was on, and there was something bubbling on the stove. But inside me there was nothing but a blood-curdling, ear-splitting silence . . .'

She sat hunched over her cup of coffee. She stroked its rim carefully with one index finger – like the shadow of a caress. Softly she said: 'Ever since then I've lived alone.' She looked up at me almost defiantly. 'Don't you think it's absurd when women of nearly sixty start talking about love?'

'No.'

'You're young and you belong to a different era. It's all different nowadays. People hurry from one marriage to the next, never settle down, are so busy meeting one another that they . . . But do they ever get time to love, really to – Oh, perhaps I was just one of the privileged few who are permitted to experience that kind of all-embracing love. I was so terribly in love with Holger that he filled me, in a way. He filled me – right up – and, when he was gone, there was nothing but emptiness left. A vacuum no living thing could enter. If you know what I mean . . . The love I had experienced had exhausted my need for all that. I devoted the rest of my life to Anita: she's what's left of Holger in me.' She was looking straight at me now. 'Since then I haven't touched a man, haven't even kissed one – nothing.' And with a faint smile she continued: 'I haven't even felt I was missing anything. Can you understand that?'

I looked at her face. It hadn't been kissed since 1953, hadn't experienced the flight along the escape route of sensuality because it wasn't necessary any more. Because she had been there already. It sounded romantic – and a bit old fashioned. It really put her on the other side of sixty, or should have done. But in a strange sort of way I felt I understood her, I felt there was a form of kinship between us as we sat facing each other across the kitchen table: the woman of nearly sixty who hadn't made love since 1953 and the man with the first strands of grey in his hair and a great longing freshly chiselled in behind his skull.

I asked her: 'What does your daughter do?'

'Anita? She works in a day-care centre out in Loddefjord. She likes children but she hasn't any of her own yet. She hasn't married. She still lives here with me. She rents a little flat in the attic and she most often has her meals down here. So I still have someone to keep me company.'

'How did Anita take the loss of her father?'

'It's hard to tell. After all, she was very young when it happened. She probably didn't really understand what had taken place. But she would get completely hysterical if I wanted to go out for the evening, say. It was as if she were afraid I might disappear too, as her father had done. But I often think that it was what happened later that had a really damaging effect on her – all the trouble I had with my nerves, because it took so long for the insurance company to pay up, and then all the slander, the accusations against Holger, the investigation that never led to anything, the interviews with insurance people, lawyers, policemen . . . It was a nightmare that lasted for five or six years, before it finally subsided and we were able to try to get on with our lives like ordinary folk once more. I think the things she went through later on may have been connected with all that.'

'Are you thinking of anything in particular?'

'No, no. But everyone has – emotional problems nowadays. That's my impression, at least. She's had her fair share of them. I don't believe any child emerges completely unscathed from a period spent without one of its parents, whether it's due to divorce or to death.'

'That could well be so.'

'But perhaps I'm just old-fashioned.' She fell silent. The light from the sky outside was reflected in her large spectacles, creating a kind of distance: it was as if she were sitting on the other side if a window looking out at me.

'Tell me,' I said. 'Did you ever talk to Hellebust about what happened?'

She shook her head. 'I wrote to him, several times. I begged him to tell me what had really happened, to admit that Holger had been to see him and had complained about the leak.' Her voice became bitter. 'He never even bothered to reply.'

'No. Company directors all have one thing in common, by and large. They never admit to making mistakes.'

'I tried to telephone him but I never got further than his secretary.'

'Alvhilde Pedersen?'

'Yes, possibly. I've no idea what her name was. When I was at my most desperate, I even thought of going up there and sitting down outside his door until he had no option but to talk to me. But they'd only have called the police – and I'd talked to *them* already. Anyway, within a short space of time the factory went into liquidation and Hellebust left the country.'

'When you spoke to the police – who did you talk to there?'

'Oh, there were several different men. I remember the man you mentioned on the telephone. Nymark, wasn't it? He was a steady, reliable kind of man – the sort of person one trusts instinctively. I think he was on my side, in a manner of speaking. I also had a depressing feeling that what Hellebust had to say carried more weight. If it was his word against mine, he'd be the one they'd believe. No one else stood a chance . . . But you said Nymark was dead and something new had come to light?'

'Well, new and not new. I can tell you that Hjalmar Nymark was very preoccupied by this case, right up until the time he died. It never let go of him. He died very suddenly and, in a way – in a way, I'm trying to take up where he left off. You see, what I'm doing is attempting to investigate the circumstances surrounding Nymark's death – because the police are unwilling to do it. Those circumstances include, among other things, the fire at Peacock in 1953 – and a mysterious death that occurred in 1971. But I personally believe that the solution to the whole business lies buried at the site of the Peacock fire.'

'A death, you say . . .'

'Does the name Harald Wulff mean anything to you?'

She shook her head.

'He used to work at Peacock. As an office messenger.'

'We never had any contact with the people who worked in the office. I sometimes met some of Holger's work-mates but that was all.'

'I see. It's a long, complicated story and I promise you that, if I ever succeed in getting to the bottom of it, I'll come here and tell you everything. And if you don't think there's been enough of a hullabaloo made already, we'll go to the newspapers and I'll help you get your husband's name cleared once and for all, even though it's twenty years too late.'

She smiled weakly – and sadly – as though she didn't really believe me.

'But to put it briefly: Harald Wulff was convicted of being a traitor and he was strongly suspected of being behind a series of mysterious deaths that took place during the war years. Nymark – and, I would assume, Konrad Fanebust, who led the commission of public inquiry – had a more than fleeting suspicion that the fire at Peacock might have been started intentionally . . .'

'Yes, I remember Konrad Fanebust well. He was always so kind and he helped me later on, too, when it came to dealing with the insurance company. Perhaps he might be able to tell you something . . .'

'He'll soon be the only living survivor of those involved – apart from Hagbart Hellebust – so I really hope you're right. I'll certainly have a word with him.'

'But what happened to this – Wulff?'

'He was murdered, in 1971. At least, that's the official explanation.'

'Official?'

'I mean that it might not have been Wulff who was killed. He may have survived, after a manner of speaking. What I mean is that he may not be dead. He may be out there somewhere.' I found myself looking towards the window. I noticed that my own words were creating a sense of fear in me against my will, producing a constricted sensation in the area of my stomach and turning my mouth dry. I didn't much care for the thought I had just uttered and the town suddenly seemed even darker in the overcast day – darker and more dangerous. If Harald Wulff really was out there in the semi-darkness, a life or two here or there weren't going to cost him greatly. Perhaps I'd already said too much.

Her sceptical, uncertain smile was there again. 'But . . .'

'I suppose you don't believe in ghosts?'

'No – o.'

'No, but a person whose description distinctly resembles Harald Wulff's was observed near the scene of Hjalmar Nymark's murder in what *I* would call suspicious circumstances. And since I don't believe in ghosts either, there can only be one other explanation, can't there?'

'Can't there?'

I could see that I had made her uncertain and confused, that she was no longer one hundred per cent sure she could trust me. And I didn't blame her. I realized I was going to meet a lot of sceptical faces if I continued to go around talking about crimes that were ten or nearly thirty years old, suspicious war-time deaths, and ghosts.

I bent over my cup and raised it between both hands, as though it were a holy chalice I were offering her. 'Do you think it sounds unlikely?'

She looked at me through her large spectacles. 'I don't know. It's so difficult to readjust oneself, to start all over again, as it were. Perhaps . . . Perhaps it's better just to leave things as they are, perhaps it will only cause more trouble to go digging about in it all like that again.'

I watched her over the rim of my cup. 'I don't blame you for being sceptical. But – I feel I at least have an obligation to Hjalmar Nymark. I'm going to continue the investigation right as far as I can take it. But I'll try not to bother you again.'

'You're not bothering me at all, that's not what I meant. I just . . . I'm fifty-nine now and I've been a widow since the age of thirty-one. I lost the life I once had. I love Holger – yes *love* . . . in the present tense. For me he'll always be in the present tense. But, because of that, I've lived these past twenty-eight years in a kind of vacuum. The years I should have had with him, I've lived without love, without contact. I've given all that tenderness to a bed of flowers on a grave and the happiness we shared has become attached to memories – and to Anita. You must realize that a person gets – that I'm getting tired.'

Gently, I said: 'Of course. I don't want to . . .' I twisted my head to the side and stared desperately around me, looking for something to talk about, something different. I said: 'What – else do you do? Are you working?'

She took off her spectacles and put them down on the table in front of her. Her gaze was narrow and unfocused. She rubbed her eyes hard with the backs of her hands. 'Yes, I've a part-time job in the county council offices, three days a week.'

'So you work – down there?' I looked down towards the gloomy Hordaland council administration building and felt a chill run down my spine. The building with the brown metal plates on its façade rose like the wall of a dam facing Strandgaten, in glaring contrast to the pretty little wooden houses on the other side of Yttre Markevie. When the storms of autumn or the rains of summer set in, Hordaland could indeed be a gloomy and inhospitable county – but it wasn't *that* bad: it hadn't deserved such an ugly monument.

'Yes.' As if she had read my thoughts, she said: 'I remember when we first moved in here. We could see right down on to Vågen. The ships coming and going. The big passenger liners at Skolten – the USA line . . .'

'Yes. Those were the days, as they say. And they're probably going the same way as the old fairy-tales, too. Soon there'll be no one left who believes them either.' I got up and stood irresolutely in the middle of the room. 'Thank you.'

She had risen, too. 'You're welcome. Thank you, too.'

She followed me out to the vestibule where I got my coat on and opened the door. Before I left, she said: 'You'll be in touch if you find out anything, won't you?'

'If you want me to.'

She merely nodded silently, without saying anything further.

I nodded back, gave her a helpless smile, and stepped out into the daylight again.

22

Daylight can bring a sense of relief with it but it can also be as ruthlessly penetrating as an X-ray lamp. I wasn't in the mood for being X-rayed and I followed the shadow side of the street back into the centre of town. It was time to find out if Konrad Fanebust would agree to see me.

In a town with a shortage of heroes, Konrad Fanebust was one of the chosen few. If he had lived in more bombastic times, somebody would probably have put up a pedestal in the market square and stuck a statue of him on top of it. Several books had been written about his heroic deeds and exploits during the fighting in 1940 and also later on, in defiance of the law, during the occupation. In my boyhood days of the 1950s we had spoken his name with the same degree of awe with which we uttered those of Hopalong Cassidy, Roy Rogers and Shetland Larsen.

After the war he soon became a kind of figurehead. If he had belonged to a different party he would almost certainly have been given a cabinet post – as it was, he had to make do with a term as mayor of Bergen; he might have had several such terms had he not chosen to withdraw from political life of his own free will. After that, he more or less disappeared from view. But it appeared from the newspapers that he was director of a prosperous and enterprising shipping firm throughout times that were not exactly easy ones for the shipping trade. Then, of course, he was always called forth from obscurity whenever there was any war-time anniversary to be celebrated, whether connected with the occupation or the liberation, even though every time he was interviewed he declared it unfair that he should be the one to be given the honour of appearing in public, when there were all those anonymous resistance fighters who had been his comrades-in-arms during the war.

Konrad Fanebust's offices were on the second floor, with a view of the town park. Here his private secretary defended him from the outside world in a reception office of the stately variety, with heavy, brown-black items of furniture, oriental carpeting on the floor and a large, dark green potted palm that stood in one corner. Even getting as far as the reception office took quite an effort.

Fanebust's secretary was polite, charming and dismissive. She was a woman in her late thirties, with smooth, golden-brown hair, dressed in a black pullover and grey skirt; she had neatly manicured white hands, with shiny nail varnish on her well-clipped fingernails. She knew exactly what to say. 'Do you have an appointment?'

Sadly, I shook my head. 'No, I'm afraid I don't.'

'Then I'm afraid . . .'

'Don't be afraid. Just tell Fanebust I'm here about the death of an old mutual friend. Hjalmar Nymark. Tell him it's important. Very important.'

She looked at me thoughtfully. 'Very well. Have you time to wait?'

I stretched my arms out, generously. 'If time were money, I'd be a rich man by now.'

'Really.' She smiled, a little sharply. Even so, she got up and knocked on a door, waiting for a reply from inside before entering.

Offices of that type always seem to be in darkness. Their windows are narrow and old-fashioned, their walls so thick you can hardly hear the noise of the traffic outside, the central heating creates an even temperature throughout all twelve winter months of the year; they could drop an atom bomb outside those windows and you wouldn't notice it. That was what it felt like anyway.

She came back, leaving the door ajar behind her. That was a good sign. 'You can go in. He has a moment to spare.'

I thanked her and smiled. I knew she was a good secretary, guarding her boss's moments with care.

I went in, pulling the door firmly shut behind me.

Konrad Fanebust was sitting at his desk, writing. He looked up at me and gave me a brief, searching stare. Then, with his free hand, he motioned me towards a chair, while he continued to write. He was a man with a sense of order: one thing at a time.

I had an opportunity to study both Fanebust and his office before either of us had said a single word.

The office was large. Its walls were lined with glass-fronted bookcases and its tall windows were made to seem even narrower by the addition of a set of dark green velvet curtains. The pile on the carpet was so thick that my feet sounded like cat's paws when I crossed the room in the direction of the empty chair. It was an old-fashioned chair with a tall, slender back but not at all uncomfortable.

Fanebust's desk could, of course, have been bigger, if you'd wanted to dance the polonaise on it. As it was, there would have been plenty of room for a compressed tango, as long as you took care when turning round.

Konrad Fanebust must have been about sixty-five. I recognized him from newspaper photographs I had seen but his hair was whiter that I remembered it. His face was sharp-featured and bony and indicated a strong character. His blue eyes glittered beneath bushy eyebrows and his complexion was a fresh, reddish brown, receiving emphasis from its contrast with his white hair. He was wearing a discreet, coke-grey suit with a waistcoat, a light-blue shirt and a pearly-grey tie.

Finally, he put the pen down, read the last lines through and made some silent movement with his mouth, before putting the sheets of paper away in a folder and laying it to one side. Only then did he look up at me again. His gaze was open and direct.

Gently rubbing his hands together, he said: 'Very well.' He got up from behind the desk and extended his hand across it without coming round to the other side. I had to get up and bend forward over the desk in order to shake hands with him and it made me feel clumsy. It was an effective way of dealing with visitors and I made a note of it for use later on. If you want to get the upper hand right away, stay on your own side of the desk.

'Veum.'

'Fanebust.'

We shook hands briefly, like duellists. Fanebust sat down again before I did. He had the initiative, of that there was no doubt.

'Mrs Larsen said you'd come to see me about the death of my old friend Hjalmar Nymark?'

'Yes. I was a friend of . . . You weren't at the funeral, were you?'

'No, unfortunately not. I was in Athens and I only read about it in the paper when I got back. It's sad, I wish I had been there. You know – when old friends go and die like that, one always feels one's neglected them – and so one has, in a way. One feels one ought to have looked them up more often, shown them a bit more consideration – but then suddenly it's too late and all one's left with is a guilty conscience. Well, it's true that it was a good many years since Hjalmar Nymark and I had worked together but I've always tried to stay in touch with the lads from the old days. Those of them who're still alive.' He gave me a searching look. 'But enough of that. Tell me why you're here.'

'I'm here because of two things – or possibly three. In the first instance, I'm here because of certain circumstances surrounding Hjalmar Nymark's death . . .'

He raised his eyebrows. That was his only comment.

'I'm also here in connection with the fire at Peacock and a man who used to be known as Rat Poison.'

I gave the words time to sink in properly. His eyebrows had come down again but his face didn't give anything away. He had the congenital poker face of the hardened politician and businessman. All he said was: 'Indeed . . .'

Very briefly, I recounted what Hjalmar Nymark had told me about the fire at Peacock, the investigation that had followed and the suspicion that pointed to Harald Wulff. I rounded this off by saying: 'So, in other words . . . The reason I'm here is, first and foremost, to

104

try to confirm what Hjalmar Nymark told me – and also to find out if you can tell me anything else, something that Hjalmar Nymark forgot, or didn't know.' I made a gesture with one hand, to indicate that the floor was now his.

He looked at me reservedly. 'You must tell me first whom you are representing and what the circumstances surrounding Hjalmar's death are. Are you a journalist?'

'I'm a private detective but I'm here in the capacity of Hjalmar Nymark's last friend, so to speak. He was a lonely man, towards the end of his life.'

'A private detective?'

'Yes, but as I say – I'm not working for anyone. I'm here on my own intiative and, as far as the mysterious circumstances are concerned . . .' I attacked from the side. 'Do you believe that Rat Poison is dead?'

He looked surprised. 'Rat Poison? Hm. Well, we were never able to confirm our suspicions and I doubt if we ever shall now. I remember reading in the newspapers that Harald Wulff had died – that must be a good few years ago now.'

'It was in 1971.'

'Yes. That rings a bell.'

'Just how strongly did you suspect Wulff?'

He leaned back in his chair, stuck his thumbs in his waistcoat pockets and stared at a point somewhere above my head. His gaze was thoughtful. He said: 'It's so many years ago, Veum. When I think back on it now.' His gaze came down again. 'But it's not often that I can avoid thinking about it. I still have trouble from the wounds I got during the war and they keep me awake at nights.'

Then his gaze slid back up again, as if the past were situated somewhere above my head. 'I still re-live that investigation – it was more like a series of interrogations – we carried out back in 1953, after the fire. We'd been allocated a couple of offices in the old police station on Allhelgensgate. We used to sit there until late into the night sifting through technical reports, the testimonies of employees, passers-by, the people who investigated the fire. They were quiet, those evenings in the early 1950s. There wasn't as much traffic as there is now. Just a few cars and the occasional bus or taxi. It was a very small office and three people made it feel overcrowded. I would sit on one side of the desk, Hjalmar Nymark on the other, and squeezed in between the desk and the wall would sit the person we were interviewing. Directly underneath the only picture in the room – a photogaph of King Haakon. One of the people we interviewed most frequently and at greatest length was Harald Wulff.'

His face grew hard. 'He felt we were hounding him, he used to say that over and over again. We'd interrogated him in 1945, too, so he knew us quite well. The mere fact that he'd done time for treason didn't give us the right to treat him the way we were doing, he said. We didn't pay much attention to his objections. Both Hjalmar and I had had some rough times during the war and they were still quite fresh in our memories. Besides, this was before the days of the high-powered defence lawyers. Nowadays, even the most repulsive Nazi creeps get treated like royalty.'

He gave a crooked smile. 'I can see Hjalmar there at the table now – big and good-natured but hard as rock. That's how he was during the war, too. He never got tired. At 4 a.m., when I would feel like soggy spaghetti, he would still be as alert and persistent as ever. Harald Wulff would sag against the ropes while Hjalmar danced rings round him and teased him quite literally to breaking-point.'

'But he didn't break?'

His gaze slid heavily down to the present again. 'He didn't break. He never even gave an inch. And that made us even more certain that we were on the right trail. If he had broken down, begged for pity, gone down on his hands and knees to us . . . we might have hesitated. But he was – he didn't seem to feel anything except irritation and bad temper. No matter how exhausted he was, he never gave anything away. And that was exactly – that was exactly the type of person a man like Rat Poison would have to be. A black cat with nine lives, one that always landed on its feet no matter how far it fell.'

Again his face grew hard. 'Several of his victims during the war were people who were close friends of ours. He killed them without mercy, in that poisonous, invisible way of his. Men who had survived the most incredible hardships met with unfortunate accidents. Men who had climbed four hundred feet up sheer rock-faces in one go, after being dropped ashore from a fishing smack in a fresh gale – men like that don't fall down flights of stairs and break their necks. Things like that just don't happen to them. Men who've swum for two hours across Hardangerfjord when it was partially frozen over don't fall into Vågen and drown. I remember that after one of our nightly sessions, Hjalmar and I seriously discussed whether we shouldn't just bundle him into the car, drive him to some out-of-the-way spot and do away with him. We'd done things like that during the war – and, for us, Harald Wulff was a part of the same war, a representative of the same enemy, even though it was now 1953.'

He seemed to shake something from him with a movement of his shoulders. 'But we didn't do it, in the end. Hjalmar was against it. He'd become too much of a policeman by that time. The accused had to be given the benefit of the doubt. If we'd had any concrete evidence to go on, we'd have . . . but not otherwise. And that's how it was. In the end, we had to just let him go. Out into freedom again. We got on with our job. Questioned people we hadn't questioned before, attempted to find the one weak link in the chain – it had to be somewhere there, we thought.'

'What about the fire itself? The works foreman, Holger Karlsen, the man who took the rap, as it were . . .'

'That was a scandal. A man like Harald Wulff went free – and a decent, conscientious, hard-working man like Holger Karlsen got landed with the blame for the whole business. Or, at least, the responsibility, the way people saw it. I remember his wife came to see me; she was in utter despair.'

'Yes, I've spoken to her. I hear you gave her a helping hand.'

'Oh, it was nothing.'

'Hjalmar Nymark was of the opinion that Holger Karlsen might have been knocked to the ground.'

He have me a steady look. 'That's correct. He had severe head injuries. In the final report it said they were probably caused by falling roofwork but . . . it might just as easily have been a blow from a heavy object. That was about the nearest Hjalmar and I ever got to the weak link in the chain. If only we had been able to find the supposed – murder weapon . . . But we never found it and even if we had found it, we wouldn't have found any fingerprints, they'd all have been burnt away. But, listen, you still haven't told me . . . What happened to Hjalmar?'

'Hjalmar Nymark was knocked down by a hit-and-run driver, in June. Last week he was discharged from hospital, far too early in my opinion but they blame it on their staff shortage. I went to visit him, at his flat on the fourth floor of an appartment house in Skottegaten. The door should have been unlocked because he was expecting a home help. But when I arrived there the door was locked. The home help was there, too, and we broke in – and found him in bed. He was dead. There was a pillow on the floor. It looked to me as though someone had smothered him but the post-mortem report ascribed the cause of death to cardiac arrest, consequent upon overstrain and the injuries he'd sustained at the time of the accident. The police can't see any reasons for conducting an inquiry into the case.'

'But do you?'

'The home help said she saw a man leaving the building just as she was arriving. The man had a limp in one of his legs – as Rat Poison is said to have had – and as Harald Wulff certainly had.'

He gave me a sceptical look. 'I see . . .'

'And there's another thing. Before he was run over, Hjalmar showed me a box containing old newspaper cuttings, copies of reports and the like, all dating from 1953. I went over his flat after I found him and so did the police. We couldn't find the box anywhere. Someone had removed it. And who would have been interested in what was in it?'

He nodded slowly. 'You've got something there. But what about – did Harald Wulff really die in 1971?'

'*Someone* died in 1971. I'm not at all sure it was Harald Wulff. But if it really *was* him . . . Is it possible to suppose that Rat Poison was someone else, after all?'

He looked at me thoughtfully. 'Of course. Anything's possible. But, if that's the case, the trail will be so cold that it would be hopeless trying to find him now.'

'Not *this* trail!'

'No, perhaps not. But all the same. Of all the people in Norway – except, perhaps, for Rat Poison himself – I suppose Hjalmar and I were the foremost experts on him. And we would both have wagered our right arms that Harald Wulff was Rat Poison.'

'But, in that case – in that case, there's only you left . . .'

A silence descended between us. This last thought had given rise to silence. Once again I felt that sneaking sense of unease creeping up on me. Once again I had the sense of an invisible presence, as if Harald Wulff himself were sitting in the room with us, filling us with an icy chill.

Konrad Fanebust changed the mood by looking at the clock. 'Well, I'm afraid I have an appointment now, Veum. Very well. If there should be anything else you need to know, just get in touch. I have every sympathy with what you're trying to do and I'd appreciate it very much if you'd keep me informed in the event that you do discover anything. And you mustn't think that I'd want to keep you economically irresponsible, to put it in slightly formal terms.'

I got up. 'That would be nice but I'm doing all this as a favour to Hjalmar.'

He rose behind his desk. 'So, why not let me foot the bill – as another favour to Hjalmar?'

I opened my mouth to reply but he brushed me aside. 'We'll come back to that question later.'

I shrugged my shoulders and didn't protest. I said: 'Goodbye for now, then.'

He nodded, briefly. 'Goodbye for now.'

I walked towards the door, my footsteps soundless on the soft carpet. My hand was on the door-knob when he stopped me. 'Veum . . .'

I turned round.

He had come out from behind his desk and was standing beside it. 'Listen, Veum . . . If he's really got away again. Rat Poison. Find him for me, Veum. Find him!' As he stood there beside his desk – well-dressed, slim and white-haired, with an intense expression on his face and his hands gripping the desk-edge – he reminded me of some ageing US Marshal, preparing for the last, decisive gunfight. I gave him a brief nod, opened the door and got on my way before he had time to draw.

23

I ate my main meal of the day in one of those cafeterias that serve the Norwegian national character up on a plate: water-logged potatoes, overcooked greens and a frankfurter gasping for air in a puddle of fat. The afternoon mist lay low and grey above the red roof-tops of Fjellsiden and long lines of traffic radiated out from the town centre. The streets were being sucked empty of people, as though by the pull of some inexorable centrifugal force. The exhaust fumes mingled with the grey mist, giving the afternoon a ghastly reflected sheen like the light from a dirty bonfire.

Wesenbergssmauet elbows its way in from the densely built-up area around Øvregaten, just behind the wharf. Many of the houses have been given the face-lift they deserve but some of the house-owners still hold out against the tide of progress and have left the flaky paint and warped window frames of their homes as they are. Elise Blom's house was one of the latter kind. It had two floors and had once been given a coat of white paint. The vanished years had left their fingerprints on the woodwork and greyish white curtains hung in the tightly closed windows, making it impossible to see inside. The only light was a feeble glow from a standard lamp that stood in one of the windows.

Two crooked steps led up to the brown-painted front door but, before I got as far as the lower step, the door opened. The woman who came out greeted me with dark brown, smouldering eyes but there was nothing inviting about them. At school I had once had a teacher with eyes like that and she had never had any problems with keeping descipline in the classroom. 'What do you want?' she asked, as though the street were her own private property and I were guilty of a serious act of trespass.

'Elise Blom?' I asked, with a slight shiver.

Her lips tightened and she stuck her chin out slightly. It was a powerful chin and it was the feature that reminded me most strongly of the Elise Blom I had seen in the newspaper photograph that had appeared after the Peacock fire. In those days her hair had been swept back tightly from her face and this had emphasized the classical bone structure of her features which, even in a poorly reproduced photograph, had revealed her as an obvious beauty. Now almost thirty years had passed and her face had acquired a certain shapeless, indistinct quality. She still had the same chin but, otherwise, it was as though her features had lost their proportions. Her mouth had a crooked, aggressive look, as though she were the bad guy in a Western and only ever talked out of the corner of it.

She was dressed for an evening in town, in a blue coat and brown shoes and, in one hand, she held a red handbag. She had on a lot of make-up and her mouth was painted red, with an outline that enlarged her narrow, slightly spinsterish lips. As if to emphasize the fact that she really was on her way out, she pulled the door firmly shut behind her. She remained there on the upper step. 'Who are you?' she asked.

'My name's Veum and I'm here in connection with some inquiries I'm making. It has to do with the fire at Peacock, if you remember it.'

A contemptuous expression gleamed quickly in her eyes. They were the coldest brown eyes I had ever seen. 'What kind of inquiries, may I ask?'

'Certain things have happened which make it seem reasonable to take a close look at some of the events that took place back in 1953.' I purposely made no mention of 1971. Here it was definitely going to pay to take one thing at a time.

'And who are you from? The police?' Without waiting for me to reply she came down from the step, edged her way past me, and made off down the street with heavy footsteps in the direction of Øvregaten.

I hurried after her. 'No, not the police. I'm a sort of freelance.'

She gave me a quick look, sniffed contemptuously and continued along the street. A cloud of scent hung around her, a perfume of faded roses that had lain too long in the gutter. She had a strange way of walking. The upper part of her body seemed to teeter forward, while her hips hung back, and she moved heavily and flat-footedly. If I'd been badly brought up, I would have said she walked like a cow. But my mother taught me to keep thoughts like that to myself.

'Someone's been killed, you see,' I went on, as I caught up with her. I kept by her side as we emerged on to Øvregaten just behind Bredsgården, where two such disparate cultural institutions as the Asmervik Potato Company and the Norwegian Writers' Union Western Area Branch keep house together.

Elise Blom made no reply but continued on her way in the direction of St Nicholas Square.

'A policeman's been killed. Hjalmar Nymark. He was conducting an investigation into the fire.'

She suddenly came to a halt, tossing her head angrily. Her hair hung in artificial curls around her face, as though she no longer thought it appropriate to sweep it tightly back. 'Listen here, Mr whatever your name is . . .'

'Veum.'

'. . . or whatever you represent.'

'Nemesis Insurance. We have holdings in eternity.'

'What?' For a moment she forgot her lines and lost the thread of the conversation.

The prompter came to the rescue. 'Or maybe you could say I represent Hjalmar Nymark. As a final salute from those of us who're still left alive down here.'

She looked at me as though I were something that had crawled out of the woodwork and her voice came straight from cold storage. 'Just let me make one thing perfectly clear, once and for all. I'm thoroughly sick and tired of people who come poking around with questions about a fire that happened a hundred years ago. It's not much more than six months since it was that fellow, that – yes, Nymark, or whatever you said his name was – and I've nothing more to tell you. Not a thing. Got it?'

I tried to persuade her that I was one of the gentle sort.

'So Hjalmar Nymark came to see you, only six months ago? What did you tell him?'

She turned her eyes skywards and stomped resolutely off along the old, narrow pavements of Øvregaten. We passed Vikne's – the barbers, father and son – who cut my hair when I can afford it which isn't often. Six o'clock was chiming feebly from the tower of the Central Church. We were halfway into the quiet hour between working day and evening, when the town seems to hold it breath and the streets are suddenly practically empty.

Elise Blom swung resolutely down Vetrlid Square and I followed her, as silent and dependable as a well-trained husband. She pretended not to notice me.

Down by the traffic lights she stopped, as they had turned to red. I took up my position by her side again. 'If I were to tell you that Hjalmar Nymark's death had something to do with the Peacock fire, would you agree to consider answering a few questions?'

She looked straight ahead of her and began to talk out of the corner of her mouth again. 'How can the death of a stupid old man possibly have anything to do with a fire that happened thirty years ago?'

The lights changed to green and we crossed the street.

'That's just what I'm trying to find out.'

Without a word, she took a sudden turn to the side, walked in through a door on which a large, showy placard announced BINGO! and stomped, flat-footedly as before, up a steep flight of stairs. Perseveringly, I followed her.

We came out into a glaring hall which had strip lighting on the ceiling. There were greyish-white stains on the floor and there was an odd smell of weak coffee, cigarette smoke and human beings who were wearing slightly too many clothes. A reedy, high-pitched, amplified voice was reeling off a row of figures as though it were the secret liturgy of a freemasons' lodge or the evening psalms at the seamen's mission. I traced the voice to a microphone on a dais at the far end of the hall. It belonged to a woman who, even though she could hardly have been much over 25, had a face that looked strangely old beneath her peroxide blonde hair.

Elise Blom went steaming off to an empty seat at one of the rows of tables and I sat down level with her, on the other side of the aisle. In a low voice she snarled at me: 'If you don't stop pestering me I'll tell them to call the police.'

I threw up my hands in a helpless gesture and looked around me. The stares that had accompanied us on our way through the hall were now turned away again. One still persisted: a stout, middle-aged woman was staring me intently in the face, as though she were hoping to see the evening jackpot number inscribed there in characters of fire.

A few mauve-aproned women with money-holsters slung over their shoulders came down between the rows of tables. One of them came to a halt in front of me. 'How many?' she asked.

Uncertainly, I smiled, and said: 'How many am I allowed?'

'As many as you like,' she replied. She had a nice-looking face and seemed kind – at least, she didn't look as though she meant me any harm.

'I'll take two,' I said.

'Only two?'

'Five, then.'

'Right you are sir. That'll be twenty kroner.'

I paid up obediently and the woman put five playing coupons down on the table in front of me, together with a stubby, freshly-sharpened pencil. I stroked my chin and tried to look like one of the clan. Before now I had always regarded bingo halls with a mixture of wonderment and curiosity. Whenever I had passed the entrance to a hall like this one at around ten o'clock on a weekday morning, when people were queuing to get in, or at nine in the evening, when the halls were emptying, I had always wondered what the attraction of these establishments was, and what sort of people frequented them. I had always wondered where they went when the day's bingo was at an end – these quiet married couples with all those coffee filters under their arms; these sturdy, grey-clad ladies with their hats pulled firmly on as though they were afraid they might be stolen; and these lanky, pimply young lads in leather jackets that were slightly too short for them, with their ramshackle knees and slouching gait.

There was something lonely about the faces of those who left bingo halls of an evening, as though they belonged to the tribe of the lost, the ranks of the homeless, those whose souls nursed an unsatisfied hunger and whose hands held caresses they had never bestowed on anyone. Quite a few of the clients were women of a mature age, like Elise Blom. Some of them had thin, tortured-looking faces, as though they had only just managed to survive twenty years of unhappy marriage. Others were overweight and energetic and had clearly emerged from their marriages triumphant.

The striking preponderance of mature women and lads in the final years of puberty made me wonder if there might conceivably be an erotic pattern behind the whole set-up. Perhaps these places were a kind of rendezvous for the desolate – a crossroads where the lost and the wayward of two age-groups could quickly get to know one another.

This train of thought was interrupted when a man with a neat centre parting and a large gap between his front teeth, who was sitting three rows behind me, suddenly shouted 'Bingo!' He laughed loudly and noisily, as though he had said something funny. The voice over the microphone fell silent and one of the women in mauve came down to check his coupon. A tinkle of coffee cups passed round the tables. The coffee was served from large brown-and-white thermos flasks and, if you were hungry, there were vacuum-packed Viennese pastries that looked like the reject sculptures from some autumn exhibition of unimaginative art. The man who had won selected a two-kilo pack of sugar lumps as his prize. Perhaps he was going to put them between his teeth.

A powerfully built man in a suede jacket, dark brown trousers and black shoes came out from a room at the back, cast a searching gaze at the assembled congregation, exchanged a few words with the blonde at the microphone and disappeared. The blonde with the old lady's face switched on the PA system again. Another game began. Fresh numbers were called out over the heads of the faithful and were received with an expectancy like that of a troupe of seals in a zoo waiting for the salt herring to be tossed to them. All round me there was a scrabbling of pencils and ball-point pens.

Elise Blom was following the game with rapt attention, crossing off the numbers on her card. I studied her. Some of her former beauty was still visible in her profile, even though the transition between her neck and chin was more indeterminate than it must have been back in 1953. She had unfastened her coat and her figure looked erect and youthful. She was slim at the waist, something that was given emphasis by a wide brown belt, and her white sweater hugged her bulging breasts tightly in a way that touchingly reminded me of those false bosoms of the 1950s. Her brown skirt lay loosely over her knees and fell nearly to her ankles, disclosing little of her legs.

How old was she, anyway? She had been born in 1932, if I remembered correctly. In that case she was forty-nine. In 1953 she had been twenty-one and Harald Wulff had been thirty-nine. What had made a pretty young secretary fall for a man eighteen years her senior who was only an office messenger, had been convicted of high treason and was not apparently held in much esteem by the local community? Had he possessed qualities that didn't show in his photograph and that no one had told me about? Charm – sexual attractiveness – maybe even something demonic?

There must be secrets in her life, some of them possibly so dismal that it would be best to leave them alone, both for her own sake and for everyone else's.

And why was she here? Was this her life now? Did she belong to the faithful core of the bingo congregation or did she only look in here occasionally? I doubted if the latter were the case, for she was crossing off the numbers on her coupon with a skill that came of long practice and her neck and throat flushed a hectic red whenever she came close to completing a bingo series.

'Bingo!' a skinny woman squeaked loudly from the front row. There was another interval between games. I got up and went over to Elise Blom. She stared up at me with hostility. I said: 'It's really not my intention to pester you. Can't we go and talk somewhere? I'll buy you a drink. It just has to be done, that's all. And I'm not going to take no for an answer.'

She sniffed.

I added quickly: 'And, by all means, call the police. We can just as well discuss the relevant questions over there. They'd be very interested to hear them, too.'

'No, I – wait!' she said, suddenly.

Then the voice announced a new game over the microphone. Elise Blom said, abruptly: 'Wait!'

The game began. I strolled across and paid for a cup of coffee. Back in my seat again, I found I was following the proceedings with rapidly waning interest, a fact that seemed greatly to irritate an old lady who was sitting immediately behind me. She kept tapping me on the back at regular intervals, exclaiming indignantly: 'You must play! You must cross off the numbers! You mustn't just sit there, young man!'

Through the slightly dirty windows the sky took on a darker hue. Grey Gobelin tapestries were traced by invisible hands and only the *Statsråd Lemkuhl*'s old rigging stood out in sharp relief against the background. Everything else was blurred and indistinct like old, disintegrating stage scenery.

After she had taken part in five games without winning, Elise Blom rose, fastened her coat, gave me a stiff stare, and strode towards the exit. I hurriedly followed her out. Viewing my unused game coupons with a wondering look, the mauve-clad woman was clearing up the table I had been sitting at. As we were leaving the hall I could hear yet another game being announced – as though the blonde at the microphone were an archangel and the players were sitting in some absurd side room on the outer fringes of existence, where one game kept succeeding another, to all eternity.

As I stepped out on to the pavement in the company of Elise Blom it struck me that to casual passers-by we probably looked like a typical bingo couple: she in her slightly dowdy combination of blue coat and brown shoes, wearing slightly too much make-up and walking with a gait that suggested a steadily increasing degree of intoxication; I, in my slightly threadbare overcoat with its turned-up collar, my not quite freshly polished shoes, my brown corduroy trousers that had knees in them and my hair that needed a cut and was lifting gently in the evening breeze, exposing the strands of grey at my forehead. Two characterless faces on any evening late in August, as the autumn announces its arrival with angry gusts out of the north-west, empty plastic bags blow along the kerb-sides and the house-fronts look silently and threateningly into the approaching night.

I said: 'Well? Will you come with me?'

She looked at me with features that were drawn. Some of the fire had gone out of her eyes now and her voice sounded resigned when she said, in reply: 'I suppose we can go and have a glass of beer together, if you absolutely *must* go on pestering me.' Then she tore herself free and took her bearings.

'Where would you like to go?' I asked.

She shrugged her shoulders and began walking.

I followed her. She looked as if she knew where she was going.

24

The restaurant Elise Blom had selected had been tastelessly modernized since the days when it had borne a different name; even then it hadn't been much to write home about. Now it was a sort of pick-up joint for the middle-aged. The average age of the clientele appeared to be on the upper side of fifty and the mood at the tables varied from shrill-voiced intoxication to abject melancholy. On the dance floor various versions of the male species were performing obsolete exercises from the dancing academies of the 1950s with their favourite partners: themselves. For they might as well have been dancing alone. The complacent little smiles that flickered at the mouths of these ballroom Romeos revealed a whole-hearted belief in their own excellence and the conspicuous movements of their hands in the direction of the swelling hindquarters of their female partners was intended to suggest a worldly familiarity which would, no doubt, vanish like savings in the January sales when the underwear was eventually fumblingly removed. While they were still on the dance floor they looked like captivating Don Juans; in the bedroom I bet they threw brownies' caps over anything that stuck out. Long live the eternal headstart in life! You'll always be too late at the finishing post.

The faces at the tables around us expressed varying degrees of insipidity which had been lent a temporary glitter of elation; but they were also imbued with a certainty of their own mortality which lay like a hidden pattern behind their forced smiles and painted-on masks. The men concealed their hopelessness behind a blustering attempt at elegance that never quite came off, because their ties drooped crookedly, the handkerchieves in their breast pockets were dog-eared and their trousers had horizontal creases at the knees. The women, for their part, camouflaged themselves behind lacy bodices or attempted to divert attention with cleavages that would have yielded substantial gains on the Chicago meat-market. And, as a suitable accompaniment to the visual impact of all this, the two-piece band was playing a mocked-up version of 'It happened in Capri . . .' in an arrangement so mechanical and joyless that it put one strangely in mind of one of the country's gloomiest meeting houses during psalm-singing before the public dinner on Good Friday.

But as Elise Blom and I made our tortuous progression to one of the empty tables by the window, I had a depressing feeling that we didn't look at all out of place. We belonged here, just as we had done on the pavement outside the bingo hall. In a discotheque we would have looked as strange as a couple of dinosaurs at a cat show. Here, we were among our peers.

We had left our coats in the cloakroom. The close-fitting sweater emphasized the voluptuousness of her figure but the broad belt was so tight that it spoilt the effect a bit. Some of the ice-cream was dripping out.

A waitress in a pink overall took our modest order: two beers and two hamburger rolls.

The dim lighting in the place was meant to soften the contours of one's features and make them easier for others to tolerate. On Elise Blom the effect was the reverse of that intended. The lack of contour in her face stood out, its indistinct quality emphasized, and the aggressive look in her eyes acquired an intransigent gleam of irritation.

Lightly, I said: 'Do you come here often?'

'What business is that of yours?' she snapped.

'None, I suppose.'

'Precisely.'

I sighed and looked past her. Right next to our table one of the ballroom lady-killers, a greasy shine on his full-moon face, was voluptuously bending his partner backwards towards the floor in a manoeuvre he must learnt from Rudolph Valentino, while he stared entrancedly into her eyes to see if he could make out his own reflection in them. His partner hung backwards looking as though she were in some doubt as to whether she would ever be able to get back up again. A veritable avalanche was forming in her *décolletage*. I closed my eyes so as not to be swept away but luckily, at that moment, the waitress arrived with our beer and the couple were compelled to straighten up again.

Elise Blom took a mouthful of beer and put her glass down on the table with an irascible movement of her hand. Some of the foam stayed behind on her upper lip, like a wisp of cotton wool.

I stuck a finger in my collar and ran it slowly round before venturing to go on again. 'When you worked at Peacock . . . Were there many of you in the management?'

She gave me a frosty stare. 'Why do you ask about that?'

'So as to try to get an overall view of the set-up.'

'What set-up?'

'The set-up at work.'

She looked at me, thoughtfully. Then she said, slowly: 'There was the boss, Hagbart Hellebust.'

'Yes, and who else besides?'

There were the people in the sales department. There were quite a lot of them – salesmen but they were mostly away travelling. The sales director was a man called Olsen but he used to travel, too.'

'Aha.' At last it sounded as though we might be getting somewhere.

'Then there was the accounts clerk, Mrs Bugge. She had her own office.'

'I see.'

'And then there was us.'

'And who was us?'

'Those of us who worked in the outer office.'

'You were Hellebust's secretary, weren't you?'

'No, I wasn't, actually. I was just a typist and I took work for both the sales director and Mrs Bugge. Miss Pedersen was Hellebust's secretary, they even called her his "private secretary".' Her face suddenly lit up. 'And Miss Pedersen's dead now.' With a look of triumph, she went on: 'She died just a few years after the fire. She took all her savings out of the bank and went to settle down in Spain but she caught some peculiar illness or other, the kind people get out there, and she only just managed to get back to Bergen before she died. I went to see her in hospital.' She stopped in surprise, as though she were astonished at having given away so much information in the space of barely a minute.

The waitress brought our hamburgers. The rolls were drenched in fat and started to break up when you tried to eat them but the meat was edible and the lettuce was actually crisp.

In between two mouthfuls, I said: 'There was one other employee, wasn't there?'

She looked at me with hostility. 'Who do you mean?'

'Wasn't there an office messenger? . . . A man named . . .' I pretended to think hard. 'Harald Wulff?'

Her eyes had their contemptuous gleam again. 'Oh, him. I'd almost forgotten about him.' Then she lowered her eyes and continued to eat in silence.

Behind her I could see the band leaving the dais to take a break. The ballroom Romeos took advantage of this opportunity to go flocking out to the toilets. It almost looked like some kind of epidemic.

I finished eating and pushed my plate away. 'Listen . . . On one of the last days before the fire – isn't it true that the works foreman, Holger Karlsen, came to the office and made a complaint about a leakage he thought was somewhere in the production hall?'

She didn't look up from her plate. Instead, she cut her roll into tiny pieces, as if in an attempt to make her meal last as long as she could. She made no reply but shook her head decisively and negatively.

I leaned forward over the table and tried to draw her gaze up. 'Are you sure?'

She raised her head. Running the tip of her tongue over her teeth in order to clear away the crumbs and staring me straight in the eye, she said: 'That's precisely the question they asked me, over and over again, after the fire. And my answer's still the same. No. No one came to complain of anything like that – certainly not Holger Karlsen.'

I made a propitiating gesture. 'It's nearly thirty years ago now. No one'll bother to take the matter any further if you . . . if you just tell me the truth.'

I saw that, for a moment, she was unsure of how to react to this. For a second or two her defences came down and her face had the expression of someone who has run and run but finally seen that the race is lost. Then she pushed her chair back firmly and suddenly got to her feet. 'I've told the truth all along! And I'm damned if I'm going to be hauled over the coals like this by a – by a . . .' She looked me up and down contemptuously, in order to emphasize that she had no words for what I was.

I stood up, too, and felt the anger surge up in me. People in the vicinity had begun to take notice of us: one of the lady-killers at the next table turned up the volume of his hearing-aid and his face acquired a look of deep concentration. In a low, tense voice I said: 'Sit down again. We haven't finished. Not yet. You still haven't told me about Harald Wulff. Or do you want everyone in the place to hear the story as we're leaving? Take a look at Simon Smart over there with his local radio station tucked behind his ear.'

She went pale and sat down again, heavily. It had been a pretty savage attack and gentlemen weren't supposed to hit ladies below the belt. But she had given me a minimum of information and, in my mind's eye, I could still see Hjalmar Nymark lying on his bed at the rear of his dark flat, with his pillow on the floor and a cardboard box full of old newspaper cuttings that had suddenly vanished without trace.

I sat down and made a circular motion with my index finger in the direction of the monitoring station at the next table, to signal to him that he could turn his volume down now.

While I still had the upper hand, I leaned forward and said: 'Yes, because you lived with Harald Wulff. Right up until the time he died. Or have you forgotten that, too?'

'No,' she whispered. He lower lip was trembling slightly and she looked about in her handbag for a handkerchief. One soon appeared and she held it gently to her mouth as if in order to conceal the tell-tale signs of weakness at her lips. The look she gave me wasn't a very pretty one. It was as dark as a disused tunnel. Her face had narrowed and there were deep hollows in her cheeks.

I said: 'You lived together – for how many years? Fifteen? Sixteen?'

'Fr– from 1959 onwards.'

'Right up to the last?'

She nodded.

'Tell me how he died.'

She opened her eyes wide. Her voice came by fits and starts and she tripped over her words. 'I – not – that. You'd do better to go to the police. I'm through with all that, I've put it behind me. I don't know anything about it. He just went. Never came back. The police. Told me. When they came to the door. It just happened.'

'Wasn't there any warning? Nothing he said that made you suspicious?'

Silently, she shook her head.

'How did you manage to live? What did he live on?'

'We managed – like most people. I had a job, after all. And he went on taking temporary jobs as an office messenger. He – he managed to find a place for himself.'

'A place for himself in a society he hated and despised?'

'He . . .'

'Did he keep his political convictions after the war was over?'

Her eyes suddenly flashed again. 'You're damned idiots, all of you . . . If someone once makes a mistake, you never leave them alone. Not even when they're dead are they allowed to have any peace. Along you come, meddling where you're not wanted, little pip-squeaks whining about the same things all the time. He'd taken his punishment for what he'd done – back then – long before I met him. Wasn't that enough? Isn't one atoned-for crime enough? Must you get your greedy fingers on everything?'

'I'm sorry. But I belong to a generation that – the very earliest memory I have is the sound of the bombs falling on Bergen and the weird, creepy atmosphere in the air-raid shelters where we huddled together, night after night, morning after morning.'

'I remember it, too. Those were British bombs, Veum.'

'But it was the *Nazis*' war – which men like Harald Wulff were helping them to fight, on behalf of other nations, against their own fellow countrymen.'

'Well . . .' Her shoulders sagged and she grew still again. 'In that case it was a mistake he had to pay for dearly after the war was over. Yet that didn't stop me falling in love with him.'

This was a statement I couldn't think of any immediate riposte to. I stopped talking for a while. The band had come back on to the dais again. It pained me to hear them playing 'As Time Goes By' as if it were a perfectly ordinary dance tune. Around us – appositely enough – danced our fellow countrymen, couple after couple, closely and tenderly. Most of the people on the dance floor had been young at the time of the war. It was possible that some of them had actively taken part in the fighting on one side or the other. Now, forty years on, it was impossible to tell which side they had fought on. Time tames all beasts of prey. We all end up in the museum.

When I spoke again, it was in a low voice. 'I assume you know all there is to know about Harald Wulff. I don't need to tell you about all the crimes he was never punished for but which he almost certainly committed. During the war, and possibly after it as well. Accidents, they were called. Murders, others would say.'

She was looking at me round-eyed. 'What are you talking about now? What accidents? What murders?'

'Accidental deaths or regular political assassinations carried out during the war by an anonymous mass murderer for the righteous hordes. Rat Poison, they used to call him – for he was as invisible as an anonymous poisoner.'

'And this – this person – you think he was Harald?' She looked at me in disbelief.

'Yes – didn't he ever tell you anything about it?'

She pursed her lips but didn't succeed in keeping the words in. Out they came, compressed and practically inaudible. 'No, he didn't and I can tell you: I knew Harald Wulff better than anyone did and I know – I *know* – that he'd never be capable of . . .' Suddenly the tears came. Her face grew red and distorted, and she got up and swung her handbag over the table, knocking her beer-glass over so that its contents flowed out over the tablecloth; the people at the next table jumped with surprise. One of the musicians completely lost the beat of 'White Lilacs' and two of the waiters were already on their way towards us.

Elise Blom hissed at me: 'I don't want to hear from you again, Veum. If you try to contact me just one more time I'll – get in touch with the police – and I can assure you it'll be the worse for you.'

She hurled a contemptuous glance at the waiters who had now reached us. 'I'm sorry. I have to go. This gentleman will pay.' Without deigning even to look at me, she turned on her heel and marched off towards the cloakroom. The waiters started to clear up the mess and the waitress resolutely presented me with the bill. By the time I had paid it, Elise Blom had long since disappeared. The people at the other tables followed me with shy looks and two of the waiters accompanied me right to the door, as if to be certain that I really was on my way out.

Out on the pavement in front of the restaurant there was nothing to be seen. Elise Blom had gone home; there was no traffic; a gentle rain was falling from a sodden sky. It was time to be going home.

25

The climate of Bergen is an unpredictable one. The seasons pop like cards from the coat-sleeves of a heavenly conjurer: unexpected snow in March, a sudden night frost in May, a sunny, sixty-degree day in January. It's as if the weather-gods were playing some gigantic game of football with the sun which was for ever being kicked over the sidelines. Anything can happen – there are no watertight rules.

That year the summer returned just as August was giving way to September and there was a heatwave which lasted for two weeks. But the sun fell swiftly in the sky and, even though the temperature soared, no one had any illusions.

One of the last days in August saw the start of Bergen's first ever marathon. Thomas was staying with me that weekend. He arrived on my door-step early on the Saturday morning, with sun-bleached hair and wearing a Mickey Mouse T-shirt under his denim jacket. When I opened the door we stood looking at each other for a moment. He looked a little embarrassed but, when I bent down to give him a hug, he didn't try to tear himself free. He had grown over the summer and his teeth no longer looked so big.

It's not always easy to maintain contact with a child you only see every couple of weeks but, on this particular weekend, he had a lot of things he wanted to tell me about and our Saturday was an enjoyable one. Because of the marathon I asked him if it mightn't be better if I drove him home early on Sunday but, to my surprise, he said he'd like to come along too. 'I'll get back home soon enough,' was how he put it.

'But you might have a long wait,' I said. 'Four or five hours, maybe.'

'So what, I'll take a book to read.'

He took a book to read. I didn't ask him what it was. My son's reading habits might have had a disturbing effect on the organization of the race.

On Sunday morning the last of the summer's many clouds cleared away from the sky and, by the time we arrived at Fana Stadium, the sun was fairly blazing down. It was going to be hot over in Hauglandsdal.

Down on the race-track the most enthusiastic of the runners were already warming up. Others contented themselves with smearing Vaseline on strategic parts of their bodies, sticking plasters over their nipples and checking, for the umpteenth time, that their shoe-laces were properly tied. The atmosphere before the start of a marathon is a strange one. If you didn't know any better, you would suppose that all the hospitals in the land had closed their emergency wards and sent all the patients home. Muscle pains in legs and calves, stomach ailments of various kinds and enough neuroses to fill a psychiatric ward were blossoming out all over the starting area, where a mood of deep and intense pessimism held sway. It would be a miracle if even half the runners were able to complete the first kilometre.

On the inside track I caught sight of Eva Jensen, dressed in blue jeans and a green T-shirt. We said hello and I asked her if she were planning to take part in the race. She laughed an infectious sort of laugh but shook her head. 'I'm simply here to lend my moral support,' she said, passing her gaze over the race-track. The red artificial running surface stretched smoothly and invitingly in the sunshine and thousands of jogging shoes beat a muffled tattoo in intent circles around the turf in the middle. I followed where she was looking and saw Vegard Vadheim out there in his yellow police T-shirt and black trousers, a dark blue visor cap pulled well down over his forehead. The ex-long-distance champion had a clear advantage, even at warming-up stage, and he wasn't going to be easy to beat this time either.

'Could you keep an eye on my son?' I asked her, giving Thomas a clap on the shoulder.

She smiled. 'Of course. He can sit in my car and we'll cheer you on together.'

'That's great.'

Vegard Vadheim came over to us. 'So you've dared to show your face in public, have you, Veum?'

'It's worth a try, at least,' I said, doing some rapid knee-bends to work off the worst of my nervousness. When I straightened up again I said gently: 'How's the investigation proceeding?'

He gave me a sharp look. 'It isn't, as a matter of fact.'

'What do you mean?'

'They've finally decided that there's no connection between the things that happened – back then – and this recent incident. If anything new should turn up, then . . .' He shrugged his shoulders. 'If not . . .' His face was melancholic. There was a little more grey in his dark hair, I thought. His jaw-bone stood out sharply from the rest of his face and his whole body looked thin and bony. It gave him a restless, eager look, as though the race couldn't start soon enough for him.

He didn't have long to wait. Under the encouraging gaze of Thomas and Eva Jensen I positioned myself next to Vadheim on the starting line, as though I were hoping that some of his stamina might rub off on me. And so it did, for the first five hundred metres, anyway. After that he slowly began to pull ahead of me, metre by metre, second by second. As we reached the church at Fana I still had his back in view. I didn't see any more of him after that until we met far away over in Hauglandsdal, he on his way back, I still on my outward journey.

I had set myself an overall time of around three-and-a-half hours, with a kilometre time of five minutes. That held up for about thirty kilometres but after that the track started to get steeper and steeper. After thirty-six kilometres I was beginning to learn the difference between a marathon and every other type of race. During the last six kilometres the terrain grew so precipitous that I was compelled to walk, at least for part of the time. As I reached the last meeting point Thomas was watching me with worried eyes and Eva Jensen had begun to follow my progress in a slightly nurse-like fashion, as though she weren't sure if I were going to manage to stay on my feet.

But I did finish the course, in a very precise three hours, fifty minutes and ten seconds. That wasn't really all that bad for a man of thirty-nine who had never run a marathon before. Vegard Vadheim was the winner of his class, with the time of 2.55.16, and he had already emerged from the showers as I was crossing the tape. Eva Jensen asked us if we wanted a lift into town but I replied that I had my car with me. After about an hour I even felt up to driving it.

As Eva Jensen and Vegard Vadheim drove away from the stadium together I spent a long time gazing after them. Thomas asked me what the race had been like but it took me a while before I could answer.

26

The last Monday morning in August was gentle of tint and edged with sunlight. Women set off for work in blouses worn open at the throat, while men clutched umbrellas and looked sceptically up at the heavens for signs of rain to come. But there were no clouds above Askøy, and the water of Byfjorden was calm and mirror-smooth. There was not a breath of air; it was as if the weather were standing still on the divide between summer and autumn. I walked to the office with slow steps. My legs were still gently throbbing after the marathon but it was a sensation that was far from being as unpleasant as I had feared. My assiduous summer training had yielded results and the pace I had kept during the marathon hadn't been too demanding.

Outside my window lay the town with clear, sunlit contours, painted by a freshly awoken artist who was lavish with his colours. On the market square the fruit stalls were the dominant feature: golden oranges, shiny red apples, pears as green as the garden of Eden. Along at the fish-market there was a white gleam of exposed fillets and the stallholders stood with their broad hands stuck in their large pockets, lustfully ogling the women who passed by. Directly below my window, on the vegetable stalls, the season was in full swing. The leeks lay sprawled as if they were on heat, the cabbages bulged voluptuously, and there was a belated summer joy in the fresh, chalk-white onions. The stalls were busy. Business was going to be good. But, up in my office, it was quite – no one goes to see private detectives on a Monday morning. Most people wait until Tuesday.

From my desk I had a view of Bergen in miniature. The traders in the town centre, on the market square and in the little shops with which it was studded, and out along the wharf towards the new hotel complex, the building of which was still not complete. Along the mountainside above Øvregaten and out towards Sandvik lay the old workers' district: small, wooden houses in the winding, crooked lanes between Øvregaten and Skansen, tall grey apartment houses along Vetrlid Square and out towards Sverresborg. In Fjellien and along Fjellveien stood the large, ugly villas dating from the time of the First World War which had once been the residences of well-to-do families but were now inhabited mostly by old age pensioners or people who had inherited them.

On the mountainside above them, southwards towards Ulriken, in Starefossen, were the houses of the people who had struck it rich in the 1950s – white-painted façades gleamed in the sunshine and looked over a view that took in most of the town. Here and there a quiet little tennis court lay concealed behind the trees where, on a Sunday, you could see young people dressed in white engaged in physical exercise for the better-off. Above them, however, lay common land: Fløien and the nature park with its narrow paths between the trees where you could stroll on a soundless carpet of pine needles and feel the silence fill your being, find your way to sudden viewpoints, and walk hand-in-hand through warm, pale summer evenings with the one you loved, if you had anyone.

And, as if by way of natural contrast to all the houses dotted along the mountainside, a shabby group of homeless vagrants stood on the market quay, passing round the day's first bottle of beer. That was where I ought to go. It was from there that the way led back to 1971 and possibly even all the way back to 1953.

The homeless of Bergen have their own established meeting places to which most of them are attached and around which they gather almost like the members of a family. The same faces show up time after time.

One of these meeting places is the market quay; another, on colder days, is the area behind the Church of the Holy Cross. On rainy days, early in the morning, you will find them under the eaves of Shed 12, right out at the far end of Strandkaien. Later in the day you will find them in the district around Marken and Kong Oscarsgate. Most of them live in the Evangelical Hostel in Hollendergaten; some of them regularly spend the night in the drunk cells.

Another meeting place is Teaterparken and the circular open space in front of the theatre itself. You will find some of them in Nygårdsparken and down towards Møhlenpris, a few in the Viken-Danmarksplass district, while a large branch of the family frequents various sites in Sandviken, around the Salvation Army in Bakkegaten and the new Blue Cross hostel out at Rothaugen.

The homeless are never attractive to look at and there is nothing romantic about them. Their faces bear the marks of drunkenness, nervous problems, pill abuse and violence. Their complexions are a bluish red and often display bruises, either as a result of fights or of falling down while intoxicated. With the police they have a kind of tacit truce. Most of the violence occurs among themselves, over things like unpaid debts or squabbles over a bottle of liquor. The men are unshaven, the women have bad teeth. Their hair is untidy, they have worn the same clothes for as long as anyone can remember and their bodies often seem to be in a state of decay – swollen, almost.

On a fine summer's day in August, when they are sharing a carefree

126

bottle of beer down by the market quay as you are on the way to your office – briefcase in hand and tie freshly knotted – you may feel a tiny stab of envy. Any experienced social worker knows better, however. Take a look at them on a frosty November morning after a night spent under an overturned boat on Nygårdstangen in a temperature of minus ten without any solace other than a drop of methylated spirits in the bottom of a lemonade bottle. Meet them on an Easter Monday, when all supplies of alcohol have been exhausted, and even the bootleggers have nothing left, and watch them shake with the symptoms of withdrawal. Look into their eyes as they come towards you and mumblingly beg for a krone 'to buy a cup of coffee'. See if you can find any trace of freedom or independence in their eyes, instead of the signs of fear, depression and humiliation. It is a short distance, as the crow flies, between the people who live in those large villas on Fjellveien and these wretched folk at the bottom of the social ladder but, between them, a mighty gulf is fixed: they live in two different worlds.

The old drunkards who hang about on the market quay were once either seamen, dockworkers, messengers or labourers. Most of them have ended up here because of nervous problems and alcohol abuse. Some of them are also abusers of tranquillizers and sleeping pills but very few of them can really be called drug addicts. The drug addicts belong to a younger generation and you will find them around Ole Bulls Plass, at the top end of Nygårdsparken and around Lille Lungegårdsvann. Not many of them venture out by daylight. Their transactions are made under cover of darkness. The drunkards, on the other hand, do their shopping during normal hours: beer from the grocer's, spirits from the liquor store, sometimes obtained through middlemen.

I crossed the market square and strolled over towards the group on the quay. They looked at me with wet lips. Drops of beer glittered in their stubbly beards. One or two of them nodded to me. They knew me from previous occasions.

The group contained six men and one woman. Five of the men were well over fifty and the other was a comparative youngster of about thirty, with long, greasy hair that was parted in the middle, a tousled beard and ravaged-looking features. The woman was of the indeterminate age common to females in this enviroment – an age that may lie anywhere between twenty and sixty. It sometimes seems incredible that some of them can earn enough by prostitution to buy alcohol with: it makes you feel that these transactions, too, must take place in pitch darkness. This particular woman had a massive physique but was strangely thin about the face. Her mouth was sunken and partially toothless, her face was as pale as death, and her eyes floated like fish lying belly upwards in a poisoned lake. Her hair was a greyish blonde and she was dressed in an unbecoming man's overcoat with a thick Shetland sweater underneath. Her legs were covered by a pair of stiff, stained, size 44 jeans and, on her feet, she wore green seamen's boots.

One of the men was known as Barrel Hoop, for a reason that was anyone's guess. He went around in an old brown felt hat, looking like a malaria-ravaged Adolf Hitler who had gone into premature retirement somewhere in the jungles of South America. His hair was grey and his neck bore a nasty red scar. In the past he had worked at sea as a ship's engineer but now he would scarcely have been able to get down the ladder to the engine room.

I held up a folded ten-kroner note in front of Barrel Hoop, and observed the immediate interest it aroused among the others.

'Listen, friend, I want to talk to a fellow called Bombsite. Do you know where I can find him?'

He considered the banknote for a long time. 'Bombsite, eh?' he mumbled. He looked round the circle of faces.

One of the others said: 'He mostly hangs around with the Professor. Out in Sandviken. Try in front of the Petty Officers' Academy.'

Two of the other men nodded in agreement. The youngster with the parting was giving the banknote a damp stare. The woman was observing me from the other side of a petrified forest, her gaze as dead as asphalt.

As though he hadn't heard the other, Barrel Hoop said: 'I'd suggest you try outside the Petty Officers' Academy. I don't know if you remember the Professor?'

I nodded.

'Well, he's often together with him.'

I tucked the banknote into the breast pocket of his grey-brown tweed jacket and thanked him for the information. He had a green woollen scarf around his neck and his puffy face lit up in a kind of smile as he fished the banknote out from where I had put it and hid it away in his right-hand trouser pocket, guarding it with his hand.

'Also, there's a woman called Olga,' I went on. 'She used to live with Docker Johan, if you remember him.'

Barrel Hoop began to look thoughtful. 'Johan, eh? Sure, who doesn't. He got his name in the papers, too, in the end.'

The others nodded gloomily. They all remembered Docker Johan.

'Is she still alive?'

'Olga? Yes. She hangs out in Sandviken, too. Comes and goes a bit, though. She's mostly on her own but I should think Bombsite could tell you her whereabouts. She's got a flat out there somewhere. Didn't take it well, that business with Johan. She was never the same again afterwards.'

I threw out a feeler. 'Do you know anything about what happened to Docker Johan?' I looked from face to face. 'Any of you?'

Their faces closed up and they started to look like the three monkeys: see no evil, hear no evil, speak no evil. They shook their heads. 'No more than what was in the papers,' said Barrel Hoop. 'He got what was coming to him, that Johan.'

I gave a start of surprise. 'Got what was coming to him? What do you mean?'

'Eh?' He looked at me in bewilderment. 'He disappeared, you know. Went away.'

'Yes, but where to?'

He turned his head to one side and stared out across Vågen. 'The sea out there holds a lot of secrets, Veum. That much is for sure.'

I put it to him straight. 'So do you know anything or not?'

He shook his head, heavily. 'But we draw our own conclusions, don't we? And when one of us disappears, it usually means he's gone to sea. It's only natural. Down here by the docks is where we hang out. One step too far in the dark and you're in there, floundering about. If you've taken too much on board it won't be long before you pass out or just sink. That's life, Veum. Goodbye and farewell.'

'What about the rest of you? Do you remember anything?

They shook their heads in unison. I produced another ten-kroner note. 'I can pay.'

They looked at the banknote for a long time. It gave them a taste for beer.

One of them stammered: 'There was some talk . . . You know, Johan, he was in the resistance during the war. I remember Olga once telling me that shortly before Johan disappeared they had a visit from a man who was the leader of his cell, in those days, during the war. Olga said she was made to go out of the room while they talked. She thought they must be planning something or other but then Johan disappeared, as you know – and that was the end of it.'

I stared at the large bluish-red face in front of me. The man's hair was a yellowish colour, his eyes light brown, his nose lumpy like a malformed potato. Tonelessly, I said: 'A man who was the leader of his cell . . . I suppose you don't know – he didn't mention any names, did he?'

He chewed it over, staring at the banknote all the while. I was aware that the banknote was crying out for a name but I didn't want one that had simply been pulled out of the air at random. I gave him the note and asked: 'He wasn't called Fanebust, was he? Konrad Fanebust?

He shook his head. 'I don't remember. Really I don't.'

Barrel Hoop said: 'You could probably ask Olga about it. Maybe she would know.'

I nodded slowly, in agreement. 'Maybe she would,' I said, thoughtfully.

Then I raised my hands in a gesture of farewell, stuck them in my coat pockets and set off for Sandviken, along the wharf.

27

The Professor was sitting by himself in the circular area in front of the Petty Officers' Academy, as the building was still known, even though there had been no training school for NCOs there since before the last war. In front of a low wall stood a couple of red park-benches that had a view of Koengen and the old military exercise ground there, the back of the Orion Hotel and the factories of NEO, out across Vågen to Nordnes and the copious architecture over on that side.

The Professor had his winter overcoat buttoned up well, in spite of the warm weather. His cheeks were plump, his nose was hooked and his eyes were sharp behind the thick-lensed, horn-rimmed spectacles he wore. His head seemed to rest directly on top of his shoulders, giving him an owlish appearance. But that wasn't why they called him the Professor.

Human fortunes are so diverse. The Professor had completed the written part of his university final examinations, with mathematics as his principal subject, and it only remained for him to take the oral exam. During those last few days he crammed right up until the last exam and then a fuse blew somewhere inside his head. He never succeeded in taking the oral, spent six months in a psychiatric clinic, three years in a sanatorium, and re-emerged as a laconic, remote-controlled robot kept functioning by means of pills and set in motion by skilled repair technicians. Needless to say he was never quite the same again after that and he drifted around in the lower strata of society like an empty bottle in a backwater. Thirty years later he sat alone in the circular area in front of the Petty Officers' Academy wearing brown, threadbare trousers that hung down between his legs and a pair of dirty, black shoes, with a half-empty bottle of beer in between them on the ground.

But the look he gave me was not an unintelligent one. There was occasionally something disturbingly alert about the Professor, as though he were really just playing a part, and had been for the past thirty years – the part of a decrepit, middle-aged Hamlet. It was as though he had once made a resolution that was to last for the rest of his life and had kept it.

I had had enough foresight to bring along a plastic bag containing some bottles of beer, discreetly concealed beneath a few newspapers.

130

One or two beers can sometimes genuinely break the ice in the kind of company I was planning to spend the day in.

I greeted the Professor, sat down on the bench beside him, and opened the first bottle in his honour. To show I was one of the boys I took a good swig from it before handing it to him without saying anything.

Silently, he took the bottle, put its neck to his mouth and drained it in one long pull. Then a quick, Hamlet-like flicker of wit appeared in his eyes, before he returned the bottle to me.

'How's life, Professor?' I asked him, in a friendly tone of voice. His voice was hoarse.

'Oh, you know how it is, it never rains but it pours.'

He spoke in an educated manner, without any strong accent or dialect expressions. 'Does the same hold true of yourself?'

I nodded. We sat there for a while in silence. He cast a furtive glance down at my plastic bag.

I fished out another bottle and sat cradling it in my hands without opening it. 'I'm really looking for Bombsite.'

'Bombsite? What do you want with him?'

'I want to talk to him about the fire.'

'That old business? Good heavens, man!'

'And then there's Olga. The woman who used to live with Docker Johan.'

'You want to talk to Bombsite about her, do you?' He sounded curious.

'No, no. I'm looking for her, too.'

'Oh.' After a moment's thought he said: 'She comes by now and then, Olga. But she hardly ever talks to me. We never moved in the same circles, as it were.'

'What circles does she move in?'

'She . . . Docker Johan and she used to keep themselves very much to themselves. After he disappeared she really withdrew into herself completely. But Bombsite . . .'

'Yes?'

He made a lugubrious motion with his head, as though in order to stretch a stiff neck. 'On a day like this, when the sun's out and the weather's fine, I expect you'll find him out at the airport. Try there, Mr er . . .' I could see he was hesitating between my name and the bottle I was holding.

I opened the bottle and gave it to him. 'Veum,' I said.

His face lit up in a big smile but it wasn't at the sound of my name. As I got up to leave, he already had the bottle to his mouth. The sun shone through its brown glass, casting a golden reflection.

I found Bombsite on the breakwater that ran down to the sea beneath

131

the pier, close to the old seaplane port in Sandviken. He was enjoying himself. There were two couples and four bottles and some plastic bags promised more. The breakwater was built up of stones, gravel and scanty tufts of grass but, once they had taken off their coats and sweaters and rolled them together under the backs of their necks, they were able to sun themselves in comfort. The ladies had undone their blouses and there were lazy undulations both on land and at sea.

Over by the rocks the sun was glinting on the ripples. To their left were the boathouses along Sjøgaten, and to their right lay Byfjorden, where white seagulls bobbed on the waves and the Askøy ferry was moving cautiously out from the town towards the island. Both the ladies were of the same indeterminate age as their colleague on the market quay but the two gentlemen were definitely over fifty. One of them was a dwarf, swarthy and slightly gipsy-like in appearance, with a square-jawed, mischievous face that would have looked at home in a Parisian backstreet on a pimp in some lively brothel. He was naked to the waist but had kept his braces on. The skin on his chest was chalk-white, like a woman's, and the hump on his back didn't seem to embarrass him.

Bombsite was lying on his back with his hands on the back of his neck, squinting up at the sun. He was clad in a blue-and-grey-striped flannel shirt and brown trousers. He had kicked off his shoes and was stretching his toes through the holes in his socks. His face was glowing like a rising sun on a Japanese plate design. His skin was cracked and inflamed, his eyes were feebly watering, and he was one hundred per cent bald, as though the hair had been singed from his scalp. He was the only evidence I had that the fire on Fjøsangerveien in 1953 had really happened. One look at his face told me immediately what a tragedy the Peacock fire had been and I could understand the people who had wondered who had been the lucky ones: those who had died in the fire or those who had survived it.

I strode down the breakwater and met their wondering gaze. The ladies modestly adjusted the hems of the skirts and I could see that for a moment they had thought I was a cop, for the dwarf threw his jacket over a couple of the bottles.

'I'm sorry to disturb you,' I said. 'I'm not sure if you know who I am. My name's Veum and I'll pay you for the – inconvenience.'

I held the plastic bag open towards them and, when they saw what the payment was to be, they visibly relaxed and the dwarf said: 'Welcome to the fresh-air club, come and sit down.'

I found a place in the sun. We sat in silence for a while.

It was never a good idea to hurry things in circles like these. The only time these people were ever in a hurry was when it was five minutes to closing time down at the liquor store. For the rest of the time they took life easy, just as long as there was an open bottle somewhere close at hand. They didn't, of necessity, drink much, either: all that mattered was that there should be *something* to drink. The days were just as different from one another as they were for everyone else. Some days were good and on those they made do with a beer or two. Others were bad and then two bottles of schnapps wouldn't be enough.

This was a quiet place at that time of day. The traffic to and from Åsane was light and it was a long time since very many ships had put in at Sandviken in order to unload their cargoes. Behind us rose the sides of the mountains, round and plump towards Fløien, on the southern side of Skredderdalen, dark and steep towards Sandviksfjellet and Sandvikspilen, which steadfastly pointed out the direction of the wind to us. The sunshine was reflected in the windowpanes of the houses along the mountainsides and, up on a knoll, like some grey stone Dracula castle on a pinnacle, loomed Rothaugen School.

I sat hugging my knees and turned to look out over the sea. The waves were shimmering out at Nordnes Point, where the town of Ballangen tested the temperature of the water like a cautious big toe. A Westamaran hydrofoil was making its way out to sea; as it reached the Point, it rose from the water like some mighty sea-creature, roared nastily at the late summer sky and then stomped off stiffly southwards on its long stilts towards South Hordland and Stavanger.

I said: 'It's really you I want to talk to, Bombsite.'

He narrowed his eyes as he looked at me. 'What about?'

'About what happened that time.'

'What time?'

'Back in 1953, when there was that fire.'

Suddenly he raised himself into a sitting position and there was a dry crackling of facial skin as he made a grimace.

'The fire?'

'Certain facts have come to light. I've been talking to Sigrid Karlsen, Holger Karlsen's widow. And I've interviewed other people as well.' I leaned forward. 'You're the only one left. The only one who's still alive. You know that, don't you?'

He suddenly opened his eyes wide and gave me a stiff look. 'Yes, I know it. I see it in the mirror every morning. I've been seeing it every single morning for nigh on thirty years. Can you understand that?'

Helplessly, I nodded. 'Yes.'

'It ruined my life. I was an ordinary, decent working chap – but after that, what was I? It was years before I even recovered to the extent I have now. In the years immediately after the fire I was just a lump of raw, suppurating flesh and unsuccessful skin grafts. It destroyed my life – and I remember it, Veum – I know all about it!' In semi-blind fashion he picked up a bottle of beer and took a hefty swig from it. 'Don't come here trying to teach your grandmother how to suck eggs.' After another swig he said, with suddenly restored equanimity: 'What is it you want to know?'

The other three kept silent. They were listening. A seagull flew low over our heads with a thin, hoarse scream, like a memory from an evil past.

'I . . . I'd like you to – I'd just like you to tell me about the fire. The fire, the way you remember it. The way it happened.'

He repeated, softly: 'The fire – the way it happened . . .'

28

'The day of the fire . . . I can see the production hall as clearly now as if I were standing in the middle of it. Three floors high, so as to utilize the drop. The paint was manufactured in giant tanks, each of which contained several chambers. On each floor, new materials were added and new processes carried out. On each landing, there were a lot of dials – indicating the strength of the paint and so on.'

His gaze grew remote and the rest of us remained silent.

'Right down at the bottom were the tanks where the finished paint was thinned before it went out to the pumping station, where the empty cans came in on conveyor belts, were filled and then placed in cardboard boxes which, in turn, were taken out to the sales department.'

I looked at his disfigured face and tried to imagine what it must have looked like in 1953, before the fire. Olai Osvold had been about thirty then, not all that energetic maybe but thick-set and stocky and, no doubt, a dependable worker. His biceps even now were large and he had obviously been a man who was capable of lifting heavy weights. But his face . . . Had he been handsome? Clean-shaven? Had he had a small moustache, maybe? And his hair, what colour had it been? Fair? Dark? It was impossible to tell.

'We all had our fixed stations, with clearly established routines, but it wasn't the usual kind of assembly-line work – not in the production hall, at least. You had to be constantly wide awake and you might have to test a mixture, perhaps add something to it if it contained too much of some substance or other and, then, keep on making further additions. Normally you couldn't sit down, either. You had to keep checking the process throughout the whole of the station and there were measurements you had to take and a lot of physical effort was required when it was necessary to add some substance. You were using your body but that wasn't what made the work so arduous. It was the air. It was slightly polluted from all the additives that were used. They used powerful thinners in those days, substances that are banned now, from what I hear. By the end of the day your head would feel heavy and it might take several hours before you felt normal again. You also got a headache working there.'

'But didn't you take those things up with the management?'

He gave me a scornful look. 'Oh yes, we took them up all right. But you must remember, work conditions were a bit different in those days. The management didn't pay the same sort of attention to what was said on the shop floor. And you might say that Holger's weakness was that he didn't put his foot down firmly enough when it really mattered. I've never blamed Holger for what happened – even though there were folk who did. But I suppose you could say that if he was really so afraid there was a leak somewhere in the production hall, he should have just put his foot down and told us to stop work. He should have called us out on strike until everything had been properly checked.'

'You mean you think he wasn't sure?'

'I don't know what I think. What I'm saying is that if he was *really* afraid there was a leak he should have given instructions for everyone to get out of the hall.'

'So he didn't tell the rest of you about it?'

He shook his head. 'I could see he was brooding about something. My station was on the first-floor gallery, you see, while Holger – who was the foreman – usually stayed on the ground floor. He had a little office with glass windows over the door down there where he kept lists of the overtime we worked, how much of various substances we had used and so on. Now and then I'd see him in there just sitting staring into space, blind to the world. On one occasion he came up to where I was working and started looking around. Then he asked me, in a casual sort of way: "Can you smell anything, Olai?" – I took a sniff but it was as I said: there was always something in the air. The air in there was never as clear as it was outside. So I just shrugged my shoulders and didn't say anything. But on the day before the fire, he came up to me again. "Olai," he said, "I've got to go out on an errand. I may be away for a while, so can you keep an eye on things for me from up here?" Well, that was all right. I was sort of second in command, when he was away, so that was merely routine, too. When he came back from wherever he'd been he just went into his little office and I saw him staring into space again. Several times he came out and looked as though he was taking a deep breath – then he would go back inside again. Once I saw him pick up the phone and dial a number but he hung up again without waiting for anyone to reply. As we were on our way home that day I asked him if there was anything the matter. He stared straight ahead of him and said in a low voice: "To tell you the truth, I don't really know, Olai. Maybe I'm just not feeling very well." We didn't talk about it any more after that. And the next day the place went up in flames.'

He paused, briefly. His drinking companions were staring at him, wide-eyed. It was clear they hadn't heard any of this before. I was afraid to interrupt him. It was fascinating to listen to him, the sole witness of the fire, the only person still left alive who had actually been there, in the production hall at Peacock, when it had gone up in flames . . .

'I remember that day well. It was a mild, warm sort of morning – just like today – except it was spring. I biked to work that day and I set off early, because I wanted to take a shower. We didn't have a shower at home but there were some at work, in the cloakroom. We had to have them so we could wash the paint off ourselves after we'd finished work.'

'Were you married then?' The question popped out by itself but I could have bitten off my tongue for having asked it.

I saw I had knocked him off the rails. 'No. I lived at home, with my parents. There was a girl but, after the accident, it just sort of petered out, somehow.' His eyes grew thoughtful and a gloomy expression crossed his face. I held my breath and said no more.

He was slowly returning to the production hall again. 'We used to start work at seven and the early part of the day passed the way it usually did. There was nothing out of the ordinary. And when the place went up, it all happened so quickly that it almost didn't seem real. Even the explosion . . .'

'So it was the explosion that started the whole thing? There was no warning?'

He shook his head. 'None, apart from the one Holger had had, apparently. I can see it clearly now, it's as if it had been burned into my brain. And so it was, in a way. Everything went white.'

'Was the paint you made there white?' the dwarf asked, suddenly.

'No, no,' Bombsite replied, distantly. 'It was the light. The whole of that big area was suddenly outlined in a great, white flash. The explosion took place above me, in one of the uppermost tanks. I could see Holger – he was standing semi-upright in his glass office, as though he had been waiting for this to happen. Perhaps he saw something from down there before it happened. One of the chaps on the gallery above me was hurled into the air – and in that, in that white flash he just hung there, in the air, forty feet above the concrete floor at the bottom. A moment later . . .'

He swallowed heavily. 'It all happened so quickly. It's what they call St Elmo's fire, or something like that, at sea: fire that suddenly spreads over the whole rig. That's what it was like there, too: the paint in the upper chamber was burning and raining down on us, being showered out in all directions – it was as though it was raining fire – as if the whole place was just one great firestorm. The screams – my God, how they screamed, like men possessed, like devils, like – I don't know what. Holger had come out of his office, he had grabbed hold of a fire-extinguisher and was trying to spray it around him. But it was hopeless. It was like pissing on a volcano, that's about how much good it did. I scrambled down the ladder to the floor. My clothes were on fire and my face felt like a stiff mask, as though I'd been wearing a

Hallowe'en mask that had caught fire and melted to my face. On my way down I tripped over one of the men who were lying on the floor. He was lying face down on the concrete. I grabbed his arms and dragged him towards the door. Holger had thrown the fire-extinguisher away and I had a clear view of him as he opened the door – his silhouette was right in the middle of the doorway. I saw him staggering out, clutching his face. All this time everything was in flames around us and there were small explosions, the whole building was shaking, it was like an earthquake, or as if an atom bomb had dropped – I felt myself sinking to my knees. I couldn't drag him any further. I looked desperately towards the door and then he came in, Harald Wulff, the office messenger. It was him that got me out. If it hadn't been for him, I'd have . . .'

'Do you remember . . .'

'No, because right then I fainted,' he said, interrupting me. 'I can't remember anything except looking up at Wulff's face and then everything went dark and I don't remember any more until I woke up in hospital, swathed in white from top to toe and in such terrible pain that it felt as though I'd been roasted on a spit, alive. I thought I had quite literally woken up in hell.'

'God, that's terrible,' said one of the women in the little group of listeners.

'Awful,' said the other.

'You must be pretty glad you got out of there alive, Olai, my boy,' said the dwarf.

Bombsite gave him a stiff look. 'That's precisely what I've wondered all these years, since it happened. If I really was lucky or whether it might not have been better if I'd died in the blaze, too.'

'But then you would never have met *us*,' said the dwarf.

'Fifteen people lost their lives. Only I and two others survived and the other two didn't last long either, they both died a few years later. Holger, Piddi, mates I'd had for so many years – what had I done to deserve to live? Some of those men had families, a wife and kids – it would have been better if some of them had escaped . . . Now and then I almost have a guilty conscience.'

One of the women laid a plump hand on his knee. 'You've no reason to, Bombsite. You really haven't.'

'No?' He looked at her groggily. He was still back in 1953.

Slowly, I said: 'So Holger Karlsen got *out* of the door and Harald Wulff came *in* immediately afterwards?'

'Yes, yes – and he saved me. He *saved* me, do you undertand? And the chap I dragged with me was one of the other two who survived, for a while . . .'

'Yes, that's right. He saved *you*.' That was what mattered most as far as Bombsite was concerned and I realized I mustn't try to contradict him. But why hadn't Wulff saved Holger Karlsen? Why hadn't Holger

Karlsen managed to get all the way to safety, when he'd managed to get out of the production hall alive? Of course, there had been explosions going on all the time and, of course, it was possible that he had been struck on the head by a falling girder outside the production hall – but was it likely? The events of chance spin their fateful web around us all – yet there is always room for doubt.

I slowly opened another bottle of beer and offered it to Bombsite. 'Here. Your mouth must be dry.'

He looked at me vacantly, accepted the bottle, put it to his lips and drank. Then he said: 'Veum, my mouth's been dry for years.'

29

The sun was shining in obliquely from the right as we crossed Sandvikstorget and, for a moment, I saw all five of us reflected in a plate-glass window. The dwarf – whose nickname, I had discovered, was Giant Olsen – and the two ladies led the way. The ladies wanted to go to the toilet and Giant Olsen lived in a basement flat up on Sandviksveien. Bombsite and I brought up the rear. Bombsite had agreed to come with me to the flat where Olga Sørensen lived, if she were still at the same address she had occupied two years previously.

When I saw us all reflected in the window like that, it once again struck me that I didn't look at all out of place. For a private detective, a certain degree of anonymity is not to be despised; but the fact that I seemed to blend so well with my surroundings – as a player of bingo, in the old folks' pick-up joint and, now, in this dissipated company, our heavy plastic carrier bags swinging from our hands – was making me feel thoroughly depressed. I ran my free hand through my hair and attempted to straighten my clothes. But an elderly lady who happened to be passing gave us all a stern look just then and she didn't seem to make any exception for me.

'But surely Olga couldn't have had anything to do with the fire?' said Bombsite.

'No, no. This is about something else,' I replied, vaguely.

'Docker Johan?' he asked, cautiously.

I gave him a quick look and then nodded. 'Did you know him?'

'No. At least, no better than all the rest of them. You know, this world's not really a very big one once you're a part of it.' For a moment, he hesitated. Then, softly, he said: 'But a few years ago I did ask Olga if she'd marry me. Even she wouldn't have me. So you can see what sort of chances I've got. Any loving I've had during these past thirty years, I've had to pay for. Either that, or it's happened while we've been drinking and the girls will go to bed with anybody.'

I made no reply – merely nodded and bit my lip.

'Come back to my place!' said Giant Olsen, strolling over to us. 'We can go five ways on a bottle of genever – I'll take a taxi down to Dreggen and buy it. Come on.'

'We've an - errand to see to,' said Bombsite, solemnly. 'And anyway, I've no money.'

'How about you?' He gave me a hopeful look.

I fished out five ten-kroner notes from my inside pocket. 'Here, this is from Bombsite.'

He had large hands and they closed round the money like a claw around a chocolate bar in an arcade. 'You're welcome if you want to come. Bombsite knows where it is.'

Giant Olsen and the ladies went off to the right, while we continued up the steps towards Søre Almenning. Whenever we reached a landing, Bombsite had to pause for breath, so it took us some time.

Olga Sørensen lived on the first floor of a grey stone apartment house in Kirkegaten which stretches from Sandvik Church – where people are baptised, confirmed and married, to the area around the old people's home up at Formannsvei – where they die. Some shorten the interval of waiting by living there, too, in the flats nearest to the church or in large villas a bit further away.

We climbed the stairs to the first floor. The name on the door was Jensen but Bombsite insisted that it was still Olga Sørensen who lived there. This we were, however, unable to confirm as no on answered when we rang the door-bell. I looked dubiously at the name-plate. 'Are you sure she hasn't moved?'

'Yes. I'd have heard about it if she had.'

'But what about the name on the door?'

'That name-plate was there the last time I was here. She just can't be bothered to change it, that's all. She'll have her own name on the mail-box downstairs.'

The brown door gave nothing away. Behind two narrow, poorly fitting slats of glass we could make out a flower-patterned curtain but there was no light on inside.

'She'll probably be back soon,' said Bombsite. 'At least now you know where she lives. Let's go down to Giant's place and wait for a while.'

As we were on our way out I checked the mail-boxes. He was right. One of them bore the name. O. Sørensen.

We arrived outside Giant's flat just as one of the ladies was getting out of a taxi with a blue plastic bag from the State Liquor Stores in one hand and a pot plant in the other.

'They sent *me* to the liquor store,' she said. 'I think Giant wanted to get his end away while he waited. But I bought this plant. I thought it might brighten the place up a bit.' In the brilliant daylight her face looked honest and slightly naïve, with large pores and fulsome lips that were only partly camouflaged beneath an uneven layer of red paint that had contours like those of a jellyfish.

We staggered down a flight of steps and entered a dark, cold cellar. At the far end of the cellar cracks of light showed round a door and, when we opened it, we nearly fell over Giant Olsen and his lady friend. They were lying on the floor, scantily clad, and looking as though they had been checking the air-conditioning.

It was only a little room and, with three extra people in it, it resembled the stadium during one of the big semi-finals. Giant Olsen pulled on his trousers and his lady friend expertly straightened her skirt. Bombsite sat down in the room's only armchair, a relic from the Thirty Years' War, while the lady with the pot plant went through the room and into the kitchen in order to turn round. The kitchen consisted of a zinc washtub and a bucket on the floor. Beside the bucket stood an open carton of milk and ten empty beer bottles. She had evidently been there before, as she grabbed a kitchen stool and sat down in the doorway. Two down, three to go.

'Sit down,' Giant Olsen said to me, courteously. I looked round. There was the choice between an electric heater which Giant and his lady friend had kicked to one side while they had been doing their exercises and an upturned beer-crate. I chose the beer-crate and Giant Olsen sat down on the heater. 'You do the honours, Lisbeth,' he said to his lady and she went obediently into the kitchen, returning with five dirty tumblers.

The genever glinted in the tumblers and we said *skål*. There were no pictures on the walls, although on one of them he had pinned up a page from the *Bergen Times*. I couldn't think why. It was the farming page. The room lay in twilight, as the sun's rays didn't reach this far down. Maybe it was too late in the year or too early in the day. 'My, aren't we cosy?' said Giant Olsen, casting a beaming glance around him.

His lady friend had been left standing in the centre of the room with nowhere to sit down but the floor at her feet. I could see she was hesitating about doing this and I knew the reason why. Over in one corner lay her panties, which he had managed to get off her before we arrived.

Her ageless face turned in my direction. Her eyes were brown, her hair dark and unkempt, with some untidy streaks of light brown, and her mouth had a ravaged look. I had, of course, known who she was all along. I simply hadn't realized it until now.

'Hey, don't I know you from somewhere?' she asked in a husky voice, fingering one of her eyes shut, as though that might help her to get a better look at me.

'Oh, I get around quite a lot,' I said. 'Out on the town, now and then.'

'What's your job, again?'

I avoided giving her a straight answer. 'I used to work in the Child Welfare Office.'

'Oh yes.' Her face went glum. 'You took my little girl into care. First to the children's home. Then she was given foster parents. Now I don't even know where she is.'

142

'I don't think I had anything to do with that.'

'No, I know. But perhaps that's where I remember you from.'

'Yes. Perhaps,' I said, in a neutral tone of voice. I couldn't bring myself to tell her that we'd been in the same year at grammar school. She might not have appreciated being reminded of something that had happened so long ago. She had been a pretty young girl in those days but a bit reckless. And that had been many years ago.

'Well, so here we all are and we're having a swell time,' said Giant Olsen, draining his tumbler and then pouring himself another shot.

Over in the armchair, Bombsite had gone quiet. He was sitting staring straight ahead of him, seeing and hearing nothing. The lady in the kitchen doorway was still sitting with the pot plant on her lap, as though she had given up trying to find a place to put it.

'It's a shame about people,' Giant Olsen's lady said to him. Her name was Lisbeth and my memory of her was growing more and more distinct. She had been in the sixth form and she had let one of the boys make love to her in one of the new houses that were being built at the time. The rest of us had been treated to the most luxuriant descriptions of her many good points. Now she had finally sat down on the floor and, if I had the temerity, I could check the truthfulness of at least one of those descriptions.

Yes, it was a shame about people. It was a shame about girls like Lisbeth with whom we had all been timorously infatuated, those of us who, too early in life, had belonged to the ranks of the retiring. It was a shame about girls like Lisbeth who had had an awkward young girl's body dressed in a cotton skirt and jumper, and a deep, almost masculine laugh . . . It was a shame that she should be sitting here all these years later on a cellar floor, feeling it was a shame about other people and herself.

It was a shame, too, about Bombsite whose face had been disfigured and who had lived most of his life against a background of other people's indifference. It was a shame about Giant Olsen – a misfit version of Tom Thumb who was just tall enough to be able to bite his partners in the pubic hair. It was a shame about the lady with the pot plant who had been sent out to the liquor store while others were making love; and, damn me, if it wasn't a shame about myself, sitting here with my glass of genever, a light shimmer in my brain and a list of unsolved crimes on my agenda.

I looked at my watch. A couple of hours had passed since we had been up at Olga Sørensen's flat. No one had said anything much and we hadn't drunk all that much either. We had sat there in the darkness of the cellar, watching the daylight move its rectangular imprint across the floor, little by little. The light came through a narrow skylight which was covered with chicken-wire. Through it we could see the feet of passers-by on the pavement above.

In her corner, Lisbeth had nearly fallen asleep. Her mouth had

143

fallen open and her lips had grown softer, like those of a child: 'put-put-put', her mouth said. Giant Olsen put an arm round her shoulders, supporting her. For a moment I thought I saw a hint of tenderness in his eyes but then he pulled himself together and gave me an ironic look, as if to say: 'Look what I've got to put up with!'

Bombsite sat muttering to himself. The woman in the kitchen doorway was tenderly stroking the leaves of the pot plant: she was giving it sweet, soft caresses.

I got up stiffly from the beer-crate, put my empty tumbler down on it and stretched.

Bombsite suddenly looked up. 'Are you going?'

'I think I'm going to give Olga another go,' I said.

He nodded. 'I'm going to stay here,' he said.

I found a scrap of paper and wrote my office address and phone number on it. 'If you remember anything else, please get in touch with me.'

'Anything else? What about?'

'The fire.'

'Oh, that . . . There isn't anything else to say about it.'

'Yes, I know, but just in case.'

He nodded. 'Say hello to Olga for me.'

'Yes, say hello for us, too,' they all chimed in. Lisbeth had opened her eyes again.

I nodded round to them and left. As I was closing the door behind me, I could hear Lisbeth's voice saying: 'I wonder where I remember that guy from. I know I've seen him before.'

The transition from the semi-darkness into the light was a blinding one. It was as if I had emerged into a new world that had been washed white and gleaming – taken straight out of the washing machine and hung up to dry for cellar folk to look at. But only look at – not touch.

30

No one came to the door marked 'Jensen' this time, either. I leaned all my weight against the bell-bush, like some nostalgic door-to-door salesman who had once sold a pair of nylon stockings to a lady at this address and had never abandoned his hope of repeating the success. The ringing ought to have been enough to waken the dead but no one came to the door and I finally gave up.

I went slowly down the staircase. One of the doors on the ground floor quietly opened a little way and a quick pair of eyes stared out at me over a door-chain. When I met the woman's gaze she began to close the door again. 'Hey, wait,' I said. 'Don't shut the door.'

She pushed it not quite shut. Above the shiny chain her nose was large and pointed and I could see that her skin was old and wrinkled. She had sharp, blue-black eyes and I thought: 'The usual clever madam, always one step ahead of everybody else, always at the ready, always at your service.'

I came straight to the point. 'Excuse me, but you wouldn't have any idea where Miss Sørensen from the flat upstairs is, would you?'

She shook her head and gave me an inquisitive look. 'What's it about?'

'I was supposed to bring her greetings from an old friend . . .'

'Re–a–lly?' She looked as though she didn't believe me.

'Is she often gone for long periods?'

Suddenly, she said: 'She had a visitor yesterday, too. Perhaps the greetings have already been delivered.'

'Who was it?'

'I don't know. But it was a man. I only saw him from behind, as he was leaving.'

'What did he look like? Had you ever seen him before?'

'No. It was so dark. It was in the evening and he was dressed in ordinary sort of clothes. A hat and coat. He was quite well-dressed.'

A sense of unease was growing between my shoulder-blades. 'Did he have any distinguishing features? Was there anything unusual you noticed?'

'I don't know . . .'

With a hesitation, I said: 'Was there anything peculiar – about the way he walked?'

She looked as though she was thinking something over. Then her face suddenly lit up. 'Yes, now that you come to mention it – I think he had trouble with one of his legs. Yes, that's right – he had a limp!'

My blood ran cold. My lips were still numb, as I said: 'You haven't a spare key to her flat, have you?'

'Most certainly not!' She shook her head, indignantly. 'And the warden's employed by the council, so you'll never be able to find him. No, you'll just have to wait until she comes back.' She began to close the door.

I breathed out slowly. 'All right, so you saw her go out, did you?'

'No–o, I can't say that I did.'

'Well . . . I wonder if you'd come upstairs with me, then. I think I'm going to have to break in. Something may have happened to her.'

'Break in? You must have gone crazy! I'm going to call the police.' The door banged shut in my face but I could hear no sound from inside. She was standing right behind the door, listening.

To the closed door, I said: 'Very well, do.' Then I went back upstairs again.

Life goes round in circles, big ones and small ones. Every so often you get into a situation and say to yourself: 'You've been through this before.'

As I stood there facing Olga Sørensen's front door, I once again experienced the moment in which some weeks earlier, I had stood outside Hjalmar Nymark's front door.

This door caused no problems, either. I used the same method: I kicked in a pane of glass, stuck my hand inside and opened the spring-latch from within by turning the knob.

The door opened and so did the door to the neighbouring flat. The man standing there was about six foot six and was wearing braces. 'What in the name of blazes?' he said.

'Call the police this instant, before I do,' I said, staring bravely up at him.

'I'm damned if I'm having anything to do with the police,' he said and shut the door with a heavy bang.

I shrugged my shoulders and went into the flat. The hallway was dark and not very long. Some old suede boots and a pair of rubber galoshes stood against the wall and, up on some hooks, hung a grey-brown coat and an old dress apron.

I breathed in carefully. The flat stank of beer and worse.

I opened the first door I came to. It gave into the kitchen. The sink was piled with plates and glasses and some empty beer bottles stood on the floor. In the middle of the table stood an unopened can of peas. It looked incredibly lonely, like the symbol of a poor man's feast.

I went back into the hall and opened the door which gave into the living-room. I didn't need to open any more doors after that.

It looked as though there had been a party. There were empty

146

bottles everywhere. An armchair lay overturned on the floor and the worn coffee-table stood pressed against a frayed sofa. An ashtray had fallen face down on the floor and the greyish-white ash and chewed cigarette ends formed an untidy pattern on the dirty brown surface of the floor.

A woman with tangled, grey hair and an emaciated, ravaged face lay with her back partially resting against a brownish-black writing desk. On one of the desk's sharp corners there was a dark, sticky-looking stain to which some long, grey tufts of hair adhered. The stiff fingers of the woman's right hand were clutching the neck of a bottle and she lay in a pool of beer that had turned sour. She was staring rigidly up at the ceiling, as though she were able to see right into the eternal supermarkets and was already on her way towards the beer counter.

If this was Olga Sørensen, the woman on the ground floor was right. The greetings had already been delivered.

31

I went back down to the ground floor and rang the doorbell. No one opened up. 'Hello?' I shouted at the door. 'Have you called the police yet? If not, you can do it now.'

No one answered. She was probably shaking with fright somewhere just inside the door there, terrified of what I might do.

The nearest phone was in the snack-bar along on Ekrengaten. Its proprietor was a man from Haugesund but he let me use the phone, even so. The officer on duty at the police station said they would send a car over at once. I walked back up to Kirkegaten and stood outside the house, waiting.

The police car arrived and Dankert Muus got out of it. When he saw me he turned back to the car and said: 'Who took that call? Why didn't they tell me it was Veum who phoned? The corpse-lover, that's what we call him.'

He gave me a snappish look. He was still wearing the same old coat, his hat had never left his head. He looked at me like a cannibal on a strict diet. 'Who have you bumped off this time, Veum?'

I nodded towards the house. 'Come on in and see.'

I led the way up to the first floor. As we were passing through the ground floor I heard the door open slightly once more but I didn't turn round.

Dankert Muus was accompanied by Peder Isachsen – pale, blonde-haired, and sulking as usual. They made a nice pair. Neither of them was very fond of me. 'Veum's a kind of necrophiliac, if you know what that means,' I heard Muus say to Isachsen when my back was turned. As we arrived at the door to the flat he barked: 'Whose idea was it to break in?'

I gave him a measured look. 'If I hadn't knocked the window in I would never have found her.'

'So you were looking for her, were you?' His eyes lit up in a nasty smile. 'This isn't one of your junkie whores, is it?' To Isachsen he added: 'Veum does it with minors. And corpses. He's a man with a wide range of interests.'

'Her name's Olga Sørensen, she's probably over sixty, and she . . .'

'Getting to prefer them older as the years go by, eh?'

'She was the lover of Docker Johan, the man who disappeared in

1971. The case was dropped for lack of evidence. Yesterday she received a visit from a man with a limp. A man with a limp was observed leaving the house in which Hjalmar Nymark was murdered.'

'*Murdered?*'

'Yes. But that case has been dropped, too, hasn't it?'

A veil came down over his eyes. The woman hadn't moved while I'd been away. I was able to study her more closely now. She was dressed in a pair of brown slacks of the spacious variety and a yellow and brown sweater that held enough room for two. Her face was criss-crossed by greyish-white wrinkles and her false teeth were working loose in her sunken mouth.

Muus placed a large, heavy hand on my chest and stepped into the living-room. 'You stay out there, Veum.'

He took up a position just inside the door. From it, he let his gaze sweep searchingly around the room. Then he took a small, brown-scorched cigarette end out of his overcoat pocket, stuck it between his tensed lips and lit it with a cigarette lighter. Muus was the kind of man who always has his pockets full of old cigarette ends. It would have been unthinkable to see him light a long, fresh, white cigarette. It would have looked wrong in his pallid, grey face.

The view from where I stood was like a still from a 1940s crime movie. Muus in his hat and coat, with rings of cigarette smoke swirling above his head. The depressing interior. And, on the floor, the corpse of a woman who might not quite come up to Hollywood standards as far as beauty was concerned but who could be sure of receiving a well-deserved extra's fee when the filming was over.

The trouble about this scene was that it was never over. As if it were being filmed over and over again, and nobody really knew what it was supposed to be like. The only things that were certain were that this woman really was dead, that it wasn't a film, and that Dankert Muus was no Humphrey Bogart, not even an Edward G. Robinson.

Muus turned round slowly. 'Okay, tell me what you were doing here, Veum.'

'I've just told you . . .'

'And let's have the final version right away, please. I don't intend to stand here talking to you any longer than is absolutely necessary. You know what I think of corpses. We don't see eye to eye about them.'

'No, you're the one that always arrives too late, aren't you?' I said, softly.

'One more like that and we'll take you into custody until tomorrow morning,' he replied. 'It's possible we'll do that anyway, but . . .'

I raised my hands and he stopped talking. 'As I was telling you, the woman was the lover of Docker Johan, who disappeared in 1971, at the same time as a man called Harald Wulff was murdered. Harald Wulff, who was probably the same man as the war-time mass murderer known as Rat Poison, and who may possibly also have been implicated in the tragic fire at the Peacock paint factory in 1953.'

Muus looked as though he was chewing something. 'Listen, Veum. Possibly and probably, 1971 and 1953 – for Christ's sake! I want to know what you're doing here *today*. I don't want a history lesson.'

'No, very well. I'm here today because I'm doing a little investigation of those cases – both the fire of 1953 and the disappearance of Docker Johan in 1971. Those were the things I wanted to ask Olga Sørensen about.'

'Olga Sørensen? Is that her name?'

'Well, it's the name of whoever lives here. But why don't you ask the woman in the right-hand flat on the ground floor? She told me Miss Sørensen had a visit yesterday evening from a man with a limp.'

'Some people go for corpses, other prefer cripples – so what?'

'Listen, Muus. Harald Wulff had a limp. So did Docker Johan. So did the man who came here yesterday evening. And so did the man who was seen leaving the house in which Hjalmar Nymark died. Don't you think that's a bit odd?'

'Okay, so we're a nation of cripples – so what? Some of us limp, others become private detectives. I prefer the former.'

'But . . .'

'And, while we're on the subject, Veum – is there a shortage of jobs in the private detective industry just now or something? I mean, if you have to go all the way back to 1953 to find a case to go sniffing around in . . .' He turned his head faintly in the direction of Isachsen to see if his audience was still following. It was: Isachsen's laugh was polite but sarcastic.

'Muus, 1971. That's not so long ago.'

'Oh no, only ten years. But maybe that's not such a long time in your book. That's probably about how long you have to wait in between fees, isn't it?'

'I think it's odd, anyway. And I'd advice you to investigate it a little more closely. Find out who it was who came here yesterday, for example.'

Calmly, he said: 'We will, Veum. We will. You don't have to try to teach us our job. I was doing this when you weren't yet out of nappies, so don't give me that kind of talk.'

He turned away from me and walked a short distance across the room. He gave one of the empty bottles a kick with the toe-cap of his shoe. Then he stood with his legs astraddle in the middle of the floor. After taking a good look round he turned to face me again. 'The way I see it, the most probable explanation for this scene is that it's the result of an accident. The woman had one beer too many. When she was drunk, she lost her balance and struck her head against the edge of the writing desk, *there*.' He pointed to the bloodstain. 'And the blow was a fatal one.'

'Precisely. An accident. Accidents were Harald Wulff's trademark.'

'But I thought you said just now that Harald Wulff was murdered in that momentous year 1971?'

'*Apparently*, yes.'

'You've a rich vocabulary, Veum. Possibly and probably and apparently. But, in the end, it all boils down to one thing, doesn't it? You don't know.'

'You two ought to take dancing lessons,' I said, bitterly. 'You're quite a pair.'

He turned to Isachsen. 'Are the others on their way? The autopsy report will show how much alcohol she had in her blood and also what the cause of death was. If we have a few words with the neighbours, and collect whatever forensic evidence there is, we ought to have the whole business pretty well wrapped up, oughtn't we?'

Isachsen nodded.

I said: 'And don't forget that Olga Sørensen could have been an important witness in a case that's suddenly started to attract attention again.'

'Talking in riddles, are we now, Veum?' Muus said, wearily.

'If she knew more about what happened in 1971 than she's already let on, it might have been in someone's interest to get her out of the way, now that someone else has started to dig around in the case again.'

'Even if that someone else was none other than little lost Veum? Don't overestimate your own importance. And leave the worrying to us – you're quitting the scene of this crime, *now*.' He suddenly got even tougher. 'I don't want you sniffing around here one more second. If you've no more to say, clear out and leave things to folk who've got a job to do.'

'Okay, okay. Will you need me tomorrow?'

'I don't need you at all, Veum. Why do you ask? You're not thinking of leaving the country tomorrow, are you?'

'No, but I'll be busy all morning. Working on a case.' I took good care not to say that, as far as I could see, it was the same case, only with the accent on 1953. The next day was the first of September, the only day in the year that Hagbart Helle spent in Bergen. That was an event I didn't intend to miss.

'By all means, Veum – as long as you stay off my patch you can be as busy as you like. You can be sure I'll know how to find you if I have a use for you. On the right side of the dock, seen from *my* angle – I expect you have a fair idea which side I mean. Have a good working day, Veum – when was it that case dated from – 1947?' He gave a whinnying laugh that nearly made him swallow his cigarette end and Peder Isachsen joined in, mirthlessly. Their laughter followed me out into the hallway but as soon as I got to the street door it was gone.

So, once again, I'd arrived too late on the scene. For the second time in not very long, someone had got there before me. A man with a limp.

151

I didn't make as light of that fact as Muus evidently did. And I was more certain than ever that at least several corpses lay buried here. In fact, it was getting more and more difficult to find room for all the graves.

I went home, made lunch and sat in my room with a glass of schnapps in one hand and a book in the other. But I didn't read a word. I had more than enough to think about.

The room around me was quiet and dead. As quiet and dead as only a room can be in which you once used to sleep with a woman whom you really loved.

32

When the morning's first flight from Copenhagen had landed at Flesland, and the passengers were on their way into the arrival hall, I went over to the information desk and said: 'Excuse me, but could you please ask Hagbart Helle to report to this desk?'

There are certain young men who, though they don't yet have enough stubble to be able to grow a beard, nevertheless allow an inconspicuous, downy moustache to cover their upper lip, as a dubious claim that they have now reached the age of sexual maturity. The lad behind the information desk was one of them but even he was old enough to have heard the question I asked before. Measuring me all the way from my sleep-tousled hair to my unpolished shoes, he said: 'Are you from the press?'

I made no reply; simply made it plain that I expected an answer, not questions.

'In any case,' he went on, with a supercilious look, 'it hardly makes any difference now. Hagbart Helle landed at Flesland over an hour ago, in his private jet. He's no longer in the airport.' His smile was right out in the open now, like the smile of a shark off a public bathing beach.

'That was a waste of breath,' I murmured, turning away before he could see from the expression on my face that I was disappointed. Maybe I ought to grow a moustache like that, too, I found myself thinking.

I had a cup of coffee in the airport cafeteria as I waited for the hands of my watch to creep round to the time of day when most people sit down in their offices and open the first newspaper of the day. Busy men with black briefcases marched out to the morning's first plane to Oslo. The air was warm so they carried their light-coloured raincoats over their arms. There wasn't a single woman among them. They would all be back again by evening, so there was no reason for them to take their secretaries along.

At around nine I phoned the knitwear factory Hagbart Helle's brother ran and asked to speak to Mr Hellebust, the managing director. A woman's voice – morning-fresh – said that, unfortunately, the managing director was not available that day but that I could talk to the company's financial director if I wanted to. I asked her if she knew where the managing director had gone but, like the perfect secretary she was, she merely replied that he was away 'on business'. I thanked her, replaced the receiver and left the telephone booth.

When I drove back into town the sky was clear. The wide-stretching landscape of Fana lay like a green patchwork quilt around me and the mountains around Bergen loomed blue-grey on the horizon which drew nearer and nearer with every kilometre I put behind me. A low mist hung between the mountains, above luxuriant, dark-green tree-tops. That was approximately where I was headed for.

Paradise was the name someone had given to a section of the town you pass through before you start to approach the actual centre of Bergen. The name is not entirely inapposite, even though the area it covers could reasonably be extended to Kloppedal and Hop in the south and to Fjøsanger in the north. This district – on the slope that runs down to Nordåsvannet – is one of the leafiest in the whole Bergen area and here the elegant villas of several generations of Bergen families lie wrapped in a green, woollen blanket. Some of the streets are named after shipowners.

In a quiet little street approximately in the centre of this district lay the villa that was owned by Hagbart Helle's brother. As I parked my old, grey Mini on the shady side of the road, it more or less blended into the shadows cast by the foliage. The autumn's first barberries glowed scarlet from secluded gardens and here and there, above dark green hedges, a copper beech traced its majestic silhouette against the clear, blue September sky, like a tree in a Greek tragedy.

I got out of my car and strolled a little way down the street.

A large, black wrought-iron gate barred the entrance to Hellebust's villa. I could see that the gravel drive-way on the other side of the gate branched into two. To the right stood a white garage with two black doors; set back to the left, amid gnarled apple trees and large rhododendron bushes, lay the house itself: broad, painted white, with shiny black roof-slates. In front of the house there was a wide patio which was empty. The doors that led in from the patio were half open and I could hear distant voices and the tinkle of crockery. That must be the sound of people eating breakfast with knives and forks – the people who lived in this house.

There was a sign on the gate that said: 'Beware of the dog'. I couldn't see or hear any trace of a dog but I thought twice about going in, all the same. For the moment I was content simply to get the lie of the land. Very soon I came to the end of the little cul-de-sac. I turned round and walked back to the car.

There weren't many houses in the street and their gardens were large. The men who lived here had substantial private incomes, paid low rates of income tax, owned motor launches down in the boathouses on Nordåsvannet and had wives who attended discussion groups in the mornings and helped to organize bazaars for charity in the afternoons. Involuntarily, I straightened my tie. I was afraid I would stick out here rather more than I had done among the players of bingo, the middle-aged lady-killers and the town's flotsam and jetsam. Here, I would probably be asked for my ID.

I looked at my watch. It was still early, but I could see no reason for putting off what I had come here to do. I might as well disturb Hagbart Helle during breakfast as during dinner.

The heavy gate groaned gently as I opened it and the white marble gravel crunched beneath my feet as I walked up the long garden path, past elegantly arranged flower-beds containing early autumn flowers. There was still no dog to beware of.

The garden path didn't lead on to the patio and I hadn't planned to irritate anyone unnecessarily by walking on their lawn, so I followed the path up to the black, arched front door and rang the door-bell.

The girl who opened it was in her twenties, had long blonde hair and was wearing a black dress and a white apron. Her eyes were as blue as frozen violets and her voice was rather cool as she said: 'What do you want?'

Boldly, I said: 'I'd like to speak to Hagbart Helle.'

'Have you an appointment?'

'Unfortunately not. I couldn't get hold of him beforehand but . . .'

She began to close the door. I put my foot in the doorway and continued: 'I'm sure he'll be willing to talk to me.'

'That's what they all say,' she said. 'Please take your foot out of the door.' She was looking down at my shoe as though it was a dead cat.

'What's this about?' a rich, deep voice said behind her.

I could see past her into a grey and white hallway, the walls of which were built of real stone and were inset with alcoves containing white marble urns. A man had come up from behind and was standing beside her.

He was a young man, younger than I was. He was tall and well-built, had short, blonde hair and a facial complexion that said he spent a lot of time outdoors. He was suntanned and his teeth were white and strong. His eyes were blue and transparent, like very fine porcelain, but they were the only thing about him that was delicate. He looked as though he was made of well-trained muscles and iron will-power, and I cautiously withdrew my foot, as if I were afraid he might confiscate it.

'Who are you?' he said. 'Can I do anything for you?' He spoke with an East Norwegian accent, in the featureless way that is characteristic of the moneyed inhabitants of Oslo's West End. Some people call this style of speech 'genteel *riksmål*', even though it is really no more than a minority dialect spoken within a strictly defined area of the nation's capital.

For the occasion I adopted the Bergen version of the same

speech-style – educated, well-modulated and uvular 'r'd, with just the faintest hint of aristocracy about it. 'Good morning. My name is Veum and I should very much like to have a word with Hagbart Helle.'

'And what is the nature of your business?'

'Excuse me, sir, but I'm afraid I didn't catch your name.'

He gave me a measured look. 'Carsten Wiig's the name and I'm Mr Helle's personal secretary. You may talk freely with me. But I expect you're from the press, aren't you?'

'Most certainly not,' I said, making it sound as though I wouldn't soil my fingers with printers' ink. 'I'm an independent freelance.' This was actually a correct description of myself, even though my tax assessments would hardly have given me any special credit either with Wiig or with any of his fellow shareholders.

'I see,' he said, surveying me expectantly from under weary eyelids. He was neatly dressed in a spotlessly clean white shirt which emphasized his copper-tan complexion; a light, grey-striped cravat was neatly knotted in the shirt's open neck and he wore grey, well-pressed trousers and black shoes that were so finely polished you could see his shirt reflected in them.

'It's about a factory Hagbart Helle used to own in town. The Peacock factory. Paint.'

He had a fixed expression. 'Well?'

'I need some information concerning it.'

'I'm afraid Hagbart Helle doesn't concern himself with matters that took place so long ago.'

Persevering, I went on: 'But I'm sure he'd be interested to hear – that he'd be personally interested in . . .'

He interrupted me in a voice that was pitched somewhat higher now and was also a shade louder: 'I'm afraid I can't burden Mr Helle with matters that lie so far in the past. I must ask you to bear in mind that Mr Helle is here in town on exclusively private business. Today is one of the very few holidays he permits himself during the course of the year and I'm afraid it will be quite out of the question for me to say one word to him about your visit. Do you understand?'

'No.'

'No? What do you mean – no?' His face took on an even more florid colouring. He had come right out into the doorway now, as if to prevent me from getting inside. The girl had disappeared.

Gently, I said: '*No* is one of the words most people learn the meaning of at quite an early age. I suppose it's possible that you folk who grow up in Holmenkollåsen aren't used to encountering the word in the course of your daily lives but, over here in this part of the country, we tend to associate it with a certain type of negation. *No* signifies . . . Do you understand? No, I guess you don't. I'd still like to speak to Mr Helle, though.'

He leaned forward, towering over me by at least five centimetres.

'Listen here, Veum, or whatever your name is. I belong to an international business community and we're not Sunday-school teachers. Don't try to play Bogey with me, you haven't the guts for it. If I felt so inclined, I could fold you up, put you in an envelope and mail you to Southern Patagonia with no return address. So don't provoke me, all right, Veum?'

I gave him a steady stare. 'I've got enough on Helle to be able to report him to the police.'

'You don't say? Where I come from we buy policemen in the supermarkets.'

'Not in Bergen, you don't.'

'Oh no? I've heard a different story. What's more, I'm familiar enough with Helle's past to know that there's not a shred of evidence there. Do you suppose he'd have been coming here every year for all these years if that weren't so? And now the polite talking is definitely over, Veum. Thanks for the chat. Goodbye.' He placed a broad hand on my chest and gave me a hefty shove backwards.

I stumbled down the steps, only just managing not to fall over. By the time I had regained my balance he had shut the door behind him and was standing with his legs astraddle at the top of the steps, his arms hanging loosely at his sides and his fists lightly clenched.

I could, of course, have tried to get past him. I could also have tried to seduce a cement mixer. In each case, the result would have been practically the same.

'I'll be back,' I promised him, turned on my heel and marched off down the gravel path without looking round. 'Beware of the dog' it still said on the gate. Now I knew what they meant.

33

I got into the Mini and sat there staring at the black wrought-iron gate. After a while I got out of the car and stood leaning against its bonnet. I was restless and nothing much was happening.

On the one hand, there was definitely something attractive about all this: the big, green gardens that lay breathing quietly to themselves, the houses with their soft carpets and many rooms, the French windows that opened on a scent of apples and autumn roses, the singing of all the birds of paradise. You were in an oasis, infinitely remote from the hurly-burly of everyday life.

On the other hand, that was precisely the point: in a sense it was as if the entire district was stranded somewhere in the doldrums. The sound of the traffic was far away, no steam-hammers struck against resistant ships' hulls, and no poisonous paint fumes titillated your nostrils. Once, perhaps, in the course of every day, a green-clad postman would walk by your front gate. Twice a week, a grey refuse-disposal truck would come to empty your dustbin but they usually arrived so early that you hadn't even got out of bed yet. You seldom saw any other working people. The only noise there was made by your poodle when it discovered a stray cat but that didn't last long.

It was small wonder, then, that they weren't particularly fond of having private detectives loitering around the place. Further along the little cul-de-sac a woman emerged from a gateway. I saw her catch sight of me just as she was coming out of her garden, dressed in a short, grey fur jacket of the same colour as the small, long-haired dog she was leading on a leash. She began to walk in my direction but her steps were cautious, as though she felt she were treading on thin ice. Her legs were shapely, her skirt was black. When she got closer I put her somewhere in her forties: blonde and neat-figured and without visible blemishes. She fitted with the well-cut lawns and the regularly shaped hedges. As she approached me, it was clear that she had lost me from her line of vision. In fact, I had vanished into thin air – Mini and all – like some spirit from *A Thousand and One Nights*, before her very eyes. Her gaze was steady and clear as water as she walked past me. Gently, I cleared my throat, and a muscle tautened in the side of her neck, but she continued her way past me.

Perhaps I should have whistled after her. But I didn't. I was afraid she might pass out.

I went back up the street a short distance, passed the gate and looked up at the house. There it lay, quiet and secluded as before, with nothing to indicate that anyone might be planning to come out of it.

I walked back to the car, sat down in the driver's seat and rolled the window down. In September the light is like it is in April but there is something different about it, too. In April it filters down clear and white between the naked tree-tops and people tilt their faces skywards to try to get a breath of summer, with joy and optimism in their eyes. In September the light has a melancholic tinge of gold and it seeps down heavily through the tops of the trees whose leaves have already been touched by the first glow of autumn. September is like a rich man with a lot of gold sovereigns in his pockets and nothing except old age and death to look forward to. Someone has written on September's visiting card in invisible ink the word *sadness* . . .

September is the scent of faded red roses. One late summer evening, an infinity of years ago, I had sat on a flight of steps in a garden with a girl of my own age at my side and, in a moment of abandon, I had showered the almost white rose petals over her dark hair. I remembered the scent of those roses – almost more clearly than I remembered the girl.

Love confuses and bewilders. At regular intervals in your life you stumble into it, circle around it, let yourself be ensnared by it, before it drives you away again. And it's love that controls the game: you merely follow it blindly, obeying each slightest signal. A woman comes into your life, walks through a few years of it, like a radiant being in a dark room; and, then, is suddenly out of the room and has closed the door behind her, leaving you there in the darkness.

Sitting in a squat Mini down near the ground early on a September morning can give you the strangest ideas. There was no particular reason why I should have started thinking about those things at that particular moment. In fact, I had better things to do.

Hagbart Helle was in the house outside which I had parked. One way or the other I was going to have to get in there and have a few words with him. I had no idea of what I should say to him but at least I knew where to start.

The question was whether I was ever going to get a chance. Things had begun to happen. Young Carsten Wiig had come into view behind the gate. He was standing with both hands placed on top of the gate and was peering in my direction, as though he could hardly believe his eyes. The sun was glittering in his blonde hair, gleaming on his white shirt. When he emerged from the gateway it was with long, determined strides. I rolled the window part of the way up.

If you are sitting in a Mini it can sometimes be a smart idea to stay put when anyone wants to come and have a talk with you. The roof of the car is approximately on a level with the waistline of the person outside and it doesn't take long before whoever it happens to be starts feeling rather silly in that situation. At any rate, it wasn't making Carsten Wiig feel any the more kindly disposed towards me. 'What the hell are you sitting out here for?' he barked at me through the part-open window.

I took my time before replying, shrugged my shoulders demonstratively and gave my surroundings a casual look over. 'The view's not bad if you like slow, Italian films. This one looks as though it was made by Antonioni back in the early 1960s.'

'Who?' It was doubtful whether he had ever heard of anyone in films apart from John Wayne.

'Oh, a fellow who used to make films that consisted mostly of pauses. But pretty ones. Like this street.'

'Listen here, whatever your name is . . .'

'My name's Veum.'

'You, Veum – either get out of here this instant, or I'll call the police.'

'This instant? You're going to call the police?'

'Yes.'

'That might be interesting. Then we could all go and talk to Hagbart Helle together.'

His face grew hard. 'If you don't . . . We have other ways.'

I gave him one of my gentle smiles, as fleeting as the smile of a good-natured inspector of taxes. 'Really? Could you maybe draw some of them for me?'

He leaned forwards and tried to open the door. I opened it hard so that it struck his knees. He lost his balance. I got out, shut the door behind me and stood right in front of him.

We stood there staring at each other. He was red in the face. His fists were clenched.

'What's the matter?' I asked. 'Can't you draw?'

He bared his teeth but it wasn't a smile. 'If it wasn't for the fact that I don't want to cause Helle any trouble, I'd show you a few tricks I learned over on the other side. But we haven't seen the last of each other, so don't feel too secure. There's one thing I can assure you of: Hagbart Helle will stay in this house right up until it's time for him to go home. He won't set a foot outside this gate and you haven't a chance of getting into the house to talk to him. So, if you don't want to waste the whole of your day, I'd advise you to spend it doing something more valuable. I can assure you that no one thinks you do anything to improve the appearance of this street.'

I looked around me in astonishment. 'Really? Is that because I'm not wearing a blazer, perhaps? Or because I'm not a member of the Automobile Association? This is a free country, Wiig, or at least it's supposed to be, and I'll hang around exactly where I want to for as long as I want to.'

'Very well.' He had unclenched his fists now but his eyes were still hard. 'Don't say you weren't warned.' Then he turned round and went back where he had come from, striding determinedly as before.

I got back into the car and continued my surveillance of the house. Half an hour went by and then another.

In an attempt to get things moving, I started the engine, drove demonstratively past the gate, turned the vehicle round and revved the engine extra loud as I pulled out of the street. I parked again just round the corner, however, and kept my eye on the exit in my driving mirror. I wasn't going to let anything get past me without my noticing it.

The woman who passed me on this street was about ten years younger than the other. She had dark hair and she was sitting at the wheel of a streamlined silver sports car that streaked past me with hardly a sound. I saw the woman in a brief flash: her face reminded me of someone I knew. It had been during that same summer of long ago but before the roses had faded, in lilac-time. This girl had been a blonde and her name had had a biblical ring to it: Rebecca. She had sat in the chair beside me in a high-necked dress with a serious expression on her face; suddenly we had been alone in the room and were only eighteen. Without saying a word, but with a distinct sense of the preordained, we had slowly leaned forwards towards each other and had kissed for a long time. There had just been a thunderstorm outside, the streets were wet and the gardens were luxuriant and verdant like the ones that surrounded me now. I gave the horn a thump. It was the gardens that had set me going. For that's another thing about love: the memories fade with the years, the wounds close up, and you discover a kind of peace with yourself; but suddenly they are torn open again, suddenly you go through the same thing all over again, and it has a greater strength and clarity than ever. Little bits of the past that you will carry around with you to eternity.

But I had memories that were fresher and more painful that any I had of Rebecca and I didn't feel in a mood to bring them to life again just at that moment. The green gardens had become intrusive and the sunlight had acquired a white brilliance. Blueness hammered down from the unyielding sky and I suddenly felt weary, resigned. It was futile to sit here waiting for someone who was never going to appear. I decided to give up. But only for this round. Before the day was out we'd play another – that much I promised myself.

I started the engine and let the car find its own way back to the main arterial highway into Bergen. We drove with the traffic, while the noise increased around us. At Nygårdstangen we were greeted by something that resembled a Little Manhattan – an unbecoming remnant of a construction style the Americans had left behind them a long time ago. I found a place to park on Festplassen and walked the last bit of the way to the police station. There I asked to see Hamre.

34

Hamre seemed irritable and under stress and he drew my attention to the fact that he was extremely busy. Small furrows ran down from his nostrils and his lips were tightly pursed over his clenched teeth. His desk was strewn with piles of documents and an occasional photograph peeped out from the mass of papers.

'Do you know what day it is today?' I asked him.

'. . . and I certainly don't have the time to answer riddles!' he said, concluding a sentence he hadn't even begun.

'This is no riddle. It's in the calendar,' I replied.

He sat down heavily at his desk, passed a swift hand through his hair, and stared at me. I said: 'Okay. Today is the first of September. Hagbart Helle's in town. That's what day it is.'

Suddenly, he looked even wearier. 'Oh, it's *that* old story, is it? I'm sorry, Veum. We've uncovered no fresh evidence – and there's nothing in the papers on the case to give us the slightest pretext for disturbing a man like Hagbart Helle. Don't get the idea that it doesn't bother us. There's nothing that would give me greater pleasure than to see that case cleared up.' Softly, he added: 'If for no other reason than to get rid of you.' In a louder voice, he said: 'But you can see what this place is like. Case piled on top of case and we simply haven't got the capacity to cover them all as thoroughly as we'd like to. And, as if that weren't enough, we have to face questions about police brutality. As if anyone was in any doubt that *that* existed.' He gave me an accusing look. 'But not twenty-four hours a day, three-hundred-and-sixty-five days a year. Not every single day. We do have *other* things to do besides going up and down in the lift putting bruises on drunken troublemakers. Believe it or not.'

'I wouldn't dream of accusing you of it.'

'I know. If you'd ever worked here you'd have been part of those statistics, too. We all know that story. But it's because of that that you've seen the reverse side of the medallion. It isn't exactly negligible, the degree of violence to which we're exposed, we folk who've chosen this depressing trade as a means of earning our daily crust of bread.'

'All right, all right. Let's drop this subject, seeing you're so busy. What about the Nymark case?'

'I've already told you. His getting run over like that was an ugly

162

business but that wasn't what led to his death At least, no more than indirectly – and that would never stand up in court. You're the only person who keeps on insisting that there was something fishy about Nymark's death and, so far, we haven't found a single shred of evidence to suggest you may have a point.'

'What about the death that occurred yesterday?'

'What? What death?' He looked genuinely astonished.

'The woman, Olga Sørensen, the one I found dead in her flat out in Sandviken.'

'Oh her. She fell and injured herself while she was under the influence of drink – that's the most likely explanation. An unfortunate accident.'

'Precisely,' I said, acidly. 'There are beginning to be an awful lot of accidents in this case. Maybe this will refresh your memory. Olga Sørensen was Docker Johan's lover – he's the fellow who disappeared in 1971, at the time Harald Wulff is supposed to have been murdered. And Harald Wulff is the connecting link between all these crimes – from the war years, through the fire on Fjøsangerveien, up to and including what happened to Hjalmar Nymark earlier this year.'

'But Harald Wulff *is* dead! For heaven's sake, man!'

'I'm beginning to wonder. To me it's beginning to look as though he may be on the prowl again. What if – what if he wasn't killed in 1971 and it was Docker Johan who was executed?'

'Yes, I've thought about that, too. But, in that case, what became of Wulff? No one has heard anything of Docker Johan since then and the same is true of Harald Wulff. There was only one corpse but two men disappeared. Can you explain that to me, Veum?'

'No.' After a brief pause, I added: 'Not yet. But listen. I've talked to Olai Osvold, the man they call Bombsite. He's the sole survivor of the Peacock fire. You've got a sketch-plan of the factory, haven't you?'

He looked around him despairingly. 'Somewhere, right down at the bottom of the file.' For a moment, he hesitated. Then he got up. It confirmed what I had always known: Jakob E. Hamre was a capable policeman and he let no question ever go unanswered.

He thumbed his way down one pile of papers, then another, and then yet another. Finally he arrived at the required folder. He fished it out and a couple of other folders fell to floor. I bent down and picked them up for him, while he opened the one in his hands. After a moment's search he extracted a blueprint showing the plans of the Peacock factory. He gave it to me and I eagerly bent forward over the large, unfolded sheet of paper. I located the production hall almost at one. The exit led down a flight of stairs – it was the only exit. In other words, that meant that if Bombsite had seen Holger Karlsen leave the production hall and Harald Wulff enter immediately afterwards, they must have encountered one another on the stairs. The difference between them was that Holger Karlsen had never got any further, while Harald Wulff had had time to go into the production hall, get Bombsite and drag him out – and so must also have passed Holger Karlsen on the stairs.

With the sketch-plan in my hands I reported to Hamre what Bombsite had told me.

He nodded. 'There's nothing new about that, Veum. It's all here. And it's perfectly correct. That's exactly how he said it happened at the time. The only trouble is that Harald Wulff's version of events, the one he gave in his statement, is different. It's here, too. It was one man's word against another but, since Osvold had been badly injured and couldn't be considered as reliable a witness as Wulff – who'd escaped unharmed – no one got the chance to take the case any further. They didn't get a chance then, and they're not getting one now.'

I felt a cold knot in my stomach. 'Have you got that statement? Wulff's, I mean?'

He nodded and thumbed his way through the pile until he found it. With something akin to solemnity I took the old transcript in my hands, opened it out and read Harald Wulff's stenographed statement concerning what had happened when he had run into the burning factory:

I met Holger Karlsen, the works foreman, in the doorway of the production hall. He was only slightly injured. He shouted to me: 'Get Osvold out, he's lying over there. I'll take care of Martinsen.' I merely nodded by way of reply and hurried inside. Osvold was unconscious and he was a heavy weight to pull. When I had dragged him out, I saw that Holger Karlsen was on his way into the hall. There was thick, black smoke everywhere and all I could see of him was a dark shadow moving among the fumes. That was the last I ever saw of him. Afterwards I heard they found him, that he hadn't managed to get Martinsen, and that he hadn't managed to get himself out, either. I've often blamed myself for what happened, but there was nothing I could have done. After all, my hands were full with Osvold. . .

I closed my eyes. I could almost hear his voice: it must have been deep, possibly somewhat hoarse after the coughing caused by the smoke, and it had spoken with that distinctive mid-Hordland accent: *I've often blamed myself for what happened. . .*

It wasn't difficult to see why they had had to accept this testimony, even if it had come from the mouth of a former traitor. Fanebust, too, had said they had pressed Wulff hard but he had refused to alter a comma. Harald Wulff's version of what had happened in the burning production hall would, it seemed, remain the official one until Judgement Day when someone, thumbing through a pile of mouldering court records, would place a righteous finger on a passage or two, clear his throat sternly, and fix Harald Wulff with a wooden stare until he began to talk.

I put the papers down on Hamre's desk. 'Listen,' I said. 'That death yesterday. It's just too damned strange. Why should Olga Sørensen fall and fatally injure herself right now, of all times – just when someone had begun to rake around in certain old legal matters. It isn't – it can't be explained merely as a coincidence. Isn't that case being investigated, either?'

'Yes, yes, of course it is. But it's not in my hands, Veum.'

'Muus?'

He smiled, thinly. 'Yes. So you can take your inquiries to him, can't you?'

'It won't be any good.'

He smiled the same thin smile. 'I know.'

'Look. . . You realize that a woman on the floor below saw Olga Sørensen receive a visitor the evening before – the evening of the day before yesterday, that is – and that she saw a man leave the house – a man with a limp?'

'No – or rather yes. It was mentioned at the briefing session this morning. But, as I've told you, Muus is the one who's primarily in charge of. . .'

'For God's sake, Hamre. What I'm saying to you is that the man with the limp is the connecting link between the death of Olga Sørensen and that of Hjalmar Nymark – and, for that matter, it's the link that connects those deaths with the deaths of Harald Wulff and Docker Johan, too!'

'But. . .'

'If you look at it that way, this can actually be seen as a direct extension of the Nymark case. And that's still *yours*, isn't it?'

'It's the *Department's*, Veum. We don't own the cases we work on.'

'All right, so why don't you take it up – with the *Department*? Let someone else have a look at it. Vadheim, for example. I mean, for heaven's sake, you're decent policemen, but Muus. . .'

'We *know* you don't get along well with Muus, Veum.'

'Well? Are you willing to take a chance, on my recommendation?'

He sat motionless at his desk, considering me. A well-dressed young man, he might have been a weary section head in a commercial bank, or a stress-worn consultant in an advertising bureau. But he was neither of those things. He was a detective inspector in the crime squad and he had a desk full of unsolved cases. Softly, he said: 'Let's just put it this way: I'll have a word with Vadheim and perhaps we'll take it up with the crime chief. I say perhaps, Veum. Okay?'

'Fine.' I got up. He came out from behind his desk and followed me to the door. I said: 'I'm sorry for taking up so much of your time.'

He smiled wearily. 'That's all right.'

I opened the door and found myself standing face to face with Dankert Muus. He looked as though he had just come lumbering up from the underworld with all the lesser devils of hell at his heels. When his gaze alighted on me, it grew as cold as frost over a bare, empty wilderness. He transferred it to Hamre and it didn't get much warmer. When he spoke, his voice was tense and strained: 'Have you been discussing the investigation with Veum?'

I turned to Hamre, to see how he was going to take it. He gave Muus a measured stare. 'I've been talking to Veum about something that happened twenty-eight years ago. Have you any objection?'

Muus gave him a savage look. 'I'd have thought you've got better things to do with your time,' he said. Then he turned round and lumbered off down the passage. 'Fat-assed cop!' we heard him snort, loudly enough for both Hamre and I to be able to hear it.

Hamre had grown even paler and his mouth was now a narrow pencil line on his face. He gave me a tense nod and closed the door.

Out in the passage another door banged loudly. For a moment I found myself completely alone. From an office somewhere nearby came the sound of someone fumblingly tapping the keys of a typewriter – a hesitant love letter from an aspirant to the profession.

I found my way down and out.

35

The afternoon sunlight met me in the doorway, warm and gentle. I hung around for a while on the small square outside the police station. Facing me were the old and the new town halls – the old one with its pointed gable, sitting like a doll's house between the post office and the various banks, and the new one with its rugged concrete façade, an ill-sited Jacob's ladder leading nowhere, a tower of Babel made up of obscurantist talk and bureaucracy. It rose thirteen storeys above the town, trying to look as though it possessed some special significance, an assertion most people treated with scepticism. However that might be, it certainly wasn't an attractive sight.

I wandered through the town centre and out towards Nordnes. Along the avenue that led up from the Cloisters the trees were turning yellow. A few leaves had already fallen and had stuck fast to the asphalt, like so many over-eager death-bed kisses. It was summer that was kissing you farewell, a summer yellow as a cold Arctic sun.

I walked past Fredriksberg and went on into Nordnes Park, down past the marine baths and right out on to the Point itself. The air was chillier now and the sun was sinking in the sky. It was still relatively high but the white mist that was rising beneath it warned of shorter days and lower temperatures to come. I rounded the Point and started back in the direction of the town once more. Here, at the far end of Nordnes Park, down by the seashore behind the depot barracks, were the old warehouses. The unmistakeable aroma of dried fish still rose to greet your nostrils, even though it was many years now since the last bulk cargoes of dried fish had been unloaded here.

Here, too, it had been, down on the quayside behind the houses, that a man had been killed one cold day in January 1971. I went over to the fence and looked down. A van stood parked over there. The gate was open but there was a heavy padlock and chain on it, so it could be locked up at nights. Had the padlock been there in 1971? Had someone had a key?

I tried to picture what had taken place: the man being kicked and beaten, lying huddled and bleeding on the hard-trodden, dirty snow. The man who had later been identified as Harald Wulff. A traitor who had met the fate he deserved, twenty-six years after the ending of the war in Norway.

But had it really been him? Or was it someone else who had been killed? Yet one more innocent victim? And in that case, where was the man who had borne the name Harald Wulff?

Ten more years had gone by since then. Whatever clues there might have been had long since disappeared. The snow of ten winters had come and gone, the sun had shone and the rain had poured. The trail was cold, as cold as it could possibly be. There was nothing to be guessed from the scene of *this* crime and, with the sun on my right, I continued my way back into town.

At Nykirken I turned off to the right. There were one or two things I wanted to ask Sigrid Karlsen about.

As I was approaching the house, I looked up at her windows but there was no sign of life behind them. I checked the time. She ought to have been at home at that hour.

The street door was open, as though someone had forgotten to close it, and I went inside. When I reached the first floor, I saw that the door to her flat was also slightly open.

A shock hurtled through me. Something was wrong.

I hammered at the door and rang the door-bell simultaneously. Slowly, it opened.

The vestibule was in a state of chaos. The little bureau lay overturned on the floor; someone had taken out its drawers and had emptied their contents out. Against one wall lay the frame of the mirror which had been smashed to smithereens. Pieces of the broken mirror lay strewn over the floor like brilliant peep-holes down into another world.

Cautiously, I stepped down into the mess. With a cold shiver, I said, faintly:'Hel – lo?'

No one answered. Everything was still.

36

I opened the door into the kitchen with care. My heart was in my mouth and it was beating hard. Everything in there was a mess, too. The calendar had been ripped from the wall and flung into the sink. The picture of the child and dog playing together had been crumpled up and thrown on to the counter. The portable radio was lying face down on the floor. Beside it was a piece of black plastic that had broken off it. The kitchen stool had been knocked on its side. Beneath the counter there was a plastic bin-liner containing refuse. Potato peelings and egg-shells had flowed across the floor. There was also a strong smell of disinfectant but I couldn't make out where it was coming from.

The door to the living-room was half open. It was dark in there but as far as I could see the wreckage was less extensive. The television set had been knocked over and the power plug pulled out from the wall behind it. A flowerpot had fallen and smashed. One of the curtain rails was hanging askew, so that on one side the curtains reached the floor. A handful of books had been snatched from the bookshelf and thrown about. And hunched in one of the armchairs, her face hidden in her hands, sat Sigrid Karlsen, looking as though she had frozen stiff. She made no movement. Only a faint trembling of her shoulders indicated that she was still alive.

It was like surprising someone in an intimate situation – but one that involved grief rather than love. The one can be as embarrassing as the other. And it is never easy for a stranger to intrude on either of them.

I stooped down and picked up the radio, placed it on the kitchen counter and gave it a good shove against the wall, hoping by the sudden noise to register my presence. Then I walked slowly into the doorway of the living-room and stood there looking at her, my hands feeling large and helpless. There was a circular grey patch on the crown of her head, where the parting was. What I could see of her neck was white and exposed. She was wearing a light grey dress with a simple belt knotted like a rope around her waist. 'Mrs Karlsen?' I said cautiously. 'It's Veum.'

She didn't take her hands away from her face. But her back straightened slightly and I knew she had heard me.

I stood there, waiting.

Slowly, she opened her fingers and between their long, white joints I glimpsed her eyes. They were dark and red-rimmed. Thin stripes showed where the tears had flowed down her cheeks. I could see no sign of her spectacles. My gaze slid automatically across the floor but there was no more there than what I had seen from the kitchen.

'What happened?' I asked, making a shrugging gesture, as though she might not be sure to what I was referring.

She shook her head. Her mouth answered silently: 'Nothing.' Her lips were a bluish red colour, with a thin layer of lipstick on top.

'Nothing?' I said, without any particular inflection in my voice. 'Mr Nothing's just been to see you, has he?' said a dark voice inside me, suddenly. 'Mr Nothing has just been to see you and he's turned the whole flat upside down and now he's gone. A guest from the past – or a fugitive to the future?' 'Who was it?' I heard my own voice say out loud.

She gave me another speechless look. Her hands were on their way down from her face now. Her features were shockingly exposed. She couldn't have hidden anything – not with *that* expression on her face. I suddenly recalled two details from my previous visit to her. The bureau in the vestibule: the paint had been scraped off one of its corners. And the mirror: there had been a crack running across it.'

Carefully, I said: 'This isn't the first time this has happened, is it?'

She shook her head silently. A white pocket handkerchief had appeared in one of her hands. She carefully dried her eyes, her cheeks, her upper lip.

'Was it someone you know. . . a man?'

She gave me a frightened look, blushed and shook her head. 'It's not that,' she said faintly. It was a startling voice – anguished and quite different from the one she had spoken in the last time we had met.

Suddenly, before I had even put the question, I knew what the answer was: 'Your daughter?'

Her eyes flooded full of tears. Her lips began to tremble. The handkerchief came out again.

She cried. I came all the way into the living-room, as quietly as if I were walking on moss. I went over to the window and looked down at the street outside. The cobble-stones were flat and worn. The houses had weary façades. Such small houses, so many houses – so many people – so many things one didn't know.

'Is she. . . Does she often have turns like that?'

'It – it comes over her. It doesn't happen often. She's been having treatment and she's doing fine – at her job. She can manage there but she has to have somewhere to take it out on, doesn't she? The doctors said she was schizophrenic. She takes medicine for it but. . .' Her hands fluttered soundlessly in front of her, like butterflies on a day of sudden frost.

'I can see it in her eyes when she comes home. And then it happens.

She's too strong for me, I can't match her. . . Then she knocks over everything she can set her hands on, tears things down and breaks things and then – disappears. In the evening she comes back and then it's over. If she gets too crazy, she goes to the – hospital – herself. Takes stronger medicine for a while; then she comes back – my sweet little Anita. . . My little child.'

Our eyes met. Yes, little children grow into big ones but, for their parents, they always remain little, especially if they have problems.

'Have you – have the doctors ever told you what they think might have caused it?'

'They say it's because she lost her father so early on and in the way she did. And because of all the horrible things people said during the years that followed. She had to have somewhere to hide and she took refuge in – that.' It came mechanically, a sober statement of fact. But in the way she said it there was a good deal of suppressed rage. And I got the message: Anita Karlsen, who had been only four years old when the Peacock fire happened, was yet one more victim of that unhappy event.

Sigrid Karlsen had stopped crying. Suddenly, she clenched her fists and rose to her feet. 'I must start to clear up.'

'I'll help you,' I said, quickly.

She gave me a stern look. 'I'd rather do it myself, thank you.' Then, to soften this slightly, she said: 'I don't want there to be anyone here when Anita gets back. She's always very sorry for what she's done, afterwards.'

I nodded. 'I understand.'

'Was there something you wanted?' she asked. 'Since you've come here?'

'Yes, I suppose there must have been. But I've forgotten what it was. I really got a shock just now.' Indeed, for a moment I had thought I was going to walk into what I had walked into at Olga Sørensen's flat the evening before.

'All I wanted to say, Mrs Karlsen, was that I'm still working on this case and that I'm getting more and more convinced that your husband was in no way to blame for what happened back then and that I'm not going to give up until I've got to the bottom of the whole business. When you think the time is right, tell Anita I *know* her father was innocent.'

She looked at me with sad eyes. 'What use is that now? But thank you, all the same.'

'I'll be back when I have incontrovertible proof that I'm right,' I said in a firm voice. I noticed that I said 'when' and not 'if', and I knew I was telling the truth. I was going to find out what had really happened back then, even if I had to go all the way down to hell to bring Harald Wulff back from there. And I was getting a stronger and stronger feeling that I wouldn't need to go as far as that.

The day of reckoning was approaching, slowly but surely, for someone. Far too many years too late – but even so. . .

Outside it had begun to get dark. The contours were being erased. And it was at night that the wolves came out: both those that hunted in packs and those that hunted alone.

37

The darkness was falling swiftly now and in the big gardens of the villas the lights were being switched on. The light descended evenly across the garden, revealing damp earth under the autumn-yellow grass. Once the sun was gone, it quickly grew colder.

This time I parked a good distance away, up in the side street, and walked the last bit of the way down to Hagbart Helle's brother's house. As I walked I stayed close to the hedge, so as not to be seen from the house.

The hedge that divided the garden from the road was thick and full of thorns. The wrought-iron gate was fixed to two massive stone pillars which had been erected on the outside of the hedge. I squatted down and examined the gate thoroughly. In spite of what the notice said there was no dog to be seen this time, either. I tried to find out if any alarm device had been fitted to the gate but it didn't look like it. All the same, I was far from sure.

I walked past the gate and continued my way along the hedge. The next villa was situated more accessibly, behind a low, wooden fence that had been planted on the inside, with rose-bushes. Company director Hellebust's hedge continued around his property. After I had taken a good look round to see that no one was watching, I stepped over the fence and followed the hedge round along the back of the garage on the other side.

The hedge was as thick and impenetrable as ever. Behind Hellebust's property the land sloped gently down towards the old railway canal which was no longer in use. In one place there was a hollow in the ground, like the bed of an old creek. Suddenly there was a small cavity under the hedge.

I looked around me. It was strangely still. Away up above me, between formations of ragged cloud, the stars had pierced holes in the dark vault of the sky. The canopy of leaves stretched its handsome profile towards the west and, above the ridge of the mountains, I could see an evening jet coming into land at Flesland – soundless, almost mirage-like.

I got down on my hands and knees, ducked my head and squeezed my way through under the hedge. A moment later I was on the inside of the property. I stayed there quietly, bent down to the ground, listening.

Faint sounds were coming from the house, which was separated from me by a clump of fruit trees and a white flag-stoned patio on which there was a table and some wicker chairs. No guard dogs came gnashing their teeth at me, no angry barks announced that an intruder was on the prowl.

Cautiously, I straightened up and walked in a semi-circle up towards the house. I arrived at one of the side walls. Above me was a row of three windows: two of them were completely dark but, in the third, there was a warm, flickering glow that looked as though it was probably coming from an open fire. This was the window nearest the front of the house and I assumed that it belonged to the living-room.

The window was above head-height and I passed beneath it as far as the corner. I took a quick look round it. The flag-stoned patio lay bathed in light from the large windows that gave straight on to the garden via a sliding door. A slope planted with rock-plants led up to the patio. When I stuck my head out a bit further, I could see that the heavy, brown velvet curtains were partially drawn. I would probably be able to get up to the large windows without being seen.

Warily, I moved up through the rock garden; I avoided walking on the rocks themselves, paying no heed to the fact that some of the flowers got trodden flat in the process.

When I reached the patio I stood still, holding my breath. My observation had been correct. The velvet curtains hid me from view. No one called out. But I could hear the voices through the glass: they were monotonous and indistinct and I was unable to make out what they were saying. The double-glazing cut off the sound in both directions.

I went right up to the window and moved cautiously along towards the open area between the curtains, inch by inch, keeping my head back and pressing my body as flat against the window as I possibly could.

Now I was near the edge of one of the curtains. By moving my head round slowly I was able to get an oblique view of the room.

The light was flickering and unsteady. A couple of discreetly placed bracket-lamps provided the only fixed illumination. On a large dining table stood a seven-pronged candelabrum containing tall white candles. Their light flickered against the tall, narrow chairbacks. The chairs were empty.

I moved my head round a little further.

The light grew stronger, red and gold. Now I could see the white fireplace. Its surface was rough, executed in stucco. In front of the fireplace there were three high-backed armchairs which faced a wide sofa across a low table; the armchairs and sofa were all covered in the same warm, reddish-brown velvet material. On the low table stood an ice bucket, bottles of champagne and a selection of the more expensive types of brandy. Around the table, in the light from the fireplace, sat six people.

I recognized one of them immediately. Straight-backed and clean-profiled, Carsten Wiig sat facing into the warmth of the fire, listening. Seated next to him was a young woman, as pretty as most women are in front of dancing flames, but wearing large spectacles and with a slightly over-stiff smile on her pursed lips. In one corner, two women were having an intimate conversation with each other. One of them was white-haired and looked in her late sixties. The other was considerably younger, with a suntanned face and sun-bleached hair.

Of the two older men in the room, one was a stout, slightly bloated-looking fellow with a florid complexion and thin, whitish-yellow hair that was combed back smoothly across his scalp. The other was Hagbart Helle.

Hagbart Helle sat in sharp profile against the white surface of the wall. I wouldn't have recognized him had it not been for the blurry photograph Ove Haugland had shown me.

There was something ruthless and bird-of-prey-like about his thin, veined face, his large, aquiline nose, his dark, irascible eyes and the accentuated tautness around his mouth and jaw. He was one of those men who are always on their guard, always on the look-out for any irregularity – or possible advantage. His skin was suntanned a reddish brown but he had clearly-marked wrinkles and he looked older than I had imagined. Somehow, it was only at that moment that I realized that Hagbart Helle was really an old man of seventy-three. Success and the pursuit of his career had certainly hardened him but he was never going to be able to buy off time. The years catch up with us all, rich and poor alike.

I then became aware that there was one other living creature in the room. In front of the fireplace a large, black Dobermann suddenly raised its head, listening. Had it heard the beating of my heart? Or had it suddenly picked up the scent of something alien, something that ought not to be there?

It wasn't, however, the menacing dog's head that held me back.

There was only one window and a sliding door between me and Hagbart Helle but I suddenly realized that it was going to be no use. The pane of glass between us was little more than a symbolic divide but it might just as well have been made of concrete.

Those people in there, with their tailor-made clothes, their expensive drinking habits, their mahogany-brown, velvet-covered furniture, their massive silver candelabra, their thousand-ton ships on silent seas all the way from the tropics to Alaska, with their Swiss bank accounts, their holiday homes in the Seychelles, their orchid-gardened residences in the Caribbean: they were beyond my reach.

People like Docker Johan, Bombsite, Giant Olsen and the rest – they could steal the odd bottle of beer or two and, if they got caught doing it too many times, they got locked up. People like Hagbart Helle could destroy factories and make economic arrangements that ordinary people, if they understood them, would call fraud; could transfer the greater portion of their incomes to invisible investments, under multiple pseudonyms, in countless fake companies the world over; and could live their lives in the sunshine or in front of flickering open fires, far from the noise and hubbub of the machines, removed from every care. They possessed the power given to them by money and it would take a different social order, another system, to reach them.

The only chance you had of getting to them was if you could confront them with concrete, tangible evidence. And of that I had none. I scarcely even had a theory.

I gazed longingly at Hagbart Helle, thought of all the questions I might have put to him, all the accusations that might have provoked a reaction from him before the Dobermann leapt at my throat. Deep down inside, however, I knew even that would be futile. Hagbart Helle had navigated his way out of foul waters and on to the great, quiet deeps; he had brought international board meetings under control, put a check on colleagues too eager to do battle. . . He wasn't going to allow himself to be provoked. He sat safely in there leaning back in his comfortable armchair with a half-full highball glass in one hand and the slightly tense smile that played at his ambitious mouth. He had attained his goal. He was safe.

His brother was a different kettle of fish. Yngvar Hellebust was the usual homespun Norwegian capitalist and possessed no obvious ambitions. If you went by his appearance you might have thought he was an employee of the Inland Revenue who also just happened to be the director of a medium-sized and – if his home was anything to judge by – not at all unsuccessful knitwear firm. But there were light years between him and Hagbart Helle: the difference between the provinces and the metropolis, the boys' club and the Mafia.

Perhaps it was the dog holding me back, after all. Its head was still raised on its powerful, black and brown neck. It had strong jaws and sharp teeth. By nature it was a hunter and killer. I didn't exactly relish the idea of having a race with it out in the autumn darkness.

As slowly as I had come, I began to retrace my steps.

I cast a final glance at Hagbart Helle. Then, silently, I drew away from the window, stepped slowly down through the rock-plants, stole quietly along the wall of the house, past the garden furniture and the gnarled fruit-trees and ducked down under the hedge again.

The night gathered around me like the folds of a black sack. I had no idea what to do next.

38

That night I didn't go home.

I drove in towards the town centre along Fjøsangerveien but it was impossible to make out where the Peacock paint factory had been. The wounds had grown together. New houses had been built.

I parked my car on Tårnplass and walked down to my office. For a moment I hesitated in front of the entrance to Hjalmar Nymark's favourite café but then went on past.

Up in my office I fumbled around in the darkness, opened the bottom drawer of my desk, unscrewed the yellow cap from the new, shiny bottle, poured out a glass – and drank.

I didn't have much – not more than a sherry-glass full and I made it last a long time. It seemed to taste of moonlight and my tongue twisted in my mouth like a snake sloughing its skin. I drank to all the people who had passed on their way, people whom I'd known and who had vanished into the darkness again. I drank to freshly erected gravestones, to the sites of old fires and to crestfallen return journeys. Your health, bold countrymen, your health!

Later in the night I left the office, locked up, and went out walking in the town. It was after midnight and, out in the streets, it was shadows that prevailed, shadows and people in a hurry, with gazes that were inward-turned. I wasn't in a hurry and my eyes were alert.

I walked along Nordnes, below the tall, concrete façades of Strandgaten, all the way out to the park. Once again I passed the place where, one January evening in 1971, a man with a limp had been murdered. But I didn't stop. I continued on my way. A man in a brown overcoat was coming back from the Point: he had a grey beard and he was leading an Airedale terrier on a leash. I didn't encounter anyone else.

The sea lay black and empty. There was not a boat to be seen on it.

I walked back in the direction of the town again, past the marine baths which lay quiet and deserted, like a monument to the summer that had never really been, and then up past the Mates' School and Nordnes School.

Walking through the town at this time of night was like passing through an exhibition showing the various periods of your own life. From the Nordnes of my childhood, I walked down Galgebakken to

Strangehagen and Skottegaten and, all of a sudden, I found myself in front of one of the most recent pictures in the exhibition: the house in which I had found Hjalmar Nymark dead. On this occasion, however, I didn't stop.

I continued my walk, along Nøstet, towards Møhlenpris and up across the arched, white back of Puddefjord Bridge. Over on Gyldenpris, in my very young days, I had known a girl with blue, poetical eyes but so many blues in her heart that she had ended her days in a psychiatric clinic where she had hanged herself in one of the toilets.

Rounding Viken and crossing Danmarksplass, I approached the town centre from the south, over the old Nygård Bridge and past the hospital which is known by the sobriquet 'Florida' but not because there is any more sun there than in any other part of the town. Outside the bus station two youths in leather jackets were engaged in a brawl, egged on by a disorderly ring of supporters. A police car drew up at the kerb and a couple of police leapt out, as cautious as bats in their black uniforms.

I continued further, through Marken, Øvregaten and out towards Sandviken. Outside Giant Olsen's basement flat I stopped for a moment but all was dark and silent down there, and no Bacchic voices summoned me inside. I walked down to the airport and stopped once more. The Universe had turned upside down, The stars lay glittering in the water and the black sea stretched like a vault above the town. The Skoltegrunn quay lay like a greyish-white barrier dividing sea from sky and there, on a slope that ran down to the rocks, stood I myself.

I breathed in deeply. The air was cold and smelled of waste oil and seaweed. The hours of the night had passed, the lights had gone out all around me and everything was now quiet.

As I made my way along Sjøgaten I was able to walk in the middle of the road without hindrance. No cars passed me, even though only a few hurried morning hours later I would find myself walking in the middle of the rush-hour traffic from Åsane. It was almost eerie: as though I had entered the town and discovered that all its inhabitants had suddenly died. It hadn't been a nuclear war but a sudden plague. And I was the sole survivor. The town belonged to me alone.

When I reached Skutevikstorget, I walked a little way towards Nye Sandviksvei and stopped for a few seconds outside a white wooden house. All its windows were dark and no sound could be heard from within. She was asleep, together with her daughter.

I walked back down the hill and out on to the Skoltegrunn quay. Once again I encountered the sea. Wherever you go in this town you encounter the sea. On this particular night it was like some terse haiku lyric: 'The sea/in September is/Black'. The bollards stuck up from the edge of the pier like the inquisitive heads of seals, straining to hear the inaudible poem. The cargo ship that lay at anchor on the fortress quay had spots of rust on its paintwork. Automatically, I passed my hand over my face. The stubble on it was rough.

The town centre was dead at this hour. This was the quietest time – between five and six in the morning. Even the latest nocturnal wanderers had found their way home by now and it was too early for the people who had to be at work at seven. In front of the statue of Holberg a solitary taxi stood waiting, its 'For Hire' sign glowing on its roof. On the steps outside the flesh market sat someone else who had survived, a man in a dirty, grey overcoat, whose face was buried in his knees. I couldn't see any other signs of life.

And I continued my restless wandering. As I walked, I ran over in my mind all the things I knew – from the rumours concerning Rat Poison's activities during the war, through the Peacock fire, the murder of Harald Wulff and the disappearance of Docker Johan in 1971 to the events of the past weeks: Hjalmar Nymark's being run over, his subsequent death and now, too, Olga Sørensen's 'accident'.

Bergen had changed during that time. In 1953 it had been a town considerably smaller than the one it was now. In Fyllingsdalen, on the other side of a mountain no one had yet bored holes through, the fields had stretched broad and green between the scattered farms which had been linked by a small, winding country road. In the opposite direction, up through Åsane, it had been a day-trip to Salhus or Steinestø and people had gone to Kjøkkelvik or Flesland, and had called it 'the country' with a good conscience. The air shuttle had still operated eastwards from Sandviken Airport in those days and a local railway had run out to Nesttun. In the centre of town the old red-brick post office had stood at the end of Allehelgensgate, on the other side of the street from the old green police station, and the built-up area had extended southwards no further than the barracks at Landås. When there was a football match at the stadium the district wasn't crammed full of parked cars as it was today; instead, there was a veritable pilgrimage back into town again when the match was over and the trams looked as though they had been attacked by colossal swarms of bees, as people clung to their outsides. And my father had still had a few years left of being a tram conductor. Nordnes had still had a lot of bombsites left over from the war, I had been eleven years old and hadn't a care in the world. Hjalmar Nymark, on the other hand, had been forty-two and in the prime of his life, Konrad Fanebust had been at the summit of his career – as a politician, at any rate; Elise Blom had been twenty-one, bursting with youth and expectations of life; Holger Karlsen had been thirty-five and the proud father of a four-year-old daughter, his wife had still been happy, and Hagbart Hellebust had been an efficient, energetic forty-five-year-old. We had all been different then, inhabitants of a smaller town, back in 1953. Some of us had already been overtaken by calamity even then; others had waited – for twenty-eight years. Even the innocent little eleven-year-old from

Nordnes had been drawn into the tragedy in a strange way. And Bergen would never again be the town it was in 1953.

From Nordnes to Sandviken, from Fjøsanger to Nøstet: everywhere the trails crossed one another, like the trails of prowling beasts on some enormous mountain plateau. Some of them had crossed over a quarter of a century ago, others only a few day previously. Most of them were cold but it might still be possible to pursue one or two of them. . .

Down on Nøstet there is a little café. It is one of the first to open in the mornings and it was there that I sought shelter, re-gathering my energies after the night over a cup of scalding hot, ink-black coffee, together with a handful of the rest of the night's wolves.

They had sharply delineated features. We sat hunched forward over our cups, as silent as the night that was behind us, as impassive as the morning around us. Most of us had jobs to go to but some had none. In the half-hour between 7 and 7.30 a.m. we shared a kind of solidarity, installed as we were in the vacuum between sleepless night and working day.

Eventually, the magic wore off and our cups were empty. A narrow band containing coffee grinds lay at the bottom of them and we got up and walked out of the door.

Outside the town was full of noise. Another day had caught up with us.

39

I returned to my small flat, stole a few hours of the daytime stretched out on the sofa, took a long shower and felt just about rested enough to realize that I felt depressed. Wolves that had lain sleeping for twenty-eight years were pretty soundly asleep – perhaps they had mouldered away altogether. There wasn't much to get one's teeth into.

On my way back to the office I bought the morning newspapers. As I was unlocking my door I heard the telephone ringing but it stopped before I could reach it and, when I lifted the receiver and put it to my ear, there was nothing there but my oldest and most faithful friend: the dialling tone.

I opened one of the newspapers and glanced over the front page. Right at the bottom of its right-hand side I found a two-column story with the headline: 'PUZZLING DEATH IN SANDVIKEN'. From the text underneath it transpired that a number of 'unusual circumstances' surrounded the fact that 'a 58-year-old woman was found dead in her Sandviken flat late Monday evening'. A number of factors pointed to it being an accident but the police were 'nevertheless' looking for a witness – a man probably in his fifties, wearing a grey overcoat and dark hat, who had a slight limp in one of his legs'. The man himself, or anyone who might have seen him, was requested to report to the police as soon as possible. Apart from this, the police had no specific information for the press.

I thumbed quickly through the other papers. There wasn't much there, either. The Oslo papers hadn't yet arrived: they were usually more imaginative but didn't really tell you much more. Most of what was known about the case was probably printed here.

I read the newspaper stories through a second time. That the police bulletin had made it into print at all was a bright spot in the situation. It probably meant that Hamre, or Vadheim – or even the crime chief himself – for that matter, had achieved a breakthrough where Muus was concerned. The fact that this was all there was didn't of itself mean that the police hadn't unearthed more facts about the case; but what they refused to tell the press, they weren't going to tell me.

I laid the newspapers to one side and dialled Konrad Fanebust's number. From his secretary I learned that he was at a conference in Copenhagen and was not expected back until late that evening or on the first flight the following morning. I thanked her for the information and hung up.

Outside my windows a new day was unfolding its wings with the golden sun of September glinting in its feathers. The houses dotted along the mountainside stood out in sharp relief and there was a brown shimmer above the tree-tops, as though somebody had superimposed an ultra-fine mesh on them. That was autumn, casting her net. Soon we would all lie floundering in it.

The telephone rang again. I answered it. 'Hello?'

No one replied.

'Hello? Veum here.'

Whoever it was hung up. There was a click and then the dialling tone was there once more. I looked down at the receiver as if it might be able to tell me something. It had either been a wrong number or someone who had lost the desire to talk.

Five minutes later I heard the door from the corridor into my waiting-room open.

I waited to see if anyone was going to knock but nothing happened. People vary that way, when they visit the offices of a private detective. Some come crashing in through both doors without ever seeming to reflect that you might possibly be sitting in there with your favourite blonde on your knee. Others go into the waiting-room and almost instantly melt into the wallpaper. Finding them is like searching for concealed figures in a picture puzzle. Yet another type of visitor sits primly and properly on one of the chairs with an old issue of a respectable weekly magazine open in front of him, or her, more or less as though they're at the doctor's; while others do nothing more than knock.

The man who was waiting for me stood with his legs slightly apart. He was broad-shouldered and athletic, in the slightly stocky manner that characterizes former weightlifters. A blue woollen hat was pulled down over his forehead; his face was pale and rectangular; he had light-blue eyes and a growth of beard that was a sickly grey colour. He was sportily dressed, in a short pilot's jacket, blue denim jeans and brown, lightweight boots – but I didn't much care for the sport he practised.

Before I could open my mouth he had planted one of his large fists accurately in my stomach. I folded up like a curtseying dancing master and he performed a tango step with his knee against my temple. I was already seeing double and when his fist came down again right between my neck and shoulders, the whole room just collapsed like a Chinese fan, and then everything went blank.

Before the first blow struck home, however, one detail had had time to register itself in my brain: he hadn't been alone. Through the frosted panel that looked out on to the corridor I had seen the silhouette of a second person, dark and blurred through the glass.

40

Footsteps that come, and footsteps that go. Like waves washing over you, as you lie dead drunk by the edge of the seashore. Back and forth, back and forth.

Gently they rock you in the surf: back and forth, back and . . .

'Veum?'

The sea washes over you. September is black. The sun comes rarely.

'Veum!' A voice. It sounded familiar but it didn't belong to anyone I particularly cared for. I couldn't place it.

I opened my eyes and stared down at the worn, brown floor. My voice was mangled, my tongue galvanized. 'Hello?' It awoke an echo within me, cruel and grotesque: 'Hel – he– – lo – hel – lo hel– loooooooo. . .'

I felt sick. There was a large, heavy stone in my stomach and it was hurting me. I had a swelling on my temple and my neck felt as though it were living a life of its own, torn free of mine.

'Wake up! What's the matter?' That voice. . . It belonged to someone from Eastern Norway. When did you last meet anyone from there, Varg? No. No. It was the other way round. It was him that met me.

Powerful hands turned me over. I groaned. The ceiling came horribly close. It looked as though it could have done with a clean.

'Hey, are you awake?'

The voice above me grew more remote and the large face smaller, pushing the ceiling up as it receded. The room became taller but I remained lying at the bottom of a large, shimmering jam-jar. I had seen that face before.

Suddenly I sat up, turned round and crouched on all fours with my head hanging forward between my arms. My head felt like a mass of flames but, if I kept perfectly still, it cooled down. The footsteps moved away from me, surrounding me with a confusing pattern of echoes. Some of them were inside my head, others were out in the corridor.

A curt, unfriendly laugh. 'My God, you look ridiculous.'

I laughed. Ha ha. That was precisely how I felt. The king of the fools. The rat-catcher's favourite.

I crawled over to the wall, or where I supposed the wall to be, and raised myself slowly against it, supporting myself with the flats of my palms. *Oh, oh, oh, oh, Mrs Robinson!* The voices came filtering through my head in an echoing polyphony, like circles in water. *Heaven knows a place for those who pray, hey hey, hey. . .*

My knees felt as though they might give way beneath the strain at any moment but they held out. I stood looking around me, as though I were seeing the room for the first time: the panelling that came halfway up the wall, the old wallpaper above it, the chairs along the wall, the table with its shiny, round legs and the old copies of weekly magazines that lay on top of it.

With his hands in the pockets of his fashionable, white trousers – bagged around the thighs, tapered at the ankles – wearing a pale, lightweight dress jacket and a broad, red-checked tie, Carsten Wiig stood watching me with his eyebrows slightly raised and an acid smile on his lips. Because I was feeling as white as a sheet and as weak as an aspen leaf, he seemed even more suntanned and healthy-looking than when I had seen him last. His closely cropped hair glistened in rivalry with his flawless teeth. He was the first prize in a competition I had never gone in for. Now I was merely waiting for the certificate that said I had taken part.

'Hello – o?' he said, smiling. 'May I come in? Is there anybody home?' Then, in a different tone of voice, he said: 'Good Lord, Veum, you look as though you'd been run over by an express train!'

I just stared at him through the frayed holes in the mist around me.

'Or have you maybe been playing with fire – Veum?' His words held a concealed menace now. We had arrived at the nitty-gritty. I wasn't *that* punch-drunk and I didn't believe in coincidences. I had seen the silhouette in the window and I was in no doubt as to whose it had been.

He came closer. 'Has somebody been giving you a rough time, Veum?'

He was right in front of me now. I could see the small, burned areas above his nose and cheek-bones: they stood out red against all that brown. His voice was soft now, casual, as though he wasn't really interested in what he was saying: 'You know, people like Hagbart Helle have a lot of influence. I don't know what's been going on here but I think I have an idea, as it were.'

'As it were?' I formed the words contemptuously on my lips but no sound came out.

'You could end up getting worse treatment that this. If you're not more careful.'

The pauses were like ones in a bad performance of a play by Chekhov. I didn't feel in the mood for talking.

'That's so, isn't it, Veum? The next visit you get . . . it won't be a foregone conclusion that you'll be able to get up again at all. Afterwards.'

Then he suddenly turned away from me, as though I made him feel sick. In the doorway he turned round again. 'Have a speedy recovery, Veum. And don't forget the advice I gave you. Nothing happens by accident in this life, you know.' A quick glance at his watch, an ironic bow in my direction, and he was gone.

The door closed behind him and I stood staring at its frosted glass and at my name, which appeared on it back to front. Standing there, I felt sort of back to front myself.

At last I managed to drag myself back to the office again. I left the door into the waiting-room ajar, as a sign for anyone who might come visiting to walk right in. Once I had sat down in the chair behind my desk I didn't propose to leave it again in a hurry.

I took my seat. The scene outside the windows had altered. The perspective was squint, with a strange lack of proportion: the houses on Fjellsiden had suddenly grown larger than those on the wharf and everything was covered in a curious red tint, as if the sun were about to set or as if this were the glow from an erupting volcano. Out along the wharf the cars were coughing blood.

I sat staring out of the windows until the daylight welled up and came streaming towards me. The redness disappeared and everything turned white. I leaned my head on the desk and was only awoken by the ringing of the telephone.

I lifted the receiver and listened but said nothing. I could hear the meter of a telephone booth ticking away somewhere or other.

We kept our silence, at both ends of the line. Then a metallic voice said, in the background, through a microphone:'Flight 92. . .' The receiver was quickly replaced.

Slowly, I nodded. It was Carsten Wiig, checking up on me. He was out at Flesland and wanted to make sure I was still alive. They didn't want another 'accident' on their consciences. Or, at least, they didn't want any more publicity than they'd had already.

I had taken the point. If they had wanted to kill me, they would have sent the man in the woollen hat on his own. I had never seen him before today and put my money on him being a recruit from the Oslo underworld. Carsten Wiig had come along, too, just to make sure I didn't receive rougher handling than was strictly necessary. Now he was calling me from the airport to check that I was still up and about. Later on he would be able to deliver a satisfactory report to Hagbart Helle.

But the question that was still bothering me was: Did this mean that they actually still had something to hide, even now, twenty-eight years later? Or was it something that had happened more recently than that – barely a month ago, in a flat on Skottegaten? Not to mention the Monday of the present week. Or were they simply trying to show how powerful they were?

Several hours had elapsed and the sleep I had had at my desk had done me good. The perspective outside was back to normal again. I was just strong enough to bend down, fetch the bottle and glass from the bottom drawer and pour myself a shot of clear, bright schnapps.

I sipped, cautiously. The warmth spread out slowly, like oil on water.

I worked my shoulders loose. The nape of my neck was still tender and the upper part of my arms felt stiff. My temples ached and a dull pain beat and throbbed somewhere down in the region of my stomach. But I felt better than I had done for several hours. And I had begun to think again.

I sat there with the glass in my hand. The day hobbled onwards through me on unsteady crutches. It doesn't take much to knock a man into the grave. I should have speculated on blonde lace, not blondes. A fancy goods department, not a private detective's office.

At about three-thirty I heard the door of my waiting-room open. The door was closed again and light, female footsteps crossed the floor in there before their owner appeared in the doorway.

It was a couple of seconds before I recognized her. Then I shoved my glass of schnapps aside as though it had no business to be there and said: 'This is something of a surprise.' But I had enough presence of mind to stand up as I said it.

It was the dentist's assistant from the office next-door. She had on a turquoise coat, she was blushing like a sunset and wasn't quite sure what to do with her hands. She was terribly young. She seemed to bring twilight and sunlight into my room – both at the same time.

I came out from behind my desk, still a little unsteady on my feet.

She said: 'You said – I ought to come and see – the view.' She looked up at me a little uncertainly. When I came too close, she moved aside and walked quickly towards the window. 'Hum,' she said.

I stayed where I was in the middle of the room. 'And what does "Hum" mean?'

She laughed. 'It means – you've got the same view as we have.'

'Did you really expect anything different?'

'You said. . .' She broke off and looked down at my glass. 'What's *that*?'

Feebly, I smiled. 'It looks like water.'

She gave me a mistrustful look. The afternoon light made her facial features even softer and put me in mind of another woman, who had also stood over there by the window. She was still as red in the cheeks as before and her eyes were dark, the eyebrows black and strongly marked. I wondered how old she was – nineteen, maybe twenty.

I went a little closer. She was smiling a little half-smile. I said: 'You're – you're the type all the men fall in love with, aren't you? You know it, everyone says so . . .'

She looked at me with large, shiny eyes.

I went on: 'Just like Ingrid Bergman in *Casablanca*.'

'Who?' She looked bewildered.

186

'Oh – a woman it was easy to. . .'

'I've seen it now,' she said. 'The view.' As she passed me, she gave me a radiant smile; she passed so close that I could smell her sweet, flower-like perfume. 'Thank you.'

When she reached the door she stopped and looked around. 'Why don't you put the light on?'

But she didn't wait for me to reply. I heard her footsteps as she walked out through the waiting room, the door closing behind her, and then her footsteps out in the corridor, the sound of the lift door, the noise of the machinery and then, finally, silence.

I looked at myself in the mirror. Then I picked up my glass of schnapps, raised it to my mirror-image, and said: 'Here's looking at you, kid.' I drained the glass in one mouthful and then went across and switched the light on.

41

September has days like golden honey, mornings of heavy sunlight outside open windows. September is a mature lover: with a rounded shapeliness and the warmth of late summer in her veins. The sunlight plays on colours that have not yet been visited by the cold winds of October. These are days to which to wake up slowly, days to take your time over.

I ate a leisurely breakfast by a window that was in need of being cleaned. The summer rain was covering the glass like pale stains. Outside, washing flapped cheerfully in the breeze. A radio was playing light music from Germany. On the crest of a roof some small birds were holding a council of war: was it time for a tour of the Mediterranean, or should they spend September in Norway? There are always choices, decisions to be made.

I tried Konrad Fanebust's number again. Yes, Mr Fanebust had arrived back. No, he was in a meeting at present. If I would be so good as to give my name, Mr Fanebust would call me back when he had time.

I told her I would be greatly obliged if I could have a word with him right now. I told her to tell him that Veum was on the line and that there was something very important that I wanted to talk to him about. *Very* important.

A few moments later the secretary came back, slightly out of breath. Yes, she had talked to Mr Fanebust and, if I would look in at two-thirty, he would do his best to put some time aside for me then.

I said: 'Haven't you read the latest doomsday bulletins? The world may have come to an end by two-thirty and, besides, this is an election year.'

She said: 'Haven't you seen the newspapers? Your appointment's at two-thirty. Goodbye.'

'Goodbye.'

On my way down to the office I bought the newspapers. SHIPPING CRISIS, one of the front-page headlines said. SHIPPING SUMMIT IN COPENHAGEN, said another. MORE BANKRUPTCIES ON THE WAY? was the lead story in a third paper. The journalism varied in quality but the overall gist was the same: Konrad Fanebust had more important things to contend with than fires that happened twenty-eight years ago and disappearances that had taken place ten years ago.

And there was also the fact that this was election year. This was the year when all the politicians had studied American campaign techniques. The left-wing candidates arrived at election meetings on green-painted bicycles, the Centrists planted bushes on patchy lawns, the Labour Party's prime ministerial candidate handed out red roses on the market square, while the Conservative candidate had himself filmed by Norwegian State Television engaged in thoroughly democratic conversation right in the middle of Stavanger Vegetable Market – a bit stiff-necked, perhaps, but none the worse for that. This was the year when all the politicians promised more than they had ever promised before and everyone knew that we were going to get less than we had ever got before. It was open season for old cynics. The optimists had all gone into hibernation.

From my office I telephoned Vegard Vadheim. I asked if they had had any response to the bulletin they put out. He said he wasn't able to answer that question but, no, they hadn't had any. I thanked him and hung up.

The morning passed quietly, like a discreet guest at a funeral. I could hear the chirring of the drill from the dentist's next door. I thought of the girl assistant fastening napkins around the necks of nervous patients, mixing amalgam and arranging appointments. If ever I got a decent fee perhaps I should make an appointment for myself some time. With her.

At twenty-five minutes past two I was in Konrad Fanebust's reception office. Out in the corridor I had passed two young, close-cropped, well-disciplined young men who were having a serious, low-voiced conversation – one of them was clutching a wad of documents and the other had an armful of Oslo dailies. As I walked past them they fell silent but even before I had entered the reception office their conversation had started up again.

As I came in, Fanebust's secretary looked up. She glanced at her watch. It was a gold one. She was wearing green today: green skirt, lichen-coloured cardigan set, amber ornament in the hollow of her throat.

'Mr Veum?' she said.

I smiled. 'You never forget a face, do you?'

She said: 'It's on my memo pad.'

'My face?'

'Your name.' She dialled Fanebust's number and told him I was there. Then she put down the receiver and said: 'You can go right in, Mr Veum.'

'Thanks a lot.'

I opened the door. Konrad Fanebust was sitting at his desk writing, just as he had been the last time I had called to see him.

He motioned me towards the same chair and went on writing, as if this were a repeat performance. It wasn't like one of those films where you remember the scenes being different from how they actually are. This was a faithful copy or, perhaps, a very good imitation.

He looked possibly a shade wearier than he had at our last encounter. Whether it was the crisis in the shipping industry or the night he had spent in Copenhagen that had made the difference, it was hard to tell. But the furrows on his brow were a little deeper and his smile a little more forced as he laid his fountain-pen aside, put the sheet of paper away in the same file as last time, folded his hands in front of him on the table, and said: 'Yes. . . Veum. You had something important to tell me. Does that mean – you haven't found him, have you?'

'Wulff?' I said, lightly.

'Yes.'

'No.' I watched him across the desk. 'Did you expect me to?'

'What do you mean – expect? You yourself said – that you thought there was a chance he might still be alive.'

'Yes. Perhaps I didn't know any better. The question meanwhile is: How much do *you* know, Fanebust?'

He went slightly redder in the face. Then he separated his hands and made a gesture to me, as if demanding that I explain myself. Then he placed his elbows on the desk top and positioned his fingers precisely against one another.

I said: 'You ought to have told me that you knew Docker Johan. Or Johan Olsen, to give him his real name.'

His face betrayed nothing. 'Johan Olsen?'

'You paid him a visit in January 1971. Not long before he disappeared.' I leaned forward. 'I have the testimony of reliable witnesses, Fanebust. It's no good trying to hide anything.'

He said: 'I have nothing to hide. Johan Olsen's not exactly an uncommon name and it may well be that I used to know someone called that. But what does this have to do with what we're talking about?'

'Tell me, first, how you came to know him. He hardly moved in your sort of social circles, did he?'

'No. But Johan was one of my comrades from the war days. He didn't quite belong to the inner circle Hjalmar Nymark was a part of but he was one of us all the same. He was a good comrade. A man you could rely on. But, unfortunately, he fell on hard times after the war. He wasn't the only one – there were a lot of men who had problems with their nerves, men who began to drink. Johan started to go downhill. I used to try and help him now and then, when I could manage it. I got him that job at the docks, for example, but in the end his life became too irregular and he went off the rails altogether. It may well be that I paid him a visit in January 1971. I can't remember. I didn't often go to his home but it did happen occasionally.'

'Why did you go to his home, when you did?'

He gave me a cold look. 'For old times' sake. If you've ever fought together with someone in the kind of conditions Johan and I had to put up with, you stay in touch. No matter how many problems it may cause from time to time.'

'And then he disappeared.'

'Yes, I remember.'

'You remember. Did you ever make any attempt to find him?'

'Did *I*? I left that to the police. What are you suggesting I ought to have done – hired a private detective?'

'Well. . .'

'People disappear, Veum. As you get older, people start to go. Some of them die. Others move to other towns, other countries, they slip out of sight and are gone. Others simply vanish into thin air. They may even still be living in the same town but you never see them again. It may be the result of chance, fate, call it what you will. When I think back on my life now – how many of my old war-time comrades are still left? You must bear in mind that we lived under terrible pressure for several years and it left its mark. A lot of us died too young.'

'But, even so, Johan Olsen's disappearance was different, wasn't it?'

'Yes,' he said, all of a sudden. 'Perhaps,' he added, quickly.

'Yes – perhaps?' I said, echoing his words, slowly and questioningly.

Konrad Fanebust sat thin, lean and shaken at his desk. His face was bony, his hair white. He was like the skeleton of a sculpture that had not yet acquired a substance and contours. His eyes had a distant, thoughtful expression. Then, suddenly he was back in the office again. 'Why are you bringing Johan Olsen into all this, anyway, Veum?'

I said: 'Someone was killed out at Sandviken on Monday evening. You must have read about it in the newspapers?'

He nodded, slowly.

'A woman was found dead out there. Olga Sørensen. She was the lover of Docker Johan, the woman he lived with. On the night she died a man was seen outside the apartment house she lived in. The man had a limp.'

He considered me, tensed and on his guard. 'You surely don't think. . . Does that mean that. . .'

I waited for the sequel but it didn't come. Then I said:

'What really happened to Johan Olsen back then, in 1971?'

'He. . .' He bit the words off.

'Yes?'

Konrad Fanebust carefully scrutinized me. His gaze slid over me, examining my pockets, my buttons, everything, all the way down to my shoes and back up again. Then he laid his hands flat on the desk-top, leaned slightly forward and said in a soft voice: 'He left the country. And I helped him.'

'I see.' I waited.

191

'Yes. That time in January I went to see him on a particular bit of business. He had come to me in despair about his personal situation, to put it in formal terms. He felt he was soaked in alcohol, bogged down in a miserable love affair, part of an impoverished, depressing environment. He wanted out – away – from it all. And he wanted to make a complete break with his past life, all his previous connections. He didn't want her to know about it, this woman – didn't want anyone to know about it. And he came to me and asked for help. An old wartime comrade. . . I could hardly have turned him down.'

'No?'

'No. Anyway, I had connections in other countries. Spain, Portugal – there were enough places. So I helped him – to get out of the country, bought him a ticket, arranged for somebody to meet him at the other end, gave him enough money to tide him over for the initial period.'

'A loan?'

'I would prefer to call it the repayment of a debt. A debt of honour. I owed him that money. I'd landed on my feet but he'd had to rough it down in the lower depths.'

'And what about later?'

'Later?'

'I mean, did you continue to see him?'

'No – that was part of the deal. The way *he* wanted it. All his previous links were to be severed. He was finished with Norway for good.'

'Almost as though he had died.'

'Yes. And there were plenty of people who thought he had. So his plan worked.'

'And you did all this – free of charge?'

'That's correct, I tell you! What chance could he possibly have had of paying me back?'

I fixed him with my gaze. We stared at each other. There was an almost imperceptible twitch at the corners of his eyes and I felt my own eyes narrow.

He broke the silence: 'Docker Johan had contacts among the hold-workers. He could easily have obtained a key to the padlock on the gate out there, on Nordnes.'

'Where on Nordnes?'

'The place where Harald Wulff was beaten to death. The tracks in the snow indicated that at least two people were involved in the murder.'

His eyes were hard and steady now and his mouth had become a taut, grey trampoline. His words came out like small, thick-set acrobats: 'Yes. Well. So what? He deserved it, didn't he?'

42

Konrad Fanebust had fought a lot of hard battles with tougher nuts than I could ever pretend to be and so he quickly recovered his calm. His voice was as low as ever as he said: 'Very well, I admit it. We put an end to Rat Poison between us, Johan Olsen and I.'

He opened a cigarette case, took a cigarette from it, and then offered me one, reflectively. I refused politely and he lit his cigarette. Then he leaned back heavily in his high-backed chair. The cigarette glowed in a double reflection from the doors of two of the glass-fronted book-cases. In a sense we were no longer alone. We were sitting together in pleasant company, the cigarettes had been passed round and one of us had a small confession he wished to make to the rest. And we were on 'thou' terms, now.

Konrad Fanebust said: 'I'll tell you the whole story, Veum – the way it happened. But this is the only time I'm going to tell it – I shall never repeat it again. If you should be so foolish as to attempt to pursue the matter further, you will be the one to suffer. This is purely for your information, as they say. It won't take long.'

'Go ahead, I'm all ears,' I said, shrugging my shoulders.

'As I told you on the last occasion we talked together: we *knew* that Harald Wulff was Rat Poison but we'd never been able to prove it. The years had gone by and old comrades had died but Harald Wulff was still a free man – alive and well, with not a stain on his conscience. And our bitterness at this fact just seemed to grow worse and worse with every day that passed. Rat Poison was a piece of unfinished business, if you know what I mean. During the war we had decided that weeding him out would have top priority and that, if ever we came across him after the war, we would take our revenge. But you know how it was. Peace came and we all seemed to get so – civilized, somehow. And Hjalmar was such a stickler for the rules. Without evidence it was no dice. We had to have tangible evidence. But where on earth were we going to get it? So . . .'

'Yes?'

'So I went to see Johan. I explained my plan to him. That we would take the law into our own hands and settle Rat Poison's hash once and for all. We would lure him to some out-of-the-way spot and give him what he deserved. And Johan agreed to do it. He was the one who suggested that place out on Nordnes because it was central and out-of-the-way at the same time and because – yes. . .' A curt bow in my direction. 'He had a key.'

'But how did you manage to get Wulff out there?'

He gave me a crooked smile. 'We made him an offer he couldn't refuse. 50,000 kroner for putting his old skills to practical use. We allowed him to think – it was Johan who got in touch with him – that he'd been recommended to us by old contacts and I had just enough knowledge of the Nazi underworld to be able to make the request sound credible. I knew he didn't have much money to play with, he was still working as an office messenger in those days, and – well, he fell for it.'

'And then what happened?'

He made a face. 'We did what we'd decided to do. I'd taken part in some pretty brutal killings during the war – brutal but necessary. In a sense we were back in those days again, down there behind the warehouses, face-to-face with our old arch-enemy. Johan kept an eye on him from behind and I walked out of the shadows and let him see my face. It was snowing a bit, light flakes. It was cold as hell and there was a biting wind from the sea. I could tell he'd recognized me. He tried to shout but I made a signal to Johan and he knocked him to the ground, from behind, with an iron bar.'

'And then you turned him into ground meat?'

'We didn't torture him, the way his colleagues had often tortured *our* lads, during the war. But I suppose we worked off some of our aggression on his body – after he was dead.'

'That doesn't sound very nice.'

'War is never very nice, Veum.'

'No, especially when it's fought a quarter of a century after the event.'

'It was still war as far as we were concerned, Veum. For us, it'll never really be over.'

'Okay. I won't pass judgement. I. . . But did you help Johan Olsen to get out of the country?'

'Yes. That was his precondition for agreeing to help me.'

'And you haven't heard from him since?'

'Not a word.'

'Who else have you told this to?'

'No one, Veum. You and I are the only people who know about it.' It almost sounded like a threat.

'And Johan Olsen,' I said.

'And Johan Olsen,' he said, nodding.

'But what on earth does all this have to do with Hjalmar Nymark? There are too many loose strands, Fanebust. And what about Olga Sørensen? What if Johan Olsen came back from exile? *He* had a limp, after all. Wouldn't he have wanted to look you up? Or Olga Sørensen?'

Konrad Fanebust said: 'I've told you this, Veum, because I honestly think you're barking up the wrong tree. At any rate, that business has no connection with Hjalmar Nymark. He was never involved, not at any stage. He had no idea of what we were doing. I think you've got to look at this case from a different angle – now that you can disregard what happened in 1971. Now you *know* what happened back then.'

'But why – why were you so insistent about asking me to try to find Harald Wulff? Why did you make it sound as though you thought he was still alive?'

'Listen Veum – I've been playing this game for a good many years now. I do that kind of thing automatically. The name of the game is conspiracy. That was the way we survived. You never miss a trick. And you did have the facts on your side. Hjalmar *did* die, in mysterious circumstances, and you might as well go chasing after Harald Wulff as after some other phantom. If you can find the person who killed Hjalmar – I'm still willing to pay your fee.'

I looked at him, steadily. 'I'm not sure I can accept that offer.'

'Why not?'

'It might look as though you were paying me to keep my mouth shut.'

'And who would ever get to know about it, apart from ourselves?'

'That's just it. I would know.'

He made no reply but merely gazed at me sourly from his chair behind the large desk.

I had nothing more to say. I had been given enough to digest as it was. One mystery had been cleared up but there were several more still waiting.

I said: 'Have you ever had any business dealings with Hagbart Helle?'

'Not that I know of, Veum,' he said, lightly. 'But in our profession . . . He owns a lot of fake companies, you know. It's hard to keep to the straight and narrow. I don't know if you've been reading what's in the newspapers. . . They're keeping an eye on us. We can't make too much of a fuss right now.'

'Have you ever run into a fellow called Carsten Wiig?'

'I can't say I have. Who is he?'

'A fellow who goes around making speeches over dead bodies that aren't quite dead yet.'

'Really. Well, if you'll excuse me, Veum. . .' He reached for the file. 'I have some paperwork to take care of. So - thank you for your visit - and good luck. But remember. . .'

'Yes?'

'Those things I told you just now – you never heard them. All right?'

'You can rely on me, Fanebust. Goodbye.'

'Goodbye.'

I heard the scratching of his fountain-pen before I had even closed the door behind me. He certainly didn't believe in wasting time. And his secretary didn't exactly believe in being extravagant with her smiles, either. They made a good pair.

43

I ate my evening meal in town. At the Chinese restaurant that looked on to the market square they served ample portions at reasonable prices and the oriental music that came over the speaker system was not so loud that you couldn't hear yourself think. And I had a lot to think about. I was beginning to glimpse the outlines of a pattern.

After I had eaten I walked quickly along to Wesenbergssmauet and rang the door-bell of the house in which Elise Blom lived. No one came to the door. That gave me two possible options. I didn't want to think about a third possibility. I tried the bingo hall first.

I climbed the steep flight of stairs and stood in the doorway, looking around. The atmosphere was the same as it had been on my previous visit: a concentrated, almost servile preoccupation with the numbers that rasped from the hoarse loudspeakers. It struck me, again, that it might be the lack of religious experience in society at large that was responsible for filling all these halls with people. Perhaps the rituals and number fetishism of bingo fulfilled some deep-seated primordial need in those who went in search of them. Perhaps the glittering window ads were the stained glass painting of our time, the eternally varying numbers a kind of Roman liturgy and the bingo hostesses the high priestesses of the late twentieth century.

Elise Blom wasn't there.

I went back down the stairs and out on to the street again.

I walked in at the entrance to the restaurant we had visited. The big, hefty doorman was in the process of escorting outside a woman who was in the last stages of intoxication. They were halfway down the stairs and I stood watching them.

The doorman was attired in one of those dirty-green uniforms which they tend to wear and which make them look like some kind of private police force. The woman was wearing a cheap, bluish-pink dress with a peculiar cape-like garment draped over her shoulders. She had on a dark-coloured wig but in her intoxicated state it had fallen slightly askew and a few strands of her own hair stuck out at the nape of her neck. Her mouth was lipsticked and blurry, and she was using it in order to fire off some very juicy insults at the unruffled doorman. When they had only another couple of stairs to go, she suddenly tore herself free of him managed the last steps by herself and tumbled headlong in the direction of the door. I quickly stepped forward and caught her.

She landed in my arms like a sack of potatoes and my fingers sank right into her, as if some of the potatoes hadn't survived their time in storage.

As she hung there in my arms, her gaze slowly began to focus. She smelled strongly of beer and it took her quite a while before she recognized me. It was Elise Blom.

The doorman was by now already on his way back up the stairs, as though he had assumed that from now on I would take responsibility for her. He didn't even look back.

After she had finally got her eyes in focus, she tried to do the same for her voice. The blurry face with its angular profile bore witness to an increasing degree of recognition and I could feel her trying to get a proper foothold again, so as not to have to depend on me in order to stay upright. Her voice came haltingly up from the depths: 'Veum?'

I nodded.

'You bastard!'

'That sounded as though it came straight from the heart.'

Her mouth grew twisted. 'It came straight from the asshole.'

'That's what I meant. That's where some people keep their hearts.'

She looked up at me, insinuatingly. 'What is it you want now? Haven't you done enough damage already? Telling all that – saying all those filthy things about Harald. They were all lies, all those things you said he had done during the war. He wasn't like that.'

'Perhaps not,' I said. 'Actually, there was something I wanted to ask you about. You're going to need help if you're ever going to get home, anyway. Let's make a deal. I'll take you home and on the way you can answer a few questions.'

She gave me a suspicious look. 'What sort of questions?'

'Oh, ones about money.'

She looked even more suspicious. 'Money? I haven't got any money.'

'No,' I said lightly, opening the door to the street. 'But in 1955. . .'

She grabbed my arm and walked stiffly out on to the pavement beside me.

'In 1955 you had money.'

'How do you know?'

'You bought a house. You went straight from being a secretarial assistant to being a houseowner, all in one step. How ever did you manage it?'

'How ever did you manage it?' she said, mimicking me, and headed off on her own for the nearest corner. She had to support herself against the wall and, having taken a few steps, she stood still. Her head swung round, her eyes swivelled up and down. She clearly felt dizzy and I went right up to her with my arm ready to support her. She seized me by the elbow and started to drag me along with her.

'And your colleague, Miss Pedersen. She was suddenly able to afford to settle down in Spain. Even before she was eligible for a pension.'

She continued her way along the street but she was clinging to my arm now. We turned the corner and headed towards the market square. By now her eyes had grown a little clearer. It had done her good to get out into the fresh air. 'She'd been saving,' she said, abruptly.

'All that amount?'

She made no reply. We crossed Strandgaten and, when we came to the corner of Strandkaien, we were greeted by a refreshing breath of wind. I felt the hair lift from my head, while her wig lay on top of hers like a creature that had been run over.

The market square was wet – flushed clean. Now and then we found reflections of ourselves in puddles: two strange, distorted figures seen from a frog's-eye angle.

I said: 'Two secretaries, both employed by a firm that burned to the ground, some people said because the management took no action after warnings they had received from the works foreman that something was wrong. Warnings which, by his own testimony, he delivered to the office – and which might very easily have been overheard by Miss Pedersen and by yourself. And by Harald Wulff. But the works foreman died in the blaze and none of you were willing to confirm that he'd said anything. But at least two of you came out of it with unexpected financial gain – not to mention Hellebust himself.'

Slowly, she turned her head and looked at me. 'Hellebust was co-signatory for a loan when I bought the house after a – I inherited it.'

I stared back at her, hard. Her gaze shifted away. It might have been the alcohol. Or it might have been because she was lying.

'Did Harald Wulff have money, perhaps?' I said. 'From the war days?'

She made no reply.

We continued our way in silence. She looked gloomy. We crossed the wharf and Rosencrantzgaten and arrived at Øvregaten. Her face had acquired a certain difficult-to-define expression, as though she had just taken a decision.

As we were walking up the lane, and were on the point of arriving outside her house, she freed herself from my arm and supported herself with her back against the wall. She tilted her head back and eyed me heavily, with a kind of ersatz sensuality. If she were thinking of seducing me, she had chosen the wrong wig and the wrong day. But more likely all she was after was something to lean against. She said: 'If you'll come inside, I'll show you. . . papers. I have documents to prove it.'

'Okay.' I refrained from telling her that a document stating that

Hellebust really had been co-signatory for her loan would not necessarily speak in her favour. But it might be interesting to see her papers, all the same.

She opened her handbag – which, until now, had lived a separate life of its own on her wrist – and spent a good few minutes fumbling for her key. When at last she found it, she spent another good few minutes endeavouring to find the keyhole.

Patiently, I waited.

At last she managed to get the door open. I followed her quickly inside, in case she changed her mind or forgot that I was there.

We entered a dark, sombre stairway. She searched around for the light switch but couldn't find it; then she led the way upstairs in the darkness. The stairway ended in a narrow landing and she opened an old-fashioned-looking door into the rooms that lay on the first floor. We entered something that had once been a hallway; brown and dark. An old cupboard stood squeezed into a corner and a dusty embroidered picture of a house with a Norwegian flag flying above it hung on the wall directly opposite us.

'We'll go into the living-room,' said Elise Blom, opening another door. It hadn't been oiled for many a year. Its creaking was like the sound old branches make in a high wind.

The living-room was plain and spartan. A few green pot plants stood in the windows, which were screened by grey-white net curtains. On a writing desk stood an old memento from a trip to Germany: a miniature beer keg, with six little tankards suspended from hooks along its rim. I wouldn't have been surprised to see the words 'Greetings from Deutschland' on it. There were some old family portraits on the wall above the writing desk but I didn't recognize any of the faces.

Next to the writing desk, in the corner, there was an old TV set and, on the other side of the room, there was an old-fashioned padded sofa covered in greyish green matrial, with a couple of Hardanger pattern cushions on it. In front of the sofa stood a low coffee-table, underneath which lay some old newspapers. I could see the name of one of them: *Land og Folk*.

Elise Blom had gone nearly all the way over to the window. She could stand up without any help now but she was swaying slightly and her gaze kept roving around helplessly as before, as though she were looking for something, or someone.

I followed her gaze round . . .

A large doorway in one of the walls led through to a room in the interior of the flat. In the middle of its floor stood a straight-legged dining table, around which six high-backed chairs were placed. At the far end of the table a man was sitting with his face turned towards us. He was resting his elbows on the table-top; his powerful hands were positioned together and they held a large pistol. The pistol was pointing straight at me and, even though the only photographs of him I had seen were thirty-five years old, I had no difficulty in recognizing him.

It was Harald Wulff.

44

It was one of those moments in life when everything seems to fall into place. At the same time, everything stood still. I had a strong sense of unreality.

Elise Blom had produced a cigarette. With shaking hands, she placed it between her lips and lit it. She stood silhouetted against the window, her shoulders unnaturally hunched, like a puppet whose strings have got tangled.

Harald Wulff's hands weren't shaking. He was holding the pistol steadily. I stood in a frozen posture, motionless. With the exception of the moment when Elise Blom lit the cigarette, we formed a rigid – and improbable – triangle.

I was uncomfortably aware that what he was holding appeared to be a Luger: the only link between the man Harald Wulff and the unknown murderer who had gone by the name of Rat Poison. When they dug the bullets out of my body they'd be able to put them in an envelope and stick a label on it marked 'The Conclusive Evidence'. But I wouldn't be around when they did it.

As he spoke, Harald Wulff never took his eyes off me for one second. But it wasn't me he was speaking to. 'Who in God's name is this, Elise?' he growled in a rough, hoarse old man's voice that had said its piece a good many decades ago.

As he spoke, I kept a steady eye on him. I would have recognized him in a crowd of thousands. There was the same horsey face with the same large features, the hair smoothed back in exactly the same manner as in the photograph I had in my inside pocket. The only different thing about that hair now was that it had turned completely grey – wolf-grey. The furrows on his face were deeper, the lines around his mouth even more bitter and his skin was pale and sallow, like that of a long-term prisoner. And that was precisely what he had been, these past ten years. How old was he now? I made a quick calculation and concluded that the answer was sixty-seven. He had reached retirement age. For the moment, at least, it didn't look as though I was going to get that far.

It wasn't only Elise Blom's hands that were shaking – her voice wasn't very steady, either, as she stammered: 'H-he's th-th-at pr-pr-private detective I t-told you ab-about. . .'

His two eyes grew colder above the third which he was holding in his hands.

'A private detective?' he spat. I noticed that he rolled his r's. For a moment his eyes slid sideways, in a sceptical glance at Elise Blom. When he looked back at me, I sensed something new, even darker, in his gaze. It was fear, bottomless fear, and it made a cold shiver pass through me. Nothing is more deadly than a frightened beast of prey.

Suddenly Elise Blom screamed: 'I did it for your sake, Harald! You've got to . . .' – And then it came, so softly that I could only just hear it – 'see a doctor.'

The dark fear expanded and spread across his face to his dead mouth, the pallid grey skin under his eyes, the dry flaps of tissue on the side of his neck. The hands that held the pistol shook ever so slightly and I saw that Harald Wulff was now a mere shadow of what he must once have been.

I had no difficulty in imagining him as a young lad up on a small farm in the district of Ulven, among the gloomiest forests of the Bergen area, where the spruce trees are so tall and sombre you have to be a puritan to be able to live among them. I could see him in a pair of wide, grey trousers, supported with braces over a bare chest and shoulders, as he swung his long-handled scythe back and forth, back and forth. His powerful torso glistened with sweat and the fact that he had a slight limp in one of his legs was unimportant: it almost seemed natural out there on the grassy slope. His forelock was long and untidy but his hair was cut short at the back of his neck and round his ears. Very occasionally he would stop his scything and stand still, staring up at the blue-and-white summer sky that hung like an enticing promise above the dark crests of the forests of Ulven. Then he would go on scything again.

I had no trouble either in picturing him later on, after he had moved to town and overnight acquired a brown shirt, new friends with fresh, red cheeks, cheerful songs to sing and one real aim in life: to defend his country against the Bolsheviks and stem the tide of world Communism. There was something stooped about the whole appearance of this man on the other side of the table that accentuated the element of craftiness in him. You could picture him making his bleak rendezvous with representatives of the occupying forces during the war. You could picture him with the collar of his overcoat turned up, hidden safely away inside some gate-lodge or far up on the top floor of a house in some remote lane, while the Gestapo made their nightly excursions in accordance with the tips and advice he had given them. And you could picture him cunningly and dexterously working out the details of what would later come to be classified as 'accidents'.

There he sat, in a mausoleum to his own faith. Behind him, on the wall above the chest-of-drawers, hung two large photographs – one of

Adolf Hitler and the other of Vidkun Quisling. Both were in uniform. On the chest-of-drawers stood two three-pronged candelabra containing tall candles and forming a veritable altar before the two leading lights in his life, the two that had led him down the long, crooked road to a semi-dark room, a woman in despair and a confrontation with a man he had never seen before.

The room in which he sat was brown in tone: the wallpaper was old and grimy, the carpet worn and faded, the lacquer on the old dining table streaked and scarred. The face of Harald Wulff belonged in the frame of that room, as though he himself were no more alive than the two men in the photographs.

'You're a damned idiot, Elise. Now you've gone and ruined everything.'

His voice had a hollow, menacing quality that promised no good, either for her or for me.

I said – and they were the first words I had managed to get out so far: '*What's* the matter with you, Wulff?'

A gleam came to his eyes. 'So you know who I am?' His gaze promised no good, either.

She broke in: 'He must see a doctor. I've been trying to tell him for ages that he mustn't go on like this – he. . .' The tears were streaming down her cheeks now and she never once took her eyes off his face. 'He's bleeding internally. There's blood coming out of him. He's being eaten away, slowly, but because – because once he'd – decided to – to. . .'

'To go underground?' I said.

Her lips grew narrow.

'Yes,' she sobbed. 'He couldn't come out again after that.'

'They'd have wanted to know my name. Bloody Communist bureaucracy. The social security people would have found out who I was. But I have no name. I'm dead.'

I said: 'Maybe not quite. Not yet.' And as though it were only now that it had really dawned on me, I said: 'So you weren't killed in 1971.'

Everything was suddenly quiet. Elise Blom stood with her hands in front of her face, weeping in low, stifled sobs. I shuffled the pack and attempted to let the cards tell the story once again. When I began to speak, it was about 1953.

'It was all that sudden money that put me on the track.'

'What money?' he snarled, almost against his will.

'In 1953 – and the years that followed. The money that made it possible for Elise Blom to buy this house. And the money that made it possible for her colleague, Miss Pedersen, to settle down in Spain in a kind of premature retirement. Apart from you, Wulff, Holger Karlsen – who later died, and Hagbart Hellebust – who was least likely to give the game away, there was no one else present when those things were said.'

'When what things were said?' asked Wulff.

Elise Blom had stopped crying. Her hands had come down to the corners of her mouth and underlip. She was staring at me with big, tear-filled eyes.

Cautiously, I shifted my weight from one leg to the other. 'The things Holger Karlsen said when he came to complain about the lack of proper maintenance at the paintworks and reported the signs of a leak in the production hall.'

They stared at me in silence. It was no longer they who were the ghosts. Now it was my turn. It was as though Holger Karlsen himself were standing there, as large as life.

'That's right, isn't it? And not long after that there was the explosion. You'd been through rough times before, Wulff, and you knew what sort of pressure you would be able to put on Hellebust if you were lucky. You performed a heroic rescue feat during the fire but you saw to it that Holger Karlsen didn't get out alive. Afterwards, when the fire was over and Hellebust got back from Oslo, you'd be able to present him with the bill. You'd be able to reckon on having an easy mind. But you needed two assistants. One of them you had already, in the person of Elise Blom; and then there was Miss Pedersen: she was half blind with the kind of loyalty secretaries used to feel towards their bosses. Or maybe she was just looking forward to the money she, too, would get. The only part of the story I don't quite understand is the relationship between *you* two. You were a young, pretty girl in those days,' I said, turning to Elise Blom and then looking back at him again, 'and you were a middle-aged ex-con who'd been found guilty of treachery.'

Elise Blom gave a faint toss of her head. The red blotches on her face were turning pale and there was ice underneath them. As she looked at him, there was a strange tenderness in her voice. 'I loved him then. I would have done anything for him.' After a short pause, she added: 'Later on it was as if we grew together, in the way I think all loving couples do. The warmth of our affection turned into our everyday life together and our secrets became bitter bonds that united us.'

'And nothing binds two people together more securely than dark secrets concerning crimes they were both accomplices in,' I said. 'After those initial years, when you both kept quiet about what you'd done, you were bound together for good. You were fettered to him, Elise, and if you had wanted to be free you'd have had to go to prison, too. That is, if anyone would have believed you after all that time. If anyone could have proved anything.'

Suddenly Harald Wulff smiled – a broad, unpleasant smile that showed his large, yellow teeth. 'No, because no one could ever prove anything. And no one will ever be able to prove anything. There's been no one in this house these past ten years apart from . . . her and me. I could shoot you and put your body in a trunk in the attic and you would lie there and rot for years, before anyone found you, and no one would ever be able to prove anything.'

'But you'll soon be dead yourself,' I said. 'If you're bleeding inside, you haven't long to live – you must get help. Don't you see? It isn't worth it. You'd do better to give yourself up and get the treatment you need. You're so old and sick now that . . . No one will . . .'

'Ha! Don't make me laugh! Those who fought on our side during the war will never be allowed to get away. They'll follow us to our graves, if necessary. After we're dead they'll slander our names. The Führer – what sort of reputation did he leave behind him? And those who still follow his ideas today – how are they treated – by the press or by the majority of people, for that matter? What did you say your name was, again?' he said.

'Veum,' Elise Blom told him.

'Varg Veum,' I said, putting the emphasis on my first name.

He gave a slight nod. The name didn't mean anything to him but perhaps he just liked to know the names of the people he killed.

I said: 'You know the name they gave you during the war. . .'

He stared at me, coldly.

'Rat Poison,' I said.

He bared his teeth again. 'They deserved all they got.'

'But Holger Karlsen. . .'

'Holger Karlsen was a bloody Bolshevik!' he barked, suddenly. 'A scheming whiner who was forever complaining about working conditions merely so that he and the other union bosses could stick another feather in their caps – and get the work force out of doing any work, on full pay. Do you realize what it would have cost the company to close down the production hall and carry out a complete check? Hellebust said we should wait until the summer holidays and do it then and he asked me to keep an eye on Karlsen in the meanwhile and let him know if anything happened.'

'You mean it didn't cost you anything to kill him?'

'I didn't kill him. The roof fell in.'

I took two steps towards him and he shouted: 'Stop!' The pistol swung upwards and pointed straight at my face. 'Don't move! I'll shoot you down like a dog, Veum.' His face was wild and raw and brutal, and I had no doubt that he meant what he said.

I raised my hands in a propitiatory gesture and took two long strides backwards. 'I didn't mean to . . .' Then I stood still, with my head bowed, like a schoolboy before a stern headmaster. 'But I've spoken to someone who was in the production hall on the day the accident happened . . . And I know you met Holger Karlsen outside. Nobody saw him alive again after that. There can only be one explanation for that, Wulff.'

He snarled contemptuously at me. 'And who have you been talking to, may I ask? That drunken pig Osvold? Bombsite? How long do you think he'd hold out in court?'

'We could try. . .'

'No, we damn well couldn't because we're never going to court, you and I, Veum. The court's right here in this room, Veum, and this is the judge. . .' He nodded at the pistol. It looked like a stern sort of judge and I was conducting my own defence.

I transferred my gaze to Elise Blom. 'Talk to him,' I said. 'Make him see reason. What's wrong with him – cancer?'

Wide-eyed, she stared from me to him, and nodded briefly. 'I've been trying, ever since. . . It started nearly eight months ago, with constipation and diarrhoea, and now he's in pain, too, and he's bleeding. I find traces of the blood when I'm making the bed or doing the cleaning, and I find them in his clothes. He's dying, I know it. I thought *you* would – that he'd listen to you – that, once he realized he'd been found out, that the game was up, he'd be willing to come in out of the cold. They won't do anything to him, will they? When they find out who he is?' She looked at me with beseeching eyes.

Involuntarily, I found myself looking back at Wulff again, since it was him we were talking about.

He had altered his posture. He was leaning further forward now, as though a sudden attack of abdominal pain had made him double up and he was supporting himself against the edge of the table. A light, sickly film of sweat had appeared on the yellowish skin of his face and I could see his knuckles turning white as they gripped the heavy pistol. A bitter grimace spread like an extension of his mouth outwards to his jaws and his eyes had taken on a dazed, befuddled look. But the pistol was still pointing steadily at me and its muzzle was still as dark as ever.

'But in 1971,' I began.

'Silence!' his voice hacked. 'No more chatter now. I don't – want it.' For a second, his voice broke. 'I'll tell you about the fire. It wasn't how you think it was. It's true that Hellebust didn't pay any heed to the warnings. He was after the insurance money but, of course, he thought his employees would be able to get out alive. All of them except. . .'

'Holger Karlsen.'

'I remember when the explosion happened. . . I was convinced that everyone in there must be dead but I was compelled to go in, I *had* to find out what had happened to Holger Karlsen. And it's just as well I did.'

'Otherwise he'd have got out alive?'

'Otherwise he would. . .' He broke off, baring his teeth, but now it was from pain rather than from contempt. Softly he groaned: 'Damn it to hell!'

'Don't you realize that you've got to see a doctor?' I burst out.

'Harald!' said Elise Blom, moving closer to him.

He stared at her wildly. 'Stay where you are! I'll shoot you, Elise.'

207

The pistol swung towards her and I shifted the weight of my legs but then the muzzle was directed back at me again. I stayed where I was. Elise Blom sank to the floor on her knees and hid her face in her hands. At the back of her neck I could clearly see the dividing line between her skin and the wig. The fasteners on her dress had been torn loose and her neck looked sickly and vulnerable. But nobody stroked her hair. Nobody tried to comfort her.

I watched Harald Wulff. He was sitting like a coiled spring now, supported on a column of pain and despair, in which the black, oily glinting pistol was the only fixed point.

My legs were sore and I was beginning to wonder how long I was going to be able to stay upright myself. The tension in my body had spread downwards and my muscles were quivering. I had pain in my thighs and abdomen and the fear of death was churning in my stomach like a restless drumbeat. Blindly, I nodded in the direction of the two photographs on the wall behind him, and said: 'Have you managed to preserve your political beliefs all these years?'

'There are more of us than you think, Veum. We're coming to life again now and we have the young on our side. The newspapers try to hush it up but there are more and more of us – in Germany, Norway, even England.'

'The same old enemy?' I asked, faintly. 'The stronghold of democracy?'

'*We* are the true democrats, Veum!' he said, flaring up suddenly. 'We are the true future, the ones who will purify mankind and regenerate it. There's far too much dirt and squalor now, too much racial mixing and movement across national frontiers. But the men of the future will be pure and white – reborn.'

'In a purifying bath of blood and fire?'

'A liberating, purifying bath of iron. We shall cut them down, the dwarves and the Bolsheviks, the Jews and the blacks. All the unworthy and impure must go. . .'

For a moment, his eyes were glassy and far away, and I managed to shift my weight once more. Then his gaze suddenly came down again and the three eyes stared at me, the cold black one out in front and the two feverishly burning ones above it.

'Perhaps you're a Jew, Veum?'

'Do I look like one?'

'Or a Bolshevik?'

I pulled myself together, forcing both him and myself back to reality again. 'But in 1971, what was. . .'

'Silence, I said!' The pistol quivered. 'I said I would tell you about the fire. Afterwards it all went as I had thought it would. Hellebust gave us what we had asked for. I didn't exactly have a very good record, after all, and we were agreed that it would be a bad idea to give *me* control of the money. But Elise and I were already living together by that time and I was content to live off her. It's really true that she didn't know anything. She wasn't there when Holger Karlsen came with his complaints. Hellebust, Miss Pedersen and I were the only people present. And Hellebust had Miss Pedersen eating out of his hand. Elise was well aware that something was amiss but she put her mind at rest by telling herself it was something to do with things Hellebust and I had become involved with during the war. She really took me for what I *was*, Veum – not a traitor, as you called me, but a martyr to the cause, to the future.'

'A martyr to the future,' I repeated, tonelessly.

'And why do you think I'm telling you all this Veum?' His yellow teeth came into view again. 'Eh?'

I shrugged my shoulders and made a gesture of helplessness.

He strengthened his grip on the pistol. 'I like to watch men die, Veum.' After a tense, almost painful pause, he said: 'But most of all I like to see their fear *before* they die. Have *you* prepared yourself, Veum? Do you believe in anything? Do you know whether you'll go to heaven or hell, when death swallows you up as it's going to in a moment?'

'Yes,' I answered. 'I know where I'm going.'

'And where's that?' he asked contemptuously.

'Where you'll never make it, Wulff. And further than that. For when you've bled dry, I'll go downstairs and out on to the street.' I waved one arm in the direction of the window. 'And I'll be alive.'

'That's what you think!' he barked.

'That's what I know!' I said, and dived to one side. But I never got as far as the window. I tripped on a rag rug and stumbled blindly against the wall, felt my knees give way and heard the violent report of a shot behind me. The powerful bullet struck the wall where I had been standing and there was a sound of shattering plaster. Then there was another report and I curled up in a foetal position as a last protection against death, waiting for the next shot – the last.

But there weren't any more shots. All I heard was Elise Blom's low, squeaky sobbing and the thunderous, ear-splitting silence that follows the sound of a shot in a small room.

After a while I got up and looked around me with new, fresh eyes, as though I had risen from the dead.

The second time Harald Wulff had fired, he had pointed the muzzle of the pistol into his own mouth and pulled the trigger. The shot had sprayed a greyish-red flower of blood and brain tissue on the wall behind him, in the space between the portraits of Adolf Hitler and Vidkun Quisling.

45

I left it to Elise Blom to call the police or whoever else she felt like calling now. I myself left the house feeling as though I had a hangover. The two shots were still ringing in my ears and I was hardly aware of where I was going.

Harald Wulff was dead. He had told me nothing about Hjalmar Nymark or about any of the other things I had wanted to know. But now he didn't need to tell me. Now I knew the answers myself.

Down on Strandkaien there is one of those draughty, red telephone booths that one finds at most of the quayside terminals in West Norway. When you arrive in from the sea you can dial the numbers of people who have long forgotten your existence and listen to the engaged tone while the gale snatches at your trouser legs.

I stepped into the phone booth, inserted a coin in the slot and dialled Konrad Fanebust's home telephone number. The woman who answered the phone said Fanebust wasn't in.

'Can you tell me where he is?' I asked.

'There's a reception on at the town hall.'

I thanked her and hung up.

A few minutes later I was standing outside the town hall complex, that fortress of glass and concrete that has been raised as a monument to the megalomania of the 1970s. In the ground-floor inquiry office I found out where the reception was.

I took the lift up to the top floor – the thirteenth – and followed the sound of voices into the large reception room.

The room was approximately half full. People were dotted about in uneven groupings around a long table of smorgasbord. The gathering was made up of top people who were more or less in the news. I glimpsed at least two shipowners who were currently threatened with bankruptcy and criminal investigation, as well as several other representatives of the shipping and business communities. Two long-retired mayors had formed a little group of their own and were sunning themselves in each other's faded glory, while a Left Socialist politician helped himself liberally to the cold cuts. A well-known female member of the Labour Party was laughing, a long, rippling laughter that seemed never to end, while a town council member of the Christian Democratic Party who consistently voted against all applications for liquor licences was well into his fourth glass of rosé, if the glitter in his eyes was anything to go by. Over in one corner of the room stood the present mayor, slim and suntanned, looking as though he spent his office hours in a solarium; he was posing for press photographs with a group of short, good-natured Asiatics. I assumed they were the members of a visiting trade delegation and were the pretext for the gathering.

Konrad Fanebust was standing slightly apart from everyone else, helping himself from a plate with a long, two-pronged serving fork. I walked straight through the room in his direction and he looked up. His face betrayed nothing except mild surprise but his arm stopped in its motion and he stood still, holding the fork in one hand; a single slice of roast beef hung from one of its prongs.

I wasn't really feeling strong enough to be diplomatic and so I blurted straight out: 'It's not true that Harald Wulff was killed.'

'Really?' He grew paler by degrees. 'Have you found him?'

'Yes.' I stared him steadily in the eye and his gaze slid sideways, somewhere out across my shoulder.

'But Docker Johan – Johan Olsen – is dead. He was the man killed in 1971 and not Harald Wulff. And you and Wulff murdered him together.'

He had grown even paler. 'Listen, Veum, if you've come here. . .'

'Well, I haven't come here to eat roast beef, if that's what you mean. The real heart of this case isn't the fire of 1953 at all but what happened nearly twenty years later, in 1971 and 1972.'

'1972?'

'Most of the truth about the fire on Fjøsangerveien was evident all along; it was just impossible to prove anything, that's all. But now I've got Harald Wulff's own personal confession, and . . .'

'He confessed?' He looked at me in disbelief.

Without replying, I went on. 'The first thing I had to ask myself was: who stood to gain by Hjalmar Nymark's murder – for he *was* murdered, in cold blood. So who was it? Not Hagbart Helle, who had a huge fortune abroad to fall back on. Not Harald Wulff, either, if he were still alive – he'd been through the mill before and he knew there wasn't a shred of evidence. And not you, who were in charge of the investigation in those days, even though there would be an ever-so-tiny blot on the record if anyone were ever to come along and prove what you were unable to prove in 1953. But who cares about prestige that's thirty years old?'

Konrad Fanebust made a measured bow in the direction of a politician who was passing with a plate of fish *hors d'oeuvres*. The expression on his face was an easy one to read; he didn't want anyone joining in this conversation. There was something rearing and rampant about him as he stood there, stiff and straight-backed, with the motionless fork in one hand and the empty plate in the other.

I said:'But both Hjalmar Nymark and you were convinced that Harald Wulff really *was* Rat Poison, especially after the Peacock fire. Perhaps things were happening over which you had no control, or perhaps you had something to hide. At any rate, you wanted rid of your partner.'

'Wiger? But he . . .'

'But he died in a fire, didn't he? That was an accident, too, I suppose? Perhaps someone might have started to take a closer look at that case, too, if it were to have been established that there was a clear connection between Konrad Fanebust and Harald Wulff as late as 1971.'

'There is no such connection,' he said, faintly.

'Oh no? I got the proof of it this evening – and through our conversation of earlier today. You told me then that Harald Wulff really was dead but a few hours later I found myself face-to-face with him. So it *wasn't* Wulff who was killed in 1971 but Docker Johan, your old wartime comrade. An old friendship meant nothing when it was a question of securing your position. You yourself had noticed the resemblance – both with regard to physique and to the fact that they both had a limp – between Wulff and Docker Johan. He wasn't worth very much, was he?'

He was as grey as a corpse now, with a pair of excited red spots high up on his cheeks. 'You mean you think that I . . .'

'You used Rat Poison in order to get rid of your business partner. You bought him and thereby crossed the border between what had once been his ideals and your own.'

'This is utter nonsense,Veum!'

'Is it? Let's go and take a look at the reports on *that* fire, too. Let's do it together with the police. Against the background of what we now know to be true.'

'Listen . . .'

'For why else should you have tried to make me believe that you and Docker Johan killed Harald Wulff in 1971. You once fought a heroic battle against Nazism, Fanebust, but it looks now as though your fight was in vain. Nazism's still alive. But the really dangerous form of Nazism today isn't the one that's represented by young lads in Home Guard uniforms or by old Nazi Party nostalgists. The really dangerous form of Nazism is the one that finds its expression in the contempt for human beings that's shown by you and by those who think like you. It merely calls itself by another name.' My voice was shaking now. 'In the face of contempt like that, human lives don't matter. Not Hjalmar Nymark's, not Docker Johan's, and not Olga Sørensen's.'

'I can't find the . . .' He cut his sentence short. 'The mayor's about to give a speech.'

I spoke more softly. 'I didn't come here to listen to the mayor. You received a visit from Hjalmar Nymark and realized he was on the trail of something in connection with what happened in 1971: namely, the link no one had noticed before, the link between Harald Wulff's so-called death and Docker Johan's disappearance. You knew that if what had happened then were to be brought into the open it would have disastrous consequences for you. And so you set to work. First, you tried to kill Nymark by running him over and failed. But, the second time, you were more lucky.'

'I didn't kill him! I asked him. . .' He bit his lip and fell silent.

'You asked him to drop the investigation, and then. . .'

'He sat up in bed, raised himself violently erect and said he understood everything – and then he clutched at his heart. . . I couldn't believe it. . . I thought he'd had a heart attack.'

'Medical help could have saved him. And you took the cardboard box that contained all his material with you. I call that murder, Fanebust.'

'But you're not a lawyer, Veum. And, anyway, I had no idea where Harald Wulff was! For all I knew he might very well have been dead. I told you, didn't I, that I'd pay you if ever you found him.'

'Conspiracy, wasn't that what you called it? That was just what you were afraid of: that I'd find him for you. Because you'd lost track of him after that job he'd done for you in 1972. . .'

He was beginning to lose his grip now. 'Did he confess to that, too?'

I lied: 'Yes.' And took a chance: 'Because that was really when you paid him the 50,000, wasn't it?'

His face had lost the last vestige of an outline now and he knew he had come to the end of his tether. Now there was only the judge waiting for him. He said: 'I suppose so. . .'

'But Olga Sørensen was dangerous,too, because she was the only person who could still connect you with Docker Johan in 1971, *before* his disappearance. So you killed her, too, without realizing that she'd told people about that connection long ago. I knew about it already, so you killed her to no purpose. And now here we are, just the two of us.'

In the room behind us the mayor was droning on in a strong Bergen accent with a voice as inflectionless as that of a computer. There wasn't much variation in Konrad Fanebust's voice, either, as he said: 'Was there anything else, Veum?'

I shrugged. 'No, not for now. The police will have to come up with the final explanation. We're going to see them now.'

'Wouldn't you like to have something to eat first?'

For a moment I took my eyes off him and gazed down at the table of food. That gave him the opening he needed and with violent force he stuck the sharp serving fork into my stomach. I bent forward and seized the round handle with both hands. The pain was sudden and acute. I lost my balance and fell to my knees. I could feel my fingers getting wet and when I looked down there was blood on them.

The room spun around me and the last thing I saw before I passed

213

out was Konrad Fanebust making a dash for the exit on to the terrace where the mayor usually took his guests to show them the view of his town. And I saw what I suppose I ought to have seen a long time ago. The ugly leg fracture he had sustained during the war had left its mark. He had a clearly perceptible limp in his left leg.

People who had been passing down in the street outside said afterwards that he had looked like a great bird as he had thrown himself over. As for myself, I had to stay in hospital for three weeks before I was allowed to go home.

QUARTET  QRIME

MEL ARRIGHI
Alter Ego

MEG ELIZABETH ATKINS
Palimpsest

DAVID CARKEET
Double Negative

ANTHEA COHEN
Angel Without Mercy
Angel of Vengeance
Angel of Death
Fallen Angel
Guardian Angel
Hell's Angel

RUTH DUDLEY EDWARDS
Corridors of Death
The St Valentine's Day Murders

SHIRLEY ESKAPA
Blood Fugue

DAVID E. FISHER
The Man You Sleep With
Variation on a Theme

ALAN FURST
The Paris Drop
The Caribbean Account
Shadow Trade

JOHN GREENWOOD
Murder, Mr Mosley
Mosley by Moonlight
Mosley Went to Mow

ELLA GRIFFITHS
Murder on Page Three

RAY HARRISON
French Ordinary Murder
Death of an Honourable Member
Deathwatch
Death of a Dancing Lady